Maximilian's Treasure

Maximilian's Treasure

JAMES D. BELL

A traditional publisher with a non-traditional
approach to publishing

Maximilian's Treasure
Copyright © 2019 by James D. Bell

ISBN: 978-0-578-56050-2

Cover design by Eric Summers.

SARTORIS LITERARY GROUP
Metro-Jackson, Mississippi
www.sartorisliterary.com

This book is dedicated to the memories of:

Robert Wade, 1960 – 2010; a great Dive Master who lost his battle with cancer of his body, but overcame cancer of his soul.

Jake Sullivan, 1969 – 2017; a great patriot with a wonderful sense of humor who laughed at death's door and gave courage to his friends. Even in death, he won souls to Christ.

Robert Jackson Brantley, Jr., 1951 – 2001; a loyal friend, brilliant lawyer and true Renaissance man.

We miss them now, but we will see them again.

Chapter 1

"The past is never dead. It's not even past."
William Faulkner

1866
Caribbean Sea,
Near the Island of Hispaniola

It's odd what you think about when you know you're about to die. Frank felt relief.

He was beyond exhaustion after days of terror and hopeless struggle. The warmth of the water was comforting. He no longer heard the continuous banshee scream of the wind or the crashing of the waves over the deck of the doomed ship. The Durance seemed so large at the dock, yet so small in the endless pounding waves.

The storm sound was muffled, unimportant now. What was left of the ship was creaking, groaning, popping and breaking below him, beside him, around him. He was floating free, weightless, yet tied by some invisible hand to the fate of the ship, drawing him into the depth. Part of the ship settled upright on the bottom. He hovered above the broken deck in milky water, tiny bubbles all around. Soft light made all things blue.

What will heaven be like ... or hell? thought Frank. He knew he deserved hell. He thought of a beautiful Choctaw maiden treating a gunshot wound he suffered while robbing a bank. He felt her soft kind touch, heard her gentle voice, experienced again her loving care.

Heaven must be like Mississippi, he thought. *I should never have left her.* Then he remembered the pain of being shot and thought, *Hell must be like Mississippi.*

* * *

Neshoba, Mississippi
1500 Miles Northwest of the Island of Hispaniola

She awoke with a gasp, sucking air as though she had been unable to breathe. *He's in danger!* She knew she must do something, but what?

There would only be one man for Sankky. She would never love another. Her eyes darted around her tiny room seeking her most prized possession, a golden coin he left, promising to return. She grasped the coin, holding it tight against her chest. Whenever she desperately missed Frank she would grasp the coin, hold it tight, and remember their tender moments together. It gave her so much comfort. What she wanted most in life was Frank's return. The coin symbolized Frank until he returned.

"The well!"

The place they first kissed.

"I have to go to the well!"

She ran from her home as swift as her bare feet could carry her as Frank's doomed ship began to sink.

* * *

"How long before I die?" Regret flooded his mind. "So many things I should have done. So many I shouldn't have." He gazed at a cabin door visible in the strange light. He thought of the chest just inside that door and remembered the voice of his friend, "I trust you with the fate of the empire."

"I'm sorry, Max. I failed."

His lungs ached, burned. His head throbbed. Still, he fought the desire, the need, to breathe. A voice in his head that sounded like his own, yet different, said, "It will be so easy. Just breathe. You've done all you can. There's nothing left for you to do. Just let go. It will be painless."

"I failed everyone," Frank said to himself. "God forgive me!"

He cracked open his mouth.

* * *

Sankky fell to her knees at the well. She held the coin inches from her face, yet she did not see the coin. She saw Frank. She kissed him one last time and released the coin. It disappeared in the mouth of the dark well. "God, save him! Even if he never comes back, save him!"

She fell at the base of the well and wept until morning.

* * *

8

Maximilian's Treasure

The deck burst with a loud pop. Bubbles and a barrel erupted from within. Swooshing as it surged through the water, the barrel looked small at first. Frank noticed that the barrel kept growing larger.

Then it hit him.

Chapter 2

**"To understand the world, you must first understand a place
like Mississippi."—William Faulkner**

Jackson, Mississippi, Present Day

"A satanic cult, right here in the middle of the Bible Belt," John
Brooks said to himself as he drove to his law office. At first, he found it
hard to believe. But, on reflection he decided that wherever the enemy
was at work, God was working even harder. "I guess my State's history
is Exhibit 'A' to that hypothesis. So much good and so much bad, all in
one place."

He parked his SUV under the Pearl Street Bridge a block from his
office. John had an appointment in a few minutes with a man whose last
appointment was interrupted by the kidnapping of his assistant, Karen
Wilkes. A flood of memories from the past few months momentarily
overwhelmed him. His friends admired his ethics and acumen and used to
say, "All you need is the big case, and your career will take off like a
rocket." He finished the big case a week ago. The case was so big and the
work so intense that he called on many of those same friends to help with
the case.

He was appointed to represent a man charged with murder who
claimed the person he killed was a vampire. John and his partner, Jackson
Bradley, used an insanity defense. The case, dubbed 'The Vampire
Defense' by the news media, became an instant sensation, resulting in
constant news coverage. Unfortunately the case attracted a lot more than
just coverage. There were murders, assaults, kidnappings and arson.
Cults, witches and devil worshipers seemed to be especially attracted to
anyone associated with the case because the Defendant claimed that he
killed a vampire. Intense courtroom drama was followed by the desperate
search for Karen, who was kidnapped by members of one of those cults.
Karen was rescued and the cult was rounded up and arrested. A court
hearing for one of their leaders, Gregory Lincoln is days away. John shook
his head and cleared his mind. "Time to go see Mr. Dalton."

John was a little late getting to the office. Frank Dalton, an elderly
Choctaw gentleman who claimed that treasure was hidden on his land, was

scheduled to arrive in a few minutes. John hurried down the hallway, long strides gobbling up the distance quickly. A charcoal suit covered his 6'1" athletic frame. His shirt collar and the first button were open, the edge of his tie protruding slightly from his coat pocket.

Karen Wilkes, John's beautiful assistant, waited for him in the lobby of the office. She couldn't stop thinking about recent events. She now knew with certainty that John was the love of her life. Her love grew out of the great respect for him she developed working as his assistant for three years. Then, just one week ago, he risked his life to save her. Every night, she replayed the event in her mind. She was on an isolated island in the middle of the Pearl River Reservoir, tied to a crude altar encircled by hooded devil worshippers. Their high priest was about to plunge a knife into her chest. She was certain that she was about to die when suddenly John threw himself on her prone body to protect her from what would have been a fatal knife strike.

She found it to be the most frightening, yet thrilling event of her life. John dominated her dreams every night. Karen was determined to get him to notice her. She wanted him as her husband, and knew that John needed her to be his wife. He just didn't know it yet. She decided that John needed a few hints and soon he would realize he couldn't live without her.

As John stepped into the office of Brooks and Bradley, he was greeted with an enthusiastic, "Good Morning! My, don't you look handsome in that new suit."

John paused, caught slightly off guard. Karen seemed even more beautiful than usual. Her long red hair spilled onto a sharp gray professional suit that seemed tailored to perfectly conceal, yet highlight all of her feminine features. She gazed at him with a demure smile.

After taking in the sight for a moment, John replied, "Good morning! Thank you. You are looking quite, ah, snappy yourself." He was uncomfortable with his reply, because he normally avoided speaking about Karen's appearance. But, "snappy" was the wrong word entirely. He was determined not to use words that better described her appearance because the office was for work.

John picked up his messages and stepped into his private office. Karen followed him. Sitting in the center of his desk was a small gift-wrapped package and an envelope. John settled behind his desk and picked up the package.

"What's this?"

"Open the envelope." Karen sat a cup of steaming hot black coffee in front of John as she sat on the edge of the desk.

"Wow! This is great treatment. What's the occasion?"

"Just open the envelope."

John opened the envelope and pulled out an embossed thank you card. He read the note and smiled at Karen.

"This is an unexpected surprise."

"Well, I had to do something for the man who saved my life and signs my paycheck."

"I thought you took over the signing of the checks."

"Well, technically I do, but figuratively you pay me," she said ever so slowly as she stretched her figure slightly and leaned towards John.

John couldn't help but notice her figure as she stretched her syllables and her legs at the same time.

"Open the package," she whispered.

Her whispered words had an effect John did not expect. His ears tingled and his spine trilled. John fumbled with the wrapping, then stopped breathing for a moment as he pulled out a fine Cutterland watch.

"Karen, this is too much. You shouldn't have."

"Don't you turn down my gift!" she said with just a hint of scolding in her voice. "They don't cost that much. I want my boss looking good, and this nice watch never needs winding. It sets itself at 2 every morning, so it always has the right time. You won't have any excuse to be late for court, or, for … anything else. Ever again."

"Wow. I don't know what to say."

"Thank you would be fine, for now."

"Thank you!"

Karen again leaned across the desk and slowly pulled the tie out of John's pocket.

"We can't have you half dressed in the office. I guess I'll just have to dress you myself," she said playfully.

She turned his collar up and slipped the tie around his neck. John didn't know how to respond to all of the attention and started getting nervous.

"When does Mr., uh, Dalton get here?"

"Any minute."

Karen finished the knot, slipped it into place, turned down his collar and brushed imaginary lint off his shoulder.

There was the sound of a throat clearing.

Startled, John and Karen turned quickly to the door.

"Jackson! I was just adjusting your partner's tie."

"Well, we are 50-50 partners. I suppose I'm next."

Karen smiled at John and at Jackson as she slipped off of the desk and walked slowly towards Jackson. John couldn't help notice the pronounced hip movement. She placed one hand on the knot of Jackson's tie and then gave the end a tug and a twist, tightening the loop around Jackson's neck and leaving the tie crooked.

"There, that's about right," said Karen with a mischievous grin as she sashayed passed Jackson on her way to her desk.

Jackson Bradley straightened his tie, cleared his throat, and took a seat in front of John's desk.

"Wow! That's a whole new level of assistance from our paralegal."

John smiled and shrugged.

"If I save a beautiful woman from a homicidal maniac intent on using her as a human sacrifice at a demonic ritual, maybe she'll bring me coffee and fix my tie, too."

John laughed. "It was team work, Jackson. You played just as big a role as me. Do you want to join me when I meet with Mr. Dalton?"

"I would like to, but I am behind on so many things."

"Speaking of behind," interjected Karen, "there is a pile of telephone messages that you need to get to, John. I was hoping Jackson would return some of them, but he says he's too busy."

"Who called?"

"Lots of potential new business. All of the publicity we received from the 'Case of the Century' is making the phone ring off the hook. I need help just screening calls."

"Tell him about the lady who called about her brother," said Jackson.

"Oh yeah! Her brother was arrested in Greenville, charged with burglary. She heard about us and wants us to help."

"Greenville is a long way to go to defend a burglary charge," John responded.

"True. She says her brother suffers from multiple personality disorder and she thinks we could use insanity as a defense," said Karen as she rolled her eyes.

Jackson laughed and said, "If he has multiple personalities, how do the police know whether they've arrested the right one?"

John laughed and responded, "You're right. It could be that Larry committed the crime, but Sam is the one in jail."

"You wouldn't be laughing if you had talked to his sister. She's really worried and her story about her brother is so sad."

"You're right," said John. "But, laughter is just a fact of life if you're around Jackson. I'll call her."

"Speaking of laughter, our favorite prosecutor, Tellers, sounds like he wants to run for governor," said Jackson with a smirk.

"Well, if he wins, at least we won't have to deal with him in Circuit Court," said John. "What makes you think he's running?"

"He just made a speech about school shootings and the need for adequate gun control. He says someone gets shot every day in Mississippi and we need to do something about it." After a brief pause, Jackson continued, "I wonder, what's the poor man's name?"

"Who?" asked Karen.

"The poor man who gets shot every day. Must be painful. Tellers is right. Let's do something about it. Give the poor guy some body armor." Jackson laughed at his own joke. No one else laughed.

Jackson continued, "Bobby Creek called and told me Peter, his eighteen-year old son, got into a little trouble and he took him to the police station to get it straightened out. His son stole his father's credit card and used it to buy a computer. Mr. Creek and the police arranged for Peter to spend a few nights in the jail to get his attention."

"When is the hearing?"

"Actually, there won't be one. They did it informally, just to let him get a taste of the consequences of a life of crime. His dad won't be pressing charges."

"Really. That's interesting. How did you swing that?"

"I can't take credit for it. I just approved the idea when Creek told me what was up. He told a police friend what his boy had done, and the policeman took it from there without filing any official charge. It sounded like a good plan to me, so I said go for it. The boy might learn from it and stay out of trouble. I'm going to go see him this morning."

"Okay. What else is up? You're holding something back."

"There is something I really want to do, but I just don't have time with all the work we have."

"What's that, Jackson?"

"I really want to write a book about our experiences in the case we just finished."

"It was an exciting case," agreed John. "A little too exciting at times."

"I think I'll name the book Vampire Defense. The press already calls it that. I think it'll make a great story, but I need time to get my thoughts together. I need to get away for a while. Some place where there won't be any distractions."

"That's a great idea. You can bring me up to speed on your cases and I'll do my best to take care of them while you're away. When do you want to do this?"

"I don't know. Maybe in a couple of weeks, after I finish a few things. I was thinking that I might go to the Caribbean for a month and see if I can get inspired."

"You'll write a great story, Jackson."

John heard Karen pleasantly greet Mr. Dalton. She asked him to have a seat while she answered the phone.

"Brooks and Bradley. Well, hello! Yes, he's here, but he can't talk right now because he's with someone and has a client waiting, but I'll have him call you right back, Sandy."

"Sandy! Is that Sandy Storm?"

"Yes."

"I'll take the call!"

Sandy is an extraordinarily attractive reporter for a cable news network. She broke the Vampire Defense story to the world. Sandy interviewed John many times. There was significant on-air tension between Sandy and John that led many viewers to believe that there could be a romantic involvement between them. Indeed, their last encounter ended with a memorable kiss.

John excitedly answered the phone. "Sandy! How are you? To what do I owe the pleasure of this call? ... I see. ... That sounds great! Yes, we would be happy to do anything we could to help. ... Great. Talk to you soon. Goodbye!"

"What was that about?" asked Jackson.

"It seems that the network might want to do a follow-up story on our case. Sandy is trying to sell the network on the idea of doing some sort of a documentary on the Vampire Defense."

"That would be great! I better hurry up and get the book ready. That kind of publicity is invaluable."

"True, but the network hasn't agreed yet. Excuse me, Jackson, let me see Mr. Dalton, and we'll talk about this later."

John stepped into the waiting area and shook hands with the elderly gentleman.

"Good to see you, Mr. Dalton. Come in my office and give me all the details. I'm sorry that our last meeting was cut off so abruptly."

"Oh, I understand. There was a real emergency and you did what you had to do."

"Karen, would you mind getting us a fresh cup of coffee, please?"

"The coffee is in the break room. You can get it yourself," said Karen icily.

John looked at her with a puzzled expression. Since he saw her last, she had wrapped herself in a thick sweater that covered her slim form fitting business suit. When they made eye contact she glowered at him for a moment, then turned her attention to the computer and typed noisily.

John led Mr. Dalton into his office, retrieved his coffee cup and stepped into the break room to get fresh coffee for Mr. Dalton and himself. On his way back to his office, he stopped at Karen's desk.

"Is anything wrong?"

"Oh, no! Nothing! Why would anything be wrong?"

"I see. Well, if I did something, or didn't do something, I am sorry."

"Don't give me that innocent look."

"What?"

"'Oh Sandy, to what do I owe the pllleaasurrre of this callll?' You never take my calls that way."

"Well, Karen. It was Sandy. I was just ..."

"Oh! That explains everything!" shouted Karen as she slapped both hands against her desk and pushed away, causing her chair to roll backward. Red faced, she jumped from her chair and rushed from the room in tears. John remained in the lobby alone, a puzzled look on his face. He wondered whether he should go after her, or see Mr. Dalton. After a moment of indecision, he shook his head and entered his office to begin the interview of his new client.

Chapter 3

"I will kill them ... all!" spat Gregory Lincoln as he finished his last set of bench presses. Every day he imagined creative ways to kill John Brooks, Jackson Bradley, Karen Wilkes and that shrimp they called Skip the Middleman. He had killed before. Many times. He relished the memory of every murder. He let his anger build as he thought about the days wasted in jail. The coiled viper tattoo seemed to writhe as his left triceps flexed when he slammed the weights home in their cradle. He wiped sweat from his brow as he sat up and slowly scanned each face in the weight room. His face seemed twisted into a permanent sneer. He saw a young inmate standing alone against the wall, just on the other side of a knot of inmates lingering near the exit.

"That's him," Gregory said to no one in particular.

Determined to make a statement that all inmates would understand, Gregory puffed his chest out and walked directly at the knot of men. He looked through them as he approached. The inmates respectfully parted and he passed through their midst without breaking his stride.

Gregory turned suddenly to the young inmate, grabbed a handful of his collar and pulled the young man close to his ugly face. "I understand that those lawyers, Brooks and Bradley, represent you."

"Ye ... yeah," stammered Peter Creek.

"I want you to pump them for personal information. I don't want them to know why. I don't want them to know that you know me. Are you trackin' with me?"

"Yeah, no, I don't know."

Gregory lifted the young man by his collar and drove him backward against the wall. "Listen closely. You won't be here long, but I know how to find you and I will. I want to know where Brooks and Bradley live. I want to know when they eat. I want to know when they sleep. I want to know everything about John Brooks, Jackson Bradley, that red-headed secretary of theirs and that little twerp, Skip Schafer. You get that information for me and I will protect you while you're here. Your time here will pass quick and easy. And don't think that getting out will help you. I can reach you on the outside. I have friends on the outside and I own the inside of this jail. My friends will set you up, put a little dope in your car and you'll be back in here with me and my friends. On the other hand, if you help me now, you will be on easy street. So, choose: a curse or a blessing. Do you understand what I'm sayin'?" sneered Gregory.

"Yes, sir."

"Just so we understand each other. Take a look at that grease spot on the floor over there. No matter how hard they try, they can't clean up that spot. Do you know who that is?"

"What? Who? What do you mean who?"

"That's the last creep that crossed me. So, what's it gonna be for you? A grease spot or easy street?"

"A gr... ah, I mean, no, not a grease spot."

Gregory lifted him a little higher on the wall and slapped him lightly on the cheek. "Just do your job, and leave the rest to me."

Gregory released the collar, and Peter sank to the floor. The other inmates laughed nervously.

"Are you trackin' with me?"

"Yeah, yeah. Information good. Grease bad. I got it."

"All right kid, I think you got it," Gregory said with a smile and a nod. He leaned close to Peter's face and said, "You may be a little slow, but you can be taught. I think it may be time for your first lesson. Perhaps a little demonstration would be helpful. There is one inmate here who did not do what I asked, even though I asked him just as nice as I am asking you. He turned me down! Can you believe it? Nobody turns me down. Nobody!"

Gregory made eye contact with a heavily tattooed inmate and nodded once. Tattoo gave no indication that he received a communication, but he walked behind another inmate and threw a vicious punch into his kidney. The man gasped and bent over backward, his hands instinctively protecting his lower back. Tattoo delivered a second vicious blow to the man's exposed throat and down he went, gurgling and gasping for air.

"Fight! Fight!"

The room filled with shouts and cries. Inmates seemingly from everywhere pounced on the fallen man, kicking and stomping him. In seconds it was over. The inmates scattered and Peter stared in horror at a bloody, mangled corpse.

Chapter 4

Frank Dalton was seated when John entered his office.

"Halito! Your lady friend, she is not happy with you."

"Yes, well, let's talk about you and your case."

"I already told Ms. Karen everything. Did she not tell you? I told you some of it too, but with all the excitement that day, you might not remember so good."

"Well, you're right. Tell me about your farm."

"Don't you want to talk about the treasure? White men always want to talk about the treasure first."

"We can come to that. I understand that your farm is about to be sold at foreclosure. Tell me about that. Let me see if someone has done something wrong. Maybe we can find a way to stop the foreclosure."

"My farm, it is like," Dalton paused as he visualized his farm. Then, with a faraway look, he continued, "paradise. It has three beautiful hills and good bottomland. We live on one of the hills and we keep a few farm animals. Milk cows, chickens, goats, beef cattle, a few pigs. Sometimes we grow quail. Good fish in the pond between the hills. Then, on the bottomland along Pinishook Creek, we grow the most beautiful crops you ever seen. But the best crops ever, they came from the old Goni Swamp."

"The Goni Swamp?"

"Yeah. The men in our family, we drained the swamp, cleared the land, and planted beans. Oh my, you never seen such good beans. But, we never got to harvest them. The beans were our last hope."

"Why didn't you get to harvest them and why were they your last hope?"

"For more-n-a hundred years, we never had no mortgage. Then, my nephew Curtis got in trouble. He was charged with a string of robberies. He would never have done that. But, they found some of the stolen things in his truck. We think he was set up. We sold everything we could to hire a lawyer and we put a mortgage on the farm to cover his hundred thousand dollar bond. He didn't come to court. We don't know where he is. He would never do this to his family. He loves our land and he loves our family. Something happened to him. He's no coward. He didn't run. He couldn't have. Anyway, cause he didn't come to court, they were coming for our land."

"I see. What does the Goni Swamp have to do with it?"

"When Curtis didn't show on his court day, the judge wanted to call the bond. We got him to give us time. Me and my brothers knew we needed a bigger crop to pay the bond, so we drained the swamp. It was hard work. Especially with our nosy neighbors, the Whittakers and our cousin, Brad Dalton, always spying on us and complaining to the Deputy that we didn't have the right to drain our own swamp. Deputy Townsend harassed us some, but the Sheriff got him off our back.

"The Goni Swamp killed my oldest brother, James. He died pullin' a stump out of the muck by himself. One day we found him keeled over next to a half pulled stump. We called for help. Deputy Townsend was the first one there. He was in a dark mood, mean, angry. Said we shouldn't be drainin' that swamp and we should quit and go home. He just made us want to work that much harder."

John thought he saw a tear in the wrinkled corner of Frank Dalton's eye. The old man looked to be in his late seventies, maybe early eighties, John couldn't tell. His skin was dark and leathery, with deep furrows in his face. His thick hair was so gray it was almost white.

"I am sorry to hear about your brother, Mr. Dalton."

"James is the lucky one. He died on his farm, working hard to save it. He's not alive today to see the mess we are in. We buried him on the farm. He'll always be there. The rest of us may not be so lucky."

"What happened to the Goni Swamp crop?"

"The first time you plant a piece of land will be the best crop you ever get. The plants were heavy with beans, but the due date of the bond was on us before we could get the crop. If we sold it on the ground, before it was harvested, we wouldn't get nothin' for it. We just needed a little longer. We tried borrowing the money, but nobody would loan to us. Then, a really nice lawyer, I thought he was nice, offered to loan us $50,000 just long enough to get our crop in. We had already raised $50,000 selling everything we could. So, we gave him a $50,000 mortgage and we paid off the $100,000 bond."

"Well, that sounds like a good thing. A terrible waste of money, but then the lien on your farm was cut in half."

"That's what we thought. We just needed enough time to harvest the beans. But then came Whittaker's cows!" said Frank, disgust dripping off his tongue.

"Whittaker again?"

"Yep. Whittaker is a rancher who raises cattle. We could'a paid off the mortgage if it hadn't been for Whittaker's cows," said Mr. Dalton as he cast his eyes down and shook his aged head.

"How did Whittaker's cows keep you from paying the mortgage?"

"His cows ruined our beans, and we lost a whole year a work. They broke through the fence and ate our beans. If it had happened once, maybe we could have saved somethin'. But it happened three times. They trampled more than they ate. Such a waste. And it happened just when the note was coming due. They called the note a balloon. The whole note come due at one time. That's when the cows busted into the Goni field. Them cows could not have busted through at a worse time."

"So, now the not-so-nice man who loaned you the money is foreclosing on the mortgage?"

"No, worse than that. He sold the mortgage to the Texas Daltons. He was working for them all along."

"Do you think Whittaker knows the Texas Daltons?"

"Yes. I saw Brad Dalton, my white cousin, leaving the Whittaker place the day after the lawyer loaned us the money on the bond. I think he was plannin' this all along."

"How could he plan a criminal charge against Curtis?"

"I don't think he could, but he took advantage of it. I just can't believe Curtis ran out on us. It makes no sense to me."

After a pause, Frank continued. "After I got notice that the Texas Daltons were foreclosing on the mortgage, old man Whittaker sued me for damage to his cows. I couldn't believe it. His cows ate my beans and he sued me! They are attacking us from two directions, thinkin' we will give up."

"Did you counter sue for damage to your beans?"

"Yeah, but my lawyer wanted too much money, so we're going to court without a lawyer in a couple of weeks, unless you help us. But, I guess it don't matter much if we lose our farm. They're coming at us ever which way."

"Why did the Texas Daltons buy the mortgage?"

"They want the treasure."

"You told me about the treasure a few days ago, right after the trial."

"Yes, when you won that Vampire Defense trial, we knew you could help us if you chose to do so. And we are so relieved and grateful that you agreed to take our case."

"Tell me what you know about the legend of the treasure."

"My great-great-grand-daddy was Frank James, brother of Jesse James. He buried a treasure on my great-great grandma's family farm way back in either 1865 or 1867. He was there at least twice. We've been looking for the treasure ever since my great-great grandma died. Now, the white side of the family from Texas has bought our mortgage. They're foreclosing day after tomorrow unless you stop 'em."

"I remember when you told me about Frank James. I have a hard time believing that Frank and Jesse James were in Mississippi. I know you believe it, but it is a surprise to me."

"Yeah, their gang robbed two banks in Mississippi, one in Carthage and one in Silver City. Frank was shot and hid out on my family farm on Pinishook Creek, where my great-great grandma, Sankky, nursed him back to health. He changed his name to Frank Dalton while he was here, because everybody was looking for Frank James. He had been here a couple of years before, too. That's why he come back when he was hurt."

"I remember a coin that you showed me."

"Yes, I'll show you again if you like. We always knew Frank James, or Frank Dalton, buried his treasure on the farm. Some say that the first time he came to the farm he was carryin' Mexican gold to be delivered to the Confederates. He and his gang were Confederate Cavalry with Quantrill's Raiders. When the Civil War ended they just kept on fighting the war by robbin' banks. At least that's how he justified robbin' banks. Anyway, the war ended before Frank could deliver the Mexican gold and he hid it somewhere. We think he hid it on the farm."

"Apparently the Texas Daltons think so too," observed John.

"That's right. The second time he came to our farm was when he was hurt. I think he might have been coming back for the Mexican gold and robbed a couple of banks on the way. After Sankky nursed him back to health, they married. Word got out that Frank Dalton was Frank James and a posse nearly caught him. So, he left and said he was coming back for his gold and for Sankky. He never come back," said Frank with a lilt of sadness for his great-great grandma. "Rumor was he settled down in different places, like Virginia, Tennessee, and Missouri. Apparently he settled down in Texas and raised a family there usin' the Dalton name, but you could never convince Sankky of that.

"Sankky loved him very much. Anyway, she took his name and raised his son. She wouldn't let nobody look for the treasure while she was alive. She felt like he had trusted her with the treasure and she wouldn't let anyone look for it. She wouldn't even let anyone even talk about it. Ever since she died, our family has been searching. Now, we're about to lose everything. And we're going to lose it to those Daltons in Texas. They already got everything else. Now, they want to take what little we got."

"Frank, to tell you the truth, the treasure story seems like an old rumor, a legend."

"But I showed you part of the gold, remember?" Frank asked as he pulled from his pocket a small black velvet bag sealed with a drawstring. Frank shook the bag over John's hand and a gold coin, almost an inch wide, fell into his palm.

Maximilian's Treasure

"EMPERADOR MAXIMILIANO," read John out loud, followed by a low whistle. He turned the coin over and read, "1865. Well, I guess this is Exhibit "A". I remember you showed this to me before, but there can be a lot of explanations for this other than buried treasure. Where did you say you found this?"

Chapter 5

Peter Creek sat on the other side of the glass from Jackson, with a pleading look on his face. "You've got to get me out of here, Mr. Bradley. I'm scared."

"You want out?"

"Of course I do!"

"And you never want to come back, do you?"

"Never. I have learned my lesson. I will never be in trouble again."

"Well, I've been talking to the police and to your dad and they might let you out, if you get a job and promise to stay out of trouble."

"Just get me out of here and I'll have a job tomorrow."

"I'm afraid I need more than your promise to look for a job. Do you have any prospects? Is there anyone you know that would be willing to hire you? Can I give them a call and confirm that they would hire you?"

Peter knew of no one who would hire him, but then he remembered Gregory's threat and an idea flickered in his mind. "Mr. Bradley, you could hire me."

"I don't think so."

"I promise, I will be the best employee you ever had. I can make copies. I can run errands. I can wash your car. I'll do anything. Just get me out of here."

"I can't do that, Peter."

"Look, it will just be for a little while, until I get another job. It will be a way for me to repay you for helping me. I really want to show you how much I appreciate your help. I'll work for free until I get a real job."

"A real job?"

"Oh, you know what I mean. Please let me work for you. I'll take out the garbage and pick up the mail. I'll do anything. Please help me."

Jackson knew he shouldn't hire the boy. His clients expected him to employ people of high integrity. Hiring someone right out of jail would be hard to explain to his clients, and to his partner. Peter recognized Jackson's hesitation and added, "I saw someone get killed here today, just a few minutes ago."

"What?"

"Ask the guards. They'll tell you." Peter leaned forward, urgency in his voice. "There was a fight. A man was killed. I was there! They threatened me! I could be next."

That sealed it for Jackson.

"What the heck? What harm could come of it? Tell you what, I'll find something for you to do for a week. After that, you're on your own. You'll either have to find a 'real' job, or you will have to convince my partner that you can stay around. If I can get you out today, you start tomorrow."

"Oh thank you, Mr. Bradley. You won't regret it."

* * *

When the meeting with John was over, Mr. Dalton rose and walked slowly to the office door. Then, he turned and looked John in the eyes. "There's something I must say to you. You are doing a great service to my family and me. So, I am moved to tell you something of great importance to you. You will have to make an important choice soon. Few people in the world pick their mates out of love. The lucky ones do. Among people of the world, parents pick mates for their children, or people pick mates for many reasons; wealth, power, to have children. We Choctaw pick our mates out of love. Sankky loved Frank James. I loved my wife."

John looked at Mr. Dalton with a puzzled expression.

"Love is a rare and wonderful thing. For some, it never truly happens. They mistake other feelings for love. For most, love happens only once. Love is the most precious thing in life. Don't let it slip away. You may never have another chance."

"Thank you, Mr. Dalton. Why are you telling me this?"

"Because you have to choose. Choose wisely."

Frank Dalton's green eyes twinkled in his deeply creased face. He nodded goodbye to John and stalked down the hallway, his head turning slowly left and right as though he was on the hunt, looking for signs of game. He skipped the elevator and took the stairs. His joints creaked and ached, but he preferred the stairs.

John shook his head and returned to his office.

* * *

Karen felt that she needed to get away. She exited the building, turned left on the sidewalk and left again down the narrow alley next to the building. She took a seat on one of the benches in the alley and cried. After a few moments she began speaking in a whisper, first to herself, and then to God. "I have always imagined finding a man of character and courage, a man who knows what he wants, a Godly man, to be my husband. Is John the one? I want him to be the one. I love him so. I can't stand seeing him fawn over another woman. Make him stop! If he is the one, please show me. Please tell me. Please make it clear to me. If he isn't the one, please let me know soon, because this hurts too much. Help me, please."

Karen wiped away her tears and returned to the building. She entered the stairway on the bottom floor just as Frank Dalton reached the last step.

"Young lady. I know I speak out of turn, but at my age I don't know if I'll get another chance."

It was obvious that Karen had been crying. She was charmed by the little old man, and said, "Oh, I'm fine. Thank you for being concerned, but I'll be all right."

"Follow your heart. I have looked into his heart. He is a good man. I have looked into your heart. You are a good woman. You are meant for each other."

Karen wiped tears from her eyes.

"Thank you. I don't know what to do. He doesn't think of me the way I think of him. It's just too hard to be with him and to see him so excited about another woman. I want to hate him when I see that, but I can't. I think I should just let go. I've decided that it's time for me to move on. If he wants me, he can find me. But, I can't take this anymore. I'll end up making a fool of myself, or worse."

"Do what you think is right, but remember. True love is precious. Everyone wants to find it, but few do. If you find it, treasure it. Protect it. Defend it."

"But, what good is love if it isn't returned?"

"In spring, autumn seems far away. Your love is ready for harvest, but his is still a fine new sprig that needs to be watered and nurtured. Be patient. It will grow, bloom and produce fruit a hundred fold. Good things come in their own time." Frank Dalton smiled at Karen, turned and slowly walked away.

Chapter 6

Three hours later, Peter was being processed for release when he felt a hand on his shoulder. He turned and saw the sneering face of Gregory Lincoln.

"Glad to hear you're getting out!"

Peter's heart jumped into his throat. "Yeah, I got a job with that law firm!" exclaimed Peter. He immediately regretted saying anything.

"Perfect. Don't forget our deal," said Gregory as he smeared something on Peter's face. Peter quickly rubbed it off, looked at his hand and gasped, "Grease!"

Gregory chuckled a humorless laugh and walked away, saying, "Remember, I know how to find you."

* * *

An hour later, Gregory was ushered into the visiting area. Most inmates have to visit through a glass wall and make use of a telephone to communicate with family members or even their attorney. But, Gregory had already achieved trustee status and was free to move around most of the jail without supervision. No one had ever achieved trustee status so quickly. He was afforded the privilege of visiting with his lawyer in a private room, furnished with a table and two chairs. Harry Hoover was waiting for him in one of the chairs.

"Hoov, what's the latest?" asked Gregory as he took the other chair.

"Your preliminary hearing is day after tomorrow, but you already know that. What was so urgent that you had to see me right now?"

"We will get to that in just a minute. But first, how is the prelim looking?"

"It's really a bond hearing, but, personally, I think the underlying charges are weak. We have a chance for you to walk."

"Chance! What do you mean chance? It better be a done deal."

"Look, I'm doing the best I can. We're getting a speedy hearing and I've already gotten the D.A. to drop the murder charge against you."

"Well, I guess! What evidence is there that I had anything to do with a murder?"

"Yeah, well, there are rumors in the D.A.'s office that you are getting away with murder in the jail."

"Why, that's ridiculous!" Gregory exclaimed with insincerity. "How would I be a trustee if they thought I was involved in jailhouse murders?" Gregory grinned, obviously pleased with himself.

"Yeah, well, the rumor is not helping my negotiations."

"There are always rumors. You should never pay attention to rumors." Gregory leaned forward. "Unless they have to do with a certain little co-ed who went missing last year, Hoov."

Hoover turned pale, his mouth open, aghast. His mind flashed back a year, when he began to dabble in the occult. He ran into Gregory at an Earth Day event. Gregory was charismatic and captured his imagination with promises of supernatural power and excitement. Gregory invited him to, "Come to the black mass Friday night, and bring a date. An expendable date."

"What do you mean, expendable date?"

"Well, mass is not for everyone. If it appeals to her, she will be your slave. If she doesn't get it, she'll never want to come back and she will never want to see you again. So, bring someone who you are not too involved with, someone who won't be missed, someone who can't be tied back to you."

Hoover wasn't sure what Gregory meant, but he was intrigued by the comment.

"The mass must be something really wild."

Gregory laughed. "You have to experience it to believe it. Just come. You will have the most memorable experience of your life. Trust me, you will never be the same."

Hoover remembered Ellie, a twenty year old he represented a couple of months before on a misdemeanor. Ellie was a drug addict and college dropout. She couldn't keep a job and Hoover knew she would do anything for drugs. Her family had given up on her and she confided in him that she was alone in the world. She was surprised to hear from Hoover and jumped at the chance to go out with him. She couldn't believe that a successful lawyer had asked her out. At last, her luck had changed. She told herself that she would do anything to make sure he had a good time so that he would ask her out again.

The 'mass' started in an eerily formal manner, and soon degenerated into alcohol and dru- fueled debauchery. Every boundary that Hoov had ever known was obliterated. He soon lost track of Ellie as he allowed his lust to lead him from person to person. The mass was too much for Ellie. When she realized that she meant nothing to Hoover, she retreated to her one true love: drugs. The mass reached a climax when Gregory announced that it was time for "communion" and he thanked the congregation's new member, Hoover, for providing the "host." He invited Hoover to be the first to partake of her body and blood. There was a great cheer, and everyone eagerly lined up behind Hoover. He thought it odd that they were about to have communion, but everyone seemed so excited. Indeed, a strange intensity gripped everyone. Some rubbed their hands together, while others licked their lips and laughed with a humorless cackle. The mood changed from wildly festive to a ravenous evil. Ellie was never seen again. He shuddered as he remembered her pitiful cries for help.

"That was just …," Hoover paused.

"Yeah, that was just a night when things got a little out of hand. I hope nobody outside the Kroth ever hears about it. What would the law do? What would the Bar Association do? What would your wife do? But, that's why you have friends, Hoov. Friends who can help keep you out of a jam," Gregory paused to let silence work on Hoover.

Hoover wiped sweat from his brow. His hand was shaking.

Gregory reached across the table and slapped Hoover's shoulder. "Don't worry, Hoov, I have complete confidence in you. I know you will have me out of this wretched place day after tomorrow."

"Yeah, well, there's a lot to do between now and then to make sure that happens."

"Like I said, I have confidence in you, Hoov. By the way, have you been going to meetings?"

Hoover avoided eye contact with Gregory and looked at his hands instead. "Yeah, I make most of the meetings."

"Is the coven holding together after the Bishop's fiasco?"

"That was a set back. But, we'll recover."

"The reason I asked you to come today is we have a new recruit. A kid named Peter Creek. This is his address." Gregory stuffed a piece of paper in Hoover's coat pocket. "He's about to start a job with Brooks and Bradley."

"No way! How did you swing that?"

"It's the touch of the master my friend. Listen, I want you to keep the boy under your wing. I am assigning you to be his angel."

"His hell's angel?"

They both laughed.

"You got it. I want to know everything about Brooks and Bradley, their secretary and that little creep, Schafer. Creek is our mole."

Chapter 7

Jackson invited John to meet him at Jaco's Tacos for a Goshen Springs Beer after work. They sat on the balcony and watched a spectacular sunset over the city.

"Can you believe these nachos?"

"Best I ever had, but it's their tacos that I crave."

"Yeah, they've got great crab cakes and steaks."

"I'm reading a new book. You would love it. I can't put it down!" said Jackson.

"What's it about?"

"Anti-gravity."

"Jackson!" John chuckled then said, "Something's on your mind partner. Tell me what's up."

"John, I accidentally hired somebody today."

John laughed. "How do you accidentally hire somebody, and how do you do it without discussing it with your partner?"

"It's Peter Creek. He had to have a job as part of the deal to keep from being prosecuted."

"Jackson, he stole from his dad! How can we trust him? How can we trust him with our clients?"

"He seems like a good kid who did a stupid thing and his parents are great people. He asked for a job and I couldn't say no."

"Here, let me help you. Form your lips like this, with your tongue behind your teeth like this, and practice the 'nooo' sound."

"Seriously, John. Somebody was beaten to death in the jail today. Peter Creek was threatened by the thugs who administered the beating. Part of the deal to get him out of jail was he had to have a job. So, I told him that I would hire him myself for a week and if he could convince you that he should stay, then fine. I'll cover his pay out of my paycheck."

"You don't get a paycheck."

"Well, if I did, I would cover it."

"I am not going to second guess my partner. You wouldn't have offered the job if you didn't feel like it was the right thing to do. So, he has a job with us, but only for a week. Just keep an eye on him."

"Great. For a week, unless he proves himself."

"Deal. Besides, maybe he's been put in our lives for a reason. Maybe this is our chance to influence him to make right choices in life."

Jackson chuckled. "There you go again. Everything happens for a reason in your world."

"Yeah, I believe that."

"I think everything is just random. Nothing happens for a reason. Nothing has ultimate meaning," said Jackson as he shook his head. "What you call intervention by a Supreme Being, I call coincidence."

"I pray you receive faith, my friend."

"Faith? What is faith?"

"The assurance of things hoped for, the conviction of things not seen."

Jackson laughed as he shook his head and responded, "I should have known you'd have a quick answer. You're a smart guy, yet you believe in all those fairy tales in the Bible. I just can't understand that about you."

"The Bible is a spiritual book and is spiritually revealed. It takes at least some faith to understand it."

"So, you're saying I should just believe, and then I'll believe? That's crazy double talk."

"I was saved by grace though faith, and that was not of my own doing, it was a gift from God. I can't boast that I chose to have faith. God gave me faith."

"That's even crazier. You're saying it's not my fault I don't believe, it's God's fault because he didn't give me faith?"

"It is not God's will that even one would be lost."

"Well then why doesn't He give me faith?'

"Maybe He's letting circumstances and people work together to build faith in you until you're ready."

"Oh, come on. So, every coincidence is a sign from God?"

"I didn't say every coincidence, but sometimes coincidences are arranged by God."

"No, John, coincidences are just that. Random events."

"Maybe there will be enough 'coincidences' in your life to convince you one day that something else is going on."

"I doubt it."

"Look, even if I'm wrong about God, we still need to make the best of whatever comes our way. We don't know how long we have here on Earth, so we need to do all the good we can while we can."

Jackson grinned and took a sip of his Goshen Springs beer. "That's one of the reasons I like you, John. We agree on that. At least we can try to make things better for ourselves and others while we're here."

"You don't realize it, but your gut feeling that we need to make things better for others while we're here proves my point."

"How so?"

"God placed that feeling in your heart. It's part of the law that He writes on everyone's heart. Love your neighbor as yourself."

Jackson laughed. "No, it's just an evolutionary development. People who have a desire to help others are more likely to survive in nature, so that trait is passed on to others."

"So how do you explain the guy who pushes a stranger from the path of a train, only to get run over himself?"

Jackson grinned and nodded. "Okay, but if helping others was a law, as you think it is, it's not a very effective law. Just look at all the law breakers."

"True. One hundred percent of us break that law."

"That makes the law giver imperfect doesn't it?"

"No, it means we are imperfect. The legislature passed a law against murder. The fact that people break that law is not what makes the legislature imperfect."

Jackson laughed and said, "I agree with you there. It's all those imperfect legislators that make the legislature imperfect. I'll never understand why a perfect God would make imperfect people. It makes no sense to me."

John smiled, and continued, "I love these talks. But, on another subject, can you file an injunction first thing in the morning to stop the Dalton foreclosure? It's scheduled to take place at 11 tomorrow."

"I could file one, John, but I'm not sure I'll get the injunction. We may not find an available judge with jurisdiction, and even if we do, we may not have grounds for an injunction."

"That leaves plan B."

"You mean outbid the Texas Daltons for the chance to look for phantom treasure?"

"No, better than outbidding at an auction. We should help Frank exercise his right of redemption."

"Of course!" exclaimed Jackson. "He has a right to bring the mortgage current at anytime before the hammer falls at the auction since it's his homestead."

"That's right, but usually to bring a mortgage current takes just a few monthly payments plus the cost of foreclosure. This time there's a balloon note. He'll need to pay the whole mortgage with interest plus costs of foreclosure. I wonder what that comes to?"

"Let's see." Jackson consulted a ledger on his iPad. "$58,327."

"You just happen to have that number handy. Interesting. Can we cover it?"

"I know you, John. I was afraid you would come up with a hair-brained idea like bidding at the auction or redemption, so I checked our accounts before I left the office. Yes, we can cover it. Barely. We'll be in a bind for the next couple of weeks. We'll need a nice fee to come in really soon." Jackson paused, and then repeated for effect, "Really soon."

"What do you think? Should we do it?"

"Good grief, John. Every time I think we're getting ahead, we give away our fee, or if we get a fee, we give away the money. Someday, I would like to make a little money and maybe have a house with a mortgage that can be foreclosed when you give away my salary."

Jackson paused, sipped his beer and admired the fading embers of the sunset. "By the way, we don't get a salary either. We just draw money now and then when we need it, if we have it when we need it. I would like to have a salary that I could count on."

"So, are we going to redeem the farm or not?"

Jackson huffed, sat back, quaffed his beer, and gazed at the sunset again. After a long moment he slapped the table and said, "Dad gum it, John. Yeah. Sure. At least I know how to spend my time tomorrow. We won't have to waste time with an injunction. Instead, we can concentrate on getting the money together and getting to the auction on time."

"We made a decision. That's a relief." John sat back in his chair and gazed at the sunset, but with a puzzled look on his face.

"Why don't you look relieved?"

"I don't know what to make of Karen. She's acting strange. And Mr. Dalton talked like it was time for me to make a move on Karen."

"Actually, that's why I asked you to meet me here. Listen to the old man. He knows what he's talking about."

"What are you talking about?"

"I'll get straight to the point. Go find Karen and apologize to her."

"Apologize? I have no idea what to apologize for."

"The girl is in love with you, John."

"What? Karen? In love with me? Why?"

"Beats me. Especially knowing she could have me. But, for whatever reason she is head over heels in love with you. And you love her, I know it."

"What do you mean?"

"You know what I mean."

"Please make this simple for me, before we get to 'I know, that you know, that I know,' cause I don't even know what I know, let alone what you know that I know and that's the truth. I think."

"Could you say that again?"

"I don't know."

They laughed at each other.

Jackson continued, "I see the way you look at her when she's not looking. I don't blame you. The girl is beautiful, and she has a beautiful heart. I have known for a long time that she loves and admires you. Now that you rescued her, you're her hero. What can top that?"

"She may be confusing gratitude for love. As for me, I love her as a person, as a friend, as our paralegal. I love her in lots of ways, but not the way you are thinking."

"I'm not buying that, John. You might be fooling yourself, but you're not fooling me. Karen is an awesome woman. Loyal, smart, beautiful, resourceful, adventurous—you could do a lot worse buddy."

"Sounds like maybe you should pursue her, since you think so much of her."

"Maybe I will, when she gets over you."

"So, why is she mad?"

"Because you were so excited to talk to Sandy."

"Well, we haven't talked to Sandy in a while. I thought we would all be excited to talk to her."

"John. Sandy is drop dead gorgeous. You ignored Karen and dropped everything to talk to Sandy. Imagine how that makes Karen feel."

"I didn't intend to make her feel anything."

"Exactly. That probably hurt her more than the way you talked to Sandy. She wants you to talk to her that way and no one else."

"But we work together. We have things we have to do. Together. Everyday. I can't be worried about how she's going to feel."

"You're probably right. She'll come to the same conclusion. Soon. Then, she'll find another job. It's too bad. I'm going to miss her. And so will you."

"What? We're a team. She can't leave!"

"Oh yes she can and she will, sooner or later. Probably sooner. Things have changed, John."

"Why couldn't things stay the way they were? Everything was perfect."

Chapter 8

Peter's mother was ecstatic when he finally made it home. She hugged him and looked him over. "Oh, Peter. I missed you so much. I was so worried about you."

His dad gave him a little nod and said, "I hope you've learned your lesson."

"So many people have been worried about you," said his excited mother, "and that nice Mr. Hoover called to check on you and make sure that you made it home all right. He said he was a friend of Mr. Lincoln's, and that he had a job for you! Isn't that exciting!"

Peter sucked in a startled breath. "No, Ma. You can tell Mr. Hoover that I already have a job, but thank him for me."

"You can thank him yourself," said Peter's dad. "When he mentioned a job, I invited him over. Here he is!"

A grinning Harry Hoover stepped into the room. He wore a black suit, with a white shirt open at the collar.

"Peter, so good to see you. Mr. Lincoln told me all about our arrangement. You start your new job first thing in the morning. I'll even give you a ride to work! Mr. and Mrs. Creek, I wonder if you would excuse Peter and me for a minute while we step outside? We need to talk business. We won't be long."

"Why sure," said Mr. and Mrs. Creek simultaneously.

"A real job! I'm proud of you, son," said Mr. Creek.

Hoover opened the front door and gestured for Peter to follow him. Once outside, the grin left Hoover's face.

"Our friend, Mr. Lincoln, sends his greetings."

"Yeah, well, what do you want from me?"

"Information. Keep your eyes and ears open. If you hear anything of interest, you let me know."

"Like what?"

"It's a law office. Use your brain. Be creative. I want to know what cases they're working on. I want to know where they live. I want to know how they spend their leisure time, when they're going out of town, where they're going. And I want everything you can find out about Skip Schafer."

"Okay. How do I get all of that information?"

"Like I said, kid, use your brain. There's one more thing. I want you to install this program on their computer."

Peter took the jump drive offered by Hoover. "What does this do?"

"It helps you do your job. It will allow me to remotely access their computer."

"Cool."

"So, with you telling me what to look for, and me having access to their computer, we will soon know everything we need to know."

"But, won't I need a password or something?"

"You install the program and it will learn the password the next time someone logs on. Now, there's a meeting I expect you to attend, Friday night. Bring a friend. Someone who wants to live on the edge; someone who loves excitement, power, women, money and everything that the world has to offer! You will have the time of your life. Trust me."

***

On his drive home, John's mind wandered to the first time he saw Sandy. Skip brought her and Bret, her cameraman, to the office. Sandy was trying to get the scoop on the defense John would be using in the Butcher of Belhaven case and had used Skip to get into John's office, unannounced. John remembered that Sandy was the most beautiful woman he had ever laid eyes on - sandy hair, high cheekbones, an elegant nose, striking blue eyes, a full complement of feminine curves, and legs that seemed to reach all the way to the first floor. The details of that first meeting flooded his thoughts. The memory was so vivid that he re-lived the moment.

He remembered being so mesmerized by her stunning beauty and aura of charisma that he didn't notice he was on camera. "I remember I was embarrassing myself, stuttering and stumbling, until Karen stepped between us. Karen rescued me, once again." John shook his head, trying to clear the memory from his brain so that he could pay attention to his driving.

"Karen is so awesome," said John to himself. "I was making a fool of myself and she stood by me to defend me. Where can you find loyalty like that? It's no wonder she's so angry with me."

John parked his Trooper below the levy and walked up the pier to his home, a 1972 Drifter houseboat. As he stepped on the deck, he had a flashback of Sandy greeting him on his houseboat. She was attired in a little, short, white dress, gathered at the waist and cut revealingly low. Her dark tan was enhanced by the color of the dress. She handed him a glass of wine and smiled, revealing a deep dimple on her left cheek. He remembered her eyes, her lips and even her perfume.

John shook his head again. "Good grief! I can't get this girl off my mind!" He took a seat in a lounge chair on the front deck of his boat and let out a sigh. "Karen is the best woman I will ever know, but I am completely infatuated with Sandy. I think I'm in love with her. What am I going to do?"

Chapter 9

Peter Creek arrived at the office of Brooks and Bradley at 8:00 sharp. Karen described his job duties and took him to a desk in the file room.

"This is your desk."

"Cool, I get my own desk."

"Don't get used to it. You won't be there much. You will be filing, making copies, delivering papers and running errands."

"I'm just glad to have a job."

Jackson stepped into the file room and said, "Good morning everybody. How's your first day?"

"So far so good," said Peter as he looked lecherously at Karen.

"Great. Ready for your first adventure?"

"Sure."

"Come with me to the bank. We need to make financial arrangements for an auction. You can come with me and see what we do."

"What do you mean, 'see what we do'? How many auctions have we done, Jackson?" asked Karen.

"Counting this one? Hmm, let me see. One."

"That's what I thought. Before you go, let me run down the hall for a minute. I'll be right back. Peter, watch the lobby for me while I'm gone."

"Sure."

As Karen left, Jackson smiled and said, "Stay on her good side, and you'll do all right."

"Okay, will do."

Jackson stepped into his office. Peter could not believe his luck. He had been in the office only minutes and he was already sitting at Karen's computer. He pulled the jump drive out of his pocket and inserted it in the port. He looked at the computer screen, and nothing seemed to change. He thought he heard someone coming down the hallway. "It could be Karen! What if an icon about the jump drive pops up on the screen? I've got to get it out,'thought Peter. He reached for the jump drive.

"Peter?"

Peter jumped from his chair when he heard Jackson's voice. He looked up, startled.

"Calm down, son. Didn't mean to startle you. Would you make two copies of this for me?"

Peter's eyes darted as he looked at the papers Jackson was handing him, looked down at the jump drive still in the computer, and looked at the door. "Uh, yeah, sure. No problem. Two copies coming up," said Peter as he took the papers.

Jackson chuckled and shook his head. "You're a little nervous. I guess that's normal for your first day at your first job. Just bring me the copies when they're ready."

"Yes, sir. Will do."

Jackson turned and stepped into his office. The jump drive icon popped up on the screen. Someone walked past the office door and continued down the hall. Sweat popped out all over Peter's forehead. He clicked on the icon. A window opened on the screen with a single command button, 'Install'. His breathing was quick and shallow as he clicked the button. Another window opened, with a single command button, 'Eject'. He pressed eject, glanced around the room, and bent over to retrieve the jump drive.

"What are you doing, Peter?" asked Karen as she stepped back into the office.

"What? I didn't know you were here. I wasn't doing nothing! I just dropped my, uh, pen."

"It must be hot in here, you're sweating like you ran a mile."

"Oh, yes, ma'am. I need to make some copies for Mr. Bradley. Excuse me," said Peter as he rushed from Karen's desk to the copy machine.

Karen instinctively looked around her desk to make sure everything was all right as Peter hurried into the copy room. "Strange young man," she said to herself. She settled into her chair and entered the code to open her email program, the firm calendar and contacts program.

A few minutes later, Jackson took Peter to the bank where Brooks and Bradley conducted all of their business. Jackson explained the situation surrounding the farm to Gary, his banker.

"That does not sound like a good business transaction to me."

"Maybe not. But, it's what we decided to do."

"Well, it's your money," said Gary, then he hesitated and said, "for now. I'll help you get what you need for the auction."

After transferring funds from the firm account and from John's and Jackson's personal accounts, Gary issued Jackson a bank check in the amount of $58,327.

"If something falls through, bring this check back to me and I'll void it and put the money back into your accounts. All you have left is $1,000."

"Thanks, Gary."

"Don't mention it. Really, don't mention it. I don't want anybody to know that I helped you lose all your money."

"I will need to take the $1,000 in cash, just in case I miscalculated something."

Gary sighed and authorized the withdrawal.

When they left the bank, Peter said, "I don't understand what the banker was saying. You and your partner are going to buy this whole farm for less than $60,000? I bet it's worth a lot more than that. Y'all are getting a really good deal, aren't you?"

"No, we aren't buying it. Our client is using this money to pay off his mortgage. Otherwise, he'll lose his farm."

"But, I heard the banker say that's all the money that you and your partner have."

"Yep."

"What if your client doesn't pay you back?"

"That's what Gary is worried about. We'll cross that bridge when we come to it. In the meantime, we're not going to let this family lose their farm."

Peter seemed lost in thought while they hurried back to the parking lot behind the office. Karen was waiting next to Jackson's car.

"So, are we all going?" asked Jackson.

"I want to see where our money is going," said Karen. "If this doesn't work out, we may not have an office, and Peter's first job might be really short."

"Well, okay. Everybody hop in. John is already there. He went ahead of us to meet with our client."

Karen noticed that Peter was quiet during most of the hour-long drive to the courthouse in Philadelphia, where the auction was scheduled to occur. She asked him a few questions trying to draw him out, but he responded with brief answers, adding nothing. Karen crinkled her forehead and nose as she wondered to herself why Peter was so quiet. *Was he shy,* she thought? *Or, is it something else?*

She turned her attention to Jackson.

"So, do you think there is any gold on that farm?"

"Naw, it's just a rumor. If there were any gold, it would have been found long ago."

"What about the gold coin?"

"That really might be left over from a visitor, long ago. One coin does not mean there was a treasure."

"What is all this talk about a treasure?" asked Peter with an edge of excitement.

"Well, that got your attention," laughed Karen. "I thought it might."

"Well, tell me!"

"There's a rumor that the James Gang buried treasure on this farm. That may be why the Texas Daltons want to foreclose on the property."

"No kidding! Buried treasure! What's up with that?"

"Our client," explained Karen, "is a nice elderly Indian named Frank Dalton. He claims that his great-great grandfather was Frank James, the brother of Jesse James."

"Wow!"

"Unlikely," said Jackson.

"Maybe it is unlikely, but his name is really interesting," responded Karen.

"You mean, 'Frank'? Lots of people are named Frank."

"No, I mean Frank Dalton. There are conflicting rumors, but one rumor is that when Frank James retired from robbing banks, he changed his name, bought land, made investments with his stolen money, lived off of his earnings and died at an old age."

"Changed his name, huh. What to?" asked Jackson. "Let me guess."

"Yep. You guessed right," responded Karen. "Frank Dalton."

"Whoa!" exclaimed Peter, while Jackson laughed.

"No kidding?"

"No kidding."

"Frank Dalton. Our client really is named after Jesse James' brother. And I suppose Frank Dalton James settled in Texas?" asked Jackson.

"Some say Texas, some say Tennessee," said Karen. "Some say he didn't change his name. There are so many rumors you can't know what's true. But, people love to believe in buried treasure."

"Maybe he lived in both places," said Peter, and added eagerly, "and Mississippi is between them! And our client is named after him!"

"So it seems," said Jackson. "And the Daltons from Texas have purchased the mortgage and want to foreclose."

"So, the treasure story must be true!" said Peter with wonder on his face.

"Well, I wouldn't go that far," said Jackson

"Knowing a little history can be really interesting and can help you understand the present a lot better," observed Karen. "Don't you agree, Peter?"

"I always hated history," answered Peter. "Seemed irrelevant to me. But, now I don't know. Maybe history matters sometimes."

"Maybe so," laughed Jackson. "For instance, historically speaking, do you know why the Native Americans were here first?"

"No, why?" asked Peter.

"They had reservations."

"Ooh, don't listen to him," said Karen with exasperation. "That is not funny. Speaking of history, what's the latest on Goshen Springs Beer?"

"The rest of our payments are on hold. Apparently, our interest in the company is pledged against a loan taken out to fund the brewery and the marketing. The company is not making money yet, and payments to shareholders are on hold until the bank is confident it will get paid."

"But, I thought we were supposed to get paid first."

"As I understand it, there are some back-end guarantees from the parent company and the Faber family, but the bank insisted that the first money be used to increase the chance that Goshen Springs Beer is a success. So, the Fabers are spending money on start up, promotion and repaying the bank loan first."

"And that means we're broke once we pay off the farm, with no hope of money from the Faber family any time soon."

"Yep."

"That's what I thought, and that's why I'm coming to the auction."

"What's all this talk about Goshen Springs Beer?" asked Peter.

Karen was pleased that Peter was opening up and engaging in conversation, so she gladly responded. "We represented the man who discovered the recipe and brewing instructions for what once was the most famous beer in America."

"How do you know it was a famous beer?"

"History, my son," said Jackson. "According to the story, back in the early 1800's, it was the most popular beer in the U.S. and General Andrew Jackson proclaimed it to be the best beer in the world."

"That was way back in the 1800's. That was like a hundred years ago," observed Peter.

"Two hundred," corrected Karen.

"Yeah, whatever, that's my point. Two hundred years ago. I mean, whatever was hot last year is gone and forgotten this year. That's just the way it is. So, why would some old beer matter today?"

"Well, I'll tell you why. The beer was named after its inventor and brewer, Goren Goshen, and the little town that grew up around his brewery was called Goshen Springs," answered Jackson.

"Oh yeah, I've heard the legend of the Ghost of Goshen Springs, and then all that stuff that happened on the island on the reservoir. That was crazy."

"Yeah," said Jackson, "satanic cults and human sacrifice, right here in the Bible Belt. Pretty scary stuff."

"I'll say," said Karen with a shiver.

"You don't believe any of that really happened do you?" asked Peter.

"Well, yeah! We were there," said Jackson.

"No way! Tell me about it!"

"Not right now. You can read all about it when I finish the book," said Jackson.

"Oh man! I gotta read a book to find out? Well, tell me what's going on with this beer."

"Okay," continued Jackson, "we negotiated the sale of the recipe to a brewing company in New Orleans owned by the Faber family, and now we each own a piece of the company. If the venture is a success, we'll do well."

"Oh. What happens if it doesn't do well?"

"I think we still get paid some money, but it will be spread out over a long time," explained Jackson.

"And you are about to spend the last money you will see in a long time on someone else's farm, so that someone else can go find gold on the farm you are paying for?"

"That about sums it up. Look, here we are in downtown Philadelphia, Mississippi," observed Karen.

Chapter 10

Strategically situated in the center of the Courthouse Square, the Neshoba County Courthouse presides over the business district of Philadelphia, Mississippi. The alignment of Byrd Street, Main Street, Beacon Street and Center Street form the Square. Jackson found a parking space under a huge magnolia tree on Center Street and spotted John and Frank Dalton standing under a shade tree.

Karen introduced Peter to John and to Mr. Dalton.

"Welcome to the team," said John as he shook Peter's hand. Peter responded with a less than confident shake, a brief smile, and then looked towards the ground, away from John's eyes.

Mr. Dalton shook Peter's hand, looked him in the eye, and asked, "Is something troubling you son?"

Peter's eyes darted to the side and he lowered his head as he said, "Oh, no sir. This is just my first day and I didn't know what to expect."

"Humph," said Frank.

"Fill me in. Tell me who these characters are," said Jackson as he pointed in the direction of a knot of men standing near the courthouse steps on Main Street.

"Mr. Dalton was just about to tell me about them," said John.

Peter and Karen leaned in so they could hear.

"The tall, older man is my cousin from Texas, Shawn Dalton. I saw him two or three times when we were young. He looks the same to me, as mean as ever. The thickset fellow next to him is his son, Brad. I chased him off the farm last month with my shotgun. He's grinning at me now. He'll enjoy throwing me off our farm."

"If he gets the chance. Does Brad live in Texas, too?" asked John.

"Yes, but he has been spending a lot of time around Philadelphia for the past year or so."

"Isn't that about how long Curtis has been missing?"

"Yes, I suppose that's true," said Frank with a furrowed brow. "The skinny bald man is Whittaker. Those are his two sons getting out of the pick-up across the street. Walt and Wes. The big man is a lawyer with a funny name. He was the man who loaned us the $50,000 and had us sign a mortgage."

"The one you thought was a nice man?"

"That's the one. I don't know the other man."

"He looks like a lawyer to me," said Jackson.

"Excuse me, Mr. Dalton," said John. "Jackson, let's go meet our competition."

John and Jackson walked into the enemy camp and extended their hands. Introductions were exchanged. Karen, Peter and Mr. Dalton trailed behind them and stayed within listening distance.

"I want to watch everyone's face," said Frank. "Faces say more than words." He paused and looked at Peter's face for a long moment, then turned back toward the action. Peter's eyes grew larger as Frank looked away, and he glanced about, wondering whether anyone else was watching his face. Karen pretended not to notice.

One of the men introduced himself as Jason Collier, a lawyer from Houston.

"This is a first for me. I've never attended an auction for anything less than a hundred million dollars." He laughed a haughty laugh. "But, Shawn Dalton is a good client and this farm has sentimental value to him. I just want to make sure that the exchange of possession is accomplished smoothly, if you know what I mean."

"I see," said John, "and you are?" asked John as he extended his hand to a tall, stout lawyer in an ill-fitting suit.

"B. H. Sutton. Everybody calls me Backhoe. I'm the trustee for the deed of trust. I'm here to conduct the sale."

Jackson and John laughed and said, "What a great name."

Karen shook hands with Backhoe and introduced herself.

Backhoe's eyes widened as he shook Karen's hand. He turned away from the lawyers who were exchanging small talk, lowered his voice, and said, "Pleased to meet you, Miss Wilkes. Mr. Brooks is a lucky man to have such a lovely assistant."

"Perhaps you should tell him sometime," said Karen. "He doesn't seem to know how lucky he is."

"I see. Here's my card in case you ever want a more appreciative employer. Is it okay if I call you?"

Karen smiled, but didn't answer.

"I take that as a yes," said Backhoe as he turned back to join the conversation with the other lawyers.

Peter leaned toward Karen and whispered, "He's hittin' on you."

"Maybe he is."

"What's a deed of trust?" asked Peter.

"The mortgage," answered Karen as she studied the men, looking for clues in their body language.

Backhoe said, "I'm not in the same league as our friend Mr. Collier," as he gestured toward the Houston lawyer. "I'm just a small time local real estate lawyer. I've never done a hundred million dollar deal, or even a million dollar deal for that matter. My deals are mostly between a hundred dollars and a hundred thousand dollars."

"I think we can trust Backhoe," whispered Karen to Peter.

"I think you like him," whispered Peter to Karen.

"You are just the man I wanted to see," said John to Back Hoe. "What is the redemption price?"

"What do you mean, redemption price?" asked Collier, a troubled look on his face. The tone of his voice caught the attention of his clients, who stopped their small talk and began listening in on the conversation.

"Well, Mr. Collier," explained Backhoe, "the owner of homestead real estate can redeem the property for the amount owed, plus interest and costs, up until the time the hammer falls at the auction."

"Well, let's get this party rolling then."

"Not till 11, Mr. Collier. My watch says that it's 5 'til,'" said Back Hoe.

"Well, I believe that your watch is a bit slow."

"That may be, but today my watch is the official time. To answer your question, Mr. Brooks, the redemption price is $58,327. At least that's what it is before the bidding starts. Some say that I am entitled to a percentage of the amount recovered once the bidding starts, but I've never collected that extra fee in a post auction commencement pre-hammer redemption. Just doesn't seem right. But, once the hammer falls ending the auction and I accept an offer, it will be too late to redeem the property."

Jackson stepped up and said, "Well, you won't have to worry about that today, because it just so happens that we have a certified check in the amount of $58,327 to present to you on behalf of Mr. Frank Dalton to redeem his property by paying his mortgage in full, together will interest and costs." He presented the check with a big smile.

"Well, that looks to be in order," said Backhoe as he examined the certified check.

Jackson symbolically wiped his forehead and said, "That's a relief, because I have never redeemed property at an auction before. I checked the math backward and forward, and I came up with the same number as you, Backhoe. Would you sign this receipt please?"

"Whoa, whoa, whoa, I don't know what you are trying to pull here, but you can't do this. Don't you sign that receipt," demanded Collier.

"I most certainly will. The man is entitled to a receipt. He delivered to me a certified redemption check in the proper amount. Therefore I will give him not only the receipt, but also the note marked paid and I will cancel his deed of trust." BackhHoe turned back to Jackson. "By the way, there will be a $12 recording fee for filing that cancellation."

"Will you take cash?"

"Certainly."

Shawn Dalton stepped forward. "Just a minute, Backhoe. I hired you. You work for me. I am telling you not to take that check or sign that receipt."

"I am aware that you hired me, Mr. Dalton and I appreciate the $500 fee, plus expenses, thank you very much. However, I am unable to comply with your command. I am the trustee for this sale and I have an obligation to follow the law."

"'Unable' you say. Well then you're fired! I'll find someone who is competent and able to do as he is told."

"You may fire me, but the redemption has already taken place. The mortgage is paid in full and the property belongs to Mr. Frank Dalton. I will process the check and send your proceeds to you promptly along with the confirmation of the termination of my employment. I believe that our business here is concluded. Good day, gentlemen."

"That was awesome," whispered Karen.

Shawn Dalton thrust his hand into Backhoe's chest. "Just a minute you low life, unethical traitor. You are not leaving here with my money."

Backhoe sucked in his gut and seemed to grow six inches taller. His face turned beet red and sweat popped out all over his forehead. In a remarkably controlled low voice, he said, "I suggest you remove your hand, if you want to keep it. I will process this check in exactly the same way I process every check. Good day." Backhoe marched away from the courthouse toward his office. As soon as he was out of sight he stopped, leaned against a parked car, wiped his forehead with a handkerchief and caught his breath. "That was way too much sugar for a dime." He then crossed the street and entered his office.

Shawn Dalton, trembling with anger, watched Backhoe march away. He whirled to face John, and said, "This isn't over. You will pay for this. Mark my words." Shawn spun on his heels and commanded, "Let's get out of here." His retinue quickly followed.

Collier, a slight grin on his face, paused for a moment and gave both Brooks and Bradley a nod of respect. "Round one to you Mr. Brooks, Mr. Bradley," he said as he turned to follow the Daltons.

"Yikes. I remember what happened the last time somebody said 'you will pay for this, mark my words'," said Jackson.

"Yeah. I believe I'll skip the celebratory brownies," said Karen.

Peter exclaimed, "That was awesome! You outsmarted them. Those people were mad, mad, mad!"

"Yeah, well, life can be short and cruel if you go around making people mad, mad, mad at you all the time. But, right is right," responded Jackson.

Frank stepped forward and shook everyone's hand with both of his hands. "My family thanks you. My ancestors thank you. My family yet to be born thanks you. Please, come to my home and let us feed you. I will invite my whole family and they will be there for lunch day after tomorrow to celebrate this great day. We would do it sooner, but I want my nephew, Awesome Dalton, to be there. He is out of town and comes back tomorrow night."

"What a great name!" said Karen.

"Yeah, that's an awesome name!" said Jackson. Karen rolled her eyes again.

"You must come to our family celebration. You are family now," said Frank.

John and Jackson looked at each other, shrugged and John said, "Sure, we wouldn't miss it."

***

Across the street, Walt and Wes leaned against their pickup, glaring at Frank Dalton. Brad Dalton joined them. "Look at them gloating, acting like they really pulled one over on us," said Brad.

"Makes me sick," said Walt.

"Maybe we can pull another Curtis on them, if you know what I mean," Brad said with a sinister expression.

"I heard 'em say they were having a big family picnic day after tomorrow to celebrate."

"Why don't we pay them a little visit and watch them scatter?" suggested Wes.

"Yeah, they won't be gloatin' then!" said Walt, and they laughed as they climbed into the pickup.

Chapter 11

John, Jackson, Peter and Karen gathered under a magnolia tree on the courthouse lawn. Their mood was buoyant and upbeat.

"I don't remember ever being so happy about being so broke," said Jackson.

"You will get your money back, won't you?" asked Peter

"We hope so. But, there's many a slip between the cup and the lip," responded Jackson. Karen shook her head and John laughed.

"Huh?" asked Peter.

"The only thing we know for sure is we don't have our money anymore. I think we'll get it back but, hey, if we don't, it's just easy go, easy go," explained Jackson.

"I thought it was easy come, easy go," said Peter.

"In my experience, the only thing about money that's easy is the go."

"So, you're okay with losing all your money?"

John and Jackson looked at each other, shrugged and said simultaneously, "Yep."

Karen laughed and said, "That's one of the reasons I love working with these guys. They have never been motivated by money. They just want to do the right thing. You could learn a lot about life from them."

Peter nodded and smiled. Karen noticed that Peter became quiet and seemed detached, lost in thought. Indeed, Peter was wondering if he was on the right side. 'How did I ever get myself in to this mess? How can I get out?'

"Mr. Dalton told me about a jury trial coming up soon," said John.

"Trial? What trial?" asked Jackson.

"It seems that Mr. Whittaker is suing the Daltons for taking possession of his cows."

"You mean the cows that ate the beans?" asked Karen.

"That's them."

"What's wrong with keeping the cows that ate the beans? Sounds fair to me," said Karen.

"Well, Whittaker claims Frank took the law into his own hands, at his peril, and it just so happened that the cows were ready for market when the Dalton family took them. He claims they lost weight, and by the time they were sold, the price of beef had crashed. Hence, big losses. Frank sold the cows, and the money raised from the sale of the cows is on deposit with the court. The winner gets the money on deposit, plus damages. If Frank wins, he should be able to repay us."

"And if he loses, Whittaker gets the money on deposit plus a judicial lien on the farm which he could foreclose, just like today. But this time, we don't have any money to stop the foreclosure," observed Jackson.

"Right," said John.

"I knew it! I knew that if we gave them all our money something would happen, and we would lose our money for nothing," lamented Jackson.

"Y'all can head back," said John. "I'm going to stay a while. I want to check out the court file for the upcoming trial."

"Are you kidding?" asked Karen. "Leave you here to do all the work on your own while all of our money is at stake? Not me. I'm staying."

"Me too," said Jackson.

Peter shrugged.

A couple of hours later, they had a complete copy of the court file. Then they examined county tax maps to get an idea of the lay of the land and the location of neighbors. A young clerk named Emily Martin walked past. John called her over to the map. "Can you tell us anything about the Goni Swamp?"

"My boyfriend took me out there to go fishing a little over a year ago. The place was spooky. I would never go back. It was creepy. We heard strange animal sounds. Almost like a person moaning."

"Huh," said John. "Is that around the time Curtis Dalton went missing?"

"Now that you mention it, yeah, about that time."

"I understand that the Daltons drained the swamp and planted soybeans," said Karen.

"Well, that may be, but I have bad memories about the place. They say it's haunted. I'm never going back. Besides, that Deputy scared the heck out of us when we were there the first time."

"Deputy?" asked Karen.

"Yeah, Deputy Townsend. He told us we were trespassing, and we should never come back."

As the clerk walked away, Karen, Jackson and John looked at each other with wide eyes.

"Oh no. Not another haunted place," said Karen as she visibly shivered.

* * *

At last, they headed back. Karen climbed into the Trooper with John, and Peter rode with Jackson. John looked at Karen as he cranked the engine. "So, you're not mad at me anymore?"

"I'm pleased that we are doing the right thing for this family."

"Are we friends again?"

"Don't press your luck."

"Ooh! Ooookay."

"What do you think about Backhoe?" asked Karen.

"Back Hoe?"

"Yeah. What do you think about him as a lawyer, as a man?"

John was relieved that the subject had changed. "Well, I just met him, so it's too soon to form an opinion, but he did the right thing. I think he showed a lot of character."

"Do you think he showed courage?"

"I think so. It's easy to just go along with everybody, especially the ones who are paying you, but he did what he thought was right without regard to who was paying him. Why?"

"I'm looking for a man of character, who will do the right thing, even when it's hard, a man of courage, a man who knows what he wants."

John was silent for a moment as he turned onto Highway 16 and contemplated what Karen was saying. "I agree those are good qualities to look for. You deserve someone with those qualities."

"So, when is Sandy coming to town?"

"Are we going to talk about Sandy for the next hour?"

"If that's who you want to talk about."

"No, I thought we would talk about..." John hesitated.

"What? What did you think?" asked Karen.

"I'm not sure. I didn't mean to start anything."

"I just want to know one thing."

"Okay."

"When Sandy comes to town, are you going out with her?"

"What do you mean?"

"You know, take her to dinner or something?"

"I hadn't thought about it. I don't know"

"Don't know! Wrong answer."

"Karen! What is this about?"

Karen pulled her cell phone out of her purse and made a call. "Jackson, could you stop at the first gas station on Highway 16? Yes. John is going to drop me off there. Please give me a ride home."

John looked at Karen, puzzled beyond understanding or belief.

"This is the place. Pull over here, please. Thank you, John."

John stopped at the pump. Jackson pulled up behind him.

"What's going on, Karen?" asked John.

Karen opened the door, stepped out of the Trooper and leaned back in. "Backhoe is about to ask me out. I'm going to say yes." Karen closed the door, hard, and walked quickly to Jackson's car.

John stared at the closed door and said, "What?"

* * *

It was after 7:00 when Peter returned home from his first day at work. His mom met him at the door.

"Why are you so late?"

"We were in Philadelphia all day, Mom. Mr. Bradley just dropped me off. It was awesome. We saved a farm and the farm probably has buried treasure on it!"

"That's nice, honey. Why didn't you call?"

"Nice? Aren't you listening to me? I didn't call because dad took my cell phone away, remember?"

"Oh, yeah, I forgot about that."

"He said I could have it back when I could pay the bill. Well, I have a job now. Can I get my phone back?"

"I don't see why not. I'm sure he'll give it back when he gets home. Listen, will you run up to the store and get me a few things?"

"How am I supposed to get there? I'm grounded from the car. Don't you think that I'm too old to be grounded?"

"Your dad just wanted you to show some responsibility."

"Well, I got a job. That's responsible, right?"

"You can use my car."

"Great! I'm glad to go to the store for you."

Peter had driven only two blocks when blue lights and a siren startled him. The police car was on his bumper. He looked at his speedometer. He was well below the speed limit. Peter felt his heart in his throat. "Oh, man. Just what I need."

He pulled over and watched the patrolman climb out of his car and approach, one hand over his holster. Peter rolled the window down.

"Yes, officer, sir."

"License, insurance and registration."

Peter fumbled with his wallet, found his license, and searched the glove box. "This is my mom's car. I'm not sure where she keeps the insurance and registration."

"Get out of the car."

Peter complied.

"Hands behind your back." The patrolman whirled Peter around and cuffed him.

"What is going on? Why are you doing this? What did I do?"

"As if you didn't know."

"I don't know!"

The patrolman patted him down, and stopped at his rear pocket. "What's this? What do you have in your pocket, buddy?"

"What? I don't have anything in my pocket."

The patrolman whirled him back around. "Does this look like nothing to you?" He held a plastic bag with a white crystal substance in it.

"Where did you get that? I don't know what that is."

"Looks like crack to me. You have the right to remain silent. Anything you say or don't say will be used against you. You have a right to a lawyer, but not until I get through with you. Now, get in the back of the patrol car."

Peter was in tears, "But, that's not mine!"

"Yeah, yeah, that's what they all say."

Another car arrived as Peter was pushed into the backseat of the patrol car. Peter couldn't see who was there, but he could hear the patrolman talking to another man. Then the patrolman opened the door and said, "There's somebody here that wants to talk to you."

"Thank you officer," said Hoover as he stepped into sight. "Peter, Peter, Peter. I've been so worried. I've been trying to reach you for hours. You haven't forgotten about our arrangement have you?"

"No, no! I just didn't have my cell phone. That's all."

"Well, that's not a good enough excuse, see, there are phones everywhere. You can borrow a phone. Our arrangement is, you check in with us as agreed, and you take my call, or else. So, get a phone. Do you understand?"

"Sure. Yeah. It will never happen again. I swear."

"Now, tell me all about today."

Peter couldn't speak. He couldn't think. The shock of being stopped by a policeman, the planting of drugs, Gregory's grease threat, and Hoover's presence worked together to create fear deep in the recesses of Peter's mind. Fear welled up and almost blinded him. For a moment, Hoover's voice seemed to be coming from far away. Peter's head began to swim. He felt himself shaking. He felt as though he was at the end of a tunnel with no escape, and all he could see was Hoover.

"Did you install the program?"

Hope welled up in Peter. Suddenly, he could see a way out.

"Yes. It wasn't easy, but I got it done first thing this morning."

"Well, that's in your favor. Can you tell me anything that I would find interesting?"

Excitedly, Peter said, "You're not going to believe what I found out for you."

Peter laid it on thick. Hoover was especially interested in the farm, the treasure story, the auction, and Hoover was really pleased to hear that the people who wanted to foreclose on the farm were wealthy and that they were very angry with Brooks and Bradley.

"So, these people that are angry with Brooks and Bradley, tell me their names and where they're from again. I think they may become new friends of ours."

Peter eagerly told him everything he knew.

After telling Hoover everything, Peter, with a puzzled look on his face, added, "So, John Brooks and Jackson Bradley spent all of their money trying to save this farm for people they hardly know. I had sort of hoped they would be jerks or something."

"They're after that treasure."

"No, they talked like they didn't believe there was any treasure. If they wanted the treasure, they could have just bought the farm."

"Then they're fools, using their own money to save someone else's farm. They will never get their money back. Being a fool is a lot worse than being a jerk. Don't make the mistake of getting sentimental or teary-eyed. These lawyers are dangerous fools. They're your enemy. Remember that. Now, this little incident tonight, what with you being pulled over and found to be in possession of a controlled substance and all, our policeman friend will just put that on a shelf and forget about it. So long as you and I are friends, this will never be mentioned again. Okay?"

"Sure, Mr. Hoover. Are you a cop?"

Hoover laughed. "I'll tell you what I am. I'm your best friend, or your worst nightmare."

* * *

Shaking with excitement, Hoover was on his cell phone as soon as Peter drove away. He intended to quickly capitalize on an opportunity to gain a wealthy ally, get quality legal help for Gregory, get Gregory off his back, and make a handsome fee. He wondered what he would say and how much he should say if anyone answered his call. He knew the risk that if he shared too much, everything could come crashing down on him. But, he knew he was already in over his head. "Great gain comes with great risk," he said aloud, to reassure himself. After leaving several voicemails, someone returned his calls.

"This is Jason Collier returning Harry Hoover's call to Mr. Dalton. He left some interesting messages."

"That's me. I can help Shawn Dalton acquire something he is very interested in, a farm and everything on it, in it and under it. Could you have him call me tonight? Time is of the essence. He will not want to miss this opportunity."

"He received your messages and asked that I return your call. I'm his personal lawyer. He doesn't take unsolicited calls, especially in the middle of the night. So, he asked me to check you out. I have. How can you help Mr. Dalton acquire his family farm?"

"I know why he wants the farm."

"Sentimental reasons."

"A hundred million golden sentimental reasons. Maybe more."

"You haven't answered my question."

"I have critical inside information."

"Such as?"

"In two weeks there will be a trial against the current owners of that property."

"Public knowledge."

"Win that trial, acquire the rights to the judgment, do a judicial foreclosure and the farm is his."

"You are wasting my time. Way ahead of you."

"But, I know that this time there will be no miracle money to pay off the judgment at the last minute, and I know how to make sure of that."

"Speculation."

"Moles."

Silence.

"Moles are dangerous unreliable varmints."

"Not if one is digital and one is warm blooded. I know everything that Frank Dalton's lawyers, Brooks and Bradley are doing, before they do it."

"I cannot discuss anything unethical with you."

"Of course not."

Another pause.

"I also know how to get under their skin. I can keep them so occupied that there is no way they can focus on an upcoming trial."

"You're blowing smoke. Why would you have that kind of information about Brooks and Bradley?"

"I have a case against them. I play to win. That means that when Brooks and Bradley begin searching for," another pause, "sentimental trinkets, and they will, I'll know it in advance. I'll know when and where."

"How do you know they will be searching for these trinkets?"

"They didn't pay off that mortgage just to do a good deed. They want the gold. If Shawn Dalton wants that farm and what's on it, I can get it for him, but he's got to act fast. Tonight. And we have to be in City Court in Jackson in the morning."

"Ha! City Court! This has all the hallmarks of a good scam. I don't believe you."

"I happen to know you haven't left Jackson yet. Meet me tonight and I'll explain everything."

Chapter 12

Skip Schafer burst into the office at fifteen past eight the next morning.

"I've got to see John!"

Karen knew that John didn't have time to see Skip 'The Middleman' Schafer this morning. Skip was maybe two inches over five feet tall, but it was hard to tell because he always wore elevator shoes or tall heeled cowboy boots. He talked fast and thought of himself as a snappy dresser. Skip would be the only one who thought so. In fact, his wardrobe was, in a word, remarkable. Today, he was dressed in a matching bright paisley shirt and pants, accented with a huge gold chain around his neck and bright red cowboy boots. The combination made Karen feel a little dizzy as Skip darted about the lobby in a tizzy.

Until recently, Skip spent his life struggling to feel relevant. He shouted for attention in his dress and manner. To make himself feel important, he had come up with dozens of get rich schemes in his 37 years on earth. Some were so wild and out of this world that Jackson joked that Skip was from another planet. His schemes sometimes landed him in trouble, like his bottled dehydrated water scheme (just add water).

His first real success in life occurred just a few months ago when he managed to talk himself onto the Vampire Defense team as a volunteer. It turned out to be the case of the century. Unfortunately for Brooks and Bradley, Skip became the unofficial team spokesman. He first gained notoriety, and then fame because of his knack for mangling the English language. The press loved to get misquotes from Skip. At first they made fun of him, but soon they began to think that Skip's mangled speech was ingenious intentional double entendres. Skipisms, like, 'hindsight is fifty/fifty,' 'you misunderestimate me,' 'denial is not a river in China,' and 'the D.A. is a man of unimpeccable reputation,' had become household phrases.

To top off his moment of fame, Skip was involved in the late night raid on a group of devil worshippers ensconced on an island as they were about to perform a black mass rite involving murder and cannibalism. And it was little Skip who bagged the biggest catch of the raid, the infamous Gregory Lincoln, by using a boat anchor to knock him out cold. When

Gregory went to jail he promised that he would enjoy getting his revenge on little Skip, hence Skip's present state of high anxiety.

"Calm down, Skip. You can see Jackson in a few minutes," said Karen in a soothing voice, "John is not available."

But, I want to see John," exclaimed Skip over a protruding lip. "Never mind. I'll give Jackson the benefit of the pout. He can handle it. Gregory Lincoln has a bond hearing today! They're not going to let him out are they?"

"Jackson has it covered. He'll be in court at 9 to see what happens. Are you going to be there?"

"No! I don't want to see him again. He gives me the creeps."

Peter heard the commotion. His ears perked up when he heard 'Skip' and 'Gregory Lincoln,' so he stepped out of the file room into the lobby.

"Who's this?" asked Skip, skepticism in his voice.

"Skip Schafer, meet Peter Creek, our new runner."

"Yeah, yeah, good to meet you, Peter. I had your job, sort of, up until a week or two ago."

"So, you're Skip Schafer?"

"I know, I know, it can be hard to believe when you meet a certifiable celebrity, but it's true! It's me, in person," said Skip as he held out his arms and turned in a circle to give Peter a view of the celebrity from every angle.

"Yeah, it's hard to believe," said Peter. "I just thought you would be bigger."

"What? Well, let me tell you, the size of the frame doesn't dictate the size of the fame. What matters most is what you got right here kid," Skip said as he thumped his chest with his fist. "Heart!"

"I'll try to remember that."

"Ya hear that Karen? The kid has heard of me. That's proof that my reputation exceeds me."

"Precedes, Skip, the word is precedes," responded Karen, suppressing a smile.

"Yeah. That's what I said."

"Did you get subpoenaed to be in court today?" asked Karen.

"Well, yeah, but I don't really have to go, do I?"

"Well, yeah!"

"Aahh! Look, they already set a bazillion dollar bond at his initial disappearance. Why do they have to have another bond hearing?"

"You mean his initial appearance."

"Yeah! That's what I said. He already had that hearing, and they already set a bond. Why they gonna do it again?"

"Every criminal defendant gets an initial appearance in three days or less from the date of arrest. Often, he doesn't have his own lawyer then, so he doesn't have a real chance to state his reasons for a reduced bond or raise other issues."

"What's there to raise? He's one of the leaders of a murderous gang of devil worshipers."

"He has rights just like everybody else," explained Karen.

"How can you say that? You were one of his victims!"

"Skip! Good to see you," said Jackson as he stepped out of his office. "Are you ready to go to court?"

"Do I have to?"

"Yep."

Skip sighed. His shoulders slumped and his arms hung limp by his side for a moment. "Oh, all right. You'll make sure Lincoln doesn't get out of jail, right?"

"It's not up to me. I'm not handling Gregory's case."

"Why not? You're my lawyer!"

"Yes, but I'm not handling this case. I'm just going there to observe. The D.A. is handling the prosecution. That's his job."

"The D.A.? Tellers? He hates me! He hates us!"

"Hate is a strong word, Skip. I agree that he doesn't like us."

"Isn't that a conflagration of interest?"

Jackson laughed. Karen grinned and shook her head.

"What's so funny?"

"I think that may be a perfect description. It probably burns Tellers up that he might help us. But, I bet that an assistant will be handling the hearing. I doubt we'll see Tellers today. Did you dress for court?" asked Jackson as he gazed at Skip's unique outfit.

"Yeah, you like?" asked Skip as he slowly turned so Jackson could get a good look. "I wanted something snappy, but understated for court."

"You redefine understated," said Karen, with extra emphasis on redefine.

"Give me a minute and I'll be ready," said Jackson as he stepped into his office and picked up a file. Just then, there was a knock at the door. Skip and Karen looked up to see a man with a bouquet of flowers.

"Excuse me, I have a delivery for Ms. Karen Wilkes."

"Whoa," said Skip. "Somebody's got a boyfriend."

"I'm Karen Wilkes."

"Here you go, ma'am," said the deliveryman as he placed the flowers on Karen's desk. He smiled and said, "I see why he sent flowers to you."

"Thank you," said Karen as she removed the card from the flowers. As the deliveryman left, Karen leaned into the flowers and took a deep breath. "They smell marvelous."

Jackson returned to the lobby with his file. "Who is your secret admirer?"

Skip responded, "Let me guess. John?"

"Let's see," said Karen as she smiled and opened the card. "My, my, he moves fast."

"Who?"

"That's between me and him. You two better get going or you'll be late."

"I guessed right, didn't I?" said Skip excitedly as he bounced up and down.

"No, not John."

"What? Who?"

"Get going! Hurry up!" said Karen as she made shooing motions with her hands.

Moments later, Jackson and Skip walked the two blocks to the police station, where the municipal court is located. They walked in front of the stately City Hall, a colonial mansion that resembles the White House, crossed the street in front of the Hinds County Courthouse, and arrived at the Jackson Police Department and Municipal Court, a 1950's era concrete and glass structure that takes up most of a city block.

"So, who's sending flowers to John's girlfriend?" asked Skip as they reached the door.

"Karen isn't John's girlfriend."

"Well, she should be. Who is it?"

"I'm not sure, but I have a good idea."

They passed though security, made their way to the courtroom and found a seat on a pew near the front of the packed room.

"Can't we sit further back? I don't want him to see me when he comes in. I just want to blend in with everybody else."

"Skip, you will never blend."

"Yeah, you're probably right. Some people have panache, and some don't."

A dozen inmates shackled and chained to one another and wearing orange jumpsuits entered a side door. An officer led them to an empty pew at the front of the courtroom and another officer brought up the rear.

"I don't see Gregory," whispered Skip.

Jackson didn't say anything.

"All rise," called the bailiff as the judge entered the room. A city prosecutor entered and took a seat at one of the counsel tables, a young lady Jackson recognized as Liz Blanton. The judge called the docket, the long list of cases to be handled that morning. People responded, "present," or "here." He called a name, but heard no response. He repeated the call, paused for a moment, then announced in a loud voice, "Madam clerk, issue a warrant!"

When he called "Gregory Lincoln," the city prosecutor said, "We may have an announcement on that case shortly." The judge completed the docket call and began handling initial appearances.

"Excuse me, Skip, I'm going to go see what's going on." Jackson stepped through the gate in the bar that separates the audience area from the participant area and tapped the prosecutor on the shoulder.

"Liz, what's up with Lincoln?"

"His lawyers are in the back talking with the Assistant D.A. about bond and the preliminary. I think they're about to make a deal."

"Really? Can I step back there and see what's going on?"

"Here they are now."

Assistant District Attorney Robert Thornton entered the courtroom, followed by Harry Hoover and Jason Collier. Jackson was taken aback for a moment when he saw Collier. He quickly recovered and stepped up to speak in whispered tones to the three lawyers.

"Mr. Bradley, we meet again," said Collier.

"Yes, well, I'm not surprised to see Hoover here, but it does surprise me that a famous and expensive lawyer from Houston would get his hands dirty in a lowly city court in Jackson, Mississippi."

"What do you mean, dirty?" demanded Hoover, taking great offense at the remark.

"No, I didn't mean anything inappropriate. Mr. Collier is usually handling hundred million dollar deals. I would have thought he would have sent an associate to do city court work."

"No offense taken, Mr. Bradley," said Collier. "The case of Mr. Lincoln came to my attention last night and I felt that a grave injustice was being done, so I thought I would lend him my support."

"I see. It's your civic duty."

"That's right. That and the sizable fee paid to me late last night made this case especially interesting to me."

Jackson turned to the A.D.A. "Bobby, what's going on?"

"We don't have enough evidence to hold Lincoln on the original charge of kidnapping, or on the possible murder charges."

"What?"

"Mr. Collier points out that not one witness connects Lincoln to the cult."

"He just happened to be there, on the island, during a cannibalistic ritual?"

"He had been fishing and camped on the edge of the island," explained Collier. "He had nothing to do with cult activity."

"Well, he cut Hal Boyd with a knife and he assaulted me and Skip."

"Mr. Boyd assaulted Gregory when Gregory was trying to escape the cult," explained Collier in a silky smooth voice. "My client thought you and Skip were part of the cult."

"Wait a minute. Bobby, you can't really be buying this without any testimony?"

"Jackson, even if we put on evidence, the very best we could hope for is simple assault on you and Skip. I can't proceed on the assault on Hal Boyd, even if I were inclined to do so, because Hal Boyd isn't here."

"Did you subpoena Hal?"

"No, I didn't think it would be necessary. I thought that there would be plenty of witnesses from members of the supposed cult who would identify Lincoln. None did. I can't hold him in jail on a couple of misdemeanor simple assault cases."

"Wait a minute." Jackson exhaled in exasperation. "I am not believing this."

"Now you know what our victims feel like when you walk one of your clients out of the courtroom, Bradley," said Thornton as he turned to face the Judge. "Your Honor, the State has an announcement on the Lincoln case."

"You can approach the bench. Have the Defendant approach, too."

"I'll get him, Your Honor," said Hoover.

Hoover stepped to the door and motioned to someone. Gregory Lincoln dressed in a neatly pressed dark suit, white shirt, and blood red tie stepped into the courtroom. He paused as he entered, looked across the audience and fixed his eyes on Skip. Skip quit breathing. Skip thought his heart quit beating as well.

Gregory's face broke into a wide grin when he read fear on Skip's face. He turned away from Skip and stepped up to the bench with his lawyers and the prosecutor.

"Your Honor, the State moves to drop the charges of kidnapping and murder, and the charge of aggravated assault."

"For what reason?" asked the judge.

"Lack of evidence."

"I see. What does that leave?"

"Two counts of simple assault."

"How do you wish to proceed?"

Collier spoke up, "Your Honor, Jason Collier, Houston Texas. I request that the simple assault charges be set for trial on a date far enough in the future for the State to complete its investigation. We are confident that when the investigation is complete, the State will not find enough evidence to proceed with those charges either. In the meantime, we request that Mr. Lincoln be released on his own recognizance."

"That's quite a swing, a million dollar bond last week to no bond this week," said the judge as he shook his head.

"Yes, sir. The State made a grave error in charging Mr. Lincoln, but he harbors no hard feelings and has no intention of seeking damages for wrongful arrest and false imprisonment," explained Collier. "He just wants justice to be done today, and justice requires his immediate release."

"What says the State?"

"We join in the request for a recognizance bond," said Thornton.

Jackson's mouth dropped open.

"Very well," said the judge. "Mr. Lincoln, you are a lucky man. You have good lawyers. You will be released on your own recognizance as soon as the paperwork is properly processed."

"That has already been done, Your Honor," said Collier. "Mr. Hoover has it here. All it requires is your signature and Mr. Lincoln could be released without any further delay."

"I see," said the judge as Hoover handed him the documents. The judge reviewed the papers, signed the forms and said, "Mr. Lincoln, you are free to go."

Jackson was stunned and he looked it. Collier offered his hand to Jackson. It took a moment for Jackson to recognize the offer. At last, he took Collier's hand and shook it. Collier leaned forward and said, "Looks like round two goes to the visiting team. See you soon."

Lincoln stepped next to Jackson, leaned over and, with a broad grin on his face, whispered into Jackson's ear, "I'll be seeing you." A chill ran up Jackson's spine. Lincoln turned and left the courtroom through the side door with his lawyers, leaving Jackson standing alone in the middle of the room. Jackson was unable to move while he tried to comprehend what just occurred. The world seemed to stop, until he became aware of the judge's voice.

"Mr. Bradley. Mr. Bradley!"

"What, oh, yes, Your Honor?"

"Your case is concluded. You can move along now, we have other business to conduct."

"Certainly. Excuse me, Your Honor."

Jackson returned to the pew where Skip waited, confusion etched on his face.

"What just happened?" whispered Skip loud enough to be heard throughout the courtroom.

"I'll explain when we get back to the office. We need to go now."

"It sounded like they were dismissing charges."

"Yes, they did."

"What?" shouted Skip. "How can that be?"

Bam, bam! "Order in the court!" commanded the judge as he banged his gavel on the resounder.

"I will tell you more when we get outside," whispered Jackson. "We need to go, quickly." He took Skip by the elbow, lifted him out of the pew and guided him through the door in the back of the courtroom.

Once outside, Jackson looked quickly in every direction, until he found Gregory standing on the sidewalk engaged in conversation with his lawyers. Gregory looked up, made eye contact with Jackson and grinned, like a predator sighting its prey.

"Come on Skip. Let's get back to the office. We've got to tell everybody what just happened. For their own safety, they have to know," said Jackson as he walked toward the office at a quick pace.

"How about telling me what just happened?" pled Skip as he struggled to keep up.

"A homicidal maniac who promised revenge against you, me, Karen and John is on the loose."

Chapter 13

The next morning Peter was filing for the first time. Karen had given him a single file and showed him how to index and tab pleadings and add them to the file. The work was tedious, but required his attention. His mind began to wander as he thought about last night's call to Hoover. Hoover was pleased to hear that everyone was headed to Philadelphia for lunch.

"Our friend Gregory will be glad to hear this. Maybe we can have a little surprise waiting for them," Hoover had said. "I'll make some calls now and see what I can arrange."

Peter's mind returned to the present when he heard Karen take a call.

"Oh, hello! ... Yes, I received the flowers. They are lovely. Thank you ... This weekend? I don't know. I'll have to think about it. I'll let you know tomorrow, okay? I'll be near Philadelphia today, actually. ... No, I don't think I can see you today. It's sort of work related and everyone will be there. Thanks for calling. Goodbye."

* * *

John, Jackson, Karen and Peter piled into John's Trooper, at about 10:30.

"What do you think about Gregory getting out?" asked Karen. Peter tensed up, stopped breathing, and leaned forward, listening to every word.

"I'm not sure what to think. I know I don't like it," said John, "but I'm not sure there's anything we can do about it."

"I was dumbfounded, and Skip is beside himself," said Jackson.

"I can imagine," said Karen. "Do you think we need to take precautions?"

"We need to keep our eyes open. I called Mitch yesterday," said John.

"Good. I hope we can get the Jackson Rugby Club to help us again," said Karen. She was referring to John's rugby team. They volunteered to help John and his law firm during the "case of the century." They canvassed the Belhaven neighborhood, looking for witnesses, and provided security for John and his firm when they began receiving death threats related to their defense of the alleged "Butcher of Belhaven."

"Some of the guys will be driving past our office and our homes from time to time," responded John.

"I hope one of them is Crush," said Karen, referring to Crush Barnes, the giant rugby player who volunteered to provide security to the law firm during their big case. He thwarted more than one assault during his tenure.

John nodded in agreement and then said, "After Jackson told me what happened, I called Rico at Robbery Homicide to tell him about Lincoln getting out."

"What did he say?" asked Karen.

"He couldn't believe it. He said he would put our office on a watch list for extra patrols, night and day."

"That's cool," said Jackson. "Rico's a good guy. Even though we're usually on opposite sides, he jumps right in to help when he sees it's the right thing to do."

"Yeah, he just wants justice," observed Karen.

They followed the instructions on the GPS and cruised along back roads through the Neshoba County hills. When they were close to their destination they fell behind an old pickup.

"That's Mr. Dalton," said Karen.

They followed Frank to a small wooden farmhouse, painted yellow and green. A porch with rocking chairs wrapped around two sides of the house. A dozen flowerpots sat on the porch and hung from the eves, along with wind chimes. A remarkably large Native American woman with an equally large grin occupied one of the rockers. Great oak trees provided shade for the house and yard. Hardly a sprig of grass grew under the oaks, but the yard was neat, with fresh rake marks in the dust. A feast was spread over several tables under one of the oaks. An assortment of chairs was arranged next to the tables. Sheets covered the food until the arrival of the guests of honor.

A hay barn, a tractor barn, a livestock stall, and a small pigpen were situated to the left of the house at the foot of a long lazy hill that served as a pasture. A garden and a chicken coop sat behind the house. A few cows grazed next to a small pond at the bottom of the hill and a field of freshly harvested corn stretched to a distant tree line beyond the house.

Dogs ran to greet them as John parked his Trooper in the shade beside Frank's pickup. Flushed with excitement, Frank jumped out of his truck hollering, "Erma, come meet our new family members!" Frank turned to John and explained, "Erma is G.W.'s wife. He's my cousin, but he's like a brother to me. Erma's been taking care of the place and cooking our meals since my wife passed, and man she can really cook. You're in for a treat. She's been cookin' all day. Everybody is ready to celebrate."

Erma rose from the rocker, padded across the porch and down the creaking steps into the yard. She came to Jackson first and enveloped him in her arms.

"Thank you! Thank you! We can't thank you enough," she said as she released Jackson, wiped tears from her face, and hugged Peter. After a moment, she released Peter and pulled John and Karen, together, into her chest, drowning out the sound of an approaching tractor. Karen started to resist, but surrendered to Erma's huge hug.

"Here comes G.W.," said Erma breathlessly as she released Karen and John. Karen brushed the front of her dress, as though she were straightening it, and purposefully avoided John's eyes.

The tractor brakes let out a little squeal as the tractor stopped. G.W. climbed down and greeted everyone as the engine puttered, sighed and stopped with a final clunk. Soon, a small crowd of family members of all ages came from every direction, a huge smile on every face. Hands were shaken, introductions were made, and laughter filled the air.

One young man arrived in a pickup and Frank was excited to introduce him. "Awesome, come over here and meet our lawyers." Awesome was a little over 6 feet tall, with long black hair and muscular arms. He had an easy smile as he shook hands with John, Jackson and Peter. He paused as he took Karen's hand and said, "Pleased to meet you, ma'am."

"This is my grandson," explained Frank. "He is the only one of the young men in our family interested in the farm after Curtis left. He is the hope of our future."

"You really know how to put pressure on a man, Grandpa Frank. There are plenty of children coming along after me, just look around," said Awesome as he gestured toward the many children playing under the oaks.

Karen leaned over and whispered to John, "I can see why they call him Awesome. That is one handsome young man."

John looked at Karen and raised his eyebrows.

"Please forgive all this emotion. We can't help ourselves," said Erma. "This farm is all we know. It's our life. You have done so much more than save our farm. You have saved our family and restored our hope. Please, come inside and freshen up and then share a meal with us."

Jackson smiled and said, " We would be honored to share a meal with you."

As they stepped onto the porch, Karen noticed that Peter hadn't moved. He seemed dazed. "It's pretty overwhelming, isn't it?" she asked as she observed Peter.

"Uh, Yeah. These people really appreciate what you've done."

"Yeah. Appreciation is better than pay," said Karen. "Come on in. I bet we're about to have the meal of a lifetime."

"I'll just wait out here."

"Suit yourself."

As Karen climbed the steps, she became aware of the pleasant tinkling sound of wind chimes. She noticed that all of the chimes were little metal hummingbirds.

"That's cute. I've never seen hummingbird chimes before," said Karen.

They entered through the screen door into a small den with simple furnishings. A checkerboard, game interrupted, sat on a small table in one corner. Karen noticed a hummingbird painting.

"I see that the hummingbird is a theme in your home. This painting is beautiful, and the wind chimes are precious."

"Yes, the painting was passed down to us from Sankky, Frank's great-great grandmother," explained Erma. "She was an accomplished artist, and she loved hummingbirds. This painting is more than 100 years old. Frank loves it, 'cause it was passed down, generation to generation."

"Wow! John, look at this painting. It is over 100 years old, painted by Mr. Dalton's great-great grandmother, Sankky," said Karen.

"Really? That is a very nice painting. Did Sankky travel?" asked John.

"Oh, you are wondering about the tropical plants in the picture and the mountains, the waterfall, and the valley in the background. She said that was a beautiful place that someone described to her. No, she spent her life here on the farm. She dreamed of traveling to Mexico, and she painted what she thought it would look like. Every member of the family has at least one of her paintings. She loved to paint mountains, waterfalls and hummingbirds," explained Erma.

Chapter 14

Walt turned up a dirt road, a cloud of dust swirled behind his pickup, a top of the line extended cab four-wheel drive beauty.

"So, you're headed to Skeeters," said Wes.

"Yeah, there's always some boys there lookin' for some fun."

"Who's Skeeter?" asked Gregrory.

"He's a pothead who will do anything for a few bucks. And, he knows to keep his mouth shut," said Walt.

"I know Skeeter knows how to keep his mouth shut. But, do his friends know to keep their mouths shut?" asked Brad Dalton.

"Yeah, don't worry," said Walt.

"I worry about people I don't know," said Brad as he glanced at Gregory. A humorless smile creased Gregory's lips.

Wes said, "I don't like this. I admit, I thought it was a good idea at first, but this is a bad idea."

"I agree," said Brad. "I don't want anything that might tie back to . . . ," he hesitated, and didn't finish the thought.

"Curtis," said Gregory.

"What!" exclaimed Wes, eyes wide.

"You don't want anything to tie you to the disappearance of Curtis, who jumped the bail that you paid off for him, secured by a mortgage on the property you want. I do my homework. I like to know the people I'm with."

A telling silence enveloped the group.

"That was a pretty slick move, arranging to anonymously loan the money for bail. I'm curious. How did he happen to have such a serious charge?"

"There was a series of robberies and burglaries," said Walt. "Curtis was caught with some of the stolen goods."

"Yeah. They found the stolen goods in his pickup," responded Lincoln. "Lucky break for all of you that Curtis Dalton would get into so much trouble that he would get a high bond, then jump bail, giving you the opportunity to anonymously pay off the bond. All you asked in return was that the payment be secured by a mortgage on a farm that you believe has a buried treasure. It was just a series of lucky breaks. What I wonder is, how did you get to be so lucky that Curtis didn't show?"

Walt, Wes and Brad glanced at each other.

"I guess, sometimes you have to make your own luck," said Lincoln. "Was Skeeter your lucky charm?"

Gregory noticed that Wes seemed to stop breathing and cast a sideways glance at Brad. 'The weak link,' thought Gregory.

"Lincoln, you have a vivid imagination," said Brad.

Walt stopped in front of a ramshackle house. Skeeter and two friends were looking under the hood of a car, tinkering. Beer in hand, Skeeter sauntered over to Walt's pickup. His wide smile was unforgettable because of the absence of one of his front teeth.

"What brings you to the po' folks house? You slummin' today?"

"Just wonderin' if you wanted to have a little fun," responded Walt.

"I dunno. Last time I had fun with you rich boys, I wasted my weekend in jail. And you didn't even come see me. So, what's in it for me?"

"How 'bout a hundred bucks a piece?" said Walt as he passed a wad of money through the window.

"Sure! Who do you want killed this time?" asked Skeeter with a chuckle as he glanced at Brad and took the money. Wes tensed up. Sweat broke out on his forehead. Gregory noticed.

"Nobody," said Walt. "I just want you to drive past German's place in a few minutes and scare everybody good. Make a lot of noise, shoot in the air. They're having a picnic and I want it to be memorable."

"German's place? He ain't never done nothin' to me. I don't want to mess with his family no more. I think we'll pass."

"What's the matter, Skeeter? You afraid of that old Indian?"

"Naw. I just want to stay away, after what happened with Curtis and all. I don't want to draw no attention."

Brad and Gregory climbed out of the truck and walked up to Skeeter. Brad whispered to Gregory, "This is a bad idea. We don't need more people involved in this."

"Leave it to me," responded Gregory.

"What do you mean?"

Gregory just smiled.

Walt continued speaking with Skeeter. "I'm not asking you to do nothing but scare 'em and make 'em run. It'll be fun." He passed Skeeter another wad of money.

Skeeter's eyebrows raised as he smiled and took the second wad of money.

"It's not so much the old man, but if his nephew Awesome is there, he ain't gonna sit still while we bust up their picnic."

"So, now you're afraid of just one little Indian?" prodded Walt.

"No, I just see that it could turn into more than we bargained for."

"I know what he's afraid of," said Brad. "It was Awesome that gave you that gorgeous smile. You two got into it one time didn't you?"

"That was a long time ago. We're over that." Skeeter turned to Brad and said, "Anyway, I thought them Indians was your cousins. Why do you always want to mess with them?"

Brad yanked Skeeter's ponytail, pulling his head back. "Don't ever say that. They are no relation to me. I want to see those thieving Indians run."

Skeeter stepped back to relieve the pressure on his hair. "Except for Curtis, I never heard this bunch accused of being thieves, and we know he didn't steal nothin'," said Skeeter. "What did they steal from you?"

"More than they can ever repay," responded Brad.

"Maybe that explains a lot. Well, let go a my hair, and maybe you done bought you a party buster. Who's this with you?"

"Friend of ours from Jackson. Gregory Lincoln."

"I'd like to go along. I wouldn't want to miss this for the world," said Gregory as he handed a third wad of money to Skeeter.

"Don't be spoiling him. He'll be too expensive next time we want his help," said Walt.

Skeeter smiled, took the money and said, "Yeah, sure. Why not? You can come. You got a rifle or a shotgun?"

"Yep. Let me grab my rifle."

Skeeter walked towards his pickup and motioned for Gregory to follow him. Skeeter called to his buddies, "Grab your rifles and mount up boys, we're gonna go make some noise."

"Yee ha!"

***

John stepped outside while Erma walked Karen around the farmhouse. She told a story about every picture and every piece of furniture. Karen decided that Erma was easy to love. She had a kind, friendly manner and Karen could tell from Erma's stories that she was proud of her family.

"This looks like Andrew Jackson," said Karen as she gestured at a painting.

"It is."

"Who is this in the picture with him?"

"That's Sankky's father, Kewaah. The General and Kewaah were best friends, until Jackson betrayed us and drove us out of our homes. So,

Kewaah tore Jackson right out of the picture. Later, we put the picture back together. You can still see the tear marks."

"What do you mean, drove you out of your homes? How did he betray you?"

"Kewaah and his Choctaw warriors helped Jackson beat the British in New Orleans and the Spanish in Florida, and helped tame this country. Then, he made false promises to us and drove us out of our homes onto the Trail of Tears to Oklahoma. A few of us refused to go. Most who stayed behind ran and hid. Some of the white settlers helped us, and some didn't. It's their descendants who make up the Mississippi band of Choctaw Indians.

"But, Kewaah didn't hide. He stood his ground on this farm, he and every man in our family. They would not leave. They would not run or hide.

"The soldiers, led by a Captain infamous for his cruelty to our people, came to remove us. We do not speak his name. But Kewaah stood under these very oaks and refused to go. Kewaah told the Captain that the treaty said if he became a citizen, he could stay and keep one square mile. The Captain said, 'How do you know what the treaty said? You can't even read?' Kewaah responded, 'How would you know? And if that were true, what difference would that make?'

"The Captain said his orders were to remove every Indian by force if necessary.

"Kewaah looked at the Captain and said, 'I am ready to die here, today. Are you?' Every man in our family stood with him. It looked like war. At that moment, President Andrew Jackson himself rode up. He had come to Tennessee for a meeting with Kewaah and our leaders, but Kewaah refused to go. So, the President of the United States came here to see Kewaah. Anyway, Jackson said, 'What's the disturbance here?'

"The Captain said, 'Our orders are to remove all of the Indians from this land to make room for Americans.'

"Jackson looked at Kewaah and said to the Captain, 'All I see here are Americans. Move on Captain.' The Captain left in a huff, and never came back. So, here we are on this farm to this day, thanks to Kewaah and Andrew Jackson. And now we have you and your law firm to thank for our farm."

"Oh no, not me. I really didn't do anything."

"You helped guide the hearts of the men who helped us. So, maybe a picture of you and the man you love should go on the wall next to this picture."

"Who do you mean?"

Erma smiled and didn't answer.

"Is it that obvious?"

Erma smiled and didn't answer.

"Is your land part of the reservation?"

"No, this is our land. Technically, it is not a reservation. It is land belonging to the Mississippi Band of Choctaw Indians. Someday, maybe we will give our farm to the tribe, but for now, this is our family land. If we had turned it over to the tribe, we wouldn't have been in danger of losing it."

Just then, an old-fashioned triangle bell rang outside and everyone began gathering around the tables under the great oak. As Karen stepped outside she saw a tall, stately looking white haired Indian ringing the bell. The wrinkles on his face made him look older than the great oak beside him. Soon everyone was standing around the tables and the sheets were folded back, exposing a great feast. Bowls filled with every kind of vegetable, peppers, onions, and tomatoes surrounded platters of fried chicken and heaps of sliced ham. Iron skillets with yellow corn bread and white corn bread sat at the end of each table. Pitchers of sweet tea seemed to be everywhere. Sweet is an understatement because at least three inches of sugar had settled to the bottom of each pitcher. Pies with mile high meringue covered one of the tables. The elderly gentleman, who everyone referred to as 'Uncle German,' stood at the head of the table. Erma whispered to Karen, "Uncle German is Frank's oldest brother. He's the head of the family."

"That's an interesting name."

"Yeah, his daddy fought the Germans in the Great War. That's World War I. He respected the way they fought, so he named his son German."

Frank introduced John, Jackson, Peter and Karen to 'Uncle German' as "new family members."

Uncle German vigorously shook each hand. When he came to John and Karen, he said, "You and your wife are welcome here anytime. Our home is now your home."

John was embarrassed for a moment, and said, "Oh, we're not married. We just work together."

Uncle German looked first at John and then at Karen, and smiled. He cleared his throat to get everyone's attention. "Let's say grace." Everyone held hands and John, Jackson, Karen and Peter joined the chain. "Lord, thank you for blessing this family and saving our farm. Thank you for bringing our friends to us to share this meal. Please bless this meal to the nourishment of our bodies and please bless us to your service, in Jesus' name."

Everyone said, "Amen," and the air was quickly filled with the sound of happy voices gathered around dinner tables as everyone took a seat. Uncle German looked down his long nose toward Peter and said, "Make out your meal, son."

Bowls and platters were passed around, and plates were filled with heaps of steaming vegetables, potatoes and gravy and crunchy, spicy fried chicken.

"Ms. Erma, what makes these butter beans so good?" asked John.

"Just call me Erma darlin'. I add cream, okra, sausage and love."

"It's the love that makes it good," observed Karen.

"Yes, honey, you're right about that."

John observed the laughing men, women and children that surrounded him. Everyone was enjoying the meal. It was a pleasant fall day, but the leaves of the great oak were still a beautiful green against the cloudless blue October sky. His gaze fell on each happy face. Everyone was talking to someone, while they ate their fill. At last, his eyes fell upon Karen. Her fair complexion and red hair stood in stark contrast to the dark skin and black hair of most of the people at the table, but her smile was just as wide and happy as everyone else.

Erma tugged on John's arm and whispered in his ear, "I think she may be as beautiful on the inside as she is on the outside."

John smiled at Erma as she spooned a heaping helping of peas on his plate and responded, "You're right. She really is beautiful, inside and out." He took a bite of the peas and almost gasped.

"What are these peas? I never had any so good!"

"Really?" said Jackson. "They look like green black-eyed peas."

"No," said Erma. "Those are lady peas. They're smaller, sweeter and greener than black-eyed peas. They're my favorite." She spooned some on Jackson's plate and said, "Try some."

***

A few miles away, Skeeter was driving his pickup, with his two buddies and Gregory Lincoln in the back. He shouted over his shoulder, "Okay, we're going to make a lot of noise, shoot in the air, but don't hurt nobody. We just want to make 'em run and mess up their little party. It'll just be a quick drive-by. We're gonna have a little fun." There were nods and laughs of approval. "Hey, Lincoln," Skeeter shouted, "I'm surprised you came along. I figured you would be like those lily livered Whittakers, or their buddy Brad. They start the trouble, but they always leave the dirty work to someone else."

"I wouldn't miss this for the world," said Gregory.

"Look, all we're gonna to do is make some noise. Nobody gets hurt. Got it?"

Gregory smiled and said nothing.

***

G.W. picked up a platter of peppers, took one and passed the platter to Uncle German, who took one and passed the platter on to John. "Pass that down please. You don't want one. They're hot peppers."

Karen overheard the comment and said, "Oh, John loves hot peppers. Go ahead, try one."

"Oh, no, you don't have to do that," said Erma.

"Don't let them bait you, Mr. John. They love playing with newcomers," said Awesome.

John hesitated, and then took a round green pepper that had just started turning red on one side. G.W. and German stopped eating and watched. A boy elbowed the youngster sitting next to him and nodded at John. Soon, all conversation died down as everyone watched John.

"What kind of pepper is it?"

"Hot," said G.W.

"Go ahead John," said Jackson.

"I think I'm going to regret this," said John as he bit an inch off the end of the pepper. Cool juice squirted into his mouth. "Not so bad," he said. The taste was momentarily pleasant and slightly sweet. At first, it reminded him of the taste of a yellow bell pepper. His tongue tingled as he brought the pepper to his lips for a second bite. Then, blinding pain and heat flooded his senses. His vision turned red. His head spun. He exhaled heavily to get the heat out of his mouth, but the air rushing across his tongue seemed to increase the pain.

With tears in his eyes, John asked, "Are flames coming out of my mouth?'

Everyone laughed. Awesome smiled and shook his head. Erma grabbed a pitcher of fresh farm milk, with cream and foam on the top. She poured the milk and cream through cheesecloth into a glass and handed it to John.

"Drink this quickly. It will help."

John gladly accepted the glass, brought it to his lips and paused as he looked at all the smiling faces. Everyone expected him to gulp the milk and fan his tongue. He noticed the expressionless faces of Uncle German and G.W.

'This is a test,' he thought to himself. John saw that one youngster sitting across from him was laughing so hard that tears were running down his face. John made eye contact with the boy, forced himself to smile, sat down the glass of milk without taking a drink, picked up the hot pepper and took a second bite. Without hesitating, he finished the pepper with a third bite, his face wet with perspiration and tears.

The laughter stopped. John looked at Uncle German, who cracked a smile and nodded. Awesome was grinning from ear to ear. G.W. picked up the platter of peppers and presented it to John and said, "Would you like another?"

Laughter swept around the table.

John was almost blinded by the fire in his mouth. He didn't want to speak, because he was afraid his voice would fail him. He smiled and took a second pepper. After a pause, he decided to risk speaking. "Yes," his voice was hoarse. "I'll take one as a souvenir, but I don't believe I'll eat it."

The table erupted in hoots, hollers and laughter. The boy across from John laughed so hard he fell out of his chair.

Uncle German slapped John on the shoulder and with a broad smile, said, "Good choice. That pepper is too hot. Your pride and strength drove you to finish the pepper, but you are smart enough not to eat a second one. Frank, you made a good choice when you picked our lawyers."

A cheer went up around the table. Frank's smile seemed to stretch from ear to ear.

"Drink the milk, dear," urged Erma.

The creamy, warm milk soothed his tongue, but as soon as he swallowed, the pain returned.

"Good grief! How long does this burning last?"

"Too long," said G.W. and another round of laughter swept around the table.

Uncle German turned his head and cupped his ear. "Trouble is coming." He took an iron skillet filled with corn bread in each hand, stood, and turned to face the road, putting himself between the road and his family. By now, everyone could hear a vehicle was approaching at high speed. Skeeter's pickup came into sight, horn honking and men hollering. John watched as Uncle German took in a deep breath and rose to his full height. He spread his arms wide, a skillet extended from each hand. G.W. quickly rose and faced the road, followed by Frank, Awesome, and every other male at the table, even the boys. Erma gathered the little girls under her arms and hovered over them like a mother hen. The women and girls stood behind their men.

"What's going on?" asked Jackson.

"They're standing their ground," said Karen, urgency in her voice.

John quickly rose and stood next to Uncle German. Jackson rose to stand with John. Gunshots rang out. Jackson and John were so startled that they flinched. Peter shouted, "They're shooting at us!" He knelt behind the table.

"No, they are shooting in the air," said Erma.

* * *

76

"They're just standing there," said Skeeter as they drove by. "This is no fun, they ain't even runnin'."

"Turn around and make one more pass," demanded Gregory.

"I don't know. I think it's best we keep going."

"I said turn around," yelled Gregory.

Gregory couldn't believe his luck when he saw John, but his angle was bad on the first pass. He shouted again, "Turn around, quick!"

Skeeter sighed and swung the pickup into a hard u-turn.

* * *

"They're coming back!" shouted Peter.

* * *

Gregory was just thinking that this little escapade was a waste of time, until he saw that John Brooks and his entire staff really were just standing there. Nobody was taking cover. "Well, my master has aligned the stars once again," he said as he brought the barrel down and took aim. John was completely exposed from this direction.

"Look at that old Indian. What does he think he's doing with those fryin' pans?" said one of Skeeter's buddies.

"Let's see if he can stop bullets with skillets," said Gregory as he squeezed the trigger once, felt the recoil, and aimed again.

* * *

John stood to the left of Uncle German. He noticed that the old man pivoted as the pickup approached and drove by on its first pass, so that his chest was always facing the truck and the guns. He made himself as big a target as he could, spreading his arms wide, and extended the skillets so that he could cover as much space as possible. It was as though he was trying to will any stray bullets to hit him or a skillet rather than any other family member. He repeated his stance as the truck made its second pass.

A deafening clang exploded next to John's ear and a skillet flew out of Uncle German's left hand. Pulverized cornbread filled the air. The 'whing' sound of a ricochet split the air. John glanced at Uncle German, who still stood proud and tall.

* * *

"Can you believe those guys? Are they crazy? They just stand there. Why don't they run?" shouted Skeeter as the truck barreled past the house.

Gregory put his front-sight squarely on John's chest and pulled the trigger.

Even at his age, Uncle German's eyesight was keen. On the first pass, he saw that every gun barrel was pointed up. On this pass, one barrel was pointed at his family. As soon as the skillet was knocked from his hand he stepped to his left, his arms still extended, willing the bullet to hit him instead of anyone else.

The pickup receded from sight and sound, and Frank, G.W., Awesome and the other men turned to make sure everyone was okay.

"Is everybody okay?"

"Yes, everyone is okay. Nobody's hurt," said Erma.

"What was that all about?" asked Jackson.

"Oh no!" exclaimed Karen when she saw bright red on the back of Uncle German's shirt. G.W., Frank and Erma rushed to him as he slowly sat down. Both the front and back of his shirt was blood soaked.

"Is everyone okay?" asked Uncle German.

"Yes, everyone is okay," said Erma. Her voice was steady even though her jaw trembled.

"Did we stand our ground?"

"Yes, Uncle German, we stood our ground," said Frank.

Uncle German nodded, smiled and said, "Good. I'm going home now." His limp body slid from the chair and slumped to the ground,

Karen threw her hands to her face, "Is he?"

"Yes, sweetheart," replied Erma, tears in her eyes. "He has gone home."

Everyone stared at his body in disbelief. Awesome felt rage build up inside him. The veins in his neck stood out and his face turned red. "What good does it do us to stand our ground if we don't fight back? They will just kill us all. They murdered Uncle German. Before they killed Uncle German, they killed Curtis and got away with it. He didn't skip bond. I know it in my soul."

"Awesome, don't talk that way," said Frank. "We'll call the Sheriff and he will take care of this."

"The Sheriff can't bring Uncle German back. He can't bring back Curtis. The Sheriff can't protect us. It's time that we protect ourselves."

"Awesome!" exclaimed Erma. "Don't talk that way."

Awesome stormed to his pickup, reached behind the seat, retrieved his hunting rifle, chambered a round and drove quickly away without looking back.

"I've got to stop him!" said G.W. as he headed for his truck.

Karen grabbed John with both hands, looked into his eyes and pled, "Do something, before he kills someone."

Maximilian's Treasure

John's eyes darted left and right while he considered his options. "Jackson, please stay here and tell the Sheriff what happened. I'm going with G.W. Here's the key to the Trooper." John tossed the key to Jackson and ran to the passenger side of G.W.'s truck.

Chapter 15

"Are you crazy?" yelled Skeeter as he pulled off the road behind a stand of trees next to Pinishook Creek. "You shot the old man!" He skidded to a stop and jumped out of the pickup. "If he dies, we'll be charged with murder!"

"Just calm down," said Gregory as he climbed out of the truck, a Bowie knife strapped to one leg and a 38 at his side.

"Calm down!" shouted Skeeter as he turned to confront Gregory. "What do you mean calm down? You are nuts! This means life in prison, or worse!"

"Nobody can connect this to us," said Gregory soothingly, as he fingered the Bowie knife at his side. "I've got the perfect alibi for us."

"How do you know that? How can you say that?"

"All we have to do is keep our stories straight."

"Yeah, just keep our stories straight," repeated one of Skeeter's buddies from the back of the pickup.

"Okay, wise guy, just what is the story?"

Gregory put his hand on Skeeter's shoulder and positioned himself so that the men in the pickup could not see his other hand. "It's simple. You and your buddies were out for a joy ride, just trying to have a little fun, and things went too far. One of you killed the old man."

"What? How is that a perfect alibi?"

Skeeter's buddies were in the back of the truck watching the exchange between Skeeter and Gregory. Skeeter's back was to them and Gregory was facing them. He could see puzzled looks on their faces. He heard one repeat, "Yeah, how is that a perfect alibi?"

"Because," said Gregory as he sank the Bowie knife into Skeeter's chest. "Awesome caught up with you and got his revenge." Skeeter gasped and, with a look of horror, stared down at the knife in his chest. With both of his hands, he reached for Gregory's head, clutched a handful of Lincoln's hair, coughed, fell forward onto Gregory and breathed his last. Gregory leaned Skeeter against the front of the pickup and walked quickly to the back of the truck. Two quick shots from his 38 dispatched the men in the pickup. He returned to Skeeter and pulled the knife out of his chest.

"Now, for the icing on the cake," he said as he sliced Skeeter's forehead with the Bowie knife, grabbed the skin at the cut and ripped the scalp from Skeeter's head. A minute later he had three scalps in hand.

Gregory returned to Skeeter, grabbed his arms and hoisted the body into the back of the truck. Skeeter's bloody head lolled backward, striking Gregory on the chest as he rolled the body into the bed of the pickup. Gregory wiped blood off his hands onto his already bloody shirt.

"This is perfect," laughed Gregory as he climbed behind the wheel. Gregory drove along the bank of Pinishook creek until he came to the Goni swamp field.

"This is the perfect spot to leave them, isn't it?" he said as though talking with a companion. He parked the truck in the middle of Frank Dalton's Goni Swamp field and trod across the field, leaving three mutilated good ole boys in the back.

"This is going to work out just right after all," he said as he climbed over the fence and walked up the hill to the Whittaker place. "Yep, this was a great idea, wasn't it?" Gregory laughed as he hiked up the hill.

* * *

G.W. uncharacteristically spun his tires as he sped after Awesome.

"Where do you think Awesome went?"

"I think he probably went to Skeeter's. That looked like him and his buddies."

"Where is that?"

"We'll cross the creek, take the first left and a few more turns. We'll be there in a few minutes."

* * *

Awesome arrived at Skeeter's a few minutes ahead of G.W. and found no one home. He quickly searched the grounds, then scrawled, "You will pay!" on a note and nailed it to the door. He drove to Trail's End Bar, Skeeter's favorite hangout. Skeeter's truck wasn't there. He said to himself, "I wonder if Walt or Brad had anything to do with this. I'll pay them a visit."

* * *

Fifteen minutes after John and G.W. left to search for Awesome, two deputies arrived in separate cars. An ambulance arrived a few minutes later, and then Sheriff Rainey, followed by the coroner.

"Who did this?" asked the sheriff.

"I didn't get a good look, but I thought it was Skeeter," answered Frank.

"I'm going to need better than 'I thought it was Skeeter.' Can anyone here tell me for sure who did the shooting?"

No one responded. The Sheriff looked at Jackson and said simply, "Well?"

"It was a drive-by shooting. Several people were in a pickup, whooping and hollering. On the first pass they shot in the air. They turned around and on the second pass at least two shots were pointed at the people here at the picnic."

"They had time to turn around and shoot and there was still somebody to shoot at?"

Karen spoke up, with tears in her eyes. "Yes, Uncle German stood his ground. That's what he called it. He stood tall with outstretched arms, like he was trying to catch any bullet that might be fired at his family. All the men stood with him. They made a human barrier protecting the women and children."

"I see. Could you recognize anyone?" asked Rainey as he looked Karen over.

"No. We are guests for lunch today. We're from Jackson, and we don't know the local people."

"Did anyone here recognize any of the shooters?"

No one responded.

"Are there any other witnesses I could talk to?"

"Well, my brother G.W. and our lawyer Brooks, they saw what happened," said Frank.

"I need a statement from everybody here and from them. Where are the other witnesses?"

Frank didn't answer.

"Look, I need to know where they are. They didn't go after Skeeter did they?"

"They chased after Awesome."

"Awesome. Was he here too?"

"Yeah."

"Call them, get them back here."

"I've been calling Awesome," said Erma, with tears on her face. "He won't answer. He was chasing the pickup and G.W. is chasing Awesome. Mr. Brooks is with G.W."

Chapter 16

Moments after Awesome left Skeeter's place, G.W. and John arrived. They saw several rusty broken down cars in the yard. They didn't notice the note on the door. G.W. gestured at one car that didn't look much better than the abandoned junkers. "One of Skeeter's friends drives that car. His friends travel in packs, like rats. They left their car here so they must be with Skeeter."

"Where would they be now?"

"I don't know. I don't try to keep up with his bad habits. Best we can do is keep moving and ask everyone we see if they've seen Awesome or Skeeter."

G.W. returned to the road, turned left and saw a woman checking a mailbox at the next driveway. She was about forty, dark hair, dressed in jeans and a western shirt. He stopped and said, "Afternoon, Ms. Cage. Have you seen Awesome?"

"Afternoon, G.W., I haven't."

"What about Skeeter?"

"No, what's up, G.W.? You don't see those two together. I've never heard Awesome's name mentioned with Skeeter."

"Somebody shot and killed Uncle German."

"No! That is awful. I am so sorry G.W."

"Awesome is lookin' for the killers. I want to find Awesome before anything stupid happens."

"Did Skeeter do it?"

"I don't know."

"I haven't seen 'em, but I'll sure let you know if I do."

They continued down the road, repeating that conversation with everyone they encountered. G.W. even flagged down passing vehicles. No one had seen Skeeter or Awesome.

* * *

"Why did this have to happen?" cried Erma as she sat on the couch, her head in her hands. Karen sat next to her with her hand on Erma's shoulders, trying to comfort her. The deputies were interviewing witnesses one at a time. Most family members waited on the porch for their turn to be questioned. Jackson, Peter and Karen sat with Frank and Erma in the den.

"It's the treasure," said Frank in disgust.

"How do you know it's the treasure?" asked Jackson.

Peter sat on the edge of his chair and listened.

"He's right. It seems that everything bad that happens to this family has something to do with that old treasure. I hate that treasure," said Erma. "It has brought nothing but sadness and tragedy to us. It doesn't even exist. It never existed."

"Yes, it does. But I would give it up in a minute if I could undo all that's happened," said Frank.

"It doesn't even have to exist to kill us. People believe in it, and we get killed. Nothing good has ever come from that old rumor. I hate that treasure," repeated Erma.

"I don't blame you, after what I saw today," said Karen. "What else has happened?"

"The list is too long. So many things have happened over the years. There was the cave-in at Hummingbird Well, where Frank found that coin." Tears filled Erma's eyes. She excused herself and retreated to the bedroom.

Frank shook his head.

"I found the coin in Hummingbird Well, over near Pinishook Creek. It was an old fashioned well. We lowered a bucket on a rope. One day, when I pulled the bucket up, I found the coin. The one I showed Mr. Brooks. I always believed the gold was in Hummingbird Well. To me, it confirmed the rumors about the treasure. We searched around the well and the creek, and then we started digging up the well. The sides fell in. Erma's two boys were trapped. We could hear them calling for us because the water was rising. They drowned before we could get to them."

"Oh, no!" said Karen as she rose and tapped on the bedroom door. Karen cracked open the door, looked back at Jackson, Peter and Frank, and stepped into the bedroom, closing the door behind her.

Peter, Jackson and Frank sat in silence for a few minutes.

"Did you find any gold in the well?" asked Peter.

"No. We never found the gold. I believe it's still there."

As Frank said that, Erma returned to the room, wiping her eyes, followed by Karen. "I'm sorry. I'm all right. I dealt with this a long time ago. It's just that the murder of Uncle German brought up old wounds." Karen put her arm around Erma, who gave Karen a hug and said, "Thank you. Frank still believes that gold is in that old well. He can have the gold, for what good it'll do him."

"Maybe Frank James lost one coin or dropped just one coin down the well," guessed Jackson.

"No. We were told that Sankky's last words were something like, 'You will draw the gold from the hummingbird.' They say it was hard to understand her exact words when she died, but she said something like that. We knew that she named the old well, Hummingbird Well, so I knew we would find the gold there," said Frank.

"That's why Frank was drawing water from the well," said Erma. "He always thought he would get lucky one day and draw gold up from the well. One day he finally did. We thought that was a great day. But, then tragedy struck. That gold is cursed," said Erma, almost spitting out the word cursed.

A thought struck Karen, and she sucked in a little air. Her eyes darted around the room and came to rest on the hummingbird painting. "She said 'draw' and 'hummingbird.' Erma, may I look behind Sankky's painting?"

Erma stared at Karen for a moment, then she turned and looked at Frank, eyes wide open.

Frank said, "Well, I'll be."

"Yes, darlin', you can look," said Erma.

Everyone's eyes were glued on Karen as she walked to the hummingbird painting. She lifted the frame from the wall and laid it face down on the checker table.

"Can someone help me get the back off of this frame?"

Frank used a pocketknife to pry off the back of the picture. Everyone leaned in to get a better look.

Chapter 17

Walt, Wes and Brad were in the den sipping whiskey when Gregory entered the Whittaker house through the back door.

"What happened to you?" asked Wes.

"Is that blood all over you?" asked Brad.

"It's a long story. I'll explain in a few minutes. First, I want to wash up. Do you have a change of clothes I can use?"

"Sure," said Walt. He rose from a leather chair, paused to look at Gregory's bloody clothes, then said, "I'll bring you a bag for your old clothes. When you've changed, toss the old ones in the fireplace."

"Thanks, partner."

Walt's eyes widened for a moment as he thought about the implications of the word 'partner.'

Brad stepped up to Gregory and whispered, "Whose blood is that?"

"Skeeter's," Gregory answered as he walked off to shower and change.

Dumbfounded, Brad could do nothing for several moments but gaze in the direction Gregory had gone.

A few minutes later, in fresh clothes supplied by Walt, Gregory stepped into the den, rubbing his hair with a towel with one hand. His bloody clothes were in a brown paper bag in the other.

"Well, tell us what happened," demanded Wes.

Gregory smirked, tossed the towel over a chair and pitched the bag into the fireplace. "Let's just say that Skeeter and his buddies are more useful to us now than ever."

"What do you mean?" asked Wes.

Gregory gave a cold grin in response as he stirred the burning bag in the fireplace with a poker.

No one was sure what to say, or what to ask. Walt and Wes simultaneously concluded that it was better that they not ask any more questions. The less they knew, the better. But, Gregory didn't intend to make it that easy for them.

Everyone was startled to hear a horn honk.

* * *

Awesome stopped his truck next to Walt's pickup at the Whittaker's front door and honked.

"What the…" said Brad as he looked out the window. "Awesome! What's he doing here? You didn't leave behind any clues that led him to us did you? We don't need him to think we had anything to do with Skeeter breaking up that party. And all that blood! Did Awesome shoot back?"

Gregory saw that panic was beginning to grip Brad. Brad's eyes darted about the room and settled on a shotgun above the fireplace. He rushed to grab it.

"Wait! This is perfect. I was going to have to find him anyway," said Gregory. "Keep him occupied until I've finished giving him a little present."

"What? How?"

"Just keep him occupied."

Brad caught his breath, gathered up his courage, and stepped outside.

"Awesome. What brings you here?"

"Brad! I should have known I would find you hanging out with the Whittakers. Where are they?"

Brad noticed Gregory creeping toward Awesome's truck, using Walt's truck to provide cover. He was carrying something in his hand. Brad couldn't make out what it was. Wes and Walt stepped outside behind Brad.

"What makes you think you're welcome here, Dalton?" asked Walt.

"I'm not under the impression that I am welcome. I'm looking for Skeeter. I wonder if you've seen him today."

Gregory looked over the tailgate into the bed of Awesome's truck and saw an assortment of small tools and equipment, including a small bucket. He dropped something into the bucket and backed away.

"We don't keep up with Skeeter's activities. He hasn't been around here. Why are you looking for him?"

"Somebody just murdered Uncle German. I want to ask Skeeter what he knows about it."

Walt and Wes looked dumbfounded. They both turned and stared at Brad.

"I'm sorry to hear about that," said Brad.

"I'm sure you are, cousin. Do you know anything about what happened today?"

Brad turned red and shook with rage. "You worthless…"

Walt interrupted Brad with, "Awesome, you should leave. Now!"

"All right. If you happen to see Skeeter, tell him I'm lookin' for him. I'll be waitin' for him at Trail's End."

"If I see him, I'll be sure to tell him," said Walt.

Awesome slowly pulled away from the Whittaker house and drove to Trail's End.

* * *

As soon as Awesome was gone, Wes yelled, "Murdered? Murdered! We just wanted you to scare them!"

Gregory stepped within inches of Wes. "You and Brad hired me to get them off the farm, whatever it takes."

"But not kill them in front of witnesses! Skeeter and his bunch will never keep quiet."

"Oh yes they will. Skeeter and his bunch will never tell anyone what happened. And neither will you," growled Gregory.

Wes stepped back. "What do you mean?"

"What do you think I mean?"

Wes didn't answer.

"You've guessed right," said Gregory.

"Are you out of your mind?" asked Wes.

"Don't let your grief over the death of Skeeter and his friends drive you to the depths of despair. People make terrible mistakes when they are grieving. I once heard of a whole family on the way to a funeral dying in a fiery car crash. Such a tragedy."

"What are you saying?" asked Walt.

"I'm just saying that tragedy sometimes befalls a whole family, if they forget who their partner is."

Walt and Wes were motionless and speechless.

"It seems that Awesome was so overcome with anger that he killed Skeeter and his friends," explained Gregory.

"Killed all three of them? By himself?" asked Brad.

"Yep. That's one dangerous young man. Anyone who can kill three armed men by himself is dangerous and deserves respect. I hope the Sheriff and your deputy friend can protect you and your neighbors from Awesome."

"How is the Sheriff going to, ah, find out, that Awesome is the one who killed them?" asked Brad.

"Because he's going to find their scalps in the back of Awesome's truck."

The three young men were stunned. After a long moment, Brad let out a single chuckle and said, "So, Awesome will get convicted of three heinous murders. He'll be lucky if all he gets is life in prison. That's awesome!"

Gregory grinned and said, "That's right. Skeeter killed that old Indian and Awesome tracked Skeeter down and killed and mutilated him and his buddies. Awesome left their bodies in the Goni Swamp field of all places."

"NO!" shouted Wes. "Why did you have to leave them there!"

"Because it's the perfect place. And, it was convenient. Why are you worried?"

"We don't need people snooping around that swamp."

Gregory raised his eyebrows.

"Calm down, Wes," said Brad. "I agree with Gregory. This could turn out to be perfect."

"Yes," continued Gregory, "now, with the clan leader dead, and that proud young buck headed to prison for life, your prospects of getting the Dalton's farm just sky rocketed."

"How's that?" asked Brad.

"Who's going to run it? Two worn out, discouraged old men? How are they going to pay for a legal defense for Awesome, unless they mortgage the farm again? They're already getting sued for all they're worth. Once Awesome is convicted, they'll have no hope. They will sell. If they hesitate, I'll persuade them. I can be very persuasive."

Chapter 18

"Oh my! What is this?" asked Erma as she leaned over the picture frame. Frank had just pried the back off, exposing drawings and several handwritten pages.

"It's been here all this time," said Frank. "Behind the hummingbird drawing."

"It looks like a diary and a map. A treasure map," said Jackson breathlessly.

"No way!" exclaimed Peter. "You can't be serious."

"Deadly serious," said Karen. "This is why there's a fight over this land. Everyone thinks the treasure is here. Instead, it's the clue to the treasure that's been here. How can we test the authenticity of this?"

"Is it okay if I take pictures?" asked Jackson.

"Sure. Whatever you think," said Erma. Frank nodded.

Jackson pulled his phone out of his pocket and began snapping photos. "This looks like the diary of Frank James. He says he's the only survivor of a shipwreck off the Island of Hispaniola. I'm going to ask a librarian friend of ours to do some research, and see what she can tell us."

"Who is that?" asked Frank.

"That's Clarion Cartier, a Librarian," explained Karen. "She was part of our team in the Vampire Defense case. She has the resources of the entire Eudora Welty Library at her disposal, along with a team of research assistants. She can gather more information in less time than anybody I know. She might have something for us by the time we get back to Jackson."

Jackson dialed Clarion's number. "Claire? This is Jackson Bradley. Yes, fine. How about you and Ted? That's great! Yes, we will be at the wedding!" said Jackson, smiling at Karen. "Wouldn't miss it for the world. Look, I believe I have a project for you. We just found something very interesting behind an old picture. I think it may have to do with Frank and Jesse James, and maybe even the Emperor Maximilian. That's right. Maximilian of Mexico, or France, or wherever he was from. Oh, Austria, excuse me. I should have known you would know. Anyway, we think we have a diary and a treasure map. I'm about to text some pictures to you. Do you think you could take a look for me? Great! I'll send them now.

Yes, you are part of the team again. This time, we will be Raiders of the Lost Treasure of Maximilian. Yeah, you're right! It'll be exciting! But it could be dangerous, so we need to keep this confidential. Someone was murdered today because of this treasure so let's keep this confidential until we know what we're dealing with and who is on the other side. Okay, see you soon."

As Jackson sent the texts, he said to Frank and Erma, "Claire will help us decipher some of this diary and maybe get us a history on the treasure. Frank, you were right all along."

"Yeah, I knew there was a treasure. I was looking in the wrong place all this time. Is Claire trustworthy?"

"Completely," said Karen.

"Can she keep quiet about the treasure?"

"Yes. She and her researchers were part of our team in the Vampire Defense case and they know how to keep a secret," explained Karen.

"Just the same, I'll remind her over and over again," said Jackson, as he sent a follow up text that read, 'Make sure you keep this completely confidential.'

"Is there any way we can get people to leave us alone, now that we know that the treasure is somewhere else?" asked Erma.

"Maybe so," said Karen. "But, if they would kill for the farm, they will kill for this diary and this map."

"Yes, I suppose you're right," said Erma.

Peter stared with wide eyes at Karen and then at the diary.

***

It wasn't long before Sheriff Rainey pulled up to the Whittaker house and asked Walt if he had seen Skeeter or Awesome.

"Haven't seen Skeeter, but Awesome came by talking bad about him. Said he murdered his Uncle German. Said he was going to see to it that Skeeter and all of his friends got what's coming to them. His eyes looked crazy. Looked to me like he had murder on his mind."

"Did you call my office to see if you could stop Awesome from doing anything crazy?"

"I was just talking to Wes about that. He said I should give you a call. I was just about to call when you drove up."

"Did he say what Skeeter's got coming to him?"

"Sounded like he said, 'Blood will flow."

"You have any idea where he went?"

"He asked me if I knew where any of Skeeter's friends hang out. I told him I don't hang out with them, but I see their trucks at the Trail's End all the time."

"I see. Why do you suppose Awesome came here looking for Skeeter?"

"Who knows what that crazy Indian was thinking?"

"Hmm. I thought maybe you were a mind reader, since you thought he had murder on his mind."

Walt felt the sting of blush as blood rushed to his head, turning his face red. "What, what are you getting at?"

"Don't know if I'm getting at anything, but judging from your face, maybe I should reconsider. I was just wondering why Awesome would come here looking for Skeeter, that's all."

"Well, you came here looking for Skeeter."

"Yeah, I did, didn't I? For some reason, this seemed to be the logical place to start looking for Skeeter. Funny that Awesome thought the same thing. I'll be seeing you. Real soon," said Sheriff Rainey as he pulled away.

As Walt watched Sheriff Rainey drive away, he realized that his hands were shaking.

Brad and Wes stepped out of the house behind him. Brad asked, "What about that Deputy buddy of yours? He owes us a couple of favors, doesn't he?"

"He thinks we owe him," answered Walt.

"He owes his job to us," said Wes.

"And that pickup he drives," said Walt.

"Time to earn his keep," said Brad.

"I'll call him," said Walt.

* * *

After disconnecting the call from Walt, Deputy Wayne Townsend, lights on, siren blaring, skidded to a stop behind Awesome's pickup at the Trail's End. He found what he was looking for in a bucket in the back of Awesome's truck. Bile rose in his throat. "I'm goin' to enjoy this," he said to himself as he burst through the bar door, gun drawn.

"Awesome Dalton!"

"Over here."

"Hands where I can see 'em," he shouted as he approached Awesome. "I just hope you try somethin'. I've always known one day there would be a reckoning for you. Today's the day."

"What's the problem, Deputy Townsend?"

"Don't get smart with me. Hands behind your back! I can tell you two things. I'm going to enjoy this, and you're not."

Chapter 19

The mood at the Dalton farmhouse was somber. There was sadness over the death of Uncle German, there was worry about Awesome, what he might do, what might happen to him, and there was an ambivalent feeling about the treasure.

"I just don't know what to feel," said Frank. "I've been looking for this treasure all my life and this is the best clue since I found the coin. But, I just wish Uncle German was here to see this. And I wish Awesome was here."

"If only Uncle German could see this," said Erma. "But, I am so worried about Awesome that I can't get interested in gold."

While everyone was talking, Peter slipped outside. Karen heard the screen door make its creaking sound, and looked up in time to see Peter step off the porch and walk behind one of the great oaks. Karen furrowed her brow for a moment as she wondered what Peter might be doing. Then she turned her attention back to the conversation.

Once he felt he was out of sight, Peter pulled his cell phone out of his pocket and placed a call. "Mr. Hoover? This is Peter. You won't believe all that's happened at this rickety old farmhouse today. There's been a shooting, someone's dead, and we found a treasure map hidden behind a picture frame! They said it was a map to Maximilian's gold!" whispered Peter. He was so excited that his words ran together.

"Good work, son. Calm down and give me the details."

Peter told him everything he had seen and heard. As soon as he hung up with Peter, Hoover called Gregory. Gregory was in the den of the Whittaker house with Brad, Walt and Wes. He had just proposed a toast to their good fortune concerning the probable arrest of Awesome when he received Hoover's call. He excused himself and stepped into another room.

"What have you got for me Hoov?"

"They found a treasure map behind a picture frame at the Dalton farm."

"No kidding!"

"It is supposedly a map to Maximilian's treasure, a vast treasure that Mexico and France fought a war over. That must be what our benefactors are after."

"So, they've been holding out on us. It was a map they were after," said Gregory with a growl.

"Well, it had to be something. They hired that Texas lawyer and paid handsomely to get you out of jail so that they could get the farm and find that map. But Brooks' team beat us to it. They'll be taking the map with them to Jackson to get some experts to look at it. One of them took pictures of the map with their phone and emailed the pictures to someone."

"When are they leaving?"

"Sometime tonight."

"Interesting. I doubt there is anything to this treasure angle, but if there is, we want to be the ones who collect. But for now, my interest is getting to those lawyers."

"Can we use the bug you put on the computer to capture a copy of that email?"

"Maybe. Over time, it will learn all of the passwords and we can copy everything on their computer and maybe on their phones."

"Over time. I'm not a patient man, Hoov. Do you have anything from that computer yet?"

"I know where Brooks lives."

"That's something. Give it to me." After Hoover gave him the address, Gregory said, "I'll see if I can arrange a little surprise for the Brooks team tonight when they're returning to Jackson. Slow them down a little. I need a little time to work out some details. Maybe we can even find a way to get the map from them."

Gregory hung up with Hoover and stepped into the den. He had a choice. Seek revenge or treasure. Sometimes, revenge is a more powerful emotion than greed. A quick mental calculation led him to the conclusion that he could use Brad and the Whittakers to get the map from Brooks. He judged that it would be easier to get the map from them than from Brooks. By playing his cards right, he could have revenge and the treasure.

"Gentlemen, I've got business to take care of back in Jackson. I have a mission for you."

"What's that?"

"Those lawyers will be leaving the Dalton farm sometime today with a diary and a treasure map."

Brad gasped and leaned forward. Walt and Wes turned and stared at each other. "You mean the treasure is real?" asked Walt.

"I suggest that you find a way to keep them from leaving town with that map. Get it from them somehow."

"Why don't you do it? That's what we paid you for," said Brad Dalton.

Gregory stepped toward Brad. "Like I said, partner. I've got pressing business back in Jackson. Your family has been trying to find this treasure for a hundred years. I've been here for a day and already I've told you where to find the map. If you're unable to take care of this little task, then maybe I will handle it for you after I get finished with my business in Jackson. Or, maybe I'll just take the map for myself. So, are you going to get it or not?"

* * *

Claire quickly assembled her research assistants.

"Ladies, ladies, come quick. We have a new Brooks and Bradley assignment!"

Twittering and excitement followed that announcement, along with exclamations of "Another case!" "Will it be as exciting as the Vampire Defense?" "Will we get to work with the Rugby team?"

Claire used a projector to display the pictures Jackson had texted to her on a wall-sized screen. She also displayed the 'confidential' text. All of the researchers were even more thrilled when they realized they would be working on a highly confidential project. Within minutes an excited, motivated group of professional researchers was hot on the trail of Maximilian's treasure.

Claire was too excited to keep the news to herself, so she called her fiancé, Ted Lively, who was driving into town from New Orleans for a visit. After telling him all about her new Brooks and Bradley project she said, "Ted, I am so sorry, but I will be working late. Can you find something to do for a few hours? I do want to see you so, but this new project just came in, and there is a rush on it, and it is really exciting. Will that be all right?"

"Sure, baby. I'll stop at Tommy's and visit with the boys. We'll catch up later."

"Remember, Ted, this is top secret. Tell no one."

"Gotcha!"

Ted pulled into the parking lot at Tommy's Trading Post in Goshen Springs to visit Tommy and his buddy, Skip.

"Ted! Good to see you!" exclaimed Tommy as he shook Ted's hand and Skip slapped him on the back.

"How's New Orleans?" asked Skip.

"I've been too busy at the brewery to see much of the city. I don't even have a place to live yet." A year ago Ted found a lock box containing the long lost recipe and brewing instructions for Goshen Springs Beer, a famous frontier beer that Andrew Jackson proclaimed was the 'best beer in the world' two hundred years ago. A brewery in New Orleans bought the rights to the beer and made Ted the brew master.

"Still staying in a hotel?" asked Skip.

"No, I'm renting a room from one of the guys at work. It's a lot cheaper for me, and helps him out, so that's all right for now."

"Maybe you can take Claire back with you and look for a place for the two of you, for, you know, after you get married," suggested Skip.

"Yeah, that was my plan. I was going to suggest that tonight but she just called. She's all excited about some project that Jackson and John have her working on."

"Really!" exclaimed Tommy.

"Tell us about it," said Skip, breathlessly.

"I can't. It's confidential."

"You can tell us, we're all part of the team. Hey, if it weren't for us, the most interesting cases Brooks and Bradley would get would be in traffic court," said Skip.

"Yeah, I guess you're right. We are all part of the team. I'll tell you, but don't tell anybody," said Ted as he leaned forward. "You remember that old Native American from Philadelphia, the one who had the gold coin?"

"Yeah, yeah, sure, sure," said Skip.

"They just found an old diary and a treasure map for Maximilian's treasure."

"No kidding!" exclaimed Skip, almost shouting. "This is big! This is bigger than Goshen Springs Beer! This is bigger than the Vampire Defense! We need a piece of the action!" Then Skip paused. "What exactly is Max's Million Dollar Treasure?"

Tommy leaned in and explained, "No, Skip, he said Maximilian's Treasure."

"Yeah, that's what I said. Max's Million Treasure," responded Skip. He leaned over to Tommy and asked, "So, what is it, smarty?"

Tommy looked embarrassed. "Actually, I don't know. Why don't you tell us, Ted?"

"She said something about gold, lots of gold, sent here during the Civil War by the Emperor of Mexico. She said her initial research indicated it may be the Hummingbird Hoard."

"Yeah, just what I said, Max's Million Dollar Treasure. See? I was right!"

Tommy and Ted laughed, and Tommy slapped Skip on the back. "Yeah, Skip, I guess you are right about Max's Million Dollar Treasure."

"Listen guys, this is confidential. Nobody but us can know anything about this, okay?" asked Ted, seeking reassurance.

"Sure. My lips are sealed," said Skip, making a zipping motion across his open mouth. Then he had a puzzled look on his face, and said, "What is a hummingbird hoard and what does it have to do with treasure?"

"They mean a hoard of treasure," said Ted, "like a whole bunch of treasure, named after a hummingbird."

"Why is the treasure named after a hummingbird?" asked Tommy.

"Beats me," responded Ted.

Chapter 20

It was after 4 in the afternoon when John and G.W. returned to the farm, without Awesome. He didn't recognize the pickup parked in front.

"I wonder whose truck that is?" asked G.W.

John recognized a large fellow standing beside the truck talking to Karen. "Backhoe!" said John. "I wonder what he is doing here?"

Almost as soon as G.W. pulled to a stop, John hopped out of the pickup.

"Backhoe! What brings you here?"

"I heard what happened. I came by to see if Karen was okay, and to see if there was anything I could do."

"Yeah, it's been an awful day. Have you seen Awesome?"

"No, but if I run into him, I'll try to keep him occupied while I give you a call." Backhoe turned to Karen, took her hand and said, "Are you sure you're all right?"

"Yes, I'm fine. Thank you for checking on us."

"Any time." Backhoe turned to John, shook his hand and said, "If I can do anything for you, please give me a call." He climbed into his truck, waved at Karen, and drove off.

"Nice fellow," said John.

"Yes, he is," said Karen.

Frank walked up from the side of the house and asked, "Did you find Awesome?"

The screen door creaked and Jackson, Erma and Peter emerged from the house and rushed to join everyone under the oak.

"We didn't find Awesome."

"They found them boys that shot Uncle German," said Frank.

"Good."

"It's not so good. I don't know where Awesome is, but them boys were found dead."

"Oh no! Where did they find them?" asked John.

"In our Goni Swamp field."

"Uh, oh. How did you hear about it?"

"The Sheriff told us. He said that his deputies saw buzzards circling and followed them to the bodies," said Jackson.

"This is a nightmare," said G.W. as he leaned against the truck.

G.W. shook his head. "I don't believe Awesome is that dumb. I believe he was mad enough to do it, but I don't believe he would be so dumb as to kill them and leave them in our field," he said with conviction.

The four of them heard the crunching of tires on gravel and turned in time to see the Sheriff's car stop under the trees. Sheriff Rainey climbed out and said, "We found Awesome at Trail's End. We had to arrest him."

"Why? You don't know he done this," said Frank.

"Skeeter and his buddies were scalped and we found three scalps in Awesome's truck," responded Sheriff Rainey.

* * *

"Scalped," gasped Karen. Erma threw her hand over her mouth. G.W. did not respond. He looked first at the ground, and then looked far away, past the tree line, but he did not utter a sound. His facial expression didn't change at the news, but more wrinkles appeared on his weathered face, as though he suddenly aged another ten years.

"I'm sorry to bring you this bad news, G.W. Somebody had to tell you, and I thought it should be me."

G.W. nodded once, kicked the ground, and said, "Thank you, sheriff. I appreciate you coming all the way out here to tell us. You didn't have to do that."

"I knew you would take it hard, and I didn't want just anybody telling you. Besides, I thought you needed to know the gruesome details. It's possible that some of Skeeter's family or friends might want to take the law into their own hands, and you needed to be warned."

G.W. just nodded.

Frank said, "Thank you, sheriff."

"I've arranged for extra patrols in the area, just in case. If there is anything else I can do, let me know," said Sheriff Rainey. "Anything except recommend a bond. The judge has already said there will be no bond, considering the charges and the fact that your other grandson skipped out on a bond."

G.W. responded with a single nod. Sheriff Rainey turned and walked slowly to his patrol car. He settled into the seat and just before he closed the door, G.W. called out to him.

"Sheriff! There is something you can do for us."

"Name it."

"Take me to the place where the bodies were found."

"I can't do that, it's a crime scene."

"Those are rain clouds in the west. If we go now, before the rain comes, we may find signs that could tell us what happened."

"You won't see any useful tracks. My men have already been all over the place. And so have ambulance crews, the coroner and half the volunteer fireman from two counties. There's nothing left to find, and if there had been anything, so many trucks and people have been there that any tracks, or any other evidence for that matter, have been covered up or compromised. We don't get multiple homicides often, so my deputies acted like they forgot how to preserve a murder scene."

"Still, I would like to go. We may see something that your deputies missed," insisted G.W.

"Come to think of it, it's your property. You can go anytime."

"Yes, but if you are with us then no one will say that we made up what we found."

"What if you find something that incriminates Awesome?"

"If he did this, he should be punished. We live in this community, too, and we will live up to our responsibilities."

"That's a mighty big statement, considering what Skeeter and his boys did to your family."

"If my people feel like you did not look for every clue and Awesome is found guilty, we would never be able to accept the verdict. If Awesome did this, I need to know. If he did this, he needs to accept responsibility and take his punishment, for the sake of everyone. If he didn't do it, everyone needs to know. The fact that scalps were taken means that trouble is coming to everyone if we don't get solid proof, one way or another, soon."

Rainey hesitated, his brow furrowed, as he weighed his decision. "Scalps in his truck is pretty good evidence that he did this."

"I would say that the killer probably put the scalps in Awesome's truck. If Awesome didn't do this, I have to do everything I can to help him. Without Awesome, we cannot keep this farm. If he did do this, then so be it. But if he didn't, I will prove him innocent, or die trying."

Sheriff Rainey sighed. "All right. Follow me. I'll take you to the spot where we found the bodies. Don't make me regret this."

"Let me ride with you," said G.W. "You can tell me what your men found while we're on the way."

"We'll follow you," said John as he gestured to Frank and Jackson to follow him.

Frank looked at Peter and said, "I want you to stay here with Erma and Miss Karen."

Jackson called out to John, "I'll stay behind to check out an angle here. I'll explain later."

"I'll fill John in on what we found here at the house," Frank said to Jackson as he tossed John the keys to his pickup. "You drive. I want to concentrate on looking for signs."

* * *

Townsend booked Awesome, took his fingerprints and, as directed by Sheriff Rainey, took a lock of Awesome's hair. "This is ridiculous. We got all the evidence we need. What's a little hair goin' to show?"

He slipped Awesome's hair into a clear plastic evidence bag. His hair was straight and pitch black. He sealed the bag, recorded collection information on the bag and initialed it. He placed it with the growing cache of evidence related to the murder of Skeeter and his buddies, and saw another clear envelope containing hair taken from Skeeter's hand. Brown. Slight curve. Not straight.

Townsend gasped. "I'll be." He turned the two envelopes over in his hands for a moment. Weighed the possibilities. He thought about the call from Wes giving him the tip about where to find Awesome and the scalps. He was momentarily overwhelmed by distain for the Whittakers and their friend Brad Dalton. Then he thought about the gifts, and his new pickup. Greed replaced distain.

"Here we go again. I've been covering for those spoiled rich kids my whole life. They owe me big time," he said to himself as he pocketed both envelopes. "One day they will pay. Big time."

* * *

After spending a couple of hours with his buddies, Skip said his goodbyes, left Tommy's Trading Post and headed home. When he finally got home, Skip began imagining the excitement of discovering a famous treasure and all the opportunity and fame that would surely result. He remembered his fifteen minutes of fame during the Vampire Defense. "Wow! What if we could repeat all that notarizing with another really big case? We'll all be set for life. What Brooks and Bradley need is a good press agent, again. They just don't know it yet. And I'm their man."

Skip scrambled through a pile of business cards until he found the one he wanted. "Here it is. Sandy Storm!"

* * *

Skip met Sandy Storm, a reporter with the world's largest cable news network, CTN, when she covered the Vampire Defense, a murder trial in which the defendant claimed that the victim was a vampire. She was the first reporter on the scene and she parlayed the novelty of the defense into a career case for herself. Her daily coverage built the reputations of Brooks and Bradley as two of the nation's leading criminal defense lawyers.

Her first big job in front of a camera was in Cleveland. Her extraordinary good looks and rich feminine voice made her an instant hit. She was told that she was destined for the big time. She was assured that major networks, maybe even movies, were in her future. So, she hired an agent. But, her agent told her that her name had to change. "Storcovsky just doesn't do anything for me," he said.

"But I'm proud of my name."

"You don't have to change your name, sweetheart. We just want an AKA you can operate under. We need something catchy, memorable, so that you'll stand out in the crowd. Let's face it. There are a lot of pretty faces out there and even more who have a lot of talent. But, most of them don't make it. If you get your one big shot, you need to be remembered."

"I don't know. Maybe you're right."

"Of course I'm right. I'm always right. The sooner you realize that, the sooner I can get you to the big time."

And so, Storcovsky became Storm, and Sandy Storm was born. She landed a coveted job at CTN, and after a few months operating in obscurity, she thought she was assigned to purgatory when she was sent to 'Podunk, Mississippi' to cover a multiple homicide. It turned out to be the case of the century and she became the most well known journalist on television.

She also fell for a lawyer, in Mississippi of all places. John Brooks. She realized that it would never work out between them, so as she wrapped up the story, she kissed him goodbye. It was their only kiss. And she couldn't stop thinking about it.

* * *

Skip whipped out his cell phone, and a few moments later said, "Sandy! This is Skip. Skip Schafer. You remember me?"

"Yes, hey, Skip. How could I forget? How are you?"

"Yeah, great. Couldn't be better. Have I got a scoop for you? You can keep a secret right."

"I'm a reporter, Skip. I report scoops to the world."

"Yeah, well, I know. Anyway, let me tell you about the next big case of the century, and Brooks and Bradley are at it again."

"No kidding! I'm all ears! Tell me everything you know."

Chapter 21

John and Frank followed Sheriff Rainey across Pinishook Creek, where they took a hard left onto a dirt path just wide enough for their vehicles. Slanted sunbeams shining through the trees illuminated the path as they bounced and bumped their way down the trail.

"Stop, I see something!" exclaimed Frank.

John stopped and honked his horn twice. Sheriff Rainey stopped, looked back, and put his car in reverse. Frank was already out of the truck, studying the ground on the left side of the trail. Moments later, he was joined by Sheriff Rainey, G.W. and John.

"What is it?" asked John.

"Blood," G.W. answered for Frank.

"Good eye, brother. We drove right past it."

"Easy to miss it. Most of the blood has been covered by all of the traffic and the dust that's been kicked up. But, look at this grass," Frank said to Sheriff Rainey. Rainey looked at the grass, then back at Frank. He stooped to get a closer look.

"Well, I'll be."

Frank stirred the dirt with his pocketknife, exposing dark red dirt under the dust. Within a few minutes he outlined a large bloody patch of ground.

"The killing happened here on the ground," said Frank.

"Sheriff says the bodies were in the back of the pickup," said G.W.

"That means somebody moved one or more of the bodies from here. They probably put the body in the truck," said Frank.

"Sounds right to me," said Rainey. "You proved me wrong already. I said there was nothing left to be found. You've already found something."

"This means that somebody drove the truck with the bodies from here to the Goni field to put the blame on us," observed G. W.

"That's speculation. This don't mean that Awesome didn't do it," said Rainey.

"Take us to the spot where the truck was found. Let's see what the earth tells us there," said Frank.

Rainey drove slowly down the farm trail, with John following in Frank's truck, until they reached the edge of the Goni Swamp field.

"Stop here," said G.W. to Rainey. "Let's walk the rest of the way. Your car will bog down as soon as we get off the trail into the field."

"Okay. The truck was found near the edge of the field, not far from the fence," said Rainey as he pointed to the area.

Frank and G.W. led the way, walking side by side, about six feet apart. Sheriff Rainey and John followed along behind. John observed Frank and G.W. as they scrutinized the ground. About half way to the destination they both stopped.

"Why are we stopped?" asked Rainey.

"What do you see?" Frank asked G.W.

"A fire truck was out here. It stopped here. I think they were afraid they might bog down. Four pickups, a car and three or four other heavy trucks were out here, I think, but I'm not sure. The car got stuck right here and had to be pulled out," said G.W.

Frank nodded in agreement.

"Huh," said John. "You can see all that?"

"Yeah, but it is hard to read. There's been too much traffic. Sheriff might be right. There might not be any good trail left," said Frank.

John looked at Rainey and asked, "Are they right?"

"Pretty much. No way I would have been able to tell."

"Me neither. I grew up in the city," said John.

"Yeah, if you live on a farm, you learn to let your land talk to you," said Frank.

Frank and G.W. spread further apart, so that they were outside the track marks. At last they came to the area where the pickup had been parked.

"Skeeter's truck was here," said G.W.

"How can you tell, with all these track marks?"

"A tow truck hooked up to it and towed it out. You can see the truck tracks coming in," said G.W. as he gestured at the tracks. "The tracks stop here, and then reverse and go back over themselves. That would be the tow truck lining up to tow Skeeter's truck." Continuing to point, G.W. said, "The tow truck stopped here near Skeeter's truck. The driver climbed out of the tow truck here, on the driver's side, left footprints in the mud, dropped to his knees here, and lifted the back of the pickup. Skeeter's rear tires don't make a mark as the tow truck drives off. So, that tells us, it was a tow truck. What else could it be?"

"Oh. I think I see that now. So, that's how you could tell the car was stuck back there and was towed out?"

"Yes. The marks were similar. There's much more we can read, but we need to look for other signs. We don't need to read all the signs, just the signs that would have been left by the killer, or killers."

John looked at Sheriff Rainey quizzically. Rainey pursed his lips, raised his eyebrows and said, "Sure, that's all we need. Lead on."

"No," said Frank with eyes downcast. "With all respect Sheriff, I think it better that you and Mr. Brooks wait here a minute while we take a look."

Rainey nodded.

Frank and G.W. began circling the area where Skeeter's truck had been. They moved in opposite directions, making concentric circles that spiraled out, away from Skeeter's truck tracks.

"There's been a lot of tragedy in this field and on this farm," observed Sheriff Rainey. "It's a lot to happen to one family."

"Yeah, four murders today, and one of the brothers died in this field," said John.

"You know about that?"

"Frank told me."

"Yes, and those two boys killed, buried alive in a cave-in at the well."

"What?"

"You didn't know about that?"

"No, sir. What happened?"

"G.W. and Erma's boys. They were just kids. And then Curtis disappears. Then Uncle German is murdered. It's just too much tragedy for one family to handle. I hated to bring them the news about Awesome. That's a lot bad to happen to one family just by coincidence."

"Interesting observation, Sheriff. A couple of days ago I spoke to a young lady, Emily Martin."

"The deputy clerk in the Chancery Clerk's office?"

"That's her. She thinks this swamp is haunted because she heard strange moaning sounds."

"When?"

"Around the time Curtis disappeared."

"Huh. That was a few months before James Dalton died in this swamp. There's another one of those coincidences again. I always had a nagging feeling that I should have requested an autopsy for James."

"I like the way you think, Sheriff."

"Bein' suspicious of everybody is a burden. Don't get the idea that I think that Awesome is innocent. The odds are he's the killer."

"I appreciate your professional curiosity, Sheriff."

"You butterin' me up?"

"Just telling you how I feel."

"Yeah, well, maybe I'll drop in and talk to Emily."

Frank and G.W. stopped. They gestured toward the ground, back towards the spot where Skeeter's truck had been, then toward the fence. After nodding to each other, they motioned for Sheriff Rainey and John to join them.

"Circle to the left of the tow marks and come to us," called Frank. "Don't come straight to us from where you are. You might step on tracks we want to show you."

Rainey shrugged and motioned for John to follow. "There must have been 15 or 20 people out here, with lots of vehicles. How are you going to pick out one set of tracks?" asked Rainey, incredulously.

"I'm not interested in everyone's tracks, just the killer's. So, we can ignore all the other tracks," explained G.W.

Rainey laughed. "Okay, I'll bite. How can we pick the killer's tracks out of all the others?"

"The killer drove here in the pickup."

"Okay."

"How did he leave?"

"I don't know," admitted Rainey, "How did he leave?"

"He either had to drive out, be carried out in another vehicle, or he walked out."

"Sounds logical. How does that help?"

"It means that we look for his tracks leaving."

"What if he didn't leave tracks? What if he had a truck here waiting for him? What if he had help? What if someone followed him?"

"Yes, and what if he caught a ride out of the swamp with one of your deputies?"

"What do you mean by that?"

"I mean, all of your questions are good questions, and it would be hard to find his tracks if any one of those things happened, but that's not what happened."

"How do you know?"

"Because he walked out of the field. Here is a set of tracks going one way, from Skeeter's truck to the fence and out of the field," said Frank as he gestured at a footprint at his feet. "Here is the killer's print. Look. The prints start at Skeeter's truck. You will lose sight of them when you get close to the truck, because of all of the traffic. But, you can see that they continue, alone, to the fence. They don't come back."

Rainey looked at the tracks at his feet. He looked back to where Skeeter's truck had been, and then he looked toward the fence. "Huh! I see what you mean."

A clap of thunder startled everyone.

"The rain will be here in a minute," exclaimed Rainey. "I've got to measure and photograph this, and maybe make a cast. And we have to see where these tracks go! We'll never make it before the rain. My car's too far away."

"What do you need," asked John. "I can run pretty fast. I'll get it."

Rainey tossed him the keys. "My evidence bag. It's a kit in the trunk. Run like crazy."

John caught the keys and sprinted across the field. He still played rugby with the Jackson Rugby Club, but work had been so demanding that he had not made it to practice regularly. His position was wing, which demanded a sprinter's speed. But, the car was further away than he realized, and lots of missed practices meant his condition was less than ideal. He was breathing hard before he was half way to Rainey's car.

"While he's getting the kit, let's see what we can see before the rain comes."

"Okay, Sheriff. Follow me," said Frank, and the three of them followed the footprints. Not every footfall left a print that they could see in the fading light, but enough did that, with the help of Frank and G.W., Rainey could clearly see the trail.

Sheriff Rainey stuck a stick in the ground next to one particularly clear print. "I like this specimen," said Rainey. "It'll make a good cast." They continued following the trail all the way to the fence.

John fumbled with the keys. A fat ran drop smacked him on his cheek. He popped open the lid. The trunk was full of more junk than he could imagine. A second raindrop hit his forearm as another clap of thunder boomed. John began tossing things out of the trunk. Rain fell harder. "There it is!" he exclaimed as he uncovered a bag, marked "Evidence." He grabbed it, started to run, and then thought, "I better look." He unzipped the bag and saw a camera, plastic bags, tape measure, and other items. He quickly zipped the bag and threw it over his shoulder without breaking his stride, just as a sheet of rain enveloped him. A seemingly impenetrable curtain of rain chased him as he ran. He didn't look back, knowing it would cause him to lose speed. His eyes focused on his goal. "What? They've moved! They're twice as far away!"

Rainey was just about to cross through the barbwire fence when he felt a rain drop. He whirled around, "Oh, what a fool I am! Quick, get back to the mark! Cover it!" The three of them ran, albeit slowly, toward the stick in the mud that marked the specimen chosen by Rainey. The second clap of thunder spurred them to run faster, but Rainey was overweight and G.W. and Frank were overage.

"Where's that lawyer?" huffed Rainey as they arrived at the mark.

They looked toward Rainey's car, but all they could see was a curtain of rain. The car wasn't visible.

"There!" pointed G.W. John emerged at a dead sprint from the curtain of shower.

"Oh, God, help him or he'll never make it," said Frank.

John used mind tricks to get every millisecond of speed out of his sprint. He visualized himself as a cheetah, with springs on its paws, being shot out of a cannon. He concentrated on staying on the balls of his feet, never letting his heels touch the ground. He focused on pushing hard against the ground with his toes. He tried everything he knew to get more speed out of his sprint. Still, the gap between John and the others closed agonizingly slow. He was sucking air by the gallon, but with forty yards to go and rain falling all around him, John transferred the energy required for breathing to his legs, putting every ounce of remaining strength into the final stretch.

Rainey stripped off his shirt and placed it gently over the footprint. Frank and G.W. did the same. "We have to use our bodies to make a tent over the foot print and keep as much water off as we can until he gets here. He'll never make it before the rain," said Rainey as he bent down to his hands and knees and covered the track with his body.

"Let's help him," said Frank. "I don't think this is going to work, but we've got to try."

Rainey reached for his wallet, pulled out a dollar bill, pulled the shirts back and placed the bill beside the track.

"What are you doing sheriff?" asked Frank.

"Frank, your lawyer ain't getting here in time. A dollar bill is about six inches long, so I'm going to do the best I can to measure this print before the rain washes it away," said Rainey as he marked the first dollar bill spot, slid the bill forward and tore it to mark the curvature of the print at the toes.

"That's smart," said Frank.

"Good idea," agreed G.W.

In order to save every instant he could, John didn't slow down as he reached Rainey. He dropped the bag in Rainey's reach as he sprinted past, then he slid to a stop, like he was sliding into second base. When his slide stopped, John lay on his back, gasping for air, completely spent. Sheets of rain swept over the four men, so thick that John thought he would drown. He coughed and gagged.

"Well, son, if all you're gonna do is lay around, at least you could come over here and block some of the rain," said Sheriff Rainey.

John rolled over in the mud and crawled back until he was positioned where Rainey wanted him to be. Then he lay on his side gasping for air and tried not to drown in the heavy rain.

Chapter 22

Sandy hung up with Skip and instantly called Bret, her cameraman.

"Bret, get your things together. I think I'm onto the next big story. Maybe the biggest yet."

"Whoa. You've got my attention. I can't argue with your nose for news after what we experienced with your last big story. Where are we going?"

"Philadelphia."

"Great. Independence Hall, the Liberty Bell and Philly cheese steaks."

"Not that Philadelphia. The one in Mississippi."

"Really? Okay, the Choctaw Indian Reservation, the Silver Star, the Golden Moon, Williams Brothers Grocery, the Giant House Party."

"Do you know something about every place?"

"Every place I like."

"What are you talking about, the Giant House Party and Williams Brothers Grocery? What is that?"

"You know, the Neshoba County Fair and Olivia Manning."

"What?"

"Never mind. You either get it or you don't."

"Oh, no you don't. I am a professional reporter. Don't talk to me that way. Philadelphia must be where that girl is from, the one you're talking about all the time."

Bret laughed. "You have good instincts. How can the next big story be in Mississippi, again? Does this have something to do with that lawyer you have the hots for?"

"Yes. No. I don't have the hots for him, and yes he just might be involved."

"Okay, fine, but you better clear this upstream, because, I like my job. I also like my paycheck. If somebody gets the idea that your hormones are overruling your journalistic instinct, then we'll both go down."

"Bret. Don't talk that way."

"What? I'm just saying. Anyway, I hope you can work it out, because there is a girl I would like to see."

Maximilian's Treasure

* * *

Sheriff Rainey pondered the puzzle of the prints leading away from Skeeter's truck toward the Whittaker place. He couldn't let it rest. As soon as he cleaned up, he returned to his office and went directly to his evidence room. He removed the boots taken from Awesome when he was arrested. He looked inside and noted the size, 13 ½ C. He compared it to the cast taken from the scene. Awesome's boot was three inches longer than the cast of a boot print he retrieved from Goni Swamp. He scraped dirt off one boot of Awesome's boots into a plastic bag.

After making a few notes for his investigative file, he wrapped the plaster cast of a boot print in newspaper and carefully placed it in a shoebox. A few minutes later he walked into Williams Brother's Grocery, carrying the shoebox. Williams Brother's Grocery is a general store, where a country boy can find just about anything.

"Good evening, sheriff," said a cash register clerk. "You here to pick up some bacon?"

"Yep, my wife ran out of your good bacon. But, I want to ask Earl something first. Is he in the back?"

"Sure, you know where to go."

Sheriff Rainey worked his way through the crowded aisles until he found the man he was looking for.

"Earl!"

"Hey, sheriff! Heard about them boys getting' scalped. I don't much blame Awesome for killin' em, but you can't take the law into your own hands. And scalpin' em, why, that's going way to far."

"Yep, that's what I was thinking, too. I'd like your help with something."

"Sure, anything to help the law. Does it have to do with Skeeter's murder?"

"Not at liberty to say. I just want to know what size foot would fit into this boot."

Rainey opened the box and unwrapped the cast. Earl Horton glanced at it, then at Rainey. He stepped away and moments later returned with a footplate traditionally found at shoe stores, used to measure feet, called a Brannock. After placing the cast on the Brannock, Earl responded, "I can't tell you the size of the foot in the boot, because people wear wrong size shoes all the time. But this boot was a 10 ½."

"Would a 13 ½ foot fit that boot?"

"Nope."

"Will you follow me to the jail, and bring your fancy measuring device with you?"

"Glad to, sheriff, but I might could save you some time if you want me to measure Awesome's foot."

"You see right through me, Earl. That's exactly what I want you to do."

"I've sold boots to Awesome for years. No way his foot would fit this boot. And this tread is not his tread."

"How do you know?"

"Awesome always buys the same boot. A 'Hike King' by Arrow. It's what he likes. I keep it in his size in stock for him. Every time he buys the one in stock, I re-order. He's hard on boots."

"Do you recognize the tread that left this print?"

Earl turned the cast upside down. "Not at first glance. If you give me an imprint of the tread, I can do a little research for you."

"Thanks, Earl. I'll do that."

"Glad to help, Sheriff."

Rainey cogitated on the evidence while he drove back to the Sheriff's office. He began talking to himself. "This is good evidence that Awesome didn't kill them boys. But, somebody wanted me to think he did." He turned into his parking space, but left the car running, with the headlights on the door to his office. He let his eyes trace the emblem on the door, the badge representing law and order, justice.

"It's mighty peculiar that one boy would have evidence of crime found in the back of their pickup, he disappears, and a year later another boy from the same family has evidence of crime found in the back of his pickup. And the second boy didn't do it."

Rainey climbed out of his car and entered his office. He called the jail. "Bring me Awesome. Make it quick."

Awesome was wearing a standard jail issue jumpsuit and flip-flop sandals. His hands were cuffed behind his back, his legs encumbered by chains. Rainey stared at Awesome's feet for a moment and then turned his gaze to Awesome's eyes. Rainey tried to look deep into Awesome, willing himself to detect any deception, reservation or hesitation.

"Did you kill them boys?"

Awesome looked directly at Rainey, let out a soft sigh, and responded, "No sheriff, I didn't kill them. I was mad enough to kill 'em, but it wasn't me."

"Did you get someone else to do it?"

"No, sheriff. I would have wanted to keep the pleasure all to myself."

"You're not making this easy for me."

"Sheriff. I wasn't going to kill them. I just wanted to make sure they were the ones, and that they weren't about to hurt anyone else in my family. I respect you enough to let you do your job."

"Humph. Well, I believe you. I'm releasing you tonight. It'll take an hour or two. Don't make a fool out of me."

Awesome exhaled with relief, took in a deep breath and said, "Never, Sheriff. You can count on me."

Awesome was escorted from his office. Rainey was dead tired and wanted to go home, but something was nagging him. He went to a cabinet and searched for the file on Curtis Dalton. "That's odd. Curtis' file is not here."

* * *

John was able to shower at the Dalton farm, while Erma washed and dried his clothes. She made sure they ate, ate and ate leftovers. At last, it was time to go. The Brooks and Bradley crew said their sad goodbyes and promised to be back for the funeral as they climbed into the Trooper for the hour-long drive home. The happy news of Awesome's release had not yet reached the household.

"Claire says she has something for us at the library. She can't contain herself and wants us to come tonight," said Karen

"I'm beat. Can we see it tomorrow?" asked John as he steered the Trooper onto Highway 16. Clouds blotted out the stars, and the night seemed darker than black.

"Claire will be really disappointed," continued Karen. "And, she said that what she has for us is of extreme importance. She wouldn't want word to leak out about what we have found."

"Why would it leak?" asked Jackson.

"Well, we do have a team of researchers who are librarians. Professionally, they are not much on censorship and keeping secrets," Karen explained.

"Yeah, I suppose they are into disseminating knowledge, not concealing it," agreed Jackson.

"So, the two of you think we should go tonight?" asked John.

"Why not? Well, other than you're tired, why not?" asked Karen.

John took a long look at Karen, smiled and said, "Sure. Why not?"

He didn't pay much attention to the pickup passing him on the two-lane road.

Chapter 23

"Don't let them get away!" yelled Brad. "I thought you said your deputy buddy would have pulled them over by now?"

"He's running late," responded Wes.

"They'll be out of the county before he gets here. Run them off the road!"

"What?"

"You heard me, run them off the road. Maybe then Deputy Dolittle can catch up with them."

Wes swallowed hard and began his pass. He saw that the driver was looking at one of the passengers, not paying much attention to him as he passed.

"How am I going to run him off the road if he isn't even looking at me?"

"Give me that wheel!" yelled Brad as he grabbed the steering wheel with both hands and jerked the pickup to the right.

"What are you doing!" screamed Wes as the right side of his pickup smashed into the front left side of the Trooper.

"What the…?" exclaimed John as he jerked the wheel to the right.

Karen screamed.

Peter screamed.

Jackson yelled, "Look out!"

The Trooper careened off the road, across a ditch and slammed into a tree.

* * *

Sandy had become an expert at selling ideas to her producer and editor. They usually responded enthusiastically now that she was a hot commodity. But, she knew better than to overplay her hand, so she did a little research before calling in the story. Since the supposed treasure was in Mississippi, she thought she would start her research there. A quick Internet search led her to a history and archeology professor at Ole Miss. As soon as Bret arrived at her apartment she called Professor Michael Lenton who was surprised, to say the least, when he received a call at his home from a famous CTN reporter. After a little small talk, Sandy came to the point of the call.

"Professor Lenton, is it okay if I record this interview for accuracy?"

"Sure."

Sandy nodded to Bret who began recording, then said, "I am following up on a lead that actually seems too fantastic to be true. I have been told about a supposed treasure in Mississippi linked to Jesse and Frank James and to the Emperor Maximilian of Mexico."

"Oh, ha, yes, I've heard that one. Can't be anything to it."

"That's what I was afraid of. Jesse James in Mississippi? That's ridiculous."

"Well, no, not that part. There is support for the claim that the James gang was in Mississippi."

"Really?"

"Yes, they were accused of robbing a couple of banks here after the Civil War. That was never proven in court, but it does appear they passed through more than once."

"So, is it the connection with Maximilian that is not possible?"

"No," said the Professor as his voice rose slightly in a practiced manner, intended to grab the attention of his student listeners. "That might be possible too. The Jameses were part of a Confederate Calvary outfit called Quantrill's Raiders. Quantrill was a ruthless, brilliant tactician. When the war started going badly for the South, Maximilian was a natural ally to the Rebels. Maximilian was an Austrian Prince installed by the French as Emperor of Mexico. He needed the South to keep the U.S. occupied so that it would not try to enforce the Monroe Doctrine, which asserted that the U.S. would protect the sovereignty of any country in the Americas from European intrusion. The French clearly intruded in Mexico. They knew this violated the Monroe Doctrine and invited war with America. But, the U.S. was engaged in a bloody civil war that consumed all of its military resources. It could not afford to take on a war with a European power. That might be just enough to tip the scales in favor of the South. The Southerners obviously realized the same thing. There is evidence that Quantrill's Raiders went to Mexico seeking an alliance during the war.

"In fact, after the Civil War, many Southerners settled in Mexico at the invitation of Maximilian. But, when he was captured and killed by Juarez, the Southerners were no longer welcome and they came under attack. So, Quantrill put his Raiders back together and they went to Mexico to help Southerners get out of the country. Some of those Raiders later became the James gang.

"Because of those connections, lots of rumors about treasure were started and endure to this day. According to the rumors, Maximilian would rather his Southern allies get his vast treasure instead of his sworn enemy, Juarez. Those rumors persist to this day."

"What if someone claims to have a map of the location of the treasure?"

"It would be a hoax."

"Why? With all of these connections it seems feasible, doesn't it?"

"True. There are plenty of possible, probable and even actual connections, but where the rumor breaks down is at its most fundamental point."

"And what is that most fundamental point?"

"There never was any treasure."

"What?"

"Mexico was broke. It couldn't pay its debt to European powers and that's why France invaded and installed Maximilian. The French army left because they couldn't find any money to pay the debt. That, and the Mexicans fiercely fought the French. They defeated a French army at the Battle of Puebla on Cinco de Mayo."

"Was that the end of the French/Mexican war?"

"No. The war continued for another five years. But, since no gold was found, the French lost the will to continue fighting and decided to leave. They offered to take Maximilian with them when they left, but he was naive. He sincerely thought the Mexican people loved him and he genuinely believed that he could help the country. Once the French army left, he was soon in big trouble, largely because he didn't have the money to pay his own Mexican army. He was as broke as Mexico. If he had a vast treasure the French army would have stayed, and the history of the Americas would have been quite different."

"Oh, but maybe he found a treasure after the army left, or ..."

"No. I am afraid that you may be making the same mistake others have made. I don't blame you. You want the rumor to be true, so you are imagining all of the possible, even improbable ways that the rumor might be true. But, those possibilities don't line up with the known facts. Maximilian sent his wife to Europe to try to raise money and support, or to raise an army to help him, all to no avail."

"How could his wife raise money or an army?"

"His wife, Carlota, was the daughter of the King of Belgium and she was related to the King of France. Maximilian was a Habsburg, the second son of the King of Austria. Maximilian had ruled a principality in Italy and he was very popular among the ruling class of Europe. The two of them were very well connected. They were thought of as the best that Europe had to offer. Carlota truly believed she would return with help, because of her family connections. She went to every head of state, only to be rebuffed. Indeed, it is said that she lost her sanity when she was utterly unable to help her husband.

"Back in Mexico, Maximilian fought bravely, but finally Juarez captured him. It is said that Juarez admired Maximilian and liked him as a man, but he wanted to send a message to Europe to stay out of Mexico, so he executed him."

"So, there was never any treasure?"

"None. That's where the persistent rumor breaks down, at its elemental, fundamental point. "

"Oh."

"You are disappointed."

"Well, I confess that I am disappointed because I thought I was on to a great story. But, I'm a reporter. What I really want is the truth. No need to try to run down rumors and hoaxes about Maximilian's treasure and the Hummingbird Hoard."

"What did you say?"

"I said, no need to …"

"No, you said 'Hummingbird Hoard'."

"Yes, I did."

"Why didn't you say so at first? That changes everything!"

Chapter 24

Talcum powder filled the air. John coughed, struggled to remove remnants of the airbag from his chest and said, "Is everyone okay?"

There were a few moans, but everyone acknowledged they were unhurt and okay.

"Did you see that guy?" asked Jackson. "He just ran right into you! Ran you off the road!"

"Yeah," said Peter. "He could have killed us!"

John pulled the handle and pushed the door. It didn't budge. He pushed it with his foot. The door groaned, creaked and reluctantly swung open. He looked at the darkened road at the pickup that had sideswiped him. It was less than 50 yards away.

Wes was panting. "I can't believe you did that. Look what you've done to my truck!"

"Shut up and drive. All we wanted to do is give your deputy time to catch up. Now, they won't be going anywhere. Since they ran off the road, he'll have a good excuse for searching the car for alcohol or narcotics, or anything else they may have."

"Oh, yeah, like a map. That's a good idea!"

"Yeah, so get out of here before someone recognizes us."

Wes spun his tires and raced off.

"Great. There goes the other driver," said John.

"What are we going to do?" asked Karen.

"It just so happens that I have Sheriff Rainey's number. I'll give him a call. Then, we'll see if we can get the Trooper out of the ditch. I'm afraid she may be totaled."

While John was making the call, a car rolled to a stop on the shoulder of the road, and a blue flashing light came on.

"Wow, that was fast," said Jackson.

"Yeah, too fast. I guess he just happened to be driving by," said Peter.

Karen looked at the deputy climb out of the car, hand on his gun, and a strange feeling came over her. She looked around the Trooper. The diary and the map had been on the dashboard. They were gone. She felt around on the darkened floor. There! She scooped up the envelope containing the documents. She looked out the window and saw the deputy approaching John.

"So, what happened here?"

"We were run off the road."

"Looks to me like you've been drinking."

"Actually, sir, I haven't had anything to drink."

"Well, then, it must be drugs."

Karen looked left and right, trying to decide on a good hiding place. She looked around the car. Everyone's attention was on John and the deputy. She stuffed the envelope down the back of her blouse, under her bra strap, straightened her blouse, and sat back in her seat. The envelope crinkled. She looked at Peter, wondering if he heard the noise. No one seemed to notice.

Jackson climbed out, saying, "Officer, if you hurry you can catch the criminals that ran us off the road. They just sped off. You can still see where the driver spun his tires."

"Keep your mouth shut until I get to you."

"But, officer! They are getting away!"

"I have to secure the scene and I can't do it with everyone talking at once. Get back in the car until I get to you. Now, you," indicating John, "turn around."

John complied. The deputy pushed him against the Trooper and cuffed his hands behind his back. He patted him down, but found nothing of interest.

"Lie on the ground in front of the car, where I can keep an eye on you."

John furrowed his brow, pursed his lips, and complied. He positioned himself so that he could keep an eye on the deputy.

"Next, blabbermouth!" He pointed at Jackson. "That's right. You. Get out of the car." After patting Jackson down, he took him to the squad car and locked him in the back seat. He took Karen out of the car, and did a quick pat down her sides, then moved his hands forward.

"Watch I, buddy."

The deputy laughed, and moved on to Peter and patted him down.

"You two," gesturing at Karen and Peter, pointing to an area lit by the Trooper's one working headlight, "sit there on the ground where I can keep an eye on you."

After they complied, he began searching the Trooper, glancing from time to time at each of his "subjects." He shuffled through papers in the glove box and in the door pockets. It seemed to Karen that he was more interested in finding papers than in finding contraband or alcohol. She rolled her shoulders. The crinkling of the envelope reassured her.

While the deputy was searching the Trooper, a second patrol car arrived and turned on its blue lights.

"What's going on here, Wayne?"

"Sheriff Rainey! I've got a single car accident, four people involved, with suspicion of intoxication. I'm searching for whatever they got high on."

Rainey stepped over to John. "Were you driving?"

"Yes, sir."

"What happened?"

"A gray or silver pickup sideswiped me and ran me off the road. You can see the marks on my Trooper."

Rainey walked over to the Trooper and ran his hand down the left side.

"Let 'em go."

"But, sir!"

"I said let them go. I've been with them today. They aren't intoxicated. You would have to be blind not to see the damage to the side of his vehicle. They were run off the road. Why aren't you calling in the hit and run?"

"Sir, I…"

"Don't 'sir I' me. Get on the horn and get help. First, un-cuff this man and let that one out of your squad car. Do it now!"

"Yes, sir. Right away, sir."

As Deputy Wayne unlocked John's cuffs, Rainey said, "I hope you will overlook this treatment. Wayne means well. He's just a little to gung-ho sometimes."

"Well, no harm done, except the guy who ran us off the road got away, while your deputy was arresting us."

"Yeah, we probably missed our opportunity to catch him. But, you never know. Sometimes we get lucky."

An hour later, after a full slate of reports, photographs and apologies, the Trooper was somehow running again. Rainey cut away the air bag, and Deputy Wayne Townsend removed a bent fender that scraped the tire.

"Are you sure you don't want me to get you a rental?" asked Rainey.

"No, thank you. Since my trusty old Trooper is still kicking, I want to take it home. I'll get it to a shop tomorrow."

"I'm afraid it's totaled."

"Won't matter. I don't have collision, so there won't be any insurance company to total the thing."

"No collision insurance. That's too bad. Maybe you need to talk to a lawyer about that," said Rainey with a twinkle in his eye.

"Maybe I will, Sheriff. Thank you for your help. I really mean it. Really."

"Thank you for the way you handled yourself today. I'll be talking to you soon," said Rainey. "By the way, I ordered the release of your client tonight. He should be home by now."

"That's awesome news!"

"Yeah, I'm sure Awesome thought so, too," laughed Rainey at his own joke. "But, after I had time to think about what we saw today, the rest of the story just didn't add up. The only thing that makes sense to me is somebody wanted to make it look like Awesome did it. The boot prints at the scene could not have been Awesome's."

Karen noticed that Deputy Wayne stopped in mid-stride and leaned toward Sheriff Rainey so that he could hear better.

"How do you figure they got the scalps in Awesome's truck?" asked John.

"I haven't worked that out yet, but I have a few ideas."

Everyone waved goodbye and the Brooks and Bradley firm got back on the road again. As they drove away, Sheriff Rainey asked Deputy Wayne Townsend, "You worked on the Curtis Dalton case, didn't you?"

Townsend hesitated a moment and answered, "Yes, boss, we all did."

"You don't know where the file is, do you?"

"The file? In the cabinet I guess."

"No, it's not in the cabinet. Who do you think checked it out?"

"I don't know, Sheriff. Why?"

"Something just doesn't add up. I want to take another look at it, that's all."

* * *

John shared the news about Awesome's release, and the team shouted and celebrated as though they had won the Super Bowl.

"Sheriff Rainey is a great cop," said Jackson. "Not every law enforcement officer would have stepped out on a limb this soon and released the prime suspect."

"Yeah, that was a bold move," agreed Karen.

"Not only that, he told me that the only thing that makes sense to him is that someone wanted to make it look like Awesome did it," replied John.

"Exactly," agreed Jackson. "We have a great ally in Sheriff Rainey."

Karen nodded and said, "I have a feeling that the Dalton farm will be safe for as long as Sheriff Rainey is around. He is a good man. But, I am not so sure about Deputy Wayne."

Karen noticed that Peter seemed to have withdrawn again. At first, he celebrated with everyone at the great news. Now, he seemed somber as he stared out the window.

"Let's go home and see Claire tomorrow. I was tired before, but I am really beat now," said John.

"Can you believe all that's happened? This has been a crazy night," said Jackson. "I am fine with seeing Clarion the Librarian tomorrow."

"It's worse than crazy," said Karen.

"Why?"

"I think the deputy was looking for the diary," she said as she removed the envelope containing the diary and the map from the back of her blouse, where it had been tucked under her bra strap.

"What! Why do you think that?" exclaimed Jackson. At the same time, Peter said, "No, way! He wouldn't be looking for the map!"

"It seemed as though he was looking for papers instead of contraband. It just didn't look right to me," explained Karen.

"How would he know to look for the map?" asked John.

"I'm not sure," said Karen as she glanced at Peter, "but it means we better talk to Claire tonight before anything else happens."

"Good grief. Will this night ever end?" asked Jackson.

"Just hold on, and maybe we can survive the night," responded John with a humorless chuckle.

* * *

"There's one more thing I should do before we shoot footage," said Sandy. "I need some sort of confirmation of Skip's story."

"But, didn't Skip tell you it was confidential? How will you get anyone to confirm the story if they aren't talking?"

"He said he learned about this from Claire Cartier's fiancé. So, let's ask her."

"She won't tell you anything if she's been sworn to secrecy. She knows you're a reporter."

"Watch me."

Sandy used the Internet to get the phone number for the Eudora Welty Library in Jackson, Mississippi. "Good evening. Could I speak to Ms. Clarion Cartier, please?" After a moment, Sandy winked at Bret and said, "Claire! This is Sandy Storm, how are you?"

"Oh, Sandy Storm, why, I'm fine, why, this is so, exciting!" said Claire as she adjusted the large horn rim glasses on her tiny nose. "You can't imagine what an exciting day this has been already for a librarian and to have you call, why, this really tops it off. It is so good to hear from you!" Claire grabbed a handful of papers from the counter and fanned herself. Her ankle length dress was buttoned up to the top button at her neck. "But, why would you be calling me?" The other researchers overheard the name Sandy Storm and they began gathering around Claire. One mouthed, "Be careful. Don't tell her anything."

"I am following up on a lead, and I want to know if you could verify something for me."

"I'll be happy to do anything I can for you, Ms. Storm."

"I am doing some research on the Hummingbird Hoard and Maximilian's Treasure. Can you tell me anything about them?"

"Oh, well, why, oh my. I just, I don't know what to say? Why, its such a coincidence that you should call and ask me, because, why, I…" Claire hesitated, not sure what she should say.

"Yes, Claire?"

"Why, I am in such a spot. I really would love to help you, but I'm just not at liberty to say anything about that, I am so sorry. Please don't be mad at me."

"Oh, don't worry, Claire. You don't have to say a thing. I understand completely."

"You're not mad?"

"No, not at all Claire. I will be in Jackson soon. Maybe we can see each other."

"Why, that would be wonderful."

"Thank you, Claire. Goodbye."

"Goodbye."

Claire and her librarian friends were relieved. "Good job, Claire," one said to her. "You didn't tell her a thing. I don't know if I could have done what you did. I probably would have blabbed the whole story."

Everyone laughed in relief and went back to work, compiling research for the meeting with the Brooks and Bradley team.

Sandy hung up, looked at Bret and smiled.

Bret said, "That unsuspecting librarian just confirmed the part of Skip's story that she was doing confidential research on the treasure, and she doesn't realize it."

"That's right!"

"I've got to admit, you're good at what you do."

"It's why we're going to get the big bucks. I'll get approval for an onsite follow up, while you book our flights. Our interview with Dr. Lenton will run during prime time tonight!"

Chapter 25

Something was bothering Sheriff Rainey. He just couldn't let it go. Instead of going home, he returned to his office. Even though it was late, he prepared a thorough report on his investigation into the murders of Skeeter, Dirt and Robber, and the evidence that led him to believe that Awesome was not the killer. He searched the growing file for the hair evidence taken from Skeeter's hand. When he couldn't find it, he looked for Awesome's hair evidence. He knew he had asked Townsend to get a sample.

"I can't find that either! What's goin' on? Wayne didn't do what I told him." He picked up the phone and began punching Townsend's number. "I'll give him a piece of my mind!" He paused when he was about to dial the last digit. He sat still staring at the wall; hand set at his ear, hand above the dial pad. "MEEP, MEEP, MEEP, MEEP."

Rainey hung up.

Using the plaster cast of the boot print and an inkpad, he made an impression of the boot tread on a sheet of paper. While the impression was drying, he addressed a large envelope to Earl Horton, and slid the impression into the envelope.

"What did that lawyer say about Emily in the clerk's office? Might as well make one more call," he said to himself as he found the number for Emily Martin. After speaking with Emily he sat alone in his office fingering his badge and turning the data over in his mind. "I'm gonna visit that swamp."

He couldn't believe he was doing it, but he made a copy of his report and slid it into the Horton envelope. "I don't want this to come up missing, too."

* * *

As they approached the city, John's Trooper began to shimmy and shake.

"Uh, oh," said Jackson.

"Come on, baby, just a little further," coaxed John.

Maximilian's Treasure

It was after 10 p.m. when they finally pulled into the parking lot at the Eudora Welty Library. Claire Cartier and her research team met them at the door. They were all tittering with excitement.

"We have so much to tell you," said one of the ladies, while another locked the door behind them. Everyone was ushered into a meeting room with a large table, a projector and a screen. Somehow, the librarians had found the time to obtain a tray of finger sandwiches and cookies. Hot coffee and soft drinks were ready and waiting. Peter dug in and John reached for the coffee.

"We have decaf if you would rather," said Claire.

"Thanks, but I need the caffeine," said John as he poured a cup of steaming black coffee and settled into a chair.

"Thank you for coming on such short notice and so late," began Claire. "We haven't stopped since Mr. Bradley gave us the assignment. We are excited to tell you that what you have uncovered is of great historic significance. It will change our understanding of several important portions of the history of Mexico and may lead to significant archeological findings." Claire placed her hand on her chest and caught her breath.

"Those are some big claims," said Jackson.

"What about the treasure?" Peter asked.

"We will come to that. In fact, I think that Peggy should give you the summary of our findings. She made the breakthrough in our research. Once she got us on the right track, everything started falling into place. So, Peggy, please show our friends what we found."

Peggy was shy at first, but as soon as she began describing the result of the research, her shyness disappeared, and the heart of a professional researcher took over. In short order, she described how Maximilian, an Austrian prince, and his wife Carlota, came to be the Emperor and Empress of Mexico, with the help of the French army.

She quickly touched upon the connections between Maximilian and the Confederacy, Quantrill's Raiders helping southerners evacuate Mexico and the origin of the James Gang. Then she described some of the rumors of Maximilian's Treasure.

"And all of those treasure stories were discredited by the financial condition of Mexico at the time of Maximilian, and so they have been categorized as rumors and legend," said Peggy, her voice trailing off on legends. "Until now!"

All of the researchers applauded and responded with, "Yes! Yes! Until now!"

* * *

Peggy smiled and basked in the applause for a moment.

"That is exciting," agreed John, "but what has changed?"

"Please excuse our excitement. We don't get to be involved in such finds often. In fact, until your firm came along, one of the most exciting things we did was notify the Library of Congress that it made an error in categorizing a book. I remember when Claire discovered that the Diary of Jackson Nycroft was miscataloged."

All the women applauded and Claire smiled and nodded. Peggy continued, "We were able to get a new number for the book! We live to find and correct the next mistake. So, please excuse us." Peggy fanned herself, and took a deep breath. "Anyway, the diary you found changes everything."

"How?" Karen asked.

"Before the arrival of Maximilian, the political history of Mexico was a disaster. There was a new president or dictator practically every year, and each new leader pillaged the country and oppressed the common people. There were two exceptions to that sordid history, President Juarez and Emperor Maximilian. Juarez was deposed by the French, but he didn't go away. He was constantly on the run from the French, narrowly escaping capture several times. When Maximilian became Emperor, he genuinely tried to help the people of Mexico. He instituted many reforms, including land reforms, and gave new rights to the common man. This made him very unpopular with wealthy and powerful Mexicans, who were the very people who conspired with France to overthrow Juarez.

"The diary, the one you found, written by Frank James, records a meeting between Maximilian and an Indian priest who offered to provide money, weapons and warriors. He said he wanted to help fight Juarez and allow Maximilian to complete the reforms he had started."

"Why would they want to help Maximilian, a European? Wasn't Juarez an Indian?"

"Right you are, Mr. Brooks," interjected Claire. "Juarez was the first full-blooded Native American to become President of Mexico. But, not every Indian supported him. In fact, some fiercely opposed him."

"Why?" asked Karen.

"It has to do with the ancient gods of Central America," answered Claire.

"But, I thought the worship of those gods was stamped out by the Spaniards," observed Jackson.

"True," said Peggy, "but a few cults based upon one ancient god or another still existed. In fact, they probably still exist today."

"So, what could a small number of cult worshipers of an ancient god have to offer Maximilian?" asked Karen.

Claire answered, her voice quivering with awe. "According to the diary, the Hummingbird Hoard!"

Everyone was silent for a moment. The librarians seemed to believe that they had said everything necessary for the Brooks and Bradley team to fully grasp the significance of the find.

"That's not a very dramatic name for a treasure trove," observed Jackson.

"Okay," said John. "I'll bite. What is the Hummingbird Hoard? And why exactly is it named after a hummingbird?"

"Well, I'll have to dip into legend just a bit," explained Peggy.

"Here we go with legend again," said Jackson.

"But, I can supplement legend with actual history, just bear with me a moment. The Hoard is a legendary mountain of gold named after the Aztec sun god, their god of war, Huizilopochtli."

"Huitziwhat?" asked Peter.

"He is commonly referred to by his symbol, the hummingbird, because that's easier to pronounce."

Karen gasped. "The Dalton house is filled with caricatures of hummingbirds!"

"Really? That's interesting," said Claire. "There may be more clues in that house!"

Peggy continued. "In the panoply of Aztec gods, there were good gods, bad gods and gods that were sometimes good and sometimes bad. The gods were very warlike and competed with one another. Hummingbird, the god of war, supposedly adopted the Aztecs and made them a powerful people. He was also the sun god. This is important to us, because the Aztecs believed that gold nuggets were teardrops from the sun god. They believed that everything he touched turned to gold, and that gold was therefore sacred and precious.

"The relevant story also involves followers of an evil god named Tlaloc, who was known as the eater of babies."

"Eww," said everyone at once.

"These were blood thirsty gods who demanded human sacrifice. The Aztecs were in a constant state of war, capturing victims, who they would slaughter by the thousands on their temples. A few lucky victims were treated well for a short time. They were treated like a god or goddess, until they were given an elaborate feathered dress and drugged just before their hearts were cut out."

Everyone murmured disapproval.

"Anyway, before the god of war defeated him, the earth was ruled by a good and benevolent god known as Quetzalcoatl, the feathered serpent. The Mayans called him Kukulcan. The Incas called him Vericocha, the swimmer on the sea. The Hummingbird, one of the middle of the road gods, who could be good or bad, defeated Quetzalcoatl and sent him away to the east. It was believed that Quetzalcoatl would return at the end of a calendar age, defeat the Hummingbird and regain control of the Earth."

"Yes," interrupted Claire, "they believed Quetzalcoatl would return at the end of a 500-year calendar age."

"That's right," continued Peggy, "In the Central American legends, Quetzalcoatl had a beard and fair skin."

"Yes, I remember this story," said Jackson. "It just so happened that when Cortez arrived, a calendar period of about 500 years had just ended."

"That's right," said Peggy, "and the Aztecs believed that their world would end when a calendar period ended. A great comet appeared just before the arrival of Cortez, which the Aztecs read as a sign that their world was ending."

"And their world did end when Cortez arrived," said Karen.

"That's right," added Claire, "many of the Aztecs were convinced that Cortez was Quetzalcoatl returning. He came swimming across the sea from the east, and he rode on a horse, which to the Aztecs was a huge frightening animal. That's why a handful of Spaniards so easily captured Montezuma, the Aztec Emperor."

"Well, didn't the Spaniards seize all of the Aztec gold?" asked John.

"No. There is a well-documented story of the Hummingbird Hoard. Claire, you tell this part of the story best. Why don't you tell them?" urged Peggy.

"Well, all right," said Claire. "We were able to locate and tap a lot of sources, such as the History of the Conquest of Mexico, by Prescott and Maximilian and Carlota by Smith, and many others, such as…"

"Ahem," interrupted Peggy. "They probably are not as interested in the sources and the difficulties we had putting this together, and how we cleverly collaborated to understand the story. They probably just want the story."

* * *

Peter excused himself, claiming a need to go to the bathroom as an excuse. As soon as he was out of sight he used the cell phone Hoover had given him.

"Peter, I didn't expect another call tonight. What's up?"

"You might want to know that Sheriff Rainey decided to release that Indian, Awesome. He said he thinks someone tried to set him up. Mr. Brooks thinks that the Sheriff will be a good friend to them, and Ms. Karen thinks that the farm is safe for as long as the Sheriff is around."

"That's good information Peter."

"But, there's more! Right now, we are at the library learning about a huge Aztec treasure."

"The treasure that Mr. Dalton thinks is on the farm?"

"That's it. And we have a map to the treasure!"

"Now that's what I call a great report, kid. I'll be sure to let Gregory know just how good a boy you are."

Chapter 26

In the meeting room, the lecture continued.

"I guess it is late," continued Claire. "Please forgive me. Anyway, I guess the best starting point would be Noche Triste! The Sad Night.

"The year was 1520. Cortez had captured Montezuma and the Aztec capital, Tenochtitlan, a vast city built atop a man-made floating island. Huge structures, pyramids, palaces and temples, were built on rafts, linked together and fastened to the bottom of the lake with aquatic plants. Later, the Spaniards drained the lake and the city became Mexico City.

"Montezuma died in captivity. These bearded fair skinned invaders were no longer seen as the return of the good god, Quetzalcoatl. They seemed more like devils, obsessed with gold. No matter how much gold the Aztecs gave them, they demanded more. No matter how many women the Spaniards took, they wanted more. Their appetite for gold and for women was insatiable.

"A council of the new king and the high priest decided upon a final solution: all the Spaniards must be killed. The entire Spanish army of maybe 200 men was within the island city; in effect they were trapped, surrounded by a quarter of a million angry warriors. Aztec victory seemed certain. But, somehow, on the night that came to be known as Noche Triste, the "Sad Night," the Spaniards escaped. The loss of life on both sides was dreadful."

* * *

Karen noticed Peter as he stepped back into the room. "Something's not right with that boy," she said to herself.

* * *

The following is a description of an Aztec Counsel meeting, preserved by a Franciscan monk from his interview of two Aztec priests, about two years after the event:

The High Priest Huitenpec summoned his most trusted men. As he entered the temple chamber, a cry arose.

"'All hail great Huitenpec!"

"Huitenpec held up his arms and shushed the small crowd. 'This is no time for celebration.'"

"But, we have driven the invaders from the city," cried one young warrior. "We have proven they can be beaten. Surely, this is a time to celebrate."

"No. They escaped and killed thousands. A terrible plague is sweeping the city, sapping our strength. When our many enemies see how the Spaniards have hurt us, they will join them in a great war. Already the triple alliance is broken. Our friends have abandoned us. Our only hope was to destroy the Spaniards tonight. We let victory slip away."

"What shall we do?" cried a counsel member.

"We must not let them find the Sacred Sun Drops of Huitzilopochtli."

"That is the source of the power and blessing of our people," exclaimed a priest.

"We cannot risk letting them fall into the hands of these demons from the east. Our age is over. A new age is beginning. But, this new age will not last. The Sacred Drops from the Sun must be hidden. We must preserve the memory of how to use the Sacred Sun Drops. Then, we must be ready to return, like Quetzalcoatl, when this world of the white man ends, and the next world begins."

"How long must we wait?" asked the young warrior.

"It may be 500 years, my son. But, if we act now with prudence and stealth, our descendants will be able to use the Sacred Sun Drops when the time comes."

* * *

Claire paused and looked around the table at each face.

"That happened about 500 years ago," observed Karen. "Does that mean they think our world is about to end?"

"That means nothing," said Jackson. "That's just hocus pocus. Superstition."

"You are right, of course, Mr. Bradley," continued Claire. "I don't mean to suggest that there is any supernatural power in these Sun Drops, which are also called Tear Drops. I am just relating to you the history. In any event, the removal of the contents of the vaults of Huitzilopochtli, the sun god of war of the Aztecs, began that night. Much of the treasure was crafted into images of animals, gods, bowls, cups, utensils, coins, or into teardrops, teardrops of the god of the sun, shed when he had to leave

Mexico. But, most of the gold remained in its original form, just as it had been found. Tons of gold nuggets."

"Wow! Where did they take the gold?" asked Peter as he scooted to the edge of his seat.

"I am coming to that. Huitenpec appointed Cuahhtemoc, we'll call him Moc, to remove the treasure. Moc arranged for the great hoard to be concealed in covered baskets and taken from the vaults over the course of many nights. The baskets were loaded into boats and taken by slaves to a remote shore of Lake Texcoco. A train of slaves carried the treasure to the Valley of Huitzilopchtli. That is also known as the Valley of the Hummingbird, where it was hidden in a concealed tomb awaiting the end of this world and the coming of the next. The slaves were slain.

"When he returned, Moc found the great city under siege. Tens of thousands of Central American Indians had joined the Spaniards in their war against the Aztec. Moc snuck back into the city to meet with Huitenpec and reported that the treasure was safely hidden in the Valley of the Hummingbird. Huitenpec was pleased. He anointed Moc the new Emperor of the Aztecs. Moc led the war effort for 3 months, but disease and starvation took their toll on the population. A quarter million Aztecs died in just 3 months.

"Cortez promised that the killing would stop if Moc surrendered. To save his people, he surrendered. The Spaniards searched the city for gold. They had seen tons of it before they were driven out, but found very little. Many of the Spaniards were adventurers, or uneducated riffraff. Some were criminals who joined Cortez to avoid punishment in Spain.

"Some accused Cortez of hiding the gold. Others guessed that Moc knew where Montezuma's fabled treasure was hidden. There were rumors among them that Cortez made a pact with Moc to split the treasure. They threatened mutiny. This was a dangerous time for Cortez and the Spaniards. They were still in a hostile country, far from any help. Cortez knew that if the Spaniards fought among themselves, they were doomed.

"The mutineers demanded that Moc be tortured to make him reveal the location of the treasure. Cortez refused. The mutineers claimed this was proof that Cortez was in league with Moc. The standoff lasted weeks. Cortez, fearing the loss of everything, weakened and allowed Moc to be tortured. It was a shameful episode that haunted Cortez for the rest of his life. Cortez respected Moc and knew that he would never have surrendered if he had been merely a warrior. But, since he was an Emperor responsible for the lives of his people, he surrendered to save as many as he could.

"Here is the most powerful part of the story. Moc revealed nothing. His torturers forced his feet into a blazing fire until they literally roasted to nubs."

"That is awful," said Karen, cringing.

"Yikes," said Peter as he raised his feet off the floor.

Claire continued, "Moc's generals were tortured alongside him. They begged Moc to tell the Spaniards whatever they wanted to know. 'Just tell them where the treasure is,' they pleaded. Moc remained stoic. With his feet in the fire, he turned to his generals, grinned and said, 'Do you think that I am enjoying this footbath?' He said nothing else."

"Why didn't he say something?" asked Jackson.

"I understand. He was the leader of his people," said Karen. "He didn't want to leave a legacy of weakness. He showed strength of character. It was his last act of defiance."

"Exactly," continued Claire. "Moc's wife, Perca, was hiding nearby watching everything. The Spaniards literally wore themselves out torturing Moc. Finally, late at night the torturers fell asleep from exhaustion. Perca slipped past them and slit her husband's throat.

"She became disillusioned because the great god Huitzilopochtli was unable to protect the Aztecs from Cortez. So, she became a priestess of the terrible god Tlaloc, the eater of babies. She dedicated her cult to the protection of the secret of the location of the treasure and the secret of how to use the power of the Sacred Sun Drops for evil and destruction. The Tlalocans, as they came to be known, would kill anyone who got close to finding the gold."

"Wow. She was one angry..." said Jackson.

"What did this have to do with Maximilian?" asked Karen.

"Good question," said Peggy. "There is a competing second cult involving the gold, the cult of Huitzilopochtli, the Hummingbird. This cult believes that they are the rightful heirs to the Hummingbird Hoard. They, too, are dedicated to protecting the secret of the gold and the use of the Sacred Sun Drops, ostensibly for good."

"So, we have a good cult and a bad cult?" asked John.

"That's right," agreed Peggy.

"You speak of these groups in the present tense," observed Jackson.

"Yes," said Peggy. "I'm not sure if they're still around, but we now know that they were around at the time of Maximilian."

"So, they are mentioned in the diary?" asked John.

"Exactly. Very perceptive, Mr. Brooks," said Peggy. "A priest of Huitzilopochtli came to Maximilian and offered to take him to the Hummingbird Hoard, and to show him how to use the magical weapons known as the Sacred Sun Drops."

"Why would he do that?" asked Jackson.

"Because a priest of Tlaloc had become a chief advisor of Juarez."

"So, was Juarez one of these cult members?"

"There is no evidence of that, other than the presence of the Tlalocan priest."

"So, this Hummingbird priest was trying to keep the Tlalocans from getting the upper hand," observed Jackson. "Your typical religious feud."

"Yes, and it was the Tlalocan priest that encouraged Juarez to execute Maximilian because he had a Huitzi priest with him."

"Well, Juarez won. Wouldn't he have found the treasure?" asked John.

"It may be that the Tlalocan priest never knew the location, or maybe he thought that revealing the treasure was unnecessary once Juarez won."

"What happened to the information the Hummingbird priest gave to Maximilian?" asked John.

"Maximilian thought that the French army would return if they believed there was a mountain of gold. So, he loaded the priest on a ship, along with a golden chest containing Sacred Sun Drops. The inside lid of the chest contained a map of the location of the treasure hidden in the Valley of the Hummingbird. The ship was bound for Haiti, where they hoped to find French Legionnaires."

"You said 'was bound,'" noted John.

"Right again, Mr. Brooks," said Peggy. "The ship was lost in a hurricane off the coast of Hispaniola."

"I saw a reference to that in the diary," said Jackson.

"That's right," continued Peggy. "Frank James was on that ship. When the ship sank he clung to a barrel and made it to shore where he wrote about his adventures in his diary. Now we have his diary."

"Assuming the diary is authentic," Jackson pointed out.

"Correct," said Claire. "Everything fits, but in an effort to provide further evidence, we have researched the best way to confirm the age of the diary. With your permission, we'll take it to Ole Miss in the morning to get the diary carbon dated."

"Claire! Claire! Come quick! You've got to see this!" shouted one of the librarians who had stepped out of the room unnoticed. Everyone rushed to her. They saw that her eyes were locked on a television tuned to CTN.

A breathless Sandy Storm was ending her exclusive report. "To sum up, it appears irrefutable that clues to the location of Maximilian's Treasure and the ancient Aztec Hummingbird Hoard have been found in, of all places, Philadelphia, Mississippi. This is Sandy Storm, reporting for CTN."

"She just finished reporting some of the same things we've been talking about!" exclaimed the librarian who called everyone to the television.

"What? How did she find out?" asked Karen. She turned quickly to John.

"Don't look at me!"

Claire ducked and said, "Well, she did call here tonight, and I did talk to her. But, I didn't tell her anything."

"It's true," several librarians chimed in together. "I was proud of her, she didn't tell that reporter anything."

"So, how did she find out?" asked Karen.

"How did she know to call Claire?" asked John.

* * *

Within minutes of Sandy Storm's broadcast, phones began to ring in Central America, Spain, France, Austria and the tiny country, Andorra. Refrains of "Maximilian's Treasure" and "The Hummingbird Hoard" and "The Tears of the Sun God" were repeated, some in hushed tones, some with excitement.

Coma Pedrosa, Andorra.

Antoine de Sada's heart raced as he disconnected from the call describing Sandy Storm's report. One wall of his study was glass, offering a spectacular view of the Andorran Pyrenees in this principality nestled between France and Spain. The rest of the office consisted of rich wood lined walls covered with bookshelves filled with ancient and new texts, each bookshelf covered by a glass window that protected the contents. Centered on one wall was an impressive eagle, wings spread, with an elaborate crown suspended over its head. It held lightening bolts in its talons, a feature his branch of the family added to the Habsburg crest over a century ago.

"Incredible," he said to himself as he rose from a comfortable leather chair. Deep in thought, he stepped over to one bookshelf, swung open the window and removed "Maximilian and Carlota, the Habsburg Tragedy in Mexico," a book he had practically memorized. He flipped to page 263, the end of the siege of La Cruz. In his mind, he transported himself through time and space to Mexico, June 16, 1867. Betrayed by his generals after a heroic 71-day siege, the Emperor stood proud, surrounded by enemy soldiers. One officer removed his hat and approached Maximilian. Antoine repeated the officer's words, "Your majesty is my prisoner." The words still cut Antoine to his soul.

He repeated Maximilian's words three days later as he faced a firing squad. "What a glorious day! I have always wanted to die on just such a day!"

Maximillian forgave his firing squad, granted his permission to carry out their orders and, just before he died, shouted, "Long live Mexico!"

Antoine shook his head in disgust. "What a fool. Only fools forgive. At least he was a brave fool. Max failed. I won't."

He stepped over to an elaborate marble globe, spun it until he found what he was looking for and smiled. "Who would have thought the clue would be there? Pierre, get the Gulf Stream ready. We are about to fly to Mississippi."

"Mississippi? As you wish, Señor de Sada."

At that moment, his phone rang. The caller ID indicated, "Private."

"Yes, I heard. I am already on my way. You will be the first to know what I find . . . Yes, of course I understand the importance of getting there first," a hint of exasperation in his voice. "No, I won't let my interest in ancient religions stand in the way of our quest. Indeed, I am convinced that one particular ancient religion will be quite helpful to us. ... Yes, I understand you are not yet convinced. Just have faith," he said with a chuckle as he concluded the call.

One thousand miles away, Natalia Mary Garza studied a map. She smiled as she found Philadelphia, Mississippi and marked it with an X. She dialed a number. "You've heard? Yes, I am on the way." There was a pause. "Yes, I understand how vitally important it is that we get there first. Don't worry. I know de Sada better than anyone. God willing, he will never get the Golden Tear Drops. I guarantee it with my life." Natalia removed a cross from her neck, placed it in a drawer and wondered if she was ready. "Of course I'm ready," she said to herself. "I have prepared all my life for such a day as this." She knelt, said a prayer, and packed her bags.

Natalia and Antoine were not the only ones making travel plans.

Chapter 27

Crush obtained an entry-level job at Jaco's Tacos bussing tables and washing dishes. A group of 60 law students from Mississippi College stayed late, and it was after 1 a.m. when Crush was finally able to punch out. He checked his text messages. Mitch, from the Rugby Team, wanting to know if Crush could help with security tonight. He decided he would drive past the law firm, Jackson's apartment, Karen's place and finally, past John's houseboat on the way home. He texted Mitch, "I'll swing by their homes between 1:30 and 2:30, if I can stay awake." He knew Mitch wouldn't see the message until morning.

* * *

By the time John dropped everyone off it was after 2 a.m. The shimmy and shake of the Trooper kept getting worse. When he was within sight of the levy, all of the warning lights on the dashboard flashed and the engine died.

"Good grief. What a way to end a long day. I was dead tired hours ago."

John shifted into neutral and let the Trooper coast as far as it would go. He drifted onto the shoulder of the road a quarter-mile from home. He sighed, locked the SUV, and walked home. By the time John arrived home, a 1972 Drifter houseboat named 'Always Somethin', he was beyond beat.

He left his clothes in a pile on the floor, hit the bed and quickly fell asleep to the soft sound of wavelets patting the side of the boat. Soon, his dreams were filled with visions of Karen, her beautiful smiling face, bountiful red hair and sparkling eyes. Then, he felt Sandy's kiss on his lips and heard her voice whisper, "who needs a bathing suit?" He heard a splash and found himself in the lake, a curvaceous feminine form swimming underwater toward him. Her arms and bare shoulders surfaced in front of him in a splashing eruption of bubbles. Water streamed from her face as she rose like a mermaid from the deep.

John awoke with a start before he could see her face, or anything else. He wondered, 'was that a bump that woke me?' His heart was racing and he had to catch his breath. Soft orange light filled his tiny bedroom. His mind wandered back to the evening that both Sandy and Karen were guests on his boat. So much had happened since then. So much had happened in the past 24 hours! He shivered and realized he was covered with sweat.

"Jackson is right. It's time for me to make a decision about Karen or Sandy. But, I'm not ready. A family is not in my plan now." Then, he remembered Sandy saying she wasn't interested in marriage; just a relationship, and thoughts and visions of her filled his mind. His lips felt hot as he remembered her kiss.

"Why can't a long distance relationship work?" he said to himself. "We could meet often, in exotic places. Then, when we're ready, we could take the next step. That could work. I can't believe what I'm saying! I can't believe I'm talking to myself. What about Karen? She is awesome, beautiful, loyal and honest. If I pursue Sandy, Karen will be gone forever. Jackson says if I don't pursue Karen, she'll be gone soon. But, it's not fair to chase Karen if I have feelings for Sandy. I don't know what I feel for Sandy, but I know I feel something."

John found himself on his knees next to his bed. 'Always Somethin' swayed slightly as he began to pray, "God, I don't know what's going on with me. I don't want to make a mistake. I don't want to choose wrong. I don't know what I feel. God, I'm confused. Honestly, I am attracted to Sandy and to Karen. My heart is aching. What would you have me do? Tell me, please."

Pop! Pop! Pop!

"What was that?" exclaimed John. He noticed the soft orange light was flickering, and he detected the smell of smoke. 'Always Somethin' groaned and swayed too much for a boat securely tied to a pier.

"I'm adrift!"

John raced to the front of the cabin, reaching the front door in only three quick strides.

"Fire!"

The entire pier was burning from end to end and neighbors' boats were engulfed in flames.

* * *

Crush noticed a strange orange glow in the sky when he turned from Old Canton Road onto Lake Harbor Road. He pondered the cause of the unusual light as his car climbed the hill that overlooked the lake. Then, it occurred to him that only one thing could account for that strange light. "Fire!" he shouted to himself as he floored the accelerator even before he saw the flames. As he crested the hill, he still couldn't see the harbor, or the fire, but he had no doubt that a huge fire was raging near John's houseboat.

"Oh, God, don't let me be too late!"

* * *

"Always Somethin' was adrift thirty feet from its slip. The lines, hose and electrical cord had apparently burned through," thought John. "Or, maybe they've been cut," he said to himself. John put one hand on the key, which he always kept in the ignition, and quickly adjusted the choke and throttle with his other hand. As he turned the key, he completed an electrical connection that sent a spark racing through the engine compartment below the aft deck. In a millisecond, explosive gases blasted the unhinged side of the thick metal engine compartment cover with such force that the lid was ripped free of its hinges. The momentary drag provided by the hinges caused the heavy cover to arc into the cabin.

Before John was aware of the explosion, the 60-pound lid had already cut through the bedroom walls like a knife and was smashing through the bathroom and kitchen on a trajectory that would carry it all the way through the cabin three feet above the deck. The blast concussion burst all of the windows. Expanding gases in the engine compartment caused the deck to buckle and heave under John's feet. He was aware of intense heat and light and the sensation of flying.

Chapter 28

Gregory positioned his car on the levy a quarter mile away where he had an unobstructed view of 'Always Somethin' across open water. He rolled his window down and watched with delight as fire spread across the pier. As the fire progressed, boats burned in their slips. Several flaming vessels broke free and began drifting toward other piers. One flaming boat reached a second pier. In moments, the fire raged across the second pier.

"Oh, this is great!" laughed Gregory. "The whole harbor will burn tonight! This is what the earth will be like when my lord returns!" Firelight glinted off of his binocular lenses as he closely examined 'Always Somethin'. He watched as the last flaming line holding the houseboat to the pier snapped and the houseboat began to drift.

"Come on Brooks, I can't believe you sleep so hard! Oh, there you are!" he said with satisfaction as he saw John's silhouette at the front of the boat. "Come on, buddy, crank the boat!"

Even from a quarter mile away, the heat from the explosion washed over Gregory. He spread his arms to embrace the heat and laughed deliriously as he watched the top literally blow off of the houseboat. "Yes! One down, three to go! Goodbye, Mr. Brooks."

Gregory felt his phone vibrate. Still smiling, he checked his message. "Hmm. Interesting. Make that four to go. Something has to be done about that Sheriff. Why do I have to do all the heavy lifting? Seems like they could do something."

Gregory pulled away as two fire trucks rushed past. "What futility! How do they think they're going to handle a harbor full of burning boats with a couple of trucks? What fools! Ha, ha, ha!"

* * *

Crush raced up the levy and slid his car to a stop at the foot of John's pier. He leapt out of the car and ran onto the burning deck, disregarding the danger and the heat, just in time to see the top literally blown off of John's houseboat.

"No!" he screamed in defiance as the concussion washed over him. The bright flame from the blast made the surrounding darkness seem even darker. Blast debris flew in every direction, but Crush saw that one chunk of debris, a black silhouette against the bright white, orange and yellow explosion, seemed to have human form as it sailed into the night. Crush noted the location of the splash. He sprinted to the end of the flaming pier and leapt into the shimmering black and orange water. The pier collapsed behind him. Just before he hit the water, he thought he heard demonic laughter.

With single-minded determination, Crush focused on a point where he believed a body splashed. Using long, strong strokes, he settled into a fast cruise across the top of the water. With practiced ease he fell into a pattern as he sucked air on his left, turned his head down face in the water, three stokes while exhaling, suck air on the right, repeat, with a glance at the target between each transition.

Something was floating just ahead. Crush grabbed it with his big mitt of a hand. It was a body, face down in the water, floating lifelessly.

He pulled the body to him and rolled it over.

"John! Oh, God, help me. Hang on, brother! I gotcha'!"

With one arm, Crush pulled toward the closest shore with mighty strokes. The other arm clung to the body, which trailed behind him. Nearing exhaustion, he pulled himself and John onto the riprap on the levy. He quickly checked John. No breath. No pulse.

"No, God! Don't let this happen!"

He scooped John into his arms and rushed to the top of the levy, laid him on the roadbed and began CPR. He breathed into John's mouth, pressed, pressed, pressed his chest and breathed into his mouth, minute after minute, with no response.

"Wake up John! Don't leave us. Come back!" Tears streamed down the big man's face. Hope began to fade, but he didn't quit.

Chapter 29

John was in a long crowded hallway that seemed familiar. Someone was guiding him down the hall. John's hands were cuffed behind him. Shackles hindered his steps. He looked over his shoulder into the eyes of a stern faced deputy. People in the hallway sneered and hurled taunts at him. One man with a hauntingly familiar ugly face poked a finger into John's chest and said, "It's about time you finally got what you deserve!"

"Don't touch the prisoner! Stand back!" ordered the deputy.

The cloud of confusion partially lifted. John recognized that he was in the hallway just outside the courtroom where he defended Hal Boyd a few weeks ago.

"This is the courthouse! What's going on?"

"Keep moving. Don't give me any more trouble."

"What?" asked John incredulously as he stumbled.

"You heard me," said the deputy as he grabbed John's collar to keep him from falling.

The surly mood of the hallway crowd changed to one of fearful respect. The brash voices that had been taunting John became subdued. Everyone pressed against the wall to make more room in the hallway. John looked over his shoulder and saw a large entourage quickly approaching. At the center of the group was a strikingly handsome man dressed in a perfectly pressed expensive suit.

"Who's that?" asked John as he and the guard reached the door to the courtroom.

"That's the prosecutor. If you don't already know him, you will after today."

The deputy opened the door just as the prosecutor arrived. The deputy pulled John aside and allowed the prosecutor's entourage to pass through the door into the courtroom. The prosecutor paused as he reached the doorway and slowly turned to face John. He had a strong chin and high cheekbones. His black hair was coifed to perfection. John was aware of an unusually powerful charismatic presence. The prosecutor locked his dark, empty eyes directly on John's eyes. Revulsion welled up from deep within John. An extreme urge to look away swept over him. John fought the sensation, squinted and forced himself to stare back into bottomless black eyes.

"Do I know you?" asked John.

The prosecutor cracked a smile. "You've always known me, John Brooks." He laughed and said, "After today, you're mine. My case against you is airtight."

"Case? What case?"

"Denial, so typical. I expected more, but after all, you're just a man," said the prosecutor as he let out a humorless chuckle and stepped into the crowded courtroom. A reverent trill washed through the crowd as the prosecutor made his way to his table. John recognized the courtroom. It was Hinds County Courtroom Number One, the same courtroom where he tried the Vampire Defense. Yet, it seemed somehow different.

As the deputy led John into the room, hisses and catcalls fell upon him from the crowd. Puzzled, John looked at the crowd and gasped. Grotesque faces, contorted with anger and hate, stared back at him. Some of the faces seemed familiar, caricatures of people from his past.

A giant screen covered one wall of the courtroom and a movie was playing. 'That's odd,' John said to himself as the deputy led him to the defense table. As John took a seat, he began to recognize the voices and places in the movie. It was a movie of wrongs he committed.

"That's my life!" exclaimed John.

The booming voice of the prosecutor rose above the din of the crowd. "You heard it, confession from his own lips, ladies and gentlemen! Do we have any need for more proof?"

"NO!" shouted the crowd.

"Do you WANT to see more proof?"

"YES! Show us more!"

The prosecutor laughed, and turned toward John. With a smug, confident air, he called out with a commanding voice, "Bring the jury forward." A dozen members of the hate filled crowd rose and passed through the gate in the bar that separates the public area of the courtroom from the area reserved for court personnel, lawyers, witnesses and jurors. Each juror paused to scowl at John before taking a seat in the jury box. One pale young man, with dark eyes and black hair paused and bent over John on his way to the jury box. "Remember me?" he said as he chuckled with a lack of humor.

Brooks searched his memory as the young man took a seat in the jury box. Brooks muttered, "Smith. You called yourself John Smith. But, you died months ago."

From the door that leads to the judge's chamber came a thunderous knock. A bailiff with an unusually penetrating voice proclaimed, "All kneel! The Supreme Court is now in session. He Who Is presides."

Utter silence fell upon the courtroom as everyone, including John and the prosecutor, took a knee. John, from his knees, glanced at the prosecutor. It was obvious that the prosecutor resented taking a knee as the Judge entered the courtroom. His face was red with contained rage. His hands shook with anger.

"You may take your seats," said a deep, masculine voice that seemed familiar.

John could not bring himself to look up to see the Judge. John's head remained bowed as he took a seat. He stared at a spot on the table in front of him.

"Oh, God, this is judgment day." said John under his breath. "Oh, God, have mercy on me! Forgive me please, in the mighty name of Jesus Christ!"

Somehow, the prosecutor overheard him. "It's too late for that, you fool. You're mine now."

"Announce your case," commanded the Judge.

The prosecutor rose, stood straight, glanced at John and grinned. It was clear that the prosecutor was enjoying himself.

"Our next case, Your Honor, is Humanity vs. John Douglas Brooks. We seek the ultimate penalty! He earned it!"

A murmur of approval swept through the crowd.

"Silence!" commanded the bailiff.

The crowd quickly settled down. An unspeakable dread fell upon John. Fear gripped him; his limbs trembled. He didn't notice another lawyer enter the Courtroom.

"Is there no one to speak for the accused?" asked the judge.

"His lawyer has just entered the courtroom, Your Honor," said the deputy.

John felt a strong, warm, comforting hand on his shoulder. "Your Honor, this one is mine!" said the lawyer with authority.

"NO!" yelled the prosecutor. "It's not fair! I demand justice! He belongs to…"

Suddenly, there was complete silence. The prosecutor's protestations were cut off in mid-sentence.

John turned to the prosecutor and saw he was still speaking. Indeed, he was in a rage, yelling, scowling at John, and shaking his fist at the Judge and at the lawyer whose hand rested on John's shoulder. Yet, no sound came from him. He yelled, gesticulated, raged and stomped, but not one utterance emerged, not the slightest sound escaped. The courtroom was completely quiet.

John turned and looked into the kind eyes of his lawyer. A peace that surpasses understanding swept over John and he fell from his chair onto his knees at the feet of the One who saved him.

As John wept with relief and gratitude, the Judge announced, "Hearing no evidence against the accused, this case is dismissed!"

Euphoria beyond description swept over John. He knew that he had been to the threshold of hell, only to be saved. "Thank you, Jesus," was all he could say.

After a moment, the judge said, "There appears to be an irregularity with John's admission documentation. I believe that the prosecutor was a bit too eager to bring this case to the bar of justice. John's case is not ready for a full adjudication."

John felt confused and bewildered. There was tremendous pressure on his chest. His head began to spin and he fell onto his back. The Judge seemed to hover just above him. At last, John could see God's face. John coughed and smiled when he realized that God's face is black. Tears were streaming down God's cheeks as he pressed hard on John's chest, shouting, "Wake up, John! Don't leave us! Come back!"

John retched copious amounts of water, then reached up and took the black face in both hands and whispered, "God, you're black."

Crush laughed and said, "I've always been black. Thank God you're alive!"

"I had a wild dream. I thought you were God."

"You're delirious. I'll get you some help." Crush jumped to his feet and waved at a fire truck. "Help! Help! We need help!"

Chapter 30

Aircraft often fly over the Rez on approach to the Jackson airport. Bret was looking out the window when he poked Sandy on the shoulder to get her attention. "Doesn't your boyfriend live in the harbor on the Rez?"

"What, John? Yes, he does, why? And he's not my boyfriend."

"Take a look at this," Bret gestured out the window at the smoldering ruins of the harbor. Three piers were destroyed and burned hulks of boats were scattered on the rocky shore. Smoldering hulls still drifted on the water.

"Oh, no! Can the pilot put us down right now? We've got to get there, quick!"

"Hold on, Sandy, the pilot is approaching the airport now. We'll be on the ground soon."

"Well, tell him to hurry!"

"Of course I will, Sandy. I'm sure he'll make an emergency landing once he knows it's Sandy Storm who needs to be on the ground immediately. Maybe I can get him to land in the water, next to John's pier."

"Oh, Bret. You are insufferable."

* * *

A cold rain pattered against the hospital window as Karen gently stroked what was left of John's hair. Outside the window, a dull gray sky swept away the memory of summer and the announced reality of the coming winter.

Crush sat at the door where he could keep an eye on Karen and John and greet anyone who entered the room. Crush was the gatekeeper. He was determined that no one would enter John's hospital room unless they first met his approval. After four days the hospital staff had not only adjusted to his presence, they adopted him. One nurse in particular made sure that he never missed a meal, checking on him frequently to see if he wanted or needed anything.

Someone tapped on the door.

"Who's there?" queried Crush in a deep gravely voice.

"Rico."

"Captain!" exclaimed Karen. "Glad you're here. Come on in."

Rico, the captain in charge of the Robbery-Homicide Division of the Jackson Police Department had dropped by to check on John several times. Even though the explosion was outside the city, St. Dominic Hospital is inside the city. Rico believed the blast was a murder attempt, and he didn't want the 'would be' assassin to finish the job in the city; not on his watch. Besides, he respected this pesky young criminal defense lawyer, and he had a personal stake in solving his attempted murder.

Rico greeted Crush and gazed past him into the room.

"How's he doin'?"

"Doctor says the swelling in the brain is gone. That's what they worried about the most. Second degree burns all over. Most of his hair is burned away, but he'll be all right, and his hair will grow back."

"I see he has around the clock care," Rico observed as he looked at Karen with envy. "Lucky man."

"Yeah, she hasn't left his side for four days, ever since they took him out of intensive care."

Rico nodded and stepped into the room. He put his hand on Karen's shoulder as she looked up and smiled at him.

"Thanks for coming, Rico."

"Has he been awake yet?"

"Almost. They're easing him off all the drugs, and he's been stirring around. I think he'll come around anytime now."

"Will you call me when he can talk?"

"Sure," said Karen as she continued stroking John's hand.

* * *

John felt a soft, comforting hand stoke his hand. There were sweet words, someone calling his name, saying, "Come back to me." Somehow it all became part of a dream filled with visions of Karen, her beautiful smiling face, bountiful red hair and sparkling eyes. Then, his recurring dream returned once again. He always woke before he could identify the woman in his dream. He felt a hot, moist kiss on his lips and heard her voice whisper, "Who needs a bathing suit?" He heard a splash and once again found himself in the lake, a curvaceous feminine form swimming underwater toward him. Her arms and bare shoulders surfaced in front of him in a splashing eruption of bubbles. Water streamed from her face as she rose like a mermaid from the deep. At last he identified the woman of his dreams! Wet, red hair spilled over her shoulders, "Karen!"

He felt her hand behind his head, pulling his lips to hers. With his eyes still closed, he reached up and took her in his arms and pressed her lips to his! It was a long, passionate kiss. He felt her hungry hands searching across his chest, igniting pockets of pain. But, the kiss was worth it. He ignored the pain. "Oh, John, I was so worried. I thought I had lost you!"

"It's you! I'm so glad it's you!" said John. "I love you so!"

"Oh, John, I feel the same way, but let's get you well and out of this hospital."

They kissed again as he opened his eyes. He had a moment of confusion when he looked through her blonde hair and saw Karen enter the hospital room.

Karen had spent four days and nights at his bedside. John was doing better, and his doctor thought he would regain consciousness soon. She decided to stretch her legs and get some coffee. Sandy had stopped by the room twice to check on John, and she arrived for another visit moments after Karen left. Frankly, Sandy felt relieved to have a few minutes alone with John without Karen hovering over them. "Karen will have to get used to John and I spending more time together," she said to herself.

"John, Karen will probably have to go," Sandy said to John's unconscious body. "It really won't do for my man to have a secretary who loves him. It's not good for you, or for her, or for me." She stroked what was left of his hair and spoke softly to him, urging John to return to her. When he began to respond, she doubled down on her efforts and kissed his lips passionately. Her effort was rewarded by John's embrace, more kisses and his profession of love, which she naturally took to be a profession of love for herself, not Karen.

As John's confusion lifted, he realized he was kissing Sandy, not Karen, and that Karen was across the room, a look of shock on her face, which was as red as her hair. Karen spun on her heels and bolted from the room.

John released Sandy, reached past her shoulder toward the door and said, "Stop her!"

"Oh, baby, you want me to stop because it hurts? It must really hurt if you want to stop kissing. Don't worry. You're connected to a pain pump. The nurse said that if you hurt, all you have to do is press this button to release more pain medicine into your blood stream." She pressed the button. "There, that should help." John shook his head.

"Don't fight it. Just let go," said Sandy as she stroked John's hair until he drifted back into a drug induced sleep.

Chapter 31

"Jackson, I've got to tell you about the amazing dream I had, where I saw God, and He looked just like Crush."

"Well, Crush did save you, so does that make him your savior?"

"Yes, he did save me, but there's more. You've got to hear this."

"Maybe in a minute. You know, they're going to let you go home tomorrow," said Jackson as he pulled a chair next to John's bedside.

"Yeah, but I don't have a home to go to," John responded.

"You can stay at my place. In fact, I plan to be away for a while."

"What?"

"Even though I know there is probably nothing to it, I want to follow the clues to the treasure. And, I have an excuse, a cover, if you will. I'll be writing a book about the Vampire Defense."

"So that you don't have to tell people that you're treasure hunting?"

"That's right."

"Sounds like you've got gold fever."

"Nah. There's probably nothing to it. But, if I'm wrong we don't want anyone else finding it first. Now that the story is out, people will be looking, and I don't know how long our team of researchers can keep the location quiet. Especially considering Sandy Storm's broadcast of our find to the world the same night we discovered it."

"I hear you. But, I don't know."

"You know that sabbatical that I've been wanting to take, so I could have time to write about our 'case of the century,' well, all the arrangements have been made and I'll be leaving in the morning."

"In the morning?"

"Yep. Headed to the Dominican Republic."

"Yeah, that's on the Island of Hispaniola, where Frank James' ship wrecked."

"Right."

"I don't know if this is the best time to go, for our practice I mean, but I understand why you want to go now."

"Yeah, I feel bad about leaving now. But, I've cleared the decks for you. I've gotten continuances on everything of significance and I worked like crazy to get as many loose ends tied up as possible. There is nothing pending, except the Whittaker v. Dalton trial, scheduled to start Wednesday."

"Well, that's something significant."

"There is no way the Court will make us proceed with the trial. We have the best grounds for continuance I've ever seen. I've got a motion to continue set to be heard Monday. If you can't be there Monday, I have someone who can stand in."

"Wouldn't the other side agree to a continuance?"

"No, they're completely uncooperative. I've got a trial notebook ready for you with all the witness outlines and the law. The jury instructions are done, just in case the judge doesn't continue the case. But, surely he will."

"Famous last words. Okay. Don't worry, I can handle it."

"You missed the funeral for Uncle German. The whole county turned out for it."

"He deserved that respect. I hate I missed his funeral."

"That's not the only funeral you missed."

"Really? Who died?"

"Sheriff Rainey."

"What?" Startled, John sat up quickly, felt dizzy, and put his hand to his head. "That's terrible news. How did it happen?"

"Nobody knows."

"You remember Deputy Wayne Townsend?"

"How could I forget the guy who harassed us the night we were side swiped and run off the road?"

"Yeah, that's the one. He found the Sheriff face down in Pinishook Creek. Apparently he drowned."

John pondered the news for a long moment. Then shook his head. "How? That doesn't sound right."

"Smells rotten," agreed Jackson.

"How about the funeral for Skeeter and his boys?"

"A few hot heads were there. They still believe Awesome is the killer. They can't believe Rainey turned him loose. His friends and family were raising cane and sounded like they wanted to start a race war, screaming bloody murder about their family members being scalped. They want revenge against Indians. Any Indians. All Indians. But, the people around Philadelphia were having nothing to do with that."

"What's the average Joe saying?"

"The average Joe in Philadelphia is saying even if Awesome did it, they don't blame him for killing them, and maybe they deserved to be scalped. But, the media isn't reporting it that way. The drumbeat about racial animosity in Mississippi is constant on the national media.

Supposed experts on the networks are saying that they expect a return to the Native American wars of the 1800's."

"Good grief. And you're picking this as your time to take a sabbatical?"

"There is more at stake right now than ever. There's some sort of a connection between the treasure and everything that's happening, I don't know what that connection is, but I know it's there. Look, John. If I don't go, we lose the advantage we have to find Maximilian's treasure. Already people from all over the world are swarming Neshoba County looking for clues. They seem to think that everything I do and say is a clue. If I slip away on vacation to write a book, I might be able to escape some of these prying eyes and maybe I can get something done, both on the search for the treasure and on the book."

"So, you're headed to the Dominican Republic because it has something to do with the treasure."

"That's right. Frank James' diary says that they were headed for Haiti on the west side of the island of Hispaniola. But, they were caught in a hurricane, and after his ship went down, he clung to a barrel and made it to shore on the east side of Hispaniola. The Spanish side."

"I won't be the only one guessing that you're searching for the treasure when you leave."

"Well, I'll be honestly telling everyone that I am going there to write a book."

"Jackson, the odds of finding any treasure, if there ever was a treasure, are remote at best."

"I know. We probably won't find a thing. If I don't find anything, but have time to write, I'll be satisfied. This is something I have to do. The experts examined the diary that Karen found and they believe it's genuine. I have to do this. I'll never forgive myself if I don't try. Besides, I've already arranged for a dive master to meet me there. I've already paid him. He bought his tickets and made arrangements for a series of dives and everything."

"Where did you get the money?"

"We borrowed it."

"We?"

"Yeah. I used our firm credit line, such as it is."

"I must have missed that meeting, the one in which we decided to borrow the last of our credit line."

"No, you were there. We had the meeting right here in your hospital room, just before you woke up."

"Now I remember."

"I made a motion and you didn't disagree."

"So, you were able to hire a dive expert?"

"Yep. Robert Wade, with Adventure Scuba Diving. He came highly recommended by the researchers at Ole Miss, even though he's a big State fan. Several of my friends have used him and speak highly of him. In the past two years he's found two wrecks of archeological significance for the University."

"Is he trustworthy?"

"Completely."

"Can he keep a secret?"

"At least as well as Skip."

John laughed. "Okay, since the whole world found out about our little secret before we could complete an hour long drive, I guess I have no advice to offer on the subject of secrecy." John sighed. "You being gone would be so much easier to handle if Karen was here. I could do anything if she were here. Where is she?"

"I don't know. After she quit, she disconnected her phone and moved. I asked her where she was going, but she wouldn't tell me. She said I would tell you and she didn't want you to know."

"Tell her you won't tell me. And then don't tell me."

"I did. She didn't believe me. She's gone, John."

John turned and looked out the window. They were silent for a long while.

"Did she say anything?"

"She hopes you and Sandy are very happy and said that you deserve each other."

John sighed again.

The door opened and Peter Creek entered the room.

"Hey, bosses. How's everyone today?"

"John's doing pretty good. I'm just on my way out, and I'll be headed to the airport first thing in the morning."

"That's exciting Mr. Bradley. Punta Cana. I wish I could go to an exotic sounding Caribbean island."

Jackson smiled and said, "Keep a good job and stay out of trouble and you'll go plenty of times. John, I'm glad you're so much better."

"Yep. I'm as good as new," groaned John as he adjusted himself in the bed. "Peter, come join Jackson and me, and let's send him off with a prayer."

"John, that's not necessary."

"Humor me, please."

Jackson shrugged. John took Jackson's hand with his right hand and Peter's with his left. "Lord, please give traveling mercies to Jackson, but more important, please grace him with saving faith, in Jesus' name, amen."

"There you go again with that faith thing," complained Jackson as they released hands.

"It's cause I love ya' pardner," responded John. "Have a good trip, Jackson, and be on the lookout for those coincidences we talked about."

Jackson laughed as he left the room and closed the door. John looked at the closed door for a moment, then turned to Peter and said, "Well, it looks like it's just you and me kid. You think we can handle it?"

"I know we can, Mr. Brooks."

* * *

As soon as he was alone, Peter Creek gave Harry Hoover an update.

Later that night, Shawn Dalton called Jason Collier. "Those Mississippi lawyers that I cannot stand are still causing trouble for me."

"I see, Mr. Dalton. How can I help?"

"I have it on good authority that one of them, Bradley, is traveling to the Dominican Republic tomorrow, even though the bean trial involving the farm is next week. They think they will get the trial continued. I want you to make sure that case goes to trial. Tie up those lawyers in Court. Brooks, the one left behind, is in no condition to try a case, so Bradley will have to come back."

"Okay, but what if he doesn't come back?"

"I've got that covered. If Brooks manages to show up for court, keep him tied down."

"Divide and conquer?"

"Exactly. And, I want you to get a judgment big enough that we can do a judicial foreclosure on the farm. I don't want anything to stop us this time."

"Sure, but the judgment will be in favor of Whittaker. How will that help you?"

"I'm paying for this. Whittaker has already agreed to assign any judgment to me."

"You've got all the bases covered."

"Always! Never forget that."

Chapter 32

Jackson boarded the plane at 5:30 a.m. and settled into his aisle seat. The flight to Atlanta would take about an hour, then, after a two-hour lay-over, the flight to Punta Cana in the Dominican Republic would take about 3 hours. He would lose an hour traveling from Central Time to Eastern Time, so he would arrive in Punta Cana around 1pm.

More than anything else, Jackson aspired to be a writer. Having just completed the case of the century with his partner, the now famous John Brooks, he had plenty to write about. But, their law practice had been so demanding that there was no time to contemplate, let alone write about the case. It was for this reason that Jackson announced several weeks ago that he was taking a sabbatical from the law practice, so that he could get away and write. Then, when the news about Maximilian's Treasure hit the airwaves, the media attention on the law practice was every bit as intense as it had been at the height of the Vampire Defense case. So much had happened in the past three weeks, that Jackson felt if he didn't get away now, he would never get away. On top of that, clues in the diary pointed to the emerald waters off of the Dominican Republic as the probable resting place of the Durance and a golden chest containing Sacred Sun Drops and a map to what may be the greatest treasure never found.

"But, the chances of finding anything are so remote, I'll have plenty of time to write," Jackson said to himself.

As the events of the past year flashed through his mind, Jackson wondered where he should begin to tell the story of the most famous trial of the twenty-first century.

Back at his apartment, Jackson had tried to write the story in long hand, but that was too slow. He even tried using an old fashioned typewriter. He thought that would inspire him and put him into a writing mood. That didn't help, so he bought a laptop computer, but still the words wouldn't come. So, he decided to get away to a place where there would be no distractions. Then, when the treasure clues led to the Caribbean, he thought, why not? Maybe I could arrange a few dives in the vicinity of the wreck.

Jackson called Sally, an acquaintance in the travel business, and said he wanted to get away to an affordable place for an extended period so he could write the great American novel. He said he was interested in going somewhere near the Island of Hispaniola. Sally knew the perfect place, the Poetry Resort in the Dominican Republic on the Island of Hispaniola. Because she sent several clients there over the years, she could get a substantial discount. The on-line pictures were beautiful, and the description of a quiet seaside resort, with mountains in the background seemed just right to Jackson.

Next, Jackson arranged to meet Robert Wade, a dive master with Adventure Scuba Divers, and the only certified archeological dive master in Mississippi. After several hours of pouring over notes and diagrams derived from the diary and comparing those notes with maps and navigation charts, Robert selected three likely areas to search for the remains of the Durance.

"Even if we pick the right spot, the odds are against us finding anything. We could be right on top of if, but after 150 years of storms, tides, silt, decay and sea growth, we could drop an anchor on your ship and never even know it. Then, there is the probability that the ship has already been found and plundered."

"Still, I've got to try."

Jackson read about his destination while he waited for the plane to take off. Hispaniola is the second largest island in the Caribbean. The Dominican Republic, a beautiful country with lush tropical vegetation and 12 million friendly Spanish-speaking people, covers two-thirds of the island. Haiti, the poorest country in the Americas, occupies the rest of the island of Hispaniola. For over three hundred years, the people of Haiti have been desperately poor. Jackson looked at a satellite photo of Hispaniola. In the photo, the Dominican Republic is beautiful and green, while Haiti is a depressing gray. A stark line between the countries bisects the island. Haiti seems to be a cursed nation. In comparison, the Dominican Republic seems blessed.

Jackson lowered the tray attached to the back of the seat situated in front of him. He placed his laptop on the tray and waited as it booted up. When the word processing program was ready, he selected "new document" and a blank page greeted him. He tried to ignore the other passengers passing down the aisle and concentrated on the blank page. He didn't notice three burly men shuffling sideways down the aisle. The first man, Jason, purposely sat two rows ahead of Jackson, so that he would be in front of him when they deplaned. The two remaining men turned their backs to Jackson as they passed so that he would not see their faces. Clint took a seat behind Jackson so that he could be in a position to listen and observe and McKenzie took a seat two rows back in the aisle across from Jackson. They exchanged glances, acknowledging their strategic positions. None of them noticed the tall, blond man riding in first class.

To them, he was just another executive on a business trip, but Antoine de Sada observed each of them as they passed and noted where they sat.

Jackson stared at the blank screen, his hands poised over the keyboard. The blank screen stared back at him.

"Okay, let's begin. I know it's got to be here somewhere," Jackson said out loud to himself. He knew the story he wanted to write was somewhere in his brain, just waiting to come out.

Clint alerted at the words, "I know it's got to be here somewhere." He could hardly believe his luck, striking pay dirt so quickly. He sat up, peered between the seats, and saw that Jackson was studying his laptop. Clint scrawled a note on a small piece of paper and looked for an opportunity to pass it to McKenzie.

Antoine checked his Rolex and noted that the plane had missed its departure time. No worries. There was plenty of time in Atlanta to catch the next flight, and if they missed it, he would be sure to catch the same flight as Jackson. And, as always, his Gulf Stream would be available to him on short notice to whisk him to any destination he desired. He knew that it would leave Mississippi after he took off, and would arrive in Atlanta before he could deplane.

"Ladies and gentlemen," announced the flight attendant, "we are waiting on one passenger who has checked in but has not arrived at the gate. It is important that all of our passengers arrive at the gate on time. We have checked on your connecting flights and this should not cause a problem for any of you. We apologize for the inconvenience. We should be able to push away from the gate shortly."

There was a commotion at the door.

"But my ticket say 6:10!" insisted a feminine voice with a Hispanic accent.

"No ma'am, the flight is scheduled to depart at 6, but if you will take your seat, we can get underway. We are already a few minutes late."

"But my ticket say 6:10!"

"Yes ma'am, well you're here now, so please take your seat."

"Why you tell everyone my fault when it's your fault my ticket say 6:10?"

"Yes, you're right, it is our fault. Now, if you will please take a seat."

"That's right. Your fault, not mine," she said with satisfaction as she sauntered down the aisle, with a pronounced hip swing that sent her bag bouncing into the shoulders of passengers on both sides of the aisle.

De Sada quickly looked down and away, because he knew that voice well. It was Natalia Garza, an aspiring adventuress with whom he had crossed swords more than once. He knew that it was no coincidence that she was on the same flight as Jackson Bradley. This meant he would have to make his move sooner than he intended. "She does have certain, ah, advantages," said de Sada to himself.

"There no first class seats?" asked Natalia with incredulity in her voice.

"No ma'am. You lost your seat assignment at departure time. There is one seat remaining, near the back of the plane. Please take your seat so that we can get underway."

Exasperated, Natalia proceeded down the aisle, her bag bouncing behind her from passenger to passenger. As she passed Jackson, her bag whammed into his laptop, knocking it to the floor. The screen shattered.

"What? Look at what you've done!" shouted Jackson.

"Don't talk to me in that tone, Mr. young man. I done nothing. It is you that put your computadora where it could be hurted. Don't blame me for your grande mistake."

Natalia continued down the aisle to her seat, leaving Jackson to pick up the pieces of his brand new laptop.

Clint grimaced. McKenzie noticed Clint's face and looked perplexed. De Sada smiled to himself, knowing that Natalia had done insufficient research. She was a worthy opponent, but she did not know Bradley by sight and she now had at least one strike against her in Bradley's eyes.

Chapter 33

The flight to Atlanta was uneventful. Jackson, with his cohort of followers, prepared to board the flight to Punta Cana. Clint passed the note to McKenzie, who read it and passed it on to Jason. Jason unfolded the note, read it, and threw it into a nearby trash bin. Natalia, alert for opportunities, observed the exchange. 'They must be after the treasure, too,' she thought to herself. 'It is no coincidence that they were on the flight from Jackson to Atlanta and now they are on the flight to Punta Cana.'

She nonchalantly sauntered over to the trash bin. It was filled with partially eaten food. "Disgusting!" She was certain that a clue was somewhere in that trash bin. She crinkled her nose and squinched her mouth tight as she considered her options.

"Eeuoh!" she said as she looked around to make sure no one would see her reach into the trash.

"Now boarding first class and Gold Medallion to Punta Cana."

"Oh, I've got to go," she said in a huff, looked around one more time and said, "A girl's got to do what a girl's got to do." She dove in with both hands.

"Ah, it is here!" she said under her breath as she rubbed ketchup off of the note. She unfolded the message and read out loud, "The location is on the computer. Get the computer."

She thought for a moment, then remembered the computer she knocked off the tray.

"Oh, no, not him!"

Just then someone snatched the note out of her hand. Natalia whirled around to see Antoine de Sada reading 'her' note.

"Antoine! Give me back my note!"

De Sada smiled and said, "Certainly," as he handed the note back to her. "I have no use for it now. I am so glad you were here to dig it out of the trash for me. You are so much more at home there than I."

Natalia's eyes flashed with burning rage.

"You are so beautiful when you are angry."

"Then I am always beautiful when I think of you."

Natalia pirouetted and rushed towards the plane.

"You must think of me often then!" called de Sada.

"Chu wish!" Natalia replied without looking back.

On the flight to Punta Cana, at first Jackson did not notice de Sada or the three burly men on the flight, but he could not help but notice Natalia. It had been Jackson's hope to use the lay over and travel time to get a good start on his writing. But his encounter with Natalia quashed that hope. Each time he saw Natalia, he fumed.

Just as Jackson was settling into his seat, a flight attendant tapped him on the shoulder. "Excuse me, sir, but would you like an upgrade to first class?" She, like other members of the crew, spoke with a pronounced accent. 'She may be from Dominica,' thought Jackson. "It is a long flight and we have an extra seat," continued the flight attendant. "There will be no charge for the upgrade."

Jackson was stunned for a moment, then, not believing his luck, said, "Sure! I'll be glad to help you out. It would be a shame for that seat to go to waste."

"That's what I was thinking. Gather your things and follow me. Here, let me help you with that," she said, scooping up his laptop. Clint, Jason and McKenzie all sat up and exchanged glances as they watched the flight attendant carry the laptop toward the front of the plane, with Jackson a couple of steps behind.

When they reached first class, Jackson noticed Natalia in a first class window seat. He gave her the best hard gaze that he could muster. Jackson had never been a hard gazer, so Natalia was not sure how to read it. She returned his gaze with a puzzled look, until she saw the flight attendant stop at an empty seat beside de Sada.

"Here you go, sir. Make yourself comfortable. May I fix you a drink?"

"Sure. How about a gin martini?"

"Es un placer," said the attendant, still holding the computer.

"Here, let me help you with that," said the smiling man in the seat next to Jackson as he reached out and took the computer from the attendant.

"Gracias," said the attendant as she turned to fetch a martini for Jackson.

"OOH!" fumed Natalia.

"Thank you," said Jackson to both the smiling man and the attendant.

"It is nothing. Let me introduce myself. Antoine de Sada. And your name?"

"Jackson Bradley."

"Jackson Bradley! Not THE Jackson Bradley, the famous attorney who comes from the city that bears his name!"

Natalia's mouth flew open. She rolled her eyes. Jackson was momentarily flabbergasted, pleased and even thrilled that someone on a flight to the Dominican Republic would know his name.

"Well, thank you, but I'm not famous."

"Well, I have certainly heard of you and the case of the century. And I believe you have been in the news again recently," said de Sada as he glanced over Jackson's shoulder at Natalia. Natalia, who had been eavesdropping, had a sneer on her face as she mimicked de Sada's compliments of Jackson. She saw de Sada looking at her. She mouthed, "Chu suck-up."

"Tell me about yourself, Mr. de Sada."

"Call me Antoine. Not much to tell really. My family is in, ah, finance and industry in Mexico and other parts of the world. My job is to look for, ah, opportunities." He paused for a moment, and continued, "Opportunities for diversification and for trade. What brings you to Dominica?"

"The great American novel. I want to get away and write about the case of the century, as you call it. Life is so hectic at home that I thought it would be good to find a quiet place were I could be left alone and write."

"Ah, defente solo. To be left alone can be a rare and valuable thing, my friend. Where will you be staying?"

"At the Poetry Resort in Punta Cana."

"Excellent choice. It is indeed a quiet get away. I know the place well. I have a small villa nearby. I have a large family and we have villas here and there to accommodate our travel and business affairs. If it will not be too much of a distraction, perhaps you could come by while you are in Punta Cana."

"I would be delighted."

"Excellent. I am having a few people over this evening at ocho. Perhaps you could join us?"

"Sure. How will I find you?"

"I will have a driver pick you up at seven thirty and bring you to De Sada Sol, our modest Dominican home."

"Great! In the meantime, I need to replace my computer."

"Oh! What has happened?"

"Well, I um," Jackson glanced over his shoulder and saw Natalia glaring in their direction. 'What a strange woman,' he thought to himself. "It fell to the floor and the screen shattered. I think the computer still works."

"Excellent. You need only replace the screen. When I held your computer, it felt light as air, it is a MacBook Air, no?"

"Yes, it is."

"I know someone who can replace the screen for you. Why don't you let me send it to the shop and it will be delivered to you at Poetry by Tuesday."

"That is very kind of you, but I hate to let my laptop out of my sight. It has all my notes and I just don't want to chance losing it."

"I understand completely. I will give you the address and you can take it there yourself. Jamie is the owner of the shop. He is very skilled and works on computers like yours. I will ask him if he can, ahm, borrow, a monitor from a similar computer and attach it to yours, then order a new one for the one he borrowed. You may be able to get it fixed while you wait. If not, surely it will be ready by tomorrow."

"That would be awesome. Thank you."

"It is my pleasure," said de Sada dismissively.

Jackson and Antoine talked during the entire flight. The time flew by and Jackson felt he had made a great new friend, one who was wealthy and connected. Antoine listened intently to Jackson and asked open questions that kept Jackson talking. He led Jackson into discussions about the 'case of the century,' the Vampire Defense, and then to the very interesting tale of the lost treasure of Maximilian.

"Yes, I became interested in your career after that first case, and I read something about foreclosure proceedings and a farm where some people thought a treasure was buried, and then your fantastic discovery of a diary and map. How clever of you."

"Oh, that. The press is always hungry for a story they can sensationalize. There is nothing to it. It's just an old legend. And the cleverness was not mine. Our paralegal, she's more like a partner than an employee, she discovered the diary."

"Oh, you are so modest. Surely, there could not be some great Mexican treasure transported all the way to Mississippi and buried on someone's farm."

"Indeed. The whole idea is laughable. I don't think the treasure, if it exists, was ever in Mississippi anyway."

"Really! Where do you think it is?"

"Who knows? If it even exists, it's probably at the bottom of the sea."

"Oh. It was moved by boat you think?"

"I didn't mean that. I mean, it could be anywhere, if it exists."

"I see."

Antoine was astounded that it was so easy to get this naïve young lawyer to spill the beans about the treasure. Yet, he could never get Jackson to admit that he knew where the treasure was located, or even admit that there was a treasure. 'This young lawyer is not the fool I first thought he was,' de Sada said to himself.

The stewardess distributed immigration forms as the pilot announced they were beginning their descent to the Dominican Republic. Jackson looked out the window and saw a lush countryside with a range of tree-covered mountains not far from an aquamarine coast.

"It's beautiful."

"Yes, and I am sure you will find it very peaceful and relaxing."

"I am really looking forward to that. I need a break after all the excitement I've experienced lately."

After Jackson wound his way through customs, he saw a man holding a sign bearing his name. Impressed, he walked directly to him.

"Mr. Bradley?"

"Yes."

"My name is Francis. I will be your guide to Poetry Resort. Let me help you with your bags and I will take you to your bus."

"Thank you!"

"It es my pleasure."

Jackson followed Francis past several buses and mini-vans, to a Volkswagen bus. Francis loaded the bags in the back and opened the side door for Jackson.

"Julio is our driver. He es a good driver. It will be about an hour before we arrive at Poetry. You can see a little of our country on the way." Jackson was the only passenger. In moments, they were underway.

"Can you stop at this place? I need to get my computer fixed," said Jackson as he handed Francis the address de Sada had given him.

"Es no problem. It es on our way, maybe 4 miles from the resort. You will see."

Natalia scrambled to get her bags and find a taxi to follow Jackson. She saw Jason, McKenzie and Clint hurrying to do the same, but they had an advantage. Clint kept an eye on Jackson while Jason retrieved the bags and McKenzie rented a car. Five one hundred-dollar bills sped up the rental process. After getting the bags through customs, Jason went to a locker and picked up a package containing firearms.

Natalia reached the ground transportation area just in time to see both Jackson and his three shadows leave. There was not an available taxi in sight. She dropped her bags and exhaled loudly. Then, hearing a familiar laugh, she whirled around to face a laughing de Sada.

"What you find so funny?" she demanded.

"Watching the four of you scurry about trying to keep up with a man who is not even trying to elude you."

"Why you are not keeping up with him? You lose him, too?"

"No. Unlike the rest of you, I know where he's going, so I don't have to be in a hurry."

"Where?"

"Stay with me in my villa, and I will tell you," said de Sada as his Mercedes arrived. The driver rushed around and opened the back door for his master.

"Chu wish! Not a chance! I wouldn't be caught dead at your villa."

"Lo siento, me amor. That is too bad, since Mr. Jackson will be there at eight tonight."

"Uhh!"

De Sada climbed into the back seat and handed a note to his driver. "Please call Jamie for me and give him this message."

"Certainly, sir."

Natalia stamped her foot as the Mercedes began to pull away slowly. She rolled her eyes, exhaled loudly, and as the back of the car rolled past her, she slapped the trunk twice with her open hand. The Mercedes stopped and the trunk popped open.

Chapter 34

Jackson enjoyed the drive across Punta Cana. Four miles from the resort was a small shopping center, where the computer store that de Sada recommended was located. The shopping center was filled with little shops selling trinkets, T-shirts, Dominican paintings and featured a little café. The computer shop was next to the petrol station. Julio pulled the VW in front of the computer shop. Francis opened the door for Jackson and accompanied him into the store.

Francis greeted the shop owner and said, "Jamie, this is my friend, Jackson Bradley. He has come here all the way from Mississippi and he would like his computer repaired. He needs the work done soon and at your best price."

"I see. Actually, I was expecting you. Señor de Sada sent to me a message that you had an unfortunate accident with your computer. Does it need anything besides a screen?"

Francis was impressed, "Oh, Señor de Sada called about your screen! You must be very important, Mr. Bradley."

"Oh, no, I'm not important. I think that the broken screen is all that's wrong with it."

"I can have it replaced first thing in the morning. It will be ready by noon at the latest, my friend."

"I was hoping you could replace the screen while I wait."

"Lo siento, no es posible. The soonest I can have it ready is noon tomorrow, señor."

"That's fine. In fact, that's great! Much better than I originally expected. I'll see you then."

Francis and Jackson returned to the VW bus and Julio pulled away from the shopping center. Clint, McKenzie and Jason watched from the parking lot.

"Jason, why don't you see what he dropped off?" asked McKenzie. "It could be the computer. The two of us will follow them and see where they're going. Then, we'll come back and pick you up."

"Who made you king?"

"I'm driving. Make the best of it."

Maximilian's Treasure

"All right. I'll be having a beer at that joint when you get back," said Jason as he gestured towards the little café in the middle of the shopping center. Jason climbed out of the car and watched as McKenzie and Clint followed the VW bus down the highway.

Jason straightened his jacket, making sure his gun was concealed. He was aware that the jacket seemed out of place in this heat. Already, sweat was beading on his forehead. He stepped into the computer shop and looked around.

"Buenos dias!"

"Yeah, good day to you too. You can make my day a good one if you could sell me a little Apple computer. I love those things and I lost mine."

"Lo siento. I have none for sale, but I could get one for you by tomorrow. First thing in the morning, noon at the latest my friend."

"You don't have no Apple computers here? What about those?"

"Those are here for repairs. They belong to my customers."

Jason looked over his shoulder to see if anyone might see him, and felt the gun through his jacket with his right hand. He considered his options and decided there were too many witnesses and no good escape route.

"Tell you what. You and me can make a deal and you can make a lot of money. You interested?"

"Si!"

"An American just came in here with a computer. I want whatever is on that computer. You make a copy for me and I will pay you well, and no one will ever know."

"Oh, please don't ask me to do such a thing. I could never do that."

"$500 says you can."

"No, señor. If anyone find out. No. I could not. I have a family to think of, and I could lose my business. No, I could never do such a thing. Not for $500. No."

"How much?"

"Señor, why do you ask me this thing?"

"I am asking a favor of you. All I have is $1,000. Nobody will know but you and me. Won't $1,000 help your family? Please, do me this little favor."

"Well, since you put it that way. I will do this for you. But, no one is to know."

"Scout's honor. This is just between me and you."

"Twenty minutes. Maybe thirty. Come back in thirty minutes and I will have a complete copy for you."

"I want to be able to load the copy onto a computer and use the information."

"Si, I can make that for you. No problemo."

Satisfied, Jason walked to the café and ordered a beer.

Jamie looked at the computer and wondered aloud, "What es on this computer that so many people want it? It must be very valuable." He looked at the notes he took during his call from de Sada's driver instructing him to deliver the computer to de Sada Sol without fail, no excuses, by 7 p.m. and to give de Sada a disc with a copy of the contents. No one was to know about de Sada's disc. While Jamie copied the contents for Jason and de Sada, he made an extra copy for himself. Then he called a friend.

"Roberto. I have stumbled onto something very valuable. I want you to find out everything you can about an American named Jackson Bradley. I am repairing his computer and everyone seems to want it, including de Sada. Can you get back to me tonight?"

"What can you tell me about him?"

"He is from Mississippi."

"He is from a river?"

"No, it is a State. Mississippi."

"Okay, I'll let you know."

* * *

About an hour after leaving the airport, Jackson arrived at Poetry Resort, located near the northeastern tip of Hispaniola. The van stopped at a tall solid wooden gate. Jackson could not see over or through the gate, so he was unable to get a glimpse of the resort. After a few moments, someone opened the gate and welcomed the van into a circular drive surrounded by lush tropical plants. At the apex of the drive was an open-air lobby under a tall thatch roof. Smiling attendants welcomed him. A bellman took his bags to his room, while a young lady gave Jackson a tour of the facility. There were only 49 rooms, but 3 restaurants and a large, friendly staff to accommodate his every wish.

"Your money is no good here. Everything has already been arranged. Food and drink, 24 hours a day, everything is included."

"Wow! That sounds great."

* * *

While Jackson took the tour, Clint and McKenzie were greeted by a guard at the gate.

"Do you have reservations here?"

"Yes, McKenzie, Gerard."

The guard examined a clipboard. "Lo sciento. There must be some mistake. We were not expecting you. I will call the desk and have them check for you."

After a few moments a manager arrived at the gate.

"I am so sorry, Mr. Gerard, but we do not have your reservation. Do you think you might have reservations at another resort?"

"No, Poetry in Punta Cana is where we are supposed to be. You were highly recommended and we came all this way. Is there anything you can do?"

"You are in luck, sir. We do have rooms available. How long do you plan to stay?"

"Maybe a week."

"Oh, welcome, sir. That would be fine. Two of you for a week! Come right in and we will make the arrangements."

"Actually, there will be three of us."

Clint leaned across McKenzie and asked, "How much are the rooms?"

"Well, it is not just the rooms, sir, this is an all inclusive resort. Everything, including food and drink."

"Alcohol?"

"Si."

"How much?"

"$5,000."

Clint gasped. McKenzie's jaw dropped. Clint exclaimed, "What?"

"Yes, only $5,000 for the week. Each."

After a moment, McKenzie asked, "How much for one night, if we all stay in the same room? We may want to try it out before we take out a home mortgage."

Twenty minutes later, McKenzie and Clint began the tour of Poetry Resort with a trip to the first bar. "Hey, I'm getting my money's worth," said Clint. McKenzie called Jason and told him where they were.

"Okay, I'll catch a cab. And, by the way, I've got a copy of the entire computer."

"You what? Way to go, big guy!"

"Yeah, I'll see you in a few."

Clint spotted Jackson as he was being led on the tour of the property. "Pay dirt. I'll get a closer look. Wait here."

* * *

Jackson was shown the location of the coffee shop, the spa, the library, the bars, two beautiful formal restaurants, and an inviting open-air restaurant on the beach. A bungalow on the beach offered tours and excursions including scuba diving. Jackson waved at the attendant, stepped over to him and said, "I plan to dive Wednesday. I think that when my reservations were made, some arrangements were made to get me to the boat. Am I right?"

"You must be Mr. Bradley. I have been expecting you. You are in luck. You are booked for a trip Wednesday morning with Adventure Scuba Diving. I know the reef they are diving. There are so many sunken ships there, that we call it Shipwreck Reef. Perhaps you'll be lucky and find a sunken treasure, no?"

Jackson laughed nervously. "Can there be any treasure left if everyone knows the reef has sunken ships?"

"New finds are made all the time. But, the truth is, it is unlikely. You go for the beauty and the sea life. You will enjoy the dive. The dive master, Robert Wade, is very good and very safe. He has come here from America many times. Now, you need to know, there will be rules. If you get lucky and find a shipwreck, you cannot disturb anything, but you must report what you find, and you will receive an honorable mention in the annals of the Dominican Republic."

"That sounds exciting. I can't wait to go."

"Okay, just meet me in the lobby Wednesday morning at 7, and I will take care of everything."

As soon as Jackson left, Clint stepped up and said, "Tell me about the dive trip."

At last, Jackson was taken to his room, where a bottle of dark rum, fresh fruit and flowers waited. A steep thatch roof reached 20 feet above his head. Rich dark wood adorned the floors and the walls. The bathroom was spacious and contained a Jacuzzi tub and a shower without walls in the middle of a rock garden. His second floor room overlooked two pools and had a fine view of the Atlantic. He stood on his balcony and gazed at the swaying palms over the inviting beach. He breathed deep to fill his lungs with the fresh salty ocean air.

"Ah, just what the doctor ordered. Peace and tranquility."

Just below him, Clint looked up at Jackson. He instinctively reached inside his loose fitting lightweight jacket and patted the handle of his 9mm semi-automatic. He slid his hand away from the pistol and looked around making sure that no one was paying attention to him.

* * *

Natalia was sullen as she settled into the Mercedes' comfortable leather seat. A curtain and privacy window separated the driver from the passengers. Antoine mixed a drink. "Your favorite as I recall," he said as he handed it to her.

She stared first at the drink, then at Antoine, then at her surroundings. She exhaled loudly and said, "Well, I suppose there are less comfortable prisons. I might as well make the best of it."

"Natalia, I am shocked. Why would you say such a thing? You came to me of your own free will, as I knew you would."

"Oh, chu did, did chu?"

"Well, let's say I had a hunch. We can make a great team, you and me. Working together, we can accomplish anything."

"True. With me, chu can get anything chu set your heart upon," she said sweetly, but her voice was filled with disdain as she continued. "And I will never see anything for my efforts. Chu will steal it all and taunt me with it."

"Why would you say such a thing? I would never take anything from you that you would not freely give."

"Only in your dreams, lover boy."

They both laughed as Natalia looked over the rim of her glass into Antoine's eyes, took a sip and settled in for the ride to De Sada Sol.

Chapter 35

John was released from the hospital the next morning and, after renting a used car, moved into Jackson's apartment, half of a duplex in Belhaven. Jackson had acquired a few funky pieces of furniture and art, strategically placed so that the apartment didn't look empty. The primary feature was bookshelves. Tons of bookshelves overloaded with a wide variety of subject, genre, and style, evidencing Jackson's wide-ranging interests. John read off a few titles and said under his breath, "Well, Jackson, you're a real renaissance man."

He checked the closet, and didn't find anything he could borrow, other than ties, so he made a quick trip to Highland Village and to Wal-Mart to buy a few clothes. He was short of cash, since all of his money was tied up in the Dalton Farm, so he looked for bargains. He returned to Jackson's place and studied the Bean Trial notebook prepared by Jackson.

"Surely, the judge will continue the Bean Trial. We're new to the case, I've been in the hospital, Jackson's out of the country. We haven't had time to gather our witnesses, get a soybean expert, or prepare for trial. No way the judge will make us go to trial this soon." Famous last words.

On Monday, the judge denied the motion to continue, saying, "Your client knew the trial date when he selected his lawyer, and your partner knew the trial date when he chose to leave the country. I'm not continuing this case just to accommodate lawyers who think they are too important to postpone a vacation to accommodate something as insignificant to them as a trial date. Be here Wednesday ready for trial, or be ready to go to jail!"

* * *

The appeal of the beach lured Jackson. He quickly changed into his bathing suit, loose shirt and floppy hat and trundled to the beach. He could hardly wait to feel the sand between his toes. He left his flip-flops at the edge of the beach and said "Ahh" as he stepped onto the coo,l soft sand. The first hundred feet of beach was shaded by palms and cooled by the ocean breeze. Hammocks, lounge chairs and tables shaded with thatch roofs invited him, but he walked straight to the surf. The sun was hot and the water warm on his legs. He stripped off his shirt, tossed it with his hat onto the beach, and dove into a wave.

Jackson emerged from the water, laughing. "Oh, that felt good." He waded away from shore to the point where the surf was breaking and waited for a big wave. He didn't wait long. The third wave rose above his head and began to crest. Jackson pushed off the sandy bottom and swam toward shore for all he was worth. The wave swirled and surged around him; then it happened: he became part of the wave. Hydraulic forces lifted him to a point just below the crest, and he felt the acceleration as the wave drove him towards the beach.

After a short exhilarating ride, the wave pushed him hard against the sandy bottom and Jackson surfaced, sputtering and laughing out loud. He returned again and again, bodysurfing for almost an hour. Fighting the waves was exhausting and refreshing. Finally, he stumbled to shore and fell on his back on the wet sand, gasping for breath.

Jason arrived at Poetry Resort and met McKenzie at the beach bar. Clint joined them a few minutes later. "Nothing. I searched everything in his room. Whatever clues he had must be on the computer."

"I can't believe he would leave the computer at that place where anybody could get it," said Jason.

"He needed to get it fixed. What choice did he have?" observed McKenzie. "This place has a library with computers. Let's take a look at Jason's copy." McKenzie nodded toward Jackson, sprawled upon the beach. "Clint, whatever you do, don't let him out of your sight. There may be more to this guy than meets the eye."

Jackson returned to his room. A complementary bottle of spiced rum and a sweating bucket of ice awaited him. He poured himself a little rum and called the front desk. He didn't notice anything out of place.

"How can I help you, Mr. Jackson?"

"What does one wear to an evening event at De Sada Sol?"

"Oh, that es very exclusive, Señor Jackson. Do you have formal attire?"

"No, I brought only beach attire."

"Es no problem. I will have something appropriate delivered to your room in a few moments."

"What will that cost?"

"Es no charge. It es all included, sir. I already know your size, so don't worry about a thing."

"How do you know my size?"

"It es my job to know these things, sir. Do you need transportation?"

"No, I am to be picked up at 7:30."

"Excellente. We will have you ready in plenty of time. It es an honor for us to host someone who es a guest of Diego Antoine de Sada."

"Impressive," noted Jackson as he hung up. "I can't believe how beautiful this place is and how friendly everyone is." A wave of guilt washed over him as he thought of John back home having to deal with everything by himself. Jackson picked up his cell phone and texted John. "This place is amazing. Great to be away from all the action and the prying eyes for a change. I was tired of people watching my every move. Looking forward to a little R&R. Wish you were here."

He pondered for a moment, then decided it would be good to let John know that at least a little work was going on, so he sent a second text. "Going to dive site Wednesday with Robert."

* * *

Two bungalows to Jackson's left, McKenzie stared at the computer screen and then turned to Jason and asked, "How much did you pay for this?"

"$1,000."

"This gig is getting expensive," moaned Clint.

"You've been taken to the cleaners. There's nothing useful here," sighed McKenzie.

"It could be in code, or there could be hidden files," said Jason, hopefully.

"Hidden files?" asked Clint.

"Yeah. You can hide files on a computer. I don't know how to find them, but an expert could."

"You know any experts?" asked McKenzie.

"Just the one who took me to the cleaners."

"We need to pay Jamie the computer guy a little visit. This time, I want to leave with the computer, not a rip-off copy."

* * *

Jamie had never been to De Sada Sol. His nerves were shot following Jason's visit and the three copies he had made of the computer files. Then Roberto called back, and his anxiety skyrocketed.

"The computer belongs to a famous American lawyer. He was in the Vampire Defense case everyone was talking about."

"Vampire! I want nothing to do with vampire."

"No, he es not a vampire. That es what they called his case. It was famous."

"So, he es famous. Why es he aqui?"

"He es in the news again because a client claimed to know how to find Maximilian's Treasure! Maybe he es here for that!"

Maximilian's Treasure

"Maximilian?"

"Chu know, the emperor of Mexico."

"Oh. Da French guy."

"Si! Cinco de Mayo, lime in tourists cervezas! That es the guy."

"He's got a treasure? Why would Maximilian's Treasure be here?"

"It has to be somewhere. Why not here?"

That seemed to be a good enough answer to Jamie, so he nodded agreement as he said, "Okay! Thanks, Roberto."

"Wait a minute. You are going to include me in on the treasure aren't you?"

"Of course, my friend. You are the first person I will call."

After they hung up, Roberto began to doubt that Jamie would call him if he found the treasure. "I better hedge my bet," he said as he picked up the phone.

Jamie checked the time. "6:45! Oh my." He gathered the computer, locked the door and climbed behind the wheel of his tiny car.

* * *

At 7:30 sharp, Jackson arrived at the lobby, attired in a tropical weight, vented tuxedo. A driver called to him by name and led him to a black Mercedes limousine. In twenty minutes they arrived at an impressive gate. The guard recognized the car and quickly opened the gate. They drove through flowering tropical vegetation and arrived at an opulent palace, with a circle drive dominated by an extravagant fountain.

"Modest little villa," Jackson said to himself, recalling the words of Antoine de Sada.

An attendant opened the car door for Jackson and led him to a doorman who ushered him into the palace. Just past the foyer was a ballroom with at least 200 well-dressed guests spread across a marble floor. Someone was playing a grand piano, and floor to ceiling windows offered a spectacular view of tropical gardens, a manicured beach, the Atlantic and an infinity pool that seemed to stretch to the horizon. Guests were scattered in little clusters around the pool and even on the beach. Although the sun had set behind them, tall clouds still reflected sunlight onto the beach, and every object was bathed in the soft light of dusk.

Even more beautiful than the view was the woman perched near the top of a long, curved staircase. Her back was turned to Jackson. He could not see her face, but he could see the edge of her profile. Her black dress sparkled in the evening light. It was cut low in the back exposing rich, light brown skin. Luxuriously long black hair curved across the back of her neck and fell over one shoulder. Jackson was captivated as she glided with grace down the stairs. He didn't notice anything else in the room, not the sunset, not the people, not the fine paintings, not even his host. To Jackson, she was more than a beautiful woman. She was evocative, intriguing, mysterious. She was dangerously beautiful.

Chapter 36

After dropping off the computer and the copy, Jamie turned his little car around and returned to his shop. Everyone at De Sada Sol had treated him so well, and with such respect that he felt guilty for making the extra copy of the computer files for himself.

McKenzie decided to take Clint with him to the computer shop as a look-out. Leaving Clint outside, McKenzie made sure that the computer shop was closed and no one was around. The lock on the back door hardly slowed him down. The shop was full of computers. Laptops were everywhere. McKenzie knew that Jackson's laptop was a small Apple with a broken screen. Before he had time to find it, Jamie entered the broken back door.

"Es someone here? You better leave or I will call the police!"

At that moment, Clint hit him on the back of the head with the barrel of his pistol. Jamie collapsed. Clint shoved him out of the doorway and closed the door.

"Why did you do that Clint? We need him to help us with the computer."

"Well, excuse me for coming to your rescue," Clint said with exasperation. They pulled the shop owner into a corner, found some water and splashed it on his face. Nothing happened.

"That always works in the movies."

"Yeah, maybe he's dead."

"No, he's breathing."

"Look, he's coming around."

Jamie opened his eyes and groaned. "What do you want? I don't have much. Take it and leave."

"We want the Apple computer with the broken monitor that the American brought in today."

"You would break in and crack my skull for a broken computer?"

"Yeah, buddy. And we will do a lot worse if you don't give it to us pronto. Savvy?"

"Why everyone want that computer?"

"What do you mean?"

"Someone asked about it today and Senor de Sada wanted it. Rush job. He paid premium, but not worth getting hit on de head."

McKenzie and Clint exchanged glances.

"Where is it?"

"I took it to Señor de Sada's villa, De Sada Sol, just now. He want to surprise Mr. Jackson tonight."

"Yeah, I bet. Some surprise. Where is de Sada's Sol?"

"Maybe 10 kilometers up this road, on the beach."

"Listen, Mister. I am sorry about all of this, but it has to be this way. You were just in the wrong place at the wrong time and I got a job to do. It's nothing personal."

"What do you mean?"

Clint found rags and piled them in a corner with some boxes and set them ablaze. A stunned look was on Jamie's face, followed by terror when McKenzie wrapped a towel around the pistol and placed it against Jamie's forehead.

"No, I will show you where it es!" cried Jamie over the crackling fire. "I will take you to the computer. Don't shoot me. I have a family. What would my children do? Let me help you get computer. I help you find treasure!"

"Treasure! What do you know about a treasure?"

"It es why everyone wants the computer, no?"

Clint shrugged and McKenzie jerked Jamie up.

"One peep out of you and you and your family are dead."

"No peeps from me, no, I help you, you see. No peep."

They returned to the car and squeezed Jamie into the front between them, with McKenzie driving and Clint on the passenger side. There were only two seats in front, so Jamie sat on the console. Smoke was billowing from the roof of the computer shop when they drove away. The petrol station next door shared a wall with the computer shop.

The phone rang. McKenzie fumbled for a moment with the gun and the phone and the steering wheel. The car swerved into the other lane. He found an awkward way to handle all three and keep an eye on the road and an eye on Jamie. He steered back into his lane.

"Yeah, what?" he shouted.

"Bradley is gone!" Jason franticly replied.

"You let him get away!"

"No, he got into a limo and left."

"I can't believe this. Do I have to do everything myself?" McKenzie waved his hands in the air in frustration and the car veered into the other lane again, just missing an oncoming car.

"Why didn't you follow him?"

"I had no way to follow him. There was no cab, and you've got the car."

"Find out where he went. We'll be there in a few minutes."

* * *

Roberto picked up his cousins, Umberto and Renaldo. They were busy watching a soccer game and didn't want to go, until Roberto told them that his mother's sister's husband's brother, Jamie, was about to steal a vast treasure and he wasn't going to share it with his own family.

"Not share with your family! That's like stealing it twice," said Umberto.

"I am not sure if not sharing is the same as stealing," said Renaldo.

"Of course it is. He wouldn't even have known about the treasure if it weren't for me. We need make sure we get our fair share," said Roberto indignantly.

The three of them piled into Roberto's car and raced to Jamie's computer shop. As they were approaching the shop they saw a car pull out of the parking lot and swerve erratically.

"It's Jamie! He is on the way to get the treasure!"

"That's not Jamie's car. Even if it was Jamie's car, he is probably just going home," said Renaldo. "Not everything everybody does is an effort to do harm to you, Roberto."

Suddenly McKenzie's car swerved into their path and Roberto steered into the ditch to avoid a head-on collision. Roberto's car crashed into the bank on the opposite side of the ditch, crumpling the hood.

"Did you see that? They tried to kill us!"

"I saw Jamie in the car!" shouted Umberto.

"He was driving!" yelled Roberto.

"No, it was another guy," Umberto asserted.

"No, it was Jamie!" insisted Roberto.

"Quick, let's follow them," urged Renaldo. "They are getting away!"

Roberto put the car in reverse, but his back wheels spun. The car didn't move.

"Quick, get out and push! Hurry! Hurry, they are getting away!"

Umberto and Renaldo jumped out of the car, rushed to the front and pushed while Roberto spun the wheels. In a moment, the tires found purchase and the car whipped out of the ditch onto the road. As they were climbing back into the car, Renaldo noticed the smoke and paused with one foot in the car and one foot still on the ground.

"Look at that! The computer shop is on fire!"

Umberto and Roberto looked back for a moment, mouths agape. Then Roberto hollered, "Quick, get in!"

Maximilian's Treasure

They sped down the highway after Jamie.

* * *

McKenzie's phone rang again.

"Clint," said McKenzie as he handed the phone over. "See who it is. I can't drive this junk heap and answer the phone."

"Jason, what's up? . . . Got it. We'll meet you there."

Clint hung up and said, "Bradley has gone to de Sada's place. Jason is on his way."

"Here it is!" said Jamie. "We are here now! See, I told chu I would get you here."

Chapter 37

"She is beautiful isn't she," said de Sada.

"Oh, Señor de Sada. I didn't see you standing there."

"Call me Antoine, and don't worry, I understand why you did not notice me. She is a vision to behold. Let me introduce you. Natalia, please join us and let me introduce you to my new friend, Jackson Bradley."

Natalia turned and made eye contact with Jackson, whose look of hopeful expectation and delight turned first to confusion and then his countenance soured.

"You!" said Jackson as recognition overwhelmed his beautiful vision with the force of a spring flood.

"So, you have already met?" Antoine quizzed, with a knowing smile.

Natalia smiled demurely and said, "Oh, Mr. Jackson, please forgive me. I am so sorry about dhur computador. It was all my fault. It had been such a bad day and I was in too much of a hurry. I know that was not dhur fault that I had a bad day, but I am afraid that I took some of my bad day out on chu and made yours a very bad day. I was so rude. Please forgive me!"

"Well, no harm done, not really. Antoine arranged for my computer to be repaired. They will have it ready tomorrow."

"Really?" said Natalia with a slight edge in her voice as she looked at de Sada. "I wish chu had told me, Antoine. I would have been glad to take care of it myself. In fact, let me pay for the damage. Just tell me where the computer es, and I will pay all the expense. I will even have it delivered to chu."

"Don't worry, Natalia," assured de Sada. "It has all been taken care of."

"Yes, well, that is such a relief. Antoine is so, how should I say, thorough. He leaves no stone unturned," her smile turned to a glower for just a moment as she looked at Antoine, then she finished, "in his efforts to help a friend in need. One can always count on Antoine."

"Thank you for that compliment, Natalia."

"Don't mention it. I'm serious. Don't. Mention. It."

A small orchestra assembled next to the grand piano and began playing a familiar piece.

"Oh, Mr. Bradley," said Natalia with a mischievous smile and a touch of excitement. "I believe they are playing a tango. Do chu tango?"

"Please don't call me mister. Call me Jackson. May I call you Natalia?"

"Certainly."

"Well, Natalia, let's dance!"

Jackson danced a respectable tango, but Natalia was in a league of her own. She let Jackson feel as though he was leading, but she encouraged him to engage in steps and maneuvers he never imagined he could perform. He was soon breathing hard, but he didn't know if it was from exertion or from holding her body so close to his.

As the song ended, Natalia laughed and threw her arms around Jackson and kissed him on the cheek, marking him with the red imprint of her lips. Onlookers applauded their display of dancing prowess and Natalia politely waved and gracefully pointed her arms towards Jackson, giving him the credit for the applause. The small crowd appreciated her gesture and applauded even more. Jackson, embarrassed but pleased, redirected the applause to Natalia, prompting even more applause. His cheek still tingled from her kiss.

Natalia put her arm around his waist and laughed again as she leaned back playfully and looked up at him through long lashes. "I have never had that happen before," she said as she batted her eyes twice. "Imagine, applause on the dance floor. You must be a professional dancer, Jackson. Chu have been holding out on me?"

"Oh, no, no, it's just, no . . . Would you like a glass of champagne?"

"Oh, yes, please. That would be perfect."

From somewhere, she produced a fan and swished it quickly to cool her face. The gesture made her seem even more attractive to Jackson. He thought, *'this girl is HOT.'* Jackson guided her towards an attendant with a tray of champagne, took two glasses and handed one to Natalia.

"Who would have thought, after this morning, that we would be here, sipping champagne, and looking into each others eyes? Isn't life full of wonderful surprises?" asked Natalia as she playfully peered over the edge of her fan. She allowed one side of the fan to drop just enough to expose her moist red lips, which were pursed ever so slightly.

As he looked into her eyes, Jackson felt dizzy, as though the earth was moving.

The earth shook and Natalia stumbled into Jackson's arms, spilling her champagne. "Lo siento!" she said as she wiped the champagne off his jacket. "What was that?"

"It's all right. Really it is," said Jackson, grateful that she was in his arms and stroking his chest with her hand. He couldn't care less about a little champagne on his jacket.

Then the sound of a tremendous explosion rocked the house. Women screamed and men dove for cover.

"Something in the town has exploded," said de Sada. Everyone stepped outside onto the veranda and looked with amazement at the fireball in the night sky.

"It's the petrol station," someone said.

"That's next door to the computer shop," said de Sada. "Miguel, find out what has happened. Call Jamie."

Chapter 38

The gates to De Sada Sol, usually closed, were open tonight for the event. Two security guards checked everyone entering against a guest list. Clint asked Jamie as they approached, "How do we get in?"

Jamie said, "They are having a big party here tonight. You have to have invitations."

McKenzie stopped at the security station, rolled down his window, "We are guests of Mr. de Sada, here for the party."

The smiling guard replied, "Si. Please, your name?"

Jamie leaned forward, "It es me, Jamie, I was here delivering the computer a little while ago, remember?"

"Si."

"I have to deliver one more thing, and these gentlemen are with me. I don't think we are on the guest list, but we are expected. We won't be long."

There was an anxious moment before the guard nodded and motioned the car through the gate.

"That was lucky," said Clint. "We're in! Good job, Jamie."

Jamie felt a ray of hope. 'Maybe they won't kill me after all,' he thought.

* * *

Roberto was driving hard, trying to catch up with Jamie.

"There they are! They are going into De Sada Sol!"

"That traitor! He is sharing the treasure with the rich and leaving his family out! De Sada already has all the money he needs. Why does Jamie share with him instead of his own family?"

"What do we do? We can't go in there!"

"Pull over. We're going over the fence."

Going over the fence was easier said than done. Normally, de Sada's security system would detect someone scaling the fence, but not tonight. Fence security was turned off for the event. Still, the fence was high and laced along the top with broken glass and razor wire. Fortunately, Roberto was prepared for such inconveniences. He pulled the car next to the fence, to use the car as a ladder. In the trunk he just happened to have a handy heavy rubber mat, perfect for occasions when one might need to jump over a fence protected by broken glass or razor wire.

Jason arrived by taxi from the opposite direction.

"Here es De Sada Sol, on the left. The gate es jus around the bend. Do you haf an invitation?" asked the cab driver.

"Just drive past. I am looking for my friends who have my invitation. I'm not sure they are here yet."

"As chu wish."

As Jason studied the landscape a glint of metal or glass reflected from the taxi headlights caught his eye. He peered into the dark just in time to see Umberto slide over the fence.

"You can let me out here!"

"Chu sure? We have not even reached the gate. I don't mind waiting for your friends."

"No, this is fine. They will be along any minute and pick me up."

* * *

McKenzie parked the car between two others, within sight of the main house, and said to Jamie, "So, where is the computer?"

"Upstairs in the office, there on the side of the house."

"How do we get in?" asked Clint.

"Jamie will do it for us."

Jamie saw this as an opportunity to escape his captors. "Si. No es problemo. I can go right in the front door. They know me. I will be back with the computer in two minutes."

McKenzie growled, "I'm not buying it, Pedro."

"Jamie."

"What?"

"My name is Jamie."

"Whatever. Clint here is going with you."

"No, no, no! They don't know Clint. He can't get in."

"You won't be going through the door."

"What do you mean, not going through door?"

Staying in the shadows, they worked their way to the side of the house. McKenzie pointed to a massive tree with thick limbs that provided access to the balcony.

"I cannot do this!"

"Quiet, or I'll slit your throat!"

"I am not a young man!" whimpered Jamie. "I cannot climb tree and jump to balcony!"

"You can and you will," said Clint as he shoved the barrel of his pistol under Jamie's chin.

"Si, si, I can do it," exclaimed Jamie with newfound conviction. "No problemo. I no want slit throat and bullet in head. I can do it."

In a moment, they were on the balcony. With little effort, Clint had one French door open. He motioned for Jamie to follow and the two of them entered the office.

* * *

"There they go," whispered Umberto. "Jamie is breaking into De Sada Sol!"

"I didn't know my cousin had it in him!" exclaimed Roberto proudly. "He es not a traitor after all! I told you he was okay! He es my cousin!"

"No, you told us he was a thief who would steal from his own family."

"Focus my friend on the facts at hand," urged Roberto. "He would not be breaking into De Sada Sol unless the treasure was vast!"

Renaldo nodded in agreement and added, "It must be huge!"

"He will need our help carrying all that treasure," observed Umberto.

"Si. And our help spending it!" added Renaldo.

"Now you are focused my friends. Let's go!"

The three of them moved through the shadows toward the side of the house.

* * *

Jason scaled the fence, using the handy heavy rubber mat left behind by Roberto. He soon spotted the cousins. He followed them as they moved to the side of the house.

A great fireball lit the sky! The sudden, unexpected light exposed those lurking in the shadows. The earth shook, followed by the sound of an enormous explosion. McKenzie, Roberto, Umberto, Renaldo and Jason froze in place. De Sada's personal guard Miguel called Jamie's cell phone, as ordered by de Sada.

Jamie had just picked up the computer and was about to hand it to Clint when there was an unusually bright light and the ground shook, followed by the sound of a massive explosion. And, his cell phone rang.

He dropped the computer.

Clint dove to catch it, knocking over a table.

The phone kept ringing.

Downstairs, everyone was still enthralled by the spectacular fire in the distance when Miguel and de Sada heard commotion upstairs.

"What's going on in my office?"

De Sada nodded at several large, well-dressed men, who instantly charged up the stairs.

Clint, hearing a stampede approach, retrieved the computer, ran to the balcony and called, "McKenzie! Catch!" He dropped the computer to McKenzie and dove for the nearest limb.

Jamie panicked. He did not want to be found inside the office of De Sada Sol, uninvited. He ran to the balcony. Clint was in the tree already, climbing down. Jamie started to jump, but it seemed too far. He hesitated. There was shouting in the yard below. He turned back, looking for a place to hide. He scurried behind a wicker chair, but quickly realized it would not conceal him. De Sada's guards burst into the office. Seeing no other way out, Jamie climbed the rail and jumped for the limb.

He missed.

Roberto and his cousins saw Clint lean over the rail with the computer and realized that he was about to drop it to the man waiting below. They charged McKenzie, determined to get the computer from him at all cost.

The charge of de Sada's guards up the stairs to the office did not escape Natalia's notice. Already alert, she detected something going on outside. "What's that noise?" she asked as she squeezed Jackson's hand and moved to an exit door on the side of the house, under the balcony. They stepped outside just in time to see three small men tackle one large man, who dropped a computer.

"That's mine!" exclaimed Jackson as he picked up his computer, just as Jason arrived.

"Not anymore," said Jason as he grabbed the computer and pointed a gun at Jackson.

Natalia screamed!

Startled, Jason turned toward Natalia and away from Jackson for a moment. Jamie fell on Jason with a loud thud. He and Jason emitted a double "Oof!"

Jason dropped the computer.

Natalia scooped up the computer.

Clint leaped from the limb and grabbed the computer from Natalia. Jackson yelled, "Hey, leave her alone!" He stepped closer to intervene. Clint balled his fist and turned to confront Jackson, prepared to dispatch him with the skill of a boxer.

Jackson is not a fighter, but he knew he was about to be hit by a bigger man. Unpracticed in the art of boxing, he knew nothing about blocking and counterpunching. Instead, he pulled his fist well behind him and twisted his body to deliver what he imagined would be a haymaker. Before Jackson swung his punch, Clint let out a roar of agony and stumbled forward a few paces, blood on the shoulder of his shirt.

Jackson swung, missing his mark. Fortunately, Clint stumbled into the path of the punch, which landed squarely on Clint's temple. Clint fell to his knees, dazed. Jackson grimaced and shook his hand, wondering who was hurt more by his punch, him or his assailant. That's when Jackson noticed Natalia's fan protruding from Clint's shoulder. Jackson's head was on a swivel, looking first at Clint, then at Natalia, then Clint and back to Natalia.

"How? What?"

"Well, a lady has to be prepared for, uh, eventualities," she explained as she retrieved her fan and the computer.

McKenzie scrambled out from under the scrum of his attackers, found his pistol and fired without aiming. The sound apparently reminded Umberto, Roberto and Renaldo that they were late for an urgent appointment. They scurried off into the dark, leaving Jamie behind, moaning.

"I'll take that," insisted McKenzie as he grabbed the computer, trying to snatch it away from Natalia.

"Oh, no chu won't!" she said as she held on so tight that McKenzie lifted her off the ground as he pulled the computer to him.

Jackson grabbed Natalia and pulled her back. "No! Natalia, let go! He can have the computer! Take it!"

Natalia let go, with a puzzled and angry expression on her face. "Why chu let him have it?"

"I can get another computer. Take it and go!"

With one eye on Jackson and Natalia, McKenzie helped Jason and Clint to their feet. The darkness enveloped them a moment later as they ran to their car.

De Sada and his entourage of security arrived in time to see Jackson embracing Natalia, who was weeping against his shoulder, while Jamie lay moaning on the lawn.

"Now, this is a touching scene," said de Sada. "What could possibly make you so upset?"

Jackson was gently stroking her hair as Natalia snuffled. She sucked in air in two short gasps before responding, "They tooked his computador."

Chapter 39

McKenzie sped away from De Sada Sol with his two wounded warriors.

"What happened back there?"

"I don't know," said Jason. "I had the drop on him, and I glanced away for a moment when that woman screamed. That's when he hit me like a ton of bricks. I never saw it coming. I've never been hit so hard."

"Yeah, he popped me a good one, too," said Clint as he rubbed his temple.

"You're bleeding like crazy!" exclaimed Jason. "What happened?"

"I have no idea."

"And who were those guys who tackled me?" asked McKenzie.

"They showed up at the same time Bradley did," explained Clint. "I think they were with him. Maybe they're his bodyguards or something."

"This guy, Bradley, he's good," observed McKenzie. "Real good. We underestimated him."

"Yeah. I don't want to cross him again," said Jason.

"We won't have to. We've got the computer."

"But, they've got Jamie. How are we going to find the hidden files?" asked Clint.

"He's not the only computer expert on this island," said McKenzie.

* * *

Jamie was whimpering in a chair in de Sada's office. He had been half carried, half shoved into the office by de Sada's security staff. They were none too happy with Jamie. De Sada paid them handsomely to provide first-rate security, which had been breached by a mere computer merchant.

"I promise, I don't know the men. They made me come. I delivered the computer to your house, just as you asked, so that you could give it to your American friend tonight. They were waiting for me when I returned to my shop. They demanded I give them the computer. When I told them I didn't have it, they burned my shop and threatened to kill my family. I told them the computer was here. I had to tell them to save my family. I am so sorry. They made me come with them. I didn't want any of this to happen. I have lost my shop and your respect. I am so sorry."

"Why?" asked Bradley. "Why did they want my computer?"

"The treasure. They say there es clues to the treasure on the computer."

Bradley laughed while Natalia and de Sada exchanged glances.

"What so funny?" asked Natalia.

"There is nothing on the computer."

"What?" cried Jamie, de Sada and Natalia simultaneously.

"No. Nothing. I bought it to write a book while I was on this trip. I wanted to get away for a while because back home I was followed everywhere by media and fortune seekers who thought I knew something about a treasure. I don't! Now, the curse of the mummy's tomb has followed me to Punta Cana."

"Your mommy's tomb is cursed?" gasped Natalia.

"No, I mean, it's just a figure of speech."

"She is disfigure?" said Natalia as she fingered her smooth face with both hands, a look of shock and horror etched on her features.

"No, I don't mean disfigured. I mean, rumors of treasure tend to bring the worst out of people and bad things tend to happen," explained Jackson. "It's as though the treasure was cursed."

"Oh. And this happened to your mommy?"

"No, Natalia. He is talking about an Egyptian mummy," explained de Sada.

"Egyptian! But, I thought chu were American…"

"Jackson," interrupted de Sada as he placed a hand on Bradley's shoulder and turned him away from Natalia. He waved his free hand at Natalia behind his back to shush her. She would have none of that, so she thrust herself closer so she could hear everything.

"English is not her first language, nor her second. She is easily confused by figures of speech. This has been a terrible experience. But, I fear it is not over. These men, they think you know of a treasure. They will continue to follow you and may cause you harm, even if there is no treasure."

"What do you suggest?"

"Let me help you. I have, uh, resources that can provide security and assistance to you."

"No! I will protect him!" exclaimed Natalia urgently. "Chu no have to do it. I can do it!"

Bradley chuckled, while de Sada smiled and shook his head.

"What? Chu don't think I can help? Jackson and me, we chase off six armed men! Six! Chu tell him Jackson!"

"It's true that she didn't back down in the face of armed men."

"Chu fight for me, I fight for chu. Chu belong to me now and nobody will harm chu."

"I don't know what to say!"

"Just say jes. I take care of chu."

"I certainly agree that Natalia can be a formidable bodyguard with certain unconventional, but useful weapons," de Sada said in a condescending tone.

"What do chu mean by that?" demanded Natalia.

"But, Jackson, let me help as well."

"Well, I will be taking a dive trip, and I would not want any fortune hunters to horn in on my trip."

De Sada and Natalia answered at the same time, "I will make sure no more fortune hunters bother you!"

* * *

Hoover checked the Brooks and Bradley office computer. He had discovered that the office computer received a copy of text messages sent to the lawyers' phones. He found a most interesting text from Bradley to Brooks about diving Wednesday. He had already researched the dive master based upon information provided by Peter. Hoover called his contact in Texas. "They will be diving Wednesday. They think they've found the wreck."

"Already? Good work. Good thing I've got men standing by."

* * *

The phone call was from an unknown number, as usual. McKenzie answered, but he wasn't sure how well his report would be received.

"We got the computer, but there is nothing useful on it."

"The computer is a diversion. It flushed you out in the open."

"No kidding! This guy is a professional. This is no mere lawyer. He took down two of my men. Clint lost a lot of blood. We had to take him to a local doctor, but now he has some kind of strange tropical infection. I'm sending him home. Jason is beat up pretty bad. He's got bruises all over his body."

"Bradley did that by himself?"

"Yeah, but he had help. He had three guys on me, while he took care of Clint and Jason by himself."

"Bradley's more than you can handle. We underestimated him big time. I'm sending you help. We know where he's going. He's diving Wednesday with a guy named Robert Wade. I'm emailing you a file on him and his company, Adventure Divers. They've found the wreck!"

* * *

Gregory's phone rang. He was not surprised that the call was from an unknown number. Many of his calls were from unknown numbers.

"Speak."

"I've got another job for you."

"I'm not finished with the one here."

"The farm can wait."

"What about the Sheriff?"

"We've got it handled. What I want is in the Dominican Republic. I need you there."

"Why me? You sent your own guys there."

"Bradley was too much for them to handle."

"Bradley! You're kidding."

"Didn't he have something to do with catching you?"

"Yeah, he distracted me while somebody else sucker punched me with a boat anchor."

"A boat anchor! Sounds resourceful. Bradley is no sucker. My guys are professionals and he put two out of three of them down. Watch yourself."

"What about Whittaker?"

"He can fend for himself. Besides, he's got Collier for the next few days."

"All right. I've got a score to settle with Bradley, so I'm your man. Just send me the details."

"Check your inbox. Make sure you get what I'm looking for. Turn it over to McKenzie and I'll make you a rich man."

Chapter 40

It was getting late when Jennifer Wolfe left a client's office. She had just solved a nagging conflict between software applications when her cell phone rang. She checked the caller ID and did not recognize the number. She hesitated a moment while she considered ignoring the call. "Probably a wrong number," she sighed as she took the call. Unwilling to identify herself, she simply said, "Hello?"

"Jennifer, this is Karen."

"Karen, it is so good to hear from you. I almost didn't take the call because I didn't recognize the number."

"Yeah, I changed my number because I don't want to be found."

"I understand. I can't believe John is interested in that Sandy Storm. I am so disappointed in him."

"Jennifer, I can't talk about her. That's not why I called. I just don't want to go there."

"I'm sorry. I understand." After an uncomfortable pause, Jennifer said, "Well, how are you doing?"

"I'm good. I have a good job with a lawyer, who really appreciates me, in every way."

"Really! Sounds interesting! So, are you two an item?"

"No. Yes. I don't know. He wants to be. In fact, things are moving pretty fast. So fast my head is spinning. He has asked me to marry him."

"What! Who? That's fast!"

"Yes, it is. He told me the day after we met that I was the girl he had been waiting for, and that sooner or later I would marry him."

"Sounds a little arrogant."

"Maybe. But I don't see arrogance in the way he handles himself. He's an amazing guy. He just knows what he wants."

"Well, good for him. What do you want?"

"I'm worried about something and I wonder if you could do me a favor."

"Are you kidding? Anything, girlfriend. Just ask."

"I'm worried about the clients I left behind, and, well, I need you to . . . I don't know how to even begin explaining this."

"You are worried that John can't get along without you?"

"No. I'm not worried about John."

"Don't lie to me, Karen. More importantly, don't lie to yourself."

Karen sighed. "This is hard. But, just hear what's on my heart. First, I couldn't stay. Then, Jackson left."

"How did you know Jackson left? You've been keeping up. That's not healthy for you, girl."

"I know you're right. But, I also know John hasn't hired a replacement for me, and the only person left to help him is Peter Creek."

"Yep. He made his bed. He's got to sleep in it."

Karen's voice became agitated and almost shrill. "Jennifer! Why did you say that? Is he sleeping with that girl?"

"No, no, I didn't mean that. I mean he created the problem and he has to deal with it."

"So, he's not sleeping with that girl?"

"Karen, I don't know what he's doing when he's not at work."

"So, he is sleeping with her. You know something. Just tell me!"

"Karen, is that why you called? You want me to be your spy?"

"No. I don't even know how I got off on that subject. This is why I had to leave. This ridiculous jealousy consumes me! I hate myself when I feel this way."

"I love you like a sister Karen, so I have to tell you, you're beating yourself up. You need to just let him go. Do your best to put his memory behind you. Let this new fellow catch you and see where that leads. That's the best way to forget ole what's his name."

Karen sighed again and paused while she let Jennifer's advice sink in. "I guess you're right. But, the reason I called is I feel that there is something funny about Peter."

"There you go again. You are not John's momma."

"I know, I know. But, something is wrong with that boy and I don't trust him. Now that it's just Peter and John in the office, my gut tells me that a lot of people I care about could be hurt if I'm right. That's why I called you."

"You want me to keep an eye out?"

"Yes."

"How?"

"I have no idea. I just know something is wrong, and I don't know anyone I could trust to share my concern besides you. And, I know you care about John and Jackson, too. Even if you're disappointed in John, you still care about him."

"Yeah, you're right. I'm not sure how I can help, but I promise I'll check in on him."

"Thank you, Jennifer. You are a true friend."

"You're welcome. And, you be sure to tell me how things are going with your new boyfriend."

Karen laughed, but her laughter died into an uneasy pause. "Okay, Jennifer. Thank you. Bye."

After hanging up Jennifer just shook her head. "Poor girl. This is really unhealthy. She has got to let go." Jennifer returned to her computer, but instead of working she started thinking about Karen's request. "How in the world would I tell if anything were wrong? This is an impossible assignment." She turned the problem over in her mind and thought about Karen's statement about Peter, 'something is wrong with that boy. I don't trust him.'

"If he were doing something wrong, how would I know it? How would I catch him?" She sat back and pondered the problem and then said, "I'll start with a full diagnostic on the computer. Where I go from there, I have no idea."

Instead of going home, she went to John's office.

Chapter 41

Tuesday night Gregory was in Punta Cana placing a GPS tracker on the boat Robert Wade would be using the next morning.

Wednesday morning at 7:00 a Volkswagen bus picked up Natalia and Jackson at Poetry resort. When she met Jackson in the lobby, she was dressed in a tight fitting one-piece bathing suit that enhanced all of her assets. She carried a pack containing a snorkel, fins, a mask and her own regulator. Before boarding the bus she slipped on a neon green mesh cover-up that covered little. Her mood was as bright as her neon cover-up

"How can you be this bubbly so early in the morning?"

"I love adventure and I love diving. I go as often as I can. How about chu?"

"This will be my first actual dive. I took lessons from Robert before I left Mississippi."

"Oh! Well, chu know, chu have to have a buddy—we will be buddies, yes!" she said as she sat close to Jackson and rubbed his arm. "I will be dhur best buddy. Chu will see," she said as she pecked him on the cheek. Jackson felt a thrill run up and down his spine.

The drive across the island took an hour and a half. The scenery featured rolling hills, meadows, jagged mountains and as they neared the coast, tropical jungle. Natalia soon fell asleep in Jackson's lap. She pulled Jackson's arm over her chest like a blanket and cuddled up with it. Jackson loved her warmth and the intimate feel of her against his skin. He marveled at Natalia's simple gesture of trust in him as she quickly fell asleep. He wondered how he came to have an exotic beauty asleep on his lap. 'Just luck, I guess.' He already felt attracted to her in a way he had never felt toward a woman before. 'Could there be something between us?' he wondered.

At last, they arrived at the harbor and found Robert's boat. Robert greeted them as they trundled down the concrete pier with Natalia's gear. Robert, hands on hips, called out to Jackson, "Why didn't you tell me we were having more divers? I need to know these things." His square shoulders were suitable for carrying heavy dive equipment on his back. He had a handsome face, accentuated by blue eyes that bugged slightly from too many deep dives.

"Sorry, Robert, this is Natalia."

"You're diving, too?" he asked. "At least this one is pretty. How many times have you been diving, if I may ask, Natalia?"

"Maybe fifty, maybe one hundred, not sure. I don't count anymore."

"Do you have a dive log?"

"Si." She fished through her bag and produced a ledger. "This is the latest one. I have others."

Robert flipped through the ledger, pausing here and there, clearly impressed. "You might as well be a dive master."

"Oh, no, I could never do what chu do. It is way too dificil for me."

Robert chuckled and said, "Well, anyhoo, she's all right. I don't know about your other friends, Jackson. They're not too talkative."

"I'm not sure about them either. Let's meet them."

"So, you haven't met them yet?"

Jackson shrugged.

They stepped aboard Robert's boat, Elmo. It was rigged for diving, with a bench on each side of the main deck. A fiberglass awning covered the back deck. Air tanks protruded from slots behind the bench in such a way that divers could sit on the bench and easily strap on a tank. There were benches that doubled as storage compartments and a table. The words 'Life Raft' were stenciled across the top of a storage compartment at the stern. Steps led to the pilothouse above the deck.

"Natalia, meet Stewart. He's our pilot. Over there is Jake, he's on leave from the Air Guard in Jackson."

"Good to meet you both," said Jake.

"The Mississippi Air National Guard," repeated Jackson. "You're the guys who are doing all those practice take-offs and landings around the clock in Jackson, aren't you?"

"Yep, that's us, but we do a lot more than practice. My unit is doing some relief work in Haiti and I caught a ride here. When we're done diving, I can probably catch a ride back. No charge. One of the perks of the job."

"Must be nice," said Jackson.

"Yeah, but you have to be willing to go where the plane is going, and then only if there's an extra seat. It just happens that we're doing another relief mission to Haiti, so I hitched a ride. We fly the big C-17 Globemaster giant cargo planes that carry tanks, troops, and tons of supplies. We're on call for any military mobilization or any humanitarian project as ordered by the President or the Defense Department."

"That's interesting," said Natalia

"Yeah. We flew relief for the tsunami in Indonesia, and the earthquake in Haiti. We regularly fly to Iraq and Afghanistan. We also do all sorts of experimental special ops for training purposes. We're about to test a really cool one man glider, but I won't be able to tell you about it for a few years."

Robert continued with the introductions. "This is Neil, a brilliant programmer, and this is Jimmy. Back home, he is an Assistant D.A. Here in the Caribbean, he's our beer expert."

"Actually, Jackson and I know each other from work," observed Jimmy. "And, your Goshen Springs Beer is awesome. When will it be available everywhere?"

"Why he say 'your beer'?" asked Natalia.

"Thanks, Jimmy." Jackson turned to Natalia and explained, "I have an interest in a brewery."

"Chu didn't tell me chu are rich."

"No, just a small interest in a new company with no sales yet. I hope the public loves the beer as much as Jimmy does. Jimmy and I have worked on opposite sides a few times. He's one of the good guys. You can count on him doing exactly what he says he will do."

"Thanks, Jackson," said Jimmy with a grin.

"Anyhoo," continued Robert, "Jake, Neil, and Jimmy will be helping us today. Tonight when we get back, Jimmy will find the best beer on the island for us."

"Yeah, I meant to bring my kegulator, but Pennington wouldn't let me move it."

Jake laughed and explained, "Pennington is his cat, who has developed a taste for beer and is probably throwing a feline beer bash back home."

Neil and Jimmy laughed and Neil leaned over and said in a low voice, "Wow, Jackson, you did good," nodding at Natalia. "I didn't know you had it in ya."

"Me neither."

"And let's meet your other friends, the ones you don't know yet," said Robert as he led Jackson to two broad shouldered muscular men.

"Mr. Bradley," said one, "I am Julio. Señor de Sada sent us to keep an eye out for you. He told us to be your bodyguards. We are at your disposal. This is Francisco." Francisco nodded.

"They say they are experience divers," said Robert.

"Yes, we learned in the military."

"Which military?" asked Jackson.

"Mexico."

"Okay," said Robert. "Let's get this party started. Jimmy, what is rule one?"

"Safety, safety, safety."

"Oh, I like that rule," said Natalia. "I always take precautions. A girl can never be too safety chu know."

"Excellent," said Neil. "I like a woman who thinks ahead."

Robert nodded and said, "Neil, what's rule number two?"

"Stick with your buddy." Natalia looked up at Jackson and smiled.

"Everybody, what is rule number three?"

Neil, Jake and Jimmy said, "Deal with little problems before they become big problems."

"That's right. We are going to constantly remind each other of the rules. This dive will be unusual because we'll be doing more than site seeing. I've got a permit to do excavation at an archeological site and we have a few nifty pieces of equipment to help us, thanks to a grant from Ole Miss, of all places."

Jake laughed and explained to Natalia, "Robert is a life-long Mississippi State fan. He can't stand Ole Miss, yet they gave him enough money to buy this boat and equipment."

"Yes, and I named their boat after my dog, Elmo. Okay, is everybody ready?"

Everyone nodded and Robert gave thumbs up to Stewart, who fired up the engine. It belched a little black smoke and rumbled with controlled power.

"Let's get Elliemomo going," shouted Robert. "Julio! Francisco! Give us a hand with the lines. Prepare to shove off!" commanded Robert.

Julio went forward and Jake said, "I'll go help." Francisco went aft and Neil said, "Me too." Julio and Francisco untied the lines and leaned over to toss them on the pier with military precision. Just as they did so, Stewart gunned the engine. Julio and Francisco lost their balance, and Jake and Neil finished both off with a little nudge. Julio and Francisco tumbled into the water with twin splashes. Almost immediately they surfaced, gasping and spitting, shocked looks on their faces.

Jimmy, always helpful, called out to them, "Oh, man, we are so sorry. Here, let me help you!" He tossed their equipment bags into the water beside them. The bags sank. Julio and Francisco plunged under the surface, chasing the bags.

"Robert! What's going on? What have you done?" cried Jackson.

"Rule number three," explained Robert as he waved goodbye in the direction of Julio and Francisco. "Deal with little problems before they become big problems. They were little problems and I had a feeling they were going to become big problems, so we dealt with it."

"Won't they just be waiting for us here when we return?" asked Jackson.

"I hope so. We're not returning here."

Natalia's countenance changed from stunned to exhilarated. She laughed until she cried. "Jackson, I like dhur friends. Real men take action, and chu and dhur friends are real men. We are going to have a good time!"

Once they cleared the harbor and nearby buoy markers, Stewart set the course and Robert rolled out several charts. He held them down with dive weights.

"This is what we know, thanks to your friends at the Eudora Welty Library," Robert began. "When Hurricane Harriett sank the Durance in 1866 off the coast of Hispaniola..."

"Wait. They weren't naming hurricanes back then," interrupted Jackson.

"We call every unnamed hurricane Harriett, in honor of Jimmy's wife," explained Jake.

"Oh, okay."

"Anyhoo, three probable sites have already been identified, based upon descriptions found in the diary. Two of those sites actually have wrecks that have already been extensively explored, even plundered. The third site is here," said Robert as he indicated a point on the chart. "There is no known wreck on that site. We've been diving the area for a week, along with several volunteers from home. We've already confirmed a wreck. Yesterday, we used sub-surface sonar equipment capable of penetrating several feet below the sea floor to map the wreck site."

"You mean the equipment provided by that school up north?" asked Jake.

"The one you don't want to mention?" asked Neil.

"Excuse me, are you talking about Ole Miss?" asked Jimmy.

"Can we get to the point?" asked Robert, an edge in his voice. "Anyhoo, as I was saying, we mapped the wreck site, and this is what we found." Robert rolled out another chart as large as a blueprint. "As best we can tell, the wreck is, for lack of a better word, a wreck. It's scattered across a quarter mile of sea bottom, but most of the hull is here." He indicated a point on the chart. "You can see the bow and the stern. According to the diary, what we're looking for is not a traditional treasure chest, so don't get your hopes up."

"It's not?" asked Natalia, disappointment dripping from her lips.

"No, it's a small golden box, about yea big," indicating about 12 to 15 inches with his hands, "containing some tear drop shaped golden nuggets. The inside lid of the chest is our real target. It may be of great significance. The artifact likely would have been located in a passenger cabin, right around here."

"Not the captain's cabin?" asked Natalia.

"No. It was entrusted with Maximilian's aide de camp, Philippe Constantine."

"Who?" asked Jackson.

"Not important," said Robert. "He was washed overboard early in the storm. No one else knew where it was except Frank James, and he never had a chance to get it."

"How do you know so much?" asked Natalia.

"It helps to have a library full of dedicated research assistants."

"Why does everyone want this artifact?" asked Natalia.

"Maximilian believed that this trinket proved the existence of the Hummingbird Hoard, a treasure so vast that if it was shown to the King of France, the French army would return to Mexico to retrieve the treasure and rescue Maximilian's tottering empire," said Jimmy.

"And this trinket, I mean artifact, it proves the existence of the Hummingbird Hoard?" asked Natalia.

"That's right. But the trinket never made it..." said Jimmy.

"Artifact," interposed Robert.

"Yes, thank you, Robert. As I was saying, the trinket never made it to France," said Jimmy.

"So, here we are," added Natalia, bouncing with excitement.

"Do you think the French army will return if we find it?" asked Jake.

"It's a little late," said Neil.

"C'est la vie," said Robert.

"C'est la guerre," said Natalia.

"That's what I'm worried about," said Jackson.

Chapter 42

For John, Wednesday came like an express train. Sleep was a luxury that couldn't be afforded. He and Peter drove to Philadelphia early Wednesday morning and unloaded the file from the rental car. John carried a box to the courtroom door. He had bags under his eyes, and was wearing his new $150 suit and shirt, $40 shoes and a borrowed tie. He sported a buzz cut, because half of his hair had been singed to nubs in the blast. Jason Collier, spiffy in his $3,000 suit, opened the courtroom door for him.

"Thanks," said John as he stepped into the doorway.

Collier put his hand on John's shoulder, ran his finger along the collar of the jacket and pretended to straighten it. "Don't mention it." Collier made a point of sizing up John's appearance. "You're looking a little frazzled. Are you sure you're up to this after all you've been through?"

"Funny you should ask that today. That wasn't the position you took Monday."

Collier laughed and said, "No, I guess it wasn't. But, we have to keep up appearances, don't we? Well, may the best man win?"

John smiled and said, "May justice be served."

Collier laughed and shook his head. "Justice is only available to those willing to pay the price." He winked and took his place at one of the counsel tables.

John settled into his chair and began organizing the items he would need during trial. After a moment he felt a hand on his shoulder. He looked up to see the dark, crinkled face of his client, Frank Dalton.

"You don't look so good today."

"I'll be all right. Here, have a seat next to me. Is your family here?"

"Everyone is here. We are all counting on you today. We know you won't let us down."

A wave of angst swept over John as Frank's words pierced his heart. At that moment, Harold Hoover stepped over with someone in tow. "John, let me introduce you to our new Sheriff, an old friend of mine, Wayne Townsend."

John turned to greet the new sheriff and came face to face with the deputy who cuffed him the night he was run off the road. Steeling himself to avoid showing his disappointment, John extended his hand and said, "Congratulations, Sheriff."

Townsend ignored John's hand. Instead, with an obvious supreme effort to look stern, he said, "I've got my eyes on you, Brooks." He made a pistol sign with his finger, pointing it first at his eye then at Brooks. "We will have a surprise for you soon."

"All rise," bellowed the bailiff, "The Circuit Court of Neshoba County is now in session. The Honorable Judge Harold O'Keefe presiding."

Townsend slipped off to the side while the judge took his place at the bench. Judge O'Keefe, speaking with a high pitched nasally voice, commanded, "Be seated."

John glanced over his shoulder and saw Peter Creek on the front row.

"Is the Plaintiff ready?" asked Judge O'Keefe.

"Jason Collier here for the Plaintiff. I will be assisted by Mr. Harold Hoover, and yes, Your Honor, the Plaintiff is ready."

"What about the Defendant and Cross-Claimant?"

"Yes, Your Honor, Mr. Frank Dalton and his family are ready. I have a request."

"Yes?"

"I am usually accompanied by my partner or my paralegal, neither of which are available. I ask that my assistant, Mr. Peter Creek, be allowed to join me here at counsel table. I may need help locating documents and keeping up with witnesses, because I did not do most of the trial preparation."

"Yes, I recall that you were out of commission for a time. Is Mr. Creek a lawyer or a paralegal?"

"No, Your Honor."

"Well, this is most unusual then." O'Keefe looked at Collier and asked, "Any objection?"

Collier smiled and seemed to seriously consider the request for a moment and then said, "Considering Mr. Brooks' plea of ignorance and lack of preparation and in the interest of fairness, we have no objection."

'Why, thank you for those kind words,' John thought to himself, but he held his tongue.

"Very well. There being no objection, Mr. Creek will be permitted to join Mr. Brooks at counsel table."

John noticed that Hoover and Collier seemed pleased with themselves.

Voir dire, the jury selection portion of the trial, began. Collier was smooth. He asked extensive questions to the jury pool about the recent murder of Skeeter and his friends, explaining that he didn't want anyone on the jury pool to unfairly blame Awesome or anyone in his family for their murder. He explained that he wouldn't want the trial tainted with any such suggestions. "We wouldn't want our verdict to be set aside on appeal, you see."

When John objected, O'Keefe responded, "Mr. Collier is just trying to insure that we have a fair jury panel. Objection overruled. You may continue, Mr. Collier."

"Thank you, Your Honor. Likewise, I wouldn't want anyone on the jury to harbor any misgivings about the Dalton family just because your beloved Sheriff was found dead in the creek on their property a few days ago."

"Judge, this is improper voir dire."

"I don't agree, Mr. Brooks. Mr. Collier is performing a textbook voir dire. Perhaps you should pay attention. You might learn something."

Everyone laughed.

"I just hope he is not educated too soon," Collier added.

Everyone laughed again. John looked over his shoulder and saw Sandy Storm on the front row. She shook her head slightly in a show of sympathy. It was then that John noticed the courtroom was filling up with media. Collier was still droning on about how all he wanted was fair jurors who would commit in advance to give his client a big verdict, even before they had heard any evidence. He made it all sound so reasonable. The judge apparently thought so. It seemed that Collier just might get the jury he wanted.

John leaned over and whispered to Peter, "Go ask Ms. Storm why the media is here." Peter nodded and slipped through the gate in the bar. After a hushed exchange he returned. "She says they were tipped off that there would be an announcement of major developments in the scalping case."

"Tipped off? What's coming?"

Peter shrugged.

It seemed to John that the voir dire lasted forever. He found it hard not only to pay attention, but to even stay awake. He didn't know if his problem was lack of sleep, or whether his injury, his hospital stay and recovery had sapped his energy reserves. Whatever the cause, John felt himself losing control.

At last, the jury selection was over and the trial began. Normally, John paid attention to nuances, suggestions, fine points, and his mind raced ahead, looking for opportunities to seize, and truth to ferret out, but not today.

Collier put on his case with little opposition. He made every point he wanted to make, including the poor condition of the common fence and the failure of the Daltons to maintain the fence. He hammered away at how the Daltons had taken the law into their own hands and seized Whittaker's cows. Dalton even took them to market and sold them! Why, that was the same as cattle theft! His witnesses testified as to the quality of the cattle taken by the Daltons, the reasonable efforts of Whittaker to regain his cows without filing criminal charges, and Whittaker's efforts to mitigate his damages by not objecting to the sale of the cows before they lost even more value from mishandling. It all seemed so reasonable. Collier made Whittaker seem saintly. Finally, as a last resort, Whittaker had no choice but to sue his neighbor to get back the full fair value of his cows.

Collier demonstrated that the actual damages to Mr. Whittaker were proven without question to be over $80,000. Since the Daltons had acted with wanton and willful disregard of the rights of poor Mr. Whittaker, punitive damages of at least five times actual damages were appropriate, to make an example of the Daltons, so that in the future other innocent people might be spared the injustice suffered by Mr. Whittaker. Without a doubt, Mr. Whittaker was a suffering public servant, pursuing a lawsuit, not because he wanted to, but because it was the right thing to do.

Finally, Collier paused and said, "Your Honor, we may be through with Mr. Whittaker's proof. May I have a brief recess to make sure that I have not overlooked anything? It may be that when we return we will be able to announce that we rest our case."

"Very well," said Judge O'Keefe, clearly pleased that the case had moved along so efficiently. "Ladies and gentlemen of the jury, please step into the jury room. We will take a ten-minute recess. Please don't discuss the case during this recess." He banged his gavel on the resounder, rose and exited the courtroom through a door behind the bench.

In contrast to the mood of Judge O'Keefe, several media members were murmuring that their time was being wasted. "I thought there was going to be some major announcement today. How long are we going to have to sit through this farm border war?" one reporter asked another.

Mr. Whittaker looked like the cat that ate the canary. He couldn't be more pleased with the performance of his advocate. John overheard him say to Collier, "You're worth every penny of that exorbitant fee you charged me." Collier, Whittaker and Hoover all laughed as they gazed at Frank Dalton and John Brooks. John thought, 'I wonder if he's getting paid by both Whittaker and Shawn Dalton?'

Chapter 43

Jennifer Wolfe let herself back into the Brooks & Bradley office Wednesday morning. "I wish I were in the Caribbean like Jackson," she said to herself. The computer did not respond as quickly as usual when she began running her diagnostics. "What's this? Oh, this looks nasty! Brooks and Bradley caught a virus!" She began isolating the virus so she could completely eliminate it, but something caught her attention.

"This is spyware! It gives someone outside the office access to the computer anytime." She studied the virus code further. "This looks like it could be a copy hard drive command, coupled with a send command," she said to herself. "It copies the whole computer, every night, at 2 a.m., and sends. No, that was the first night. Every other night it copies only new entries. Send where? The recipient will have to have an IP address! If I find that I'll know who the spy is!"

Determined to find the culprit, she dug until she found the IP address to which the copy was sent. Avoiding the Brooks & Bradley computer, she used her own laptop to research the IP address location. "If it's a static address, I can narrow the address to a specific computer at a specific address. Here it is! Oh, no. It's random."

She let out a long sigh. The spy understood IP addresses were traceable. "He used a rotating random address. I still might be able to unpeel the onion since I know the time the message is sent every night. But, if it's truly random I may never find him."

She pondered the problem for a few minutes. A thought flashed in her mind. "Wait a minute! He is copying and sending everything new on the computer. I'll send him a little surprise!" She began programming a virus of her own to install on the Brooks & Bradley computer; a virus that would be sent to the spy at 2 a.m.

* * *

By ten o'clock, Stewart anchored Elmo above the wreck, and Robert instructed everyone to prepare to dive. Robert went over the pre-dive check with Jackson since it was his first real dive.

"Remember, breathe out slowly as you rise. Rise slowly to the pre-marked resting point, about ten feet below the surface. It's marked on the anchor line. I'll meet you there. Wait until I say it's okay to go to the surface. I don't want you getting the bends. All right?"

Jackson nodded. He was already feeling nervous.

"Everybody has two buddies today, because today is different. Natalia, you and I will be with Jackson. We keep each other in sight at all times, understood?"

Natalia and Jackson both nodded.

"Jimmy, Neil and Jake are buddies today. They will be operating a giant vacuum cleaner. We hope it will clear away enough silt and debris that we can get to the cabin. I'll be photographing everything. So will Neil when he can. Nothing gets removed from the bottom without my okay. Everybody on board with that?"

"I'm not bored, I'm excited," responded Natalia.

"Me too," said Robert. "Do you understand and agree with what I asked you to do?"

"Si."

"All right! Let's get this party started."

Jackson slipped on his fins and sat on the bench in front of the tank assigned to him. He slipped on the tank and stood, leaning forward slightly. He felt a little unsteady at first, but that feeling passed. Robert checked his gear and confirmed that his air valve was open. He gave an okay signal to Jackson, who responded in kind. Robert gave Natalia the same check.

Neil, Jake and Jimmy splashed off the end of the boat in turn, and then it was Jackson's turn.

"Remember. Put your hand over you mask and regulator and hold them tight so they don't come off when you hit the water," said Robert.

Jackson complied.

"Now, take a giant step off the boat."

Jackson took his first scuba step into the ocean. The first thing he noticed was the sound and the sudden change in temperature. His wet suit had been hot, but now he was enveloped in cool liquid, whooshing, surging and tugging at every limb and every piece of equipment all at once. He found himself in a world of bubbles. He couldn't see a thing for a moment until the bubbles dissipated. Then the water became crystal clear. He could see the silver surface above him and the bottom of Elmo beside him. He returned to the surface and gave Robert an okay sign. A few moments later Robert and Natalia joined him.

They began a slow descent. The pressure on Jackson's ears increased dramatically within the first few feet of his dive. He worried that he would be unable to stand the pain if it didn't ease soon. Robert anticipated his problem and motioned for Jackson to halt his descent. Robert waggled his jaw in an exaggerated manner. Jackson did the same and felt a little relief. Robert squeezed his nose with one hand and puffed his cheeks out, indicating he was forcing air into his ears. Jackson did the same and found instant relief as he heard little popping and squealing noises in his ears.

Robert questioned Jackson with an okay sign. Jackson responded, okay. He turned and found Natalia drifting beside him, and realized she was there the whole time. 'You don't have much peripheral vision when you're diving,' Jackson thought to himself. He had to purposefully swivel his head back and forth, up and down, to see as much as possible. Otherwise, he would only see what was directly in front of him.

What he could see enraptured him. A deep blue sea filled with colorful schools of fish, some darting, some floating lazily, others just passing by. None seemed to care that Jackson and his friends had intruded into their domain. A bright yellow triangular fish stopped to examine Jackson's mask, or maybe the face behind the mask. Jackson wondered, 'Is this an angel fish?'

The sea bottom was only 40 feet below, but sloped toward a dark blue abyss. A rainbow of colors exploded below him. Portions of the wreck were scattered down the slope. The cabin they were about to explore was already marked off at a depth of 60 feet. Coral of every shape and kind covered much of the sea floor. He recognized a brain coral, tubes of yellow and orange, sponges, sea urchins, featherduster worms, starfish, and strawberry anemone reaching up with tiny tentacles. Jackson felt a tap on his left shoulder. Natalia motioned that he should follow her. He kicked his fins and glided behind her.

Jake and Jimmy had already set up the equipment at the probable site of the cabin. Neil laid measuring devices on the area and was taking photographs. After Robert circled the area to be excavated, he gave a signal and they began. Silt was sucked into the hose, and Neil removed larger objects by hand. Within minutes the entrance to a cabin was uncovered. The old wood was badly deteriorated, but still held its original form. Neil eased open the door, which fell away from its old hinge and broke into two large pieces. Countless shards of water-logged wood drifted around the divers. Robert photographed everything. Neil took pictures whenever his hands were free.

At last the opening was large enough for entry. Robert signaled that only he and Neil would enter the cabin. Robert produced two lines from a pouch and attached one to himself and one to Neil. Jake held the end of one line and Jimmy held the other. Jackson and Natalia held lights.

Robert entered first, careful to avoid touching anything. There was no way to know if the structure would collapse if disturbed. Once inside, he held up both hands, indicating Neil should wait. After a quick look, and several photographs, he motioned for Neil to enter slowly. Jackson could see that they were drifting over what appeared to be a footlocker, taking photographs. Jackson felt his heart racing with excitement. He could not believe their luck, finding such a well-preserved wreck that may never have been found by other divers. 'What if this is the one?' he thought to himself.

Then he thought about luck. 'I guess it is easier to be lucky if you have a map, an explicit diary, a certified archeological diver who has the knowledge to know where and how to look and has access to all this equipment.'

Neil and Robert carefully and slowly lifted the lid off the footlocker. Even though they moved ever so slowly, detritus, debris, silt and unknown particles swirled in the light beams. They paused to take pictures. Slowly, they lifted articles out of the footlocker. First, they removed what appeared to have been cloth at one time, but now seemed to be sheets of film that dissolved and disintegrated into myriad pieces with each touch, creating clouds of debris. They paused to let some of the cloudiness clear, and took more pictures. They both pointed at something, and took pictures from differing angles.

Jackson was disappointed to see Robert give a signal to surface. Neil eased out of the room, followed by Robert, empty-handed. Once everyone was together they slowly swam as a unit toward the surface, exhaling constantly to relieve pressure from their lungs. They paused at the spot marked on the anchor line.

Natalia clapped Jackson's shoulder and reached for his air gage. After looking at it, she turned it so that Jackson could see. He was almost empty! Jackson's eyes bugged out. He was relieved that at least they were close to the surface, just ten feet away. But, he had been told that if he went to the surface too soon he could suffer the bends. The bends could be merely painful, cause permanent injury, or death. But, he was out of air!

No problem. Natalia unhooked her secondary regulator and handed it to Jackson. He removed his regulator from his mouth and took hers. She showed him her air gage. She still had over half of a tank! They stayed at the ten-foot level for several minutes and surfaced.

* * *

As Jackson and his friends were surfacing, Jennifer finished creating her own virus. "All right, John Brooks. If you were here, I would explain to you that someone has installed spyware that activates at 2 every morning, makes a copy of everything new on your computer and sends it to a practically untraceable recipient. I am adding code to your computer that will be copied and sent to the spy's computer. It will disable the randomized IP address feature on the spy's computer and cause it to be issued a traceable static IP address. Pretty slick, huh? Only problem is, I won't know that new address until after 2 a.m. Friday morning when it will be archived on the Brooks & Bradley computer when the Friday 'copy and send' occurs. Then, I've got him! Unless they find this little bug and disable it before then."

She also borrowed code from 'Find Your Phone' and 'Find Your Friend,' apps that allow the user to locate a lost cell phone or locate a friend who uses the same program. Using cell towers to triangulate a position, the location apps can be remarkably accurate. "If they use a cell phone to access Brooks & Bradley files, I'll find it," she said to herself. Finally, Jennifer added remote access to her newly created 'Find a Computer' program and downloaded it into the Brooks & Bradley computer. "This will let me run their computer from anywhere. Never mess with my clients!"

She dialed John's cell phone. His voicemail answered. "John, this is Jennifer. I have something very important to tell you. It is urgent that you call me as soon as you can. Make sure that no one can overhear our conversation. That is vitally important. We have got to talk, as soon as possible. Don't use your computer until you talk to me. Don't talk to anyone about this until you talk to me."

* * *

As soon as he hit the surface, Jackson inflated his buoyancy control device, ripped off his mask and shouted, "Did you find it? Tell us! What did you see?"

Chapter 44

With everyone floating on the surface at the rear of the boat, and Captain Stewart leaning over to hear the news; excitement and anticipation filled the air. Everyone joined in the chorus, "Tell us! Tell us!"

Robert and Neil looked at each other. Their faces were unreadable.

"Go ahead and tell them, Neil."

"All right," Neil said in a calm voice. Then he shouted, "WE FOUND IT!"

Shouts of exhilaration filled the air. One by one they clambered aboard Elmo and gathered on the main deck under the shade of the canopy, where the celebration continued.

"Robert, why didn't you bring the artifact out?"

"It's going to take time to properly remove it, and I knew you would be short of air. And I don't let anybody run out of air. It's one of the rules."

"Me? What about everybody else?"

"Jimmy, how much air did you have?"

"About a third of a tank."

"Jake?"

"A little less than half."

"Neil?"

"Half."

"Natalia?

"A little more than half."

"Likewise," said Robert. "And you were out, weren't you?"

"Yes. How did you know?"

"I teach diving. I've done it for a long time. New divers always use a lot more air than experienced divers. Use of air has to do with your level of anxiety, depth, exertion, time, size, but in your case, lack of underwater breathing experience."

"That's right," said Natalia, "with experience chu will learn to breathe slowly and deeply and conserve your air."

"So, because of me, everyone had to surface."

"Yes, we're a team," said Robert. "We go down together and we come up together."

"I feel terrible for holding us back."

"Nonsense," said Jake. "We've all been beginners, just like you."

"Yeah," said Neil as he popped open a compartment on his camera and replaced the full memory card with another, "Diving is sort of like joining a family or a club. We're always looking for more good members," he said as he absent-mindedly slipped the full memory card into a waterproof sleeve, unzipped a wet suit pocket and slipped it in. "Not one in a million get to experience what you just enjoyed, so your skills will develop fast."

"What do we do now?"

"We eat lunch, rest, let our blood gases normalize and then we dive and finish the job," said Neil.

Sandwiches, fruit, water and juice was the lunch fare, which everyone scarfed as though they hadn't eaten in a week. Natalia settled next to Jackson, leaning against his shoulder. She looked up at him and grinned.

"I need to told chu something."

"What?"

"I have never been this excited, or had this much fun, or felt so alive! I feel like I am doing something worthy, with worthy people."

"I'm feeling the same way."

"Chu really know how to show a girl a good time." She stretched up and planted a kiss on his lips. "Thank you," she said.

"Wow! You're welcome. I can't believe how well things are going. We are really lucky!"

* * *

They rigged a hoist with a wire basket with a latching top and lowered it until it was suspended a few feet from the bottom. The team returned to work. Robert and Neil slowly turned the artifact and took more photos from every possible angle. Then they lifted it carefully from the box. As soon as the artifact entered the beams of light from the lanterns, the entire cabin was ablaze in golden light.

Natalia gasped in spite of herself, and sucked in a little salty water. She coughed several times to clear her air passage, but never took her eyes from the marvelous sight.

Jake and Jimmy maneuvered the basket to the cabin door and opened the basket lid. Robert and Neil wrapped a flotation device around the artifact and inflated it, making it easier to carry. They eased the object out of the cabin and into the basket. Once the lid was closed and latched, they gave a signal and the basket slowly rose to the surface. The team gathered in a circle, high fived each other underwater, and began a slow ascent, exhaling all the way. Every one of them experienced an overwhelming feeling of accomplishment.

But something strange happened on the way to the surface.

Elmo passed them on its way to the bottom. Stunned, everyone watched as Elmo slammed onto the ocean floor, stirring a massive cloud of silt and emitting a shock wave they felt in their bones. They looked up and saw the silhouette of another boat above them. Next to the boat someone was treading water.

* * *

Robert was the first to break surface. Jackson was right behind him.

"What happened?" demanded Robert.

Stewart was treading water, tiring fast. "They scuttled Elmo and stole the gold!" he shouted.

"Who? Why?"

Jackson heard the answer from a familiar voice.

"Why is obvious. I want your gold and I want you to die. I want you all to die slowly, with fear, horror and agony, especially Mr. Bradley!"

"Lincoln! Gregory Lincoln!" shouted a startled Jackson. He felt panic wash over him like an ocean wave. "How?"

"Hahahaha! I told you I would have my revenge. And revenge in the cold ocean depths, where every kind of sea monster lurks, is oh so sweet."

The other divers were surfacing, stunned and afraid.

"Don't do this, Gregory. Pull everyone else aboard."

"You can't be serious. I have all of you right where I want you. Now, I have a little present for you."

Two of his companions lifted a large plastic garbage bin and dumped it onto Jackson. Natalia screamed with horror and revulsion when she saw it was bloody chum.

"Enjoy your swim with the fishes, Jackson. Your friends have you to thank for their predicament. Goodbye!" The motor roared and the boat was gone.

Fish began feeding on the chum immediately. Robert had everyone back away from the blood and gather into a circle.

"What do we do?" cried Natalia.

Robert responded with authority. "We've got to keep Stewart afloat, and we have to stay together."

They looked around. There was no land in sight. The only vessel was Gregory's, which was fast receding. It was late afternoon. It would be dusk soon. Never had Jackson felt so hopeless.

"What do we do?" repeated Jimmy.

"Does anybody here know how to sail?" asked Robert.

"I do," responded Jackson.

"Good. What do you need?"

"Well, a boat would be nice."

"All right then, add air to your buoyancy vest and keep Stewart afloat. We'll be back shortly."

Robert, Jimmy, Jake and Neil dove, leaving Natalia, Jackson and Stewart alone on the surface.

"Jackson, look!" said Natalia, with her voice just above a whisper. A single dorsal fin swept through the chum on the surface. She moved close to Jackson. He could feel her trembling against his side. Or was he trembling? He wasn't sure.

There was a sudden surge of water as something huge rose from the depths beside them. Natalia's scream was high pitched as she practically climbed onto Jackson's back. Jackson's and Stewart's screams were not quite as high pitched.

A large, inflatable yellow raft leapt out of the water next to them, and their screams turned into joyous laughter. They pushed Natalia onto the raft, then Jackson pushed Stewart onto the raft and finally, Natalia and Stewart helped Jackson board.

"Where are they?" asked Jackson.

"Remember, they can't come straight up," said Natalia. "They will be here soon."

At that moment the four of them broke surface at the same time.

"Boat. Check. What's next on your sailing list?" asked Robert.

* * *

"A sail, a rudder, a keel and a mast would be nice. Some stays to hold the mast, and a sheet, I mean a line or a rope to control the sail."

"Would you like fries with that?" asked Jake.

"You sure are choosy," said Neil.

"Beggars can't be choosers," said Jimmy.

"Looks like we've got our work cut out for us. You can join us if you like," said Robert as he beckoned with his hand.

"What about that shark?" asked Natalia.

"We've got him outnumbered," said Robert, as though that were the perfect explanation. "Let's get going before his friends arrive."

The guys knew there was an inflatable raft on Elmo, apparently overlooked by Gregory. They dove to Elmo and found the raft intact, undamaged. They untied the anchor line from Elmo, opened the life raft compartment, tied the anchor line to the raft, and pulled the inflation cord. The raft raced to the surface while the guys slowly followed it. There were plenty of air tanks on and around Elmo for extended work under water.

Now, the trick was turning the raft into a workable sailboat. With lines, cloth, paddles, shafts and other items salvaged from Elmo, and with a lot of ingenuity, they had a usable sailboat by sunset; none too soon, as the number of dorsal fins in the area was growing.

As they were finishing their salvage operation, everyone was on the raft except Robert and Jake. Robert had one hand on the raft, while Jake was floating on the surface fifteen feet away. Movement behind Jake caught Jackson's attention. The sharks had been warily circling them at a distance, but one dorsal fin was cutting quickly though the water straight toward Jake.

"Shark!" shouted Jackson as he stood and pointed. A helpless feeling came over him as he realized there was nothing he could do to help Jake. His foot struck something hard in the bottom of the raft. It was an air tank. Jackson instinctively scooped up the heavy tank, stepped with one foot onto the edge of the raft and hurled the tank at a spot between Jake and the shark. He used every ounce of his strength to toss the heavy object, and leveraged his body length and weight to add distance to the throw. Jackson tumbled into the sea. The tank sailed past Jake, striking the water just ahead of the charging shark.

Primal fear gripped Jackson as he fell into the water. He believed the splashing noise might attract sharks, but he couldn't calm himself. He surfaced, sputtering and splashing his arms frantically. Something gripped him. His heart jumped into his throat.

"We've got you," said Robert.

"Take it easy, buddy," said Jake. They hoisted Jackson into the raft and clambered in after him.

"I never saw anything like that," said Jake.

"Yeah, you yelled 'shark' and jumped in the water with it," said Neil.

"What happened to the shark?" asked Jackson.

"I think you hit it on the nose with the air tank," said Robert. "What were you thinking?"

"I saw it coming at Jake fast and I had to do something."

"It probably would have turned away, but we'll never know for sure," said Robert. "It did a quick 180 when the tank hit it."

"Dat was very brave," Natalia said as she hugged Jackson. "I was so scared for chu."

"Buddy," said Jake as he clasped Jackson's shoulder. "I won't forget what you did. Maybe I can repay you one day."

With everyone on board, they took a quick inventory.

"Now, if only we had a chart."

"Got it."

"A compass."

"Here's one."

"I'm out of excuses. I guess I have to actually sail now. The truth is, I haven't sailed much."

"No worries. Jimmy and Neil sail all the time," said Robert

"We should be back on shore by morning. Sooner if this thing sails faster than I think it will," said Jimmy.

"Now, if only we had food and water," said Jackson.

Jake pulled on two lines attached to the raft and hauled up two mesh bags. "Food," he said as he pulled the first bag on the raft. "Water," as he pulled up the second.

"Have you guys had to do this before?"

"No, but we've spent a lot of time imagining what we would do if the boat went down," laughed Jake.

"Yeah, we thought we were just passing time shootin' the bull," laughed Jimmy, "But, this time all the bull we shot late at night turned out to be useful."

"Okay, let's jettison the gear we don't need to make more room on the boat," ordered Robert as he tossed his diving gear overboard.

Chapter 45

After motoring away from the wreck of the Elmo, Gregory congratulated his men on a job well done and turned the wheel over to the man standing next to him. He told him the course he wanted to maintain and stepped to the back of the boat where the golden chest glittered in the sunlight.

Gregory harbored no illusions about his companions. He hired three thugs willing to perform any task for money, including dumping chum on swimmers abandoned miles from shore. They joined him in an act of piracy when they boarded Elmo, threw the captain overboard, scuttled the ship and helped him steal the prize, a priceless golden chest. He knew there was no reason they wouldn't turn on him now that they saw the prize.

The three men wore shorts. The two smaller men each wore a T-shirt. The big guy wore an unbuttoned shirt that flapped in the wind as the boat sped toward shore. The big fellow's permanent scowl had become more ominous. The thin man was at the wheel.

Scar Face, a medium sized brute, seemed to be the leader. He was the one Gregory made the deal with. He had a smirk on his face as he glanced first at the golden chest and then at Gregory. Gregory pretended not to notice the avaricious glances of all three men as he swathed the chest in bubble wrap and placed it in an empty ice chest.

Gregory's favorite weapon, a Bowie knife, remained strapped to his thigh. A harpoon gun lay on the deck near the back of the boat, exactly where he had left it before they boarded Elmo. Using the ice chest to partially conceal his activity, Gregory seemed to busy himself with his gear. He tied the anchor line to the harpoon and sat the anchor on the gunwale. Without a moment of hesitation, Gregory lifted the harpoon gun, pointed it at the big man and fired. The harpoon buried itself into his belly. The point passed through and clanged against the side of the boat.

Gregory knocked the anchor overboard. Not waiting for his companions to recover from the shock, Gregory sprang forward, Bowie knife in hand. Scar Face was quick. He stepped back defensively while he reached for his own knife. The anchor line went taught. The big man screamed and grabbed his nearest companion, Scar Face, as he was yanked overboard. They both tumbled into the sea. Gregory threw his left arm around the neck of the pilot, while he thrust his knife between the thin man's ribs. He muscled the thin man to the gunwale and rolled his limp body over the side.

Scar Face sputtered and coughed as he broke the surface. He couldn't swim. Terror gripped him. The last thing he heard was Gregory's strange, cackling laugh as the boat motored away.

* * *

"Things are not going very well, are they, Mr. John," observed Frank Dalton, worry etched on his weathered face.

"No, Mr. Dalton. I'm afraid things are not going as well as we hoped."

"I believe in you. You will do great," said Mr. Dalton.

"I'm afraid we need a miracle," said John.

"Okay, let's ask for one," said Frank. "Peter, please let my family know that we must gather to pray." Peter hesitated. "Hurry, there is little time," urged Frank.

In a few moments all the members of the Dalton family gathered in the courtroom near John's counsel table. Frank nodded to John, and said, "You are our leader, please lead us in prayer."

John looked at Frank's green eyes, brimming with conviction, faith and hope. He looked at the gathered family members; every head was bowed expectantly, humbly. He looked around the courtroom. Everyone was staring at the Dalton gathering. The media seemed puzzled. Whittaker's camp seemed amused. "God help me," thought John, and then he began.

"Lord, help us to do your will. Forgive me for not coming to you before the trial started. I tried to win this case on my own strength, and I am not up to the task, but you are. Your strength is manifest in our weakness. Show your strength, Lord. You are the God of justice. You love a truthful witness and you abhor a lie. Help us to speak the truth. Help us to make your justice so apparent that the jury will see through art and artifice, smoke and mirror, and reach a just verdict. You always lead us in triumph in Christ. Whatever the outcome, Lord, let us be truthful. Manifest through us the sweet aroma of the knowledge of you in this place, and Lord, please protect this family and their farm. In Jesus' name, amen."

All the Daltons, and several spectators said, "Amen." Frank leaned over and patted John on the back. "That was a good prayer. Jesus is with us."

"What was that?" a reporter asked Sandy.

"That was an awesome prayer," replied Sandy.

"You've really gone off the deep end. Are you going to become a wacko evangelical too?"

Sandy just smiled and said, "Let's just see what happens."

A loud knock on the door behind the bench was immediately followed by the bailiff's command, "All rise!"

Judge O'Keefe settled into his chair and commanded, "Be seated. Please bring in the jury."

As soon as the jury was seated, O'Keefe turned to Collier and asked, "Do you have an announcement?"

"Yes, Your Honor, we have just one more witness. Then we will rest."

"Very well, call your witness."

"We call Frank Dalton."

Frank looked at John, as though to ask with his eyes, "Can he do that?"

"It's all right Frank, you'll do fine. I can call you as a witness later in our case."

O'Keefe said, in his high nasally voice, "Mr. Dalton, come around and be sworn."

Frank was sworn, took the stand and identified himself. Collier jumped straight to the point.

"Tell the ladies and gentlemen of the jury about your beans."

"They was the best beans God ever made."

Several jurors chuckled.

"Why do you say that?" laughed Mr. Collier.

"I know any farmer might say that about his beans, but these beans was exceptional and I'll tell you why. My nephew and brothers and I drained the Goni Swamp, down in the Pinishook Creek bottomland. One of my brothers died pullin' stumps out of that field. His heart just give out from the hard work. At least, that's what we think happened. We found him early one mornin' layin' next to a half pulled stump near the edge of the swamp."

"Objection, Your Honor, this is not responsive," said Collier. "We will be here all day if he doesn't answer the question asked."

"Sustained, just answer the question."

John rose and asked, "May I respond to that objection before we go on?"

"I've already ruled, move along."

"Yes, Your Honor, and I certainly respect your ruling. You always give everyone a fair chance to respond. I may have been a little slow with my response and you ruled before I could get it out of my mouth. My brain seems to be slow today. I ask that you not hold that against my client."

"Well, even though objections should be timely, I'll let you make your point."

"I believe that, if you consider the question asked by the learned Mr. Collier, Mr. Dalton was in fact answering the question. I am sure Mr. Collier had a reason for asking the question as worded, and I believe that Mr. Dalton should answer the question as worded."

"Well, we agree on that point, Mr. Brooks. The witness ought to answer the question as worded. Madam court reporter, please read the question back for me."

The court reporter thumbed though the roll of paper emanating from her stenograph machine until she came to the question. She cleared her throat and read, "Tell the ladies and gentlemen of the jury about your beans."

"They was the best beans God ever created."

"Why do you say that?"

When she finished reading, the court reporter paused.

"You see, Judge, he started talking about some swamp, not about beans," protested Collier.

Judge O'Keefe held up his hand and said, "Just a minute, Mr. Collier. I know something about beans and I see your point, Mr. Brooks. I think the witness was answering the question exactly as asked, which is what I have told him to do. I reverse myself. Objection overruled. Mr. Dalton, please tell the ladies and gentlemen of the jury about your beans."

"Yes sir, Your Honor. As I was saying, after we drained that swamp, we could see that the mucky mud in the bottom of the swamp was rich and fertile. When we broke the ground and planted soybeans, that was the first crop ever growed on that land since God created it. Every farmer knows that your first crop on a field will be the best crop you ever raise."

The jurors nodded in agreement, as did the judge.

"Judge, I object to this narrative."

"Overruled, Mr. Collier. Mr. Dalton is just answering your question. Continue telling us about your beans, sir."

"Yes sir, Your Honor. I will do just as you say." The jury chuckled. "Them beans popped out of the ground faster than any I ever seen. Didn't even need no fertilizer, the ground was so rich. The beans were up and growin' faster than the weeds could catch hold. Weeds never been on that land you know, because it had been covered with water, so the soybean seeds were the first seeds properly planted in that earth, except maybe whatever had sunk to the bottom of the swamp and hadn't spoiled. The soybeans grew so high, so fast that they shut everything else out."

"How did the beans shut out the weeds?" asked Judge O'Keefe, clearly intrigued.

"Well, as some of the jurors know, soybeans have a broad leaf that spreads out as it grows. Good plants will spread out and touch the leaves on the plant next to it, shadin' the ground. If you can get your beans to do that before the weeds catch hold, then the weeds will never grow, because they can't get no sun. Usually, if you have good beans, you kill the weeds one time, and then the beans take over. But, on the Goni Swamp field, the beans grew so fast that we never had to poison the weeds. I never saw nothing grow so fast as those beans.

"Then, when the bean pods began developing, you never saw the like of it. More beans on one plant than you would see on three good plants in any other field. They was the biggest, prettiest beans God ever made. If there was ever 200 bushel an acre beans, this was them. There's never been nothing like them before and I don't see how there will ever be anything like them again. You only get to plant a field for the first time once," said Frank, with a wistful look, his green eyes sparkling, his weathered old face turned slowly side to side.

"What happened to your beans?" asked Judge O'Keefe, almost breathlessly.

"Judge!" protested Collier.

"Oh, excuse me, Mr. Collier. You should ask the question."

Collier looked exasperated. He glanced at the jury. Every one of them had been eating out of his hand moments ago, now all they wanted to know was the answer to the judge's question. *Better to get it over with now*, thought Collier. *Otherwise they won't be paying attention to the point I want to make about the fence.*

"All right, Mr. Dalton, everyone wants to know what happened to your beans?"

"Whittaker's cows ate 'em," he said, with contempt. "They broke through the fence and ate our beans. Such a waste! It all but ruined us. We may lose our farm because of them cows."

"Objection! That is an appeal to sympathy!" Collier exclaimed.

"I don't need no sympathy, I need my beans," Frank said with stern determination. Several jurors nodded in agreement.

"Sustained." The judge turned to Frank, and in an authoritative voice said, "Mr. Dalton, if the lawyer objects, I want you to stop talking and let me rule on the objection. Do you understand what I am saying?"

"Yes sir, but I was just telling the truth. I wasn't asking for sympathy," said Frank as he glowered at Collier.

"Your Honor! I object," pled Collier, feeling things were spinning out of control.

"Yes, Mr. Collier. Let me see if I can explain this to Mr. Dalton." Turning once again to Frank, the Judge said, "Please wait for the lawyer to ask a question before you respond. I sustained the objection, and that means that you don't keep talking until the next question is asked. Do you understand?"

"I think I do, Your Honor. I am sorry. I never had to do this before. Beans don't ask me no trick questions."

The jurors laughed. When the laughter subsided, Judge O'Keefe turned back to face Collier. "All right, Mr. Collier, you may continue."

Shaking off the unfortunate turn of events, Collier decided it was time to lower the boom on this pesky little man. He had wandered away from the podium during the objections. He caught his breath and his confidence returned. He sauntered up to the podium and looked down at Frank, a smirk on his face. Collier knew that he had a killer cross-examination question that would put an end to this case, and he wanted to enjoy the moment. He glanced at the jury and imagined their reaction to the brilliant line of questions he was about to unleash. He knew in his heart of hearts that the jury would be impressed with his astuteness.

"Mr. Dalton, that fence runs right down the property line, doesn't it?"

"It does."

"So, that fence is just as much your fence as it is Whittaker's, isn't it?"

"I suppose you could say that, but I never claimed it."

Collier stood a little taller, then leaned over the podium to deliver the coup-de-gras.

"Since that fence was just as much your fence as it was Mr. Whittaker's, why didn't you maintain it better?"

"I don't need no fence."

"Why not?"

"Cause beans stay where I put 'em."

The jury erupted with laughter.

Encouraged by the jurors' response, Frank leaned forward and continued speaking to Collier as though he was explaining basic farm facts to an uninformed city school boy.

"There ain't never been no case of no beans eatin' no cows!"

Jurors were laughing so hard that they had difficulty staying in their chairs. They were in the moment. They loved the fact that this little Choctaw man was getting the best of a slick, big city lawyer and was even lecturing him. They hooted and laughed for a full minute as they slapped their thighs and nudged each other. Collier slinked back to his table, a beaten man. Whittaker was aghast.

When the laughter finally stopped, Judge O'Keefe asked, "Anything further, Mr. Collier?"

"No further questions."

"Your witness, Mr. Brooks."

"Thank you, Your Honor. Frank, how do you know that Whittaker's cows ate your beans?"

"I seen 'em. I went to the Goni field at daybreak one morning, and there they were. They had tromped down beans everywhere and they were eatin' away at my beans. They tromped more than they ate that time. We got them out of our field and back in Whittaker's. Then we told Whittaker what happened."

"What did he say?"

"He thanked me for fattening his cows."

"In your answer, you said, 'that time.' So, there was more than one time?"

"Yep. The second time I hollered at my brother to come quick, cause the cows were in the beans again. He hollered back, 'Oh no, déjà moo.'"

Jurors chuckled. Two or three smiled and shook their heads. One clapped. Another slapped his thigh.

"I didn't mean to make it sound like a laughin' matter, because it really is serious. That's just what my brother said. Anyway, Whittaker's cows got in our beans three times."

"How did they get in your field?"

"Whittaker's place is next to mine. He's a rancher and he's got a fence that runs down the property line. That first time, the fence was down. Looked like it had been cut."

"Why do you say that?"

"It was a clean break on all four strands of barbed-wire. That don't happen by accident."

"Objection," called Collier in a loud voice as he sprung from his seat. "Improper conclusion. Calls for expert opinion."

"Objection overruled. You can continue your answer."

"I wasn't there, so I can't say what happened. Anyway, me and my nephew and brother rounded them cows up and drove them back through the fence. They stomped as many beans going out as they did coming in. It was plum awful. Once they was out of the field, I looked back and it was a heart breaking site. I hadn't cried since I was a baby, 'til that day."

"Did you tell Whittaker the second time?"

"Yep. He come out there and said I shouldn't a let his cows get in my field." Incredulity dripped from Frank's voice. Jurors shook their heads with disgust.

"What happened next?"

"Weeds happened. Them cows broke the leaf cover, and weeds went crazy in the field. We did what we could to control the weeds and save the rest of the crop. It was a lot of work, but we figured that since the beans that survived were so productive, we could still have an A-okay year. That's what we thought until we found them cows in the Goni field a third time. Them cows liked my beans. It looked like the cows pushed against the fence until they found a weak spot and broke some posts. They hurt us bad that time. There was no way we could break even after that."

"What happened next?"

"It was déjà moo all over again. A week later, the fence was down again and they were back. That was the end of my Goni Swamp beans. The best beans God ever grew ended up in Whittaker's cows."

"Did you tell Whittaker?"

"Sure did. He was just all high and mighty and said I shouldn't a grown beans next to his cows."

"Object to the characterization of my client."

"Sustained," ruled Judge O'Keefe. "The jury will disregard the 'high and mighty' comment." Most jurors nodded in response.

"What did you lose?"

"Well, I lost all that work of clearing and planting, but what I really lost was the best production year the Goni field will ever have."

"What was the value of that crop?"

"Objection," shouted Collier. "Calls for speculation and calls for an expert opinion."

"The owner of property is entitled to state an opinion as to the value. And, Mr. Dalton, with his experience, would qualify as an expert in the value of beans."

"Not at 200 bushels an acre he doesn't!" responded Collier.

The judge grinned and jurors laughed, but the judge overruled the objection. "I will let him testify as to his opinion of the value. The jurors will decide the weight to give to the testimony."

"At harvest time, beans was selling for $15 a bushel. The Goni field had 40 acres of beans at 200 bushels an acre. With waste and unexpected losses, and bein' generous, say 150 bushels an acre. The jury knows I'm being generous to Mr. Whittaker. Even at 150 bushels an acre, that's $60,000. That would have paid all the cost of draining the swamp, clearing the field, plowin' and plantin' and harvestin' with plenty left over."

"Because the cows ate your beans, there were some harvest and other costs that you did not incur. How much would it have cost you to finish production of your beans and get them to market?"

"Most of our work was already done. We have access to good combine operators and we pay them by the hour. Maybe 4 or 5 hours to harvest, call it a full day, what with coming and going and gathering more beans than usual. $120 per hour for 8 hours is $960. Then, we would take them to market. That would cost another $500 to $1,000. Say $1,000. That means Whittaker's cows cost me $58,040. We kept his cows and took them to market. That's why he sued me. But, they fattened up on our beans, so it seemed right. Anyway, they brought $28,000. The money is being held in trust until this case is over. We ought to apply that to what Whittaker owes us, and he should pay the difference of $30,040."

"Whittaker claims that his cows would have been more valuable if some of them had been allowed to mate, and that you cost him his next season of cattle."

"Not true."

"Why not?"

"He didn't have no bulls. Just cows."

"He said he was going to use artificial insemination."

"What do you mean?"

"He would use a large hypodermic, like a big shot."

"No kidding?"

"No bull."

More jurors laughed.

"Huh. Well, he never told me he wanted to do that. Seems like another excuse not to pay for my beans, to me. And not a very good excuse I might add."

"Objection to his opinion!" shouted Collier as he quickly rose from his seat.

"Sustained," ruled Judge O'Keefe as Collier slowly returned to his seat. "The jury will disregard Mr. Dalton's opinion concerning Mr. Whittaker's excuse for not paying him for his beans."

Collier shot back up to his feet in exasperation.

"Yes, Mr. Collier?" asked Judge O'Keefe.

Collier hesitated, wondering whether he should call attention to the judge apparently saying that Whittaker's reason for not paying Dalton was merely an excuse. In exasperation, Collier returned to his seat. "Nothing, Your Honor."

John broke the tension building in the courtroom with his own announcement. "No further questions." John returned to his counsel table. Peter nodded to him and said, "Looks good right now."

Judge O'Keefe turned to Collier, "Anything further?"

"No, Your Honor."

"Mr. Brooks?" asked the Judge.

"We rest."

"That was certainly quick. Mr. Collier took all day, and you took ten minutes. Anything else, Mr. Collier?"

"We finally rest."

The jury was out ten minutes before returning a verdict in favor of Frank Dalton for $58,040.

Even though there was no obvious outward sign of emotion, it was obvious that every member of the Dalton family was elated, joyous, thankful and grateful. They all gathered around John and Frank. Everyone was congratulating Frank, who responded, "It wasn't me, it was God answering our prayer." Awesome said, "Well then, you and God did great, Uncle Frank."

"Yes, praise God."

Whittaker gathered his things and began to leave. He stepped over to John and Frank and said, "Enjoy yourselves, your victory will be short lived. Another surprise is on the way."

"What do you mean, Mr. Whittaker?" asked Frank.

"You'll see."

"I don't want no more trouble. Let this be the end."

"No. It's war you want. It's war you'll get."

"Collier, you need to take your client away from here."

Media gathered around Frank and his family to congratulate them and ask how they felt about the outcome. Sheriff Townsend waded into the knot of people and approached Awesome from behind. Before anyone realized what was happening, Townsend handcuffed Awesome.

"You're under arrest for the murder of Sheriff Rainey, Skeeter Munson, William Bryan and Doug Fowler. You belong to me now."

"What do you mean? I would never hurt Sheriff Rainey. And he already dismissed those other charges!"

"Yeah, well, there's a new Sheriff in town, and I ain't letting any murderin' Indian run the streets to gather more scalps. Are you coming with me voluntarily, or am I going to have to bust you up? I just hope you make me bust you up."

"Sheriff," said Brooks, "he will go with you peacefully."

"Back off, Brooks," yelled Townsend, "or I'll take you in, too!"

* * *

Gregory Lincoln placed a call as the boat puttered into the harbor. When Shawn Dalton answered Gregory said simply, "I've got it."

"Great! You're worth every penny. I can't tell you how proud I am of you. I need to get it from you so that I can give it to my Aztec expert."

"What kind of sucker do you take me for?"

"What do you mean?"

"This treasure chest is not leaving my possession. If you want someone to look at it, he'll have to come to me."

"Gregory! I can't believe you would think that way of me. Haven't I shot straight with you?"

"I'm no fool. This chest is not leaving my sight."

After a pause, Dalton said, "Okay. Take the next flight to Dallas. I'll get everyone together and meet you at the airport."

"Where?"

"There are conference rooms in the terminal. I'll book one today for our use first thing in the morning."

"Now you're talking!"

* * *

"Have you heard from Jackson yet?" asked Ted as he took a seat with Skip at their usual table at the Trading Post.

"Not yet," said Skip, excitement in his voice. "But we could hear from him anytime! Can you imagine, we might be about to find the biggest treasure in history?"

"Well, that's a long shot," Ted responded. "First, they have to find the right wreck. Then, they have to find the chest somewhere on or near the wreck. And, even if they find the right wreck, the chest may not be there."

"Don't be such a persimmon."

Ted laughed and shook his head. "You mean pessimist. I bet Claire will be one of the first to hear from Jackson."

"You think?"

"Why not? They've been doing research on the treasure that helped Jackson get this far."

"You're right," said Skip. "I think I'm going to be hanging out at the library until we hear from Jackson."

"I don't blame you. It is pretty exciting."

"Yeah. I've been looking into flights to southern Mexico," said Skip. "That's where they think the treasure is."

"You think that's a good idea?"

"Sure do. As soon as I hear the location, I'm going. Jackson will go there too and he is going to need my help."

Ted laughed again.

"Why are you laughing?"

"Skip. You're right. I'm sure Jackson will be glad to see you."

That was all the encouragement Skip needed. Later that night he studied a map of southern Mexico, imagining where the treasure might be and which airport might be closest. He knew from the history given at the library that the Aztec hero Moc carried the treasure many days south from what is now Mexico City. Skip's finger stopped on the map at the city Tuxtla Gutierrez.

"Tux t la Gut tier r ez. That sounds like the perfect place to hide a treasure of golden tears. Want a ton a golden tears, got 'em herez. Spanish ain't so hard to understand. I got this." He booked a flight leaving the next day. "I'll have Claire call me with the exact location to me as soon as she knows. At least I'll be nearby when Jackson needs me."

Chapter 46

Confusion reigned at the courthouse after the verdict, followed by the unexpected arrest of Awesome. It was several minutes before John and Peter could disentangle themselves from the crowd of reporters asking, "Were you surprised by the arrest of Mr. Dawson? What are you going to do next? Did he do it? Is he guilty? Will there be a race war?"

Without answering their questions, John turned to Peter. "I've got to see Awesome in the jail for a few minutes. I need to look him in the eye and ask him a few questions. Will you gather all of our papers from the trial and get them to the car? Then walk over to see the court administrator and see if you can find out if a preliminary hearing has been scheduled. We want one as soon as possible. I'll subpoena the boot print evidence and that should take care of three of the charges."

"Sure, boss."

After visiting Awesome in the jail, John and Peter climbed into the car for the return trip to Jackson.

"Did you find out about the preliminary?"

"Yes, sir. Monday at 9 a.m."

John was quiet for a long moment, weighing options. "Peter, I'm really going to rely on you a lot. I need you to really step up. I am counting on you."

Peter looked sheepish, so John decided he needed encouragement.

"I know you can do it. In the past, I counted on Karen and Jackson, but they aren't here. I know you don't have the experience or training they have, but you're smart, honest and loyal. I'm going to need you to turn your brain on completely, think, think, think! We've got to think fast and work fast to pull off what I have in mind. I believe we can catch the new sheriff by surprise at the preliminary hearing. Maybe we can put an end to this foolishness about Awesome killing Sheriff Rainey, once and for all."

Peter smiled and nodded.

John continued. "Together, we'll make an unbeatable team. It's going to take a good bit of time to do all we have to do. I'm glad that we have until Monday. Even that is too little time, unless everything falls into place. In addition to the boot evidence, I want to subpoena each person that Sheriff Rainey spoke with, including that girl in the clerk's office. I'll see if I can arrange for you to serve the subpoenas."

"Why do you want to subpoena all those people?"

John explained his reasoning to Peter as he drove Peter home. A wave of exhaustion swept over John as he drove home after dropping Peter off. His mind was so focused on today's events that he did not check his messages. "I'll check them tomorrow."

* * *

Hoover's phone rang.

"Peter, good to hear from you my boy. Where have you been? You better have something good to tell me." After a pause, Hoover said, "Interesting. Tell me his whole plan. You may have just won yourself a big bonus, son."

After he hung up, Hoover considered the lay of the land. "I see a lot of opportunity here," he said as he dialed a number. "Sheriff Townsend, I have some information you may find interesting."

* * *

It was dark thirty when Robert finally cut the anchor line, leaving about ten feet attached to the raft in case more rope was needed. They unfurled the sail, set the rudder, adjusted the sheet and watched as the sail filled. The raft slowly began to move, then picked up speed leaving a wake. Everyone cheered, "We did it!"

They celebrated by passing around a water jug and opening cans of biscuits and Spam.

"I didn't know Spam could taste so good," said Natalia.

After a few minutes, Jimmy shook his head and observed, "What a loss, a golden chest, right in our hands, gone. It must have been worth a fortune!"

"Easy come, easy go," said Neil.

"I'm a little hazy on the easy part," added Jake.

Everyone laughed, but the chuckles faded away quickly as the realization of their loss sank in.

"Not everything is lost," said Robert.

"Yeah, we're alive," said Jake.

"Yes, but, the real value of the artifact was that it might prove the existence and location of a great treasure trove," observed Robert.

"Yeah, the Hummingbird Hoard that the archeologists have been talking about," said Jackson. "Fever for that treasure killed a lot of people and it almost killed us."

"Don't celebrate too soon. We ain't out of the woods, or the waves, yet," said Neil.

"No, I mean we haven't lost the treasure!" urged Robert with excitement in his voice as he held up his camera. "The lid was covered with drawings inside and out with some kind of glyphs. It's a map to the treasure!"

"And we've got a hundred pictures of it, from every angle," Neil said as he nodded and held up his camera.

"Yea," said Jackson. Everyone responded with "Yea!"

"I don't understand why Maximilian didn't go get the treasure?" asked Natalia.

Jackson responded, "Our researchers at the library said he received proof of the treasure, which would be on the lid of this chest, while he was losing his war with Juarez's army. He hoped that the chest would encourage the King of France to send his army back to Mexico."

"I see," said Jimmy, "If they wouldn't fight to save Max, maybe they would fight for a treasure trove."

"Exactly, but months later, he was trapped. Then, after a 71 day siege, he was captured and executed."

"And the chest never made it to France," said Natalia with a husky voice and a distant look. Then, as the idea sank in, she shouted, "It's true! There really is a huge treasure never found. Still hidden. And we have the key to its location!"

"And so does Gregory Lincoln," said Jackson.

* * *

Sandy Storm received a call from her producer. "Charles, good to hear from you. Things are really getting interesting down here. I'm so glad you sent me."

"Well, I'm beginning to wonder if my trust in you was misplaced. I think I sent the wrong person for this job."

Sandy was flabbergasted, utterly speechless for a moment. "Charles, whatever are you talking about? I'm in the middle of the biggest story in the news, and we were the first on the scene!"

"Yes, you were the first on the scene, but why is everyone else getting all the footage and all the ratings?"

"What are you talking about?"

"That's just what I thought. You're too close to the situation to see what everyone else sees. Your hormones are suppressing your journalistic instincts. Effective immediately, I am replacing you with a more seasoned reporter."

"Now, just a minute, Charles. You can't do this."

"I just did."

"Why?"

"Every other network is piling on stories about a pending race war between Native Americans and Mississippi rednecks. Everyone sees it but you."

"Charles, there is no animosity between the local white residents and the Native Americans. They get along fine in spite of the murders."

"If that were true why haven't you reported it? Everyone else is reporting bad blood, threats and protests. That's the story and you're missing it."

"Okay, Charles. I'll grant you that I haven't pursued that angle."

"No, you've been too busy promoting your boyfriend lawyer."

"Charles! You've gone too far!"

"No, I've gone too far waiting on you. I have a network to run."

"I'll tell you what, Charles. Leave me on the story and tomorrow you will have all you want about a budding race war. I'll have the scoop of the century. Again."

"Now, that's my girl. That's the reporter I know. Don't let me down."

"Never."

Chapter 47

The moonless Caribbean sky featured the Milky Way and more stars than could be counted. Starlight played on the waves, creating strange flitting highlights against the black ocean. Jimmy watched the sail as he held his makeshift tiller. He set a course on a star that seemed to be in the right direction according to the compass and constantly adjusted the rudder and the trim of the sail to stay on course with as little drift and wobble as he could manage.

"How do you know where we are going in the dark?" asked Natalia.

"Well, we are lucky enough to have a compass, but it is hard to read in the dark even though the needle glows. I used it to get a direction and then I picked a star that I could follow. That way I don't have to use the compass all the time."

"That was smart."

"Not necessarily, because most stars will seem to move during the night due to the rotation of the Earth. So, I go back to the compass from time to time to make sure we're still on course. That's why the North Star is so useful to sailors. It's always in the same place."

"Which one is the North Star?"

Jimmy pointed. "If you can find the Big Dipper, you can find the North Star. Those two stars on the edge of the Dipper line up with the North Star."

"Oh! I see!"

People began to drift off to sleep. Natalia curled up under Jackson's arm and fell asleep almost as soon as she closed her eyes. Robert sat next to Jimmy to keep him company and gazed at the marvelous night sky.

"Don't we have an awesome and wonderful God? He created this spectacular universe and allows us to share it!" said Robert.

"How can you say that? Here we are, stranded on a life raft in mortal danger, you've lost your boat, and we've lost the treasure of a lifetime!" exclaimed Jackson. "What kind of wonderful God would allow Gregory to exist? If God is so great, why do we have to suffer so?"

"You've had some terrible tragedies in your life," observed Robert.

"Haven't we all? Isn't that part of our miserable human existence?"

"You sound like me. I spent many years angry with God. I asked the same questions. Then, after more disappointments and setbacks than I care to remember, I finally managed to achieve the perfect career doing what I love most. Then, I came down with cancer."

"I'm sorry," Jackson said, pausing before continuing. "I don't know what to say."

"It's okay. I realized that I had a cancer far worse than the one attacking my body. I had cancer of the soul eating away at me, every bit as much as the physical cancer that ate away at my body."

"What did you do about it?"

"I sought refuge in every form of sin, every excess, anything to cover my anger and my pain."

"And?"

"I came to the end of myself, and said, 'God, I'm just a man. I don't understand what you're doing to me. I'm wrong, you're right. Heal me. Please.'"

"Are you saying he healed you? A miracle faith healing?"

"Yes."

"Excuse my skepticism, but I'd like to see the proof," said Jackson as Natalia stirred in his lap.

"I'm the proof."

"That's always the case with Christians. They never have real proof. Just subjective opinion."

"I'm dying of cancer, Jackson."

"What? I thought you said you are the proof! I thought you said you were healed!"

"I am. God may or may not choose to heal my cancer. He can if it fits His plan. But He has already healed me in a much more important way. He healed my spiritual cancer. I have peace. I have joy. I turned to Him like the prodigal son, and He ran to me, just like the father does in the parable Jesus told. For the first time in my memory, I feel complete, normal, whole, yet I'm mortally sick."

"I understand. You've come to terms with your mortality."

"No. I've come to terms with my immortality."

"This is too much. You sound like my partner. Next, you'll be telling me that Jesus is the only way."

"The truth will set you free. Jesus set me free."

"Well. I'm glad for you, but what's true for you isn't true for me."

"The truth is the same for everyone," said Jake.

"I thought you were asleep."

"I was resting my eyes, but this is a small boat. I couldn't help hear what was being said, because I have cancer, too."

"What?"

"Yep. That's one reason why I'm on leave from the Air Guard. I came here to clear my head and get some fresh air before the next round of chemo."

"Do you believe Robert's talk about joy and peace?"

"I sure do, brother. I have it too, and Robert is right. Jesus is the way, the truth and the life. No one comes to the Father except through Him."

Jackson shook his head and waved his hand to indicate he had heard enough. Natalia stretched and whispered, "Chu don't believe?"

"Of course not."

"Well, maybe chu should. I do. None of us know when our time is up. Better be ready." She rolled over and fell back asleep.

Jackson marveled at how easily she fell asleep. He pondered the improbability of his conversations with Robert, Jake and Natalia and thought to himself, 'What are the odds of being on a life raft in the middle of the ocean with two men dying of cancer? And both of them want to witness to me.'

"There's lightning on the horizon," said Jimmy.

"Great. There's your God at work, rewarding you for your faith. Huh?" said Jackson.

"Yes. He'll do whatever it takes to reach you. Even bring storms into your life. But you still have to do your part," said Robert.

"Yeah, yeah. I've heard this nonsense before. Let's change the subject."

* * *

The rain was cold and hard, so hard it stung. The little raft was tossed between waves. It slid sickeningly down monstrous valleys and sloshed underneath the next wave, almost to the point of being swamped, only to be driven by the wind up the surface of the next towering wave and down again, repeating the cycle. Jimmy tried to save the sail by taking it down, but the sail and the mast washed away, along with the keel and the rudder. Almost everything on board had been thrown out, either by the waves, or by the occupants in an effort to keep the raft from swamping. Neil clung to a solitary water jug. Robert's camera still hung from his neck. Everything else was gone. They were beyond seasick. Each prayed for the agony to end.

In utter darkness the raft struck something. Forward progress slowed dramatically. Some great force had slammed on the brakes. But the relentless waves didn't stop. The next wave scooped up the back of the little raft and flipped it over violently, tossing everyone onto a sandy beach. Jackson looked around him. To his relief, everyone was alive!

Coughing and sputtering, Natalia said to Jackson, "Like I said, chu really know how to show a girl a good time!"

Chapter 48

Late in the day, Shawn Dalton texted the conference room location to Gregory, who took the last flight of the day from the Dominican Republic to Dallas. He was determined to be the first person at the morning meeting. He did his homework, studying the location of the conference room and found the best vantage points for observation. With the chest safely in his backpack, he watched as Dalton and his entourage arrived. It was Shawn Dalton, three toughs, a tall, thin-framed nervous man, and a portly fellow carrying a briefcase. One of the three toughs walked with a slight limp.

Gregory waited. He studied each face and looked for any additional security that might be loitering, waiting for his arrival. He didn't want to be surprised by an ambush when he left the meeting. Gregory suspected that Dalton had no intention of sharing the treasure. Confident that Dalton's entire group was in the conference room, he made his appearance.

"Mr. Lincoln," said Dalton. "It's so good to meet a man who knows what he wants and knows how to get it. Please join us. Help yourself to some coffee and have a seat."

Gregory glanced at each person in the room before returning his gaze to Shawn Dalton, a tall man, perhaps 70. His cheeks sagged, forming a permanent scowl. His dark eyes were impenetrable. Gregory felt he had found someone he could understand. Someone like himself. He didn't trust him at all. Without taking a seat, he slipped the backpack off his shoulders and removed the chest. Everyone in the room gasped. The thin, nervous man rushed forward for a closer look. Gregory checked his forward progress with a stiff arm to the chest.

"Meet Professor Timmons," said Dalton. "He's an expert in Pre-Columbian Civilizations. He can tell us if your chest is real. He tells me he should be able to read the inscriptions."

"Oh, I am almost certain it is real! And we have learned so much in the last few years about the written language of the Mayans and even the Aztecs that I should be able to decipher this."

"We need to reach an understanding," said Gregory. "When we leave this conference room, I will be going to locate and secure the treasure. You can send your men with me," motioning to Jason, Clint and McKenzie. "Once it's secured, we'll need your help, your contacts and your resources to get the treasure out of Mexico, or wherever it is." Lincoln looked at the portly man carrying the briefcase. "My guess is that's your job."

"Very perceptive. Meet my good friend, Eduardo Lopez. International law and Mexican law are his specialties." Lopez offered Gregory his hand, which Gregory ignored.

"One thing is non-negotiable: I will be in charge of finding the treasure."

Dalton smiled and suppressed a chuckle. "What are your qualifications to lead such a quest?"

"How long have you been looking for this clue?" asked Gregory, indicating the chest. "In a century and a half, how many people have searched without success? I've been on this quest for a few days, and I've made the first significant find. More importantly, I will do anything, and I mean anything, to secure this treasure for you and for me."

Dalton's eyes fell from Lincoln to the golden chest. Four generations of Daltons had dreamed of finding Maximilian's treasure. Some had died in the quest. Some had killed. He was about to succeed. Gold fever infected him. Beads of sweat appeared on his brow. He dabbed his forehead with a handkerchief. "I believe you and I understand each other. We can reach a mutually beneficial agreement."

"I want 20 percent of the net, plus a few particular trinkets. And, I want a say in what is net and what is gross."

"You are a wise man. You understand the need we have for one another, and that there will be many costs involved in getting the treasure out of Mexico. How about 10% of gross plus your trinkets? That way you don't have to concern yourself with my costs."

"Deal."

"I have every reason to believe that we are not the only ones looking for this treasure, so time is of essence," observed Dalton.

"Yeah, that lawyer, Bradley, he's hot on the trail," said McKenzie. Worry etched his face. Jason cast an uncomfortable glance at Clint.

"What? Do I detect fear at the mention of his name?" asked Gregory as he laughed.

"Respect," said McKenzie. "He is resourceful and determined."

"Don't worry about Bradley. He ran out of resources when our paths crossed yesterday."

"You took out Bradley?" asked Clint.

"I take out anyone who crosses me."

"Bradley was not the only competition," said Dalton. "I know that several groups are on the trail, but now that we have the map, we have all the advantages. For now."

"Then, let's not waste time," said Gregory.

"My sentiments precisely," responded Dalton. In less than an hour, Professor Timmons deciphered the location of the Hummingbird Hoard.

"There is one catch," said Timmons.

"What is that?" demanded Dalton.

"There may be traps. I need to see any inscriptions on or near the entrance. That should give me the information I need. You can text pictures of those to me."

"Why don't I just blast my way in?" asked Gregory.

"Maybe you can. But you might trigger the booby-traps. Sink holes, landslides, falling boulders, who knows?"

"That settles it. You're coming with me," said Gregory.

"What? No! I can't." Although he protested, Timmons knew in his heart of hearts that there was no way he would miss this opportunity. Already, his mind was calculating how he might find a way to claim the glory and fortune for himself.

Two hours later, Gregory and his four new companions, McKenzie, Jason, Clint and Professor Timmons, were on a flight from Dallas to Mexico City, where they would then catch a flight to Tuxtla Gutierrez in the State of Chiapas, Mexico.

That morning, Skip caught a flight from Jackson to Dallas, connecting to a flight to Mexico City, where he would then catch a flight to Tuxtla Gutierrez. He sensed he was beginning a great adventure. The flight to Mexico City was crowded. Skip didn't notice Gregory until the plane was about to land. When he saw Gregory, his sense of adventure was replaced by an urgent need to find the bathroom. "Yikes!" he said to himself. "I've got to take invasive action!"

* * *

Jackson was able to phone John by noon Thursday. Uncharacteristically, John had not yet made it to the office. Weariness caused him to sleep late, and he made a couple of stops on the way to the office.

"Jackson! How's the relaxation going? Are you making progress with the book?"

"Listen, John, I've got a lot to tell you. You won't believe all that's happened."

"I've got quite an update to give you too, but first, tell me what's going on with you."

"We found, it, John. We found the treasure, or part of it. A spectacular golden chest with pictures and engravings, inside and out, with big tear drop shaped golden nuggets inside."

"Wow!"

"We think it reveals the location of the fabled Hummingbird Hoard."

"Congratulations! I can't wait to see it!"

"It was stolen from us."

"What? Good grief! I'm sorry. How did that happen?"

"The how is what I want to know. You won't believe who stole it."

"Who?"

"Gregory Lincoln."

"What?"

"You heard right. Gregory Lincoln."

"How did he find you?"

"That's what I want to know."

"Did he follow you to Punta Cana?"

"I guess he could have, but he found us at the dive site, 10 miles off shore. We didn't see any boat following us. We didn't see any boat at all near us when we were diving. Yet, when we came up with the chest, he was there waiting for us!"

"So, he had to know when and where you were diving."

"That's right."

"Is there anyone in your group who could have told him?"

"It's possible. I doubt it, because Gregory left us all to die. He sank our boat and filled the water around us with chum."

"Jackson! Was anyone hurt?"

"Miraculously, we all made it back to shore, with a lot of improvisation and luck."

"I've got to hear the full story when you have time to tell it."

"Yeah. I look forward to seeing you, if I live long enough. But I needed you to know that Lincoln found me here. And he promised to kill you, me, Skip and…"

"Karen."

"Yeah, Karen."

"Thanks, Jackson."

"John, I've got to go. Things are happening fast. Be careful, really careful. We'll talk soon."

"Sure, catch you later." After hanging up, John whispered, "I never got to tell Jackson about the arrest of Awesome and the verdict in the bean case!" He stared out the window for a moment and stroked his chin. "Gregory Lincoln. How did he find Jackson in Punta Cana?"

John dialed Jennifer Wolfe's number. "Jennifer! Glad you answered."

"John, I've been trying to get you. Why haven't you called?"

"I've been overwhelmed with problems, and I've got one I need your help on."

"Your problems may be a lot bigger than you think. I need to talk with you alone. Where no one can overhear us. We need to meet now!"

"Can you meet me at the office?"

"No, not the office. Meet me at Cups on Lakeland."

"On my way."

* * *

Jackson's next call was to Frances at Poetry Resort.

"Mr. Bradley, we haff been worried about chu. Chu did not return on time. We called and no one knew where dhur boat was. Es everything all right?"

"Yes, everything is all right now, but we did have a bit of a scare. Can you arrange transportation for us to the airport in Santo Domingo?"

"Yes. Chu won't be coming back to Poetry? Surely, your vacation is not over."

"I think I've had enough vacation. I just need a ride for my friends and me. There are seven of us."

"Okay. No problem. Tell me where chu are."

When Jackson gave Frances his location, Frances said, "Oh, Mr. Bradley, that is a long way. It may take a few hours."

"It's okay. There is a little open air, thatched roof bar here. We'll have a few drinks and get something to eat. In fact, we'll probably all take a nap. I don't remember the last time any of us slept."

"What happened, señor?"

"We were shipwrecked."

"Oh, mercy. Lo siento. Es everyone all right?"

"Yes. Just arrange to take us to the airport please."

"Es no problemo!"

Jackson returned to Pablo's Beach Bar, where Robert was passing around Tequila shots.

"We have a lot to celebrate," said Jimmy as he took a shot.

"Yeah, we're alive!" shouted Jake.

"I didn't lose a single diver!" shouted Robert.

Wrapping his arms around the group and leaning in, so that only the seven Adventure Divers could hear his voice, Neil nodded at Robert's camera and said, "And we have the map to a priceless treasure! We're all millionaires!"

"Yay!" everyone shouted.

Natalia threw her arms around Jackson's neck, squeezed him tight, and kissed him on his lips. Jackson was so surprised that he didn't respond at first. After only a moment, he leaned into the kiss and held her close.

"Woo hoo! Look at Jackson and Natalia!" exclaimed Jake.

"Atta boy, Jackson!"

"Looks like Jackson's got a girlfriend!"

Natalia broke into a wide grin and said, "Looks like Natalia has a man!"

When they finally parted, Natalia smiled, and said, "Like I said, chu really know how to show a girl a good time, Jackson Bradley." Natalia stepped to the bar and asked for the phone. After she hung up, she spoke to the bartender for a moment.

After a second round of drinks, the excitement and lack of sleep began to take hold. One by one the Adventure Divers leaned back in their chairs and dozed off. Natalia and Jackson settled into a corner table, with Natalia curled up against Jackson's chest. Jackson looked at the beautiful woman asleep in his arm, and gazed, one by one, at each of his dive buddies. "I have never felt so alive, so satisfied, so happy," he thought as he fell asleep.

Chapter 49

Gregory and his companions arrived in Tuxtla Gutierrez as Jackson fell asleep at Pablo's Beach Bar. They spent the afternoon in Tuxtla using Dalton's money to acquire a truck, camping equipment, maps and supplies. Skip spent the day improvising various disguises, partially hiding behind palms, columns, furniture and people while he struggled to decide if he would follow Gregory or run for his life. While his ultimate decision remained in doubt, he kept Gregory in sight.

"It's not too far to the valley, but we have to cross a mountain ridge," said Timmons. "I don't know the quality of the roads, but we may be able to get there in a few hours."

"We'll start first thing in the morning," said Gregory. He stepped close to Timmons and scowled. So close Timmons could feel his breath. "In the meantime, I don't want you out of my sight."

Timmons shivered and thought to himself, *What have I gotten myself into?*

Skip, was nearby pretending to read a newspaper. He heard every word. He shivered and thought to himself, *What have I gotten myself into?* Skip decided to put some distance between Gregory and himself. He stood, leaving the newspaper in front of his face and joined a group of people strolling away from Gregory and Timmons. The movement caught Gregory's attention. He glanced at Skip, returned his menacing gaze back to Timmons, and then did a double take.

"What, what is it?" asked a shivering Timmons when he saw confusion on Lincoln's face.

"It's nothing. For a second, I thought I saw someone I knew. But I couldn't have. What are the odds?"

Grateful for the change of subject, Timmons said, "Seeing someone you know here? Pretty remote I would say."

* * *

Jennifer Wolfe ordered two large Americanos with cream and met John at the door when he arrived at Cups. "I need the caffeine, and you're going to need it."

"Thanks for the Americano. Tell me what's going on?"

Jennifer motioned John to follow her into the cigar room, which was empty. She already had a table ready.

"You have a mole. You have spyware on your computer. It's not an accident. It's purposeful."

John glanced down for a moment, and then fixed his eyes on Jennifer. "You think it's Peter. Why, and who do you think he's working for?"

"You're quick. That's one of the many reasons I love working for you." Jennifer explained what she discovered and what she had done.

"So, your own spyware will be downloaded on the culprit's computer at 2 this morning, and after 2 a.m. the next day you might know who they are."

"That's right. If they don't change their protocol between now and then, I should have them."

"Why would they change their protocol?"

"If they find my spyware would be one reason."

"What's another?"

"I imagine good spies change protocol regularly to avoid incidental discovery."

"And you believe this was loaded from a jump drive?"

"That's right. It doesn't have some of the characteristics of typical Internet acquired viruses. The most likely origin is a jump drive."

"And the most likely suspect is Peter."

"Right."

"If so, he would be working for someone."

"Who do you think?"

"There is a long potential cast of characters. Shawn Dalton. His lawyer. Mr. Whittaker. Someone in the media. Gregory Lincoln."

"Lincoln?"

"Yeah. He found Jackson in the middle of the Caribbean and tried to kill him."

"What?"

John filled her in with what Jackson had told him.

"Sounds like it could be Lincoln," Jennifer agreed.

"Peter knows my plans for the upcoming hearing concerning Awesome. Since I don't know if I can trust him, I've got to make some adjustments."

"I knew you would say that. I've already called Mitch to see if the rugby team has anyone who could help you. He has eleven volunteers who can give you two days."

"Eleven! That's unbelievable!"

"They enjoyed working on the Vampire Defense so much, they couldn't wait to help you again."

"Awesome. I will send them to Neshoba County to interview witnesses. Eleven Jackson Rugby players can cover the whole county in two days. I've got a list of witnesses to start with, and then they can follow the clues wherever they lead. I would have used Peter for some of this, but not now."

"Oh, and Crush is available to help at the hearing, but he'll be late getting there."

"Jennifer, you are amazing."

"Thanks. I just asked myself, what would Karen do?"

* * *

Once everyone was asleep, Natalia slowly unfolded from Jackson's arms. She stood over him for a moment and watched him breathe, noting the smile on his face.

"You are a sweet fool," she whispered. She glanced at the bartender, who nodded to her. Then she moved quietly like a cat across the room, lifted the camera from Robert's table and stepped to the bar, her finger over her lips.

"Let them sleep as long as they can," she whispered as he handed her the keys to his car. "Gracias!"

"Oh, thank you! The payment for the car was very generous. It came a little while ago, just as you said it would."

Natalia smiled again, slipped out of the bar and sashayed across the gravel and oyster shell lot to a car parked next to thick bushes. She opened the door and started to climb in when she had a strange, unfamiliar feeling. She hesitated, looked back at the thatch hut bar, and then at the camera at her side. Contained in that camera was the key to the quest of her lifetime. She had sworn to find it. So many depended on her. Yet, she could not climb into the car. She had done everything asked of her.

"This is wrong," she said to herself as she felt something deep inside, tugging her back toward the hut. "I can't do it this way. God help me."

She sighed, closed the door, and turned back to the hut.

"Are my eyes deceiving me?" asked an all too familiar voice from somewhere behind her. "Can it be that Natalia has developed a conscience?"

"Antoine!"

Before she could utter another word, a firm hand was over her mouth. Eyes wide, she struggled, but the man who held her was too strong. She tried to scream. Maybe she could warn the others. But his hand was so large and firm that not a sound came out. As they drug her away she heard de Sada say, "Once again I find you to be a very useful and resourceful young lady."

241

One of his henchmen asked, "What do you want me to do with her friends?"

"Friends! Natalia has no friends. Let them sleep it off. They are inconsequential now. Let them believe that Natalia stole their map, which of course she did. Take the car she was about to use."

"Si."

"I will arrange another little surprise for them when they wake."

* * *

"Your former boss is back in the news," said Backhoe as he stepped into the office.

"Yes, I know. His girlfriend sees to it that he has wall to wall coverage."

"You mean Sandy Storm?" asked Backhoe, knowing the answer. "I saw her at the courthouse yesterday. She did seem to be fawning over him when he won that fence case for the Daltons. But that was followed by the dramatic arrest of Awesome. The timing of that is suspect. Like it was made for TV ratings."

"This is all so confusing. I'm really glad the Daltons won, and I am sad about Awesome, but I don't want to hear about John and Sandy. If I think about all that's going on, I'll be an emotional basketcase. It's just too much."

Backhoe smiled and kissed Karen on the cheek. "I'm sorry, Karen. I shouldn't have brought it up. I have never been happier and my office has never run better. I'm so glad you're with me."

Karen smiled. "It's nice to be appreciated."

"I would really like to show you my appreciation in a much more meaningful way."

"I know, Backhoe. Thank you, but I'm just not ready."

Backhoe detected Karen's sudden change in mood. The room temperature seemed to have decreased. "Are we still on for tonight?"

"Of course. Your place at 7, I'll bring the dessert."

"I like the sound of that!"

Backhoe glanced out the window of his office. He was so startled that he sucked in air. If he had been a smaller man it would have been a gasp. "I can't believe what I am seeing."

"What?" asked Karen as she rushed to the window. A small parade of 8 men dressed in hoods and capes were marching around the courthouse. Half a dozen members of Skeeter's family followed them, carrying signs, saying 'Justice' and 'Make Good Indians.' They chanted, "Justice, Justice, Make Good Indians!" When they tired of that shout, they chanted, "Scalp Him, Scalp Him, Scalp That Murderin' Indian!"

"The Klan! I can't believe they're here. I thought they were extinct!" said Karen.

"Apparently not," said Backhoe.

"Look at all the television cameras. That's Sandy on the street with them."

"This is all we need, with national news looking to stereotype us. Just imagine what the news will be tonight."

* * *

Robert was the first to wake. His first instinct was to check each of the divers in his care. Only Natalia was missing. He glanced toward the banos, assuming she was there. But he felt something was wrong. Then he noticed his camera was missing. He stood so quickly that his chair fell over backward. Everyone woke with a start.

"Where's Natalia?"

Jackson looked around and said, "She must be in the bathroom."

Robert knocked on the bathroom door. No answer. He went inside and returned a moment later, saying, "Not there."

"What's the matter?" asked Jake.

"The camera is missing, and so is Natalia."

A wave of nausea swept over Jackson. He felt dizzy, flush, foolish. "She couldn't have taken it."

Robert turned to the bartender. "Where is the girl who was with us?"

"She left, maybe an hour ago. Maybe more."

"Why didn't you stop her?" asked Jackson.

"What you mean? I no stop her if she wants to go. That is up to her."

Jackson collapsed into his chair. "I knew she was too good to be true! I am so sorry. I've lost a girlfriend and you've lost a priceless treasure."

"It's okay, Jackson," said Neil. "She was never really your girl-friend."

"Yeah, I feel like a fool. I am a fool."

"We've all been fools for women before. You're better off without her," said Neil in the best consoling voice he could muster.

"Maybe so, but most of us don't lose a beautiful girl and a vast treasure at the same time."

"Not so fast my friend," said Neil in a reassuring voice. "We haven't lost the treasure yet."

"What do you mean?" asked everyone at once.

Neil unzipped his pocket and produced a watertight baggy containing a memory card. "I still have my copy of the pictures!"

* * *

"How did chu find me?"

"My men have been busy traveling the coast, offering rewards. Everyone was looking for you. I've been so worried. I was so relieved to hear that you were all right," said de Sada with feigned concern.

Natalia stared at the passing landscape through the window of the Mercedes. "What will chu do with me?"

De Sada laughed. "Several things come to mind, my dear," he said with a leer, "but for now, I suppose it will be amusing to bring you with me."

"And where are we going?"

"According to the Minister of Antiquities, who happens to be on the family payroll, we should be in the Valley of the Hummingbirds by this time tomorrow."

"Sounds lovely. I just wish I were going there with someone else."

"Perhaps with your friend from Mississippi? Mr. Bradley?"

"Si."

"Well, he has been very helpful. I do appreciate his efforts, but I have no further use of him. Neither do you, my dear. There is little he can do, inebriated as he is in a Dominican beach bar, with no transportation and no clue where to go next."

"I chust wish he knew it was chu, not me, who stoled his camera."

"Oh no you don't. You can't put the blame on me. You took the camera, not me. I will see to it that the camera is returned to its proper owner, after all proper efforts are made to make sure that all proprietary information has been removed. And, I had a little surprise waiting for Mr. Bradley when he awoke."

"Chu did not hurt him!"

"No, just insurance, to cover all contingencies. Our trail will be cold long before he can disentangle himself enough to follow us. By then, he will be grateful just to be able to go home."

"Don't chu dare harm him."

"My, my, I had no idea you could actually have feelings for anyone."

After a moment of silence, Natalia changed the subject. "Just why are we going to this Hummingbirds Valley?"

"As if you didn't know. I uploaded the pictures that you stole from Mr. Bradley and sent them to our Minister friend. He was quickly able to direct to me the location identified by the chest lid in the photos, a place fittingly called Hummingbird Valley."

"Why do you say the name is fitting?"

"It's the perfect place for the lost Hummingbird Hoard. My family has been searching for the Hummingbird Hoard and the fabled Golden Tears, Sun Drops, since my foolish ancestor lost it."

"You mean, Maximilian?"

"Yes, very perceptive of you. How did you guess?"

"I do my homework. I know you are a Habsburg, like Maximilian. I know you and your family would love to be in power again. And, I know you are dabbling in the dark arts of Tlaloc worship."

"What do you know of Tlaloc worship?"

"I know it is evil, satanic and dangerous. I know it involves ripping the beating heart out of a sacrificial victim."

De Sada laughed. "You lost some of your charming accent, Natalia. There is more to you than meets the eye! And that is saying a lot. How can you know so much about me?"

A humorless smile creased Natalia's face.

"No harm in telling you that we Habsburgs already control our share of key politicians around the world," continued de Sada. "With vast wealth comes vast power and vast responsibilities. I wouldn't be surprised if one day soon Europe feels that it needs a new king. This temporary infatuation with democracy is growing tedious. You can see the discontent growing among the people daily. You can even see that discontent in American elections."

"Maximilian's empire building efforts were a failure. Why do you think your efforts will be any different?"

"Max was a fool. He thought that his land reforms would endear the peasants to him. Instead, it gained him nothing from the lower class and alienated him from his natural allies, wealthy landowners. I am no fool."

"But," observed Natalia, "perhaps it was his efforts to help the poor that lead the Aztec priest to entrust to him the secret of the treasure."

"You know more than you let on. You have been holding out on me. Playing me."

"Like I said. I do my homework. I just want a fair share of the treasure. Surely, there is enough that you would not begrudge me a few trinkets."

"I think there is much more going on here than meets the eye. You are hiding something from me. Anyway, you are in no position to bargain. But, if you are, ah, cooperative, perhaps you could earn a, small share. Here we are at the airport now."

"Speaking of foolishness, what keeps the Minister from sending you on a wild gooses chase and taking the treasure for himself?"

"He would never do such a thing. His loyalty would never permit him to break trust with me. Besides, it has just been reported that the Minister was in a tragic accident. I am heartbroken."

"You poor thing. I thought something must be wrong. You seemed much more, how do I say it in English, ah, giddy. That's it. Much more giddy than usual."

"You noticed! So, will you be cooperative?"

Natalia smiled and answered, "Aren't I always?" After a moment, she asked, "And I suppose that computer merchant, Jamie, suffered a similar fate, since he failed to remain loyal to you."

"He was introduced to Tlaloc."

The Mercedes stopped at de Sada's Gulfstream. Natalia stared at the crowned eagle Habsburg emblem on the side. "You've added lightening bolts to the eagle's talons on your family emblem."

"Yes. In honor of the god of thunder."

"Tlaloc."

"Yes. Perhaps you too will meet him soon."

Suppressing a chill, Natalia climbed out of the car and walked briskly up the steps entering the private jet ahead of de Sada.

Chapter 50

A wave of relief and excitement swept through the group as Neil held up the baggy containing the memory card filled with pictures of the golden chest.

"That is awesome!" shouted Jimmy. They were so excited they paid no attention to the crunching of tires in the parking lot. Moments later policemen swarmed the cantina shouting, "Manos arriba! Estas bajo arresto!"

Jackson and his friends were confused, but they understood the language of pointed pistols. They raised their hands. *This can't be a coincidence,* thought Neil. He closed his fist around the baggy, thinking *'I can't let them find the memory stick.'* His eyes darted around the room. The cantina was a simple thatched roof structure without walls over a concrete floor, with a bar, stools, a few tables, bathrooms on one side, and an enclosed kitchen and storage area behind the bar. Thick tropical foliage grew under the eave of the roof.

Should I keep the memory stick? Should I risk hiding it? There was no time to weigh the options. One policeman was moving toward him. The policeman turned his eyes away for a moment and Neil dropped the baggy in the middle of a purple elephant ear plant.

"Keep your hands up! Don't move!" shouted the policeman.

They were cuffed, searched and carted to the police station. "What is the charge?" asked Jimmy repeatedly. He received no answers. The six of them were crammed into a single concrete cell containing two small bunks and a drain in the floor.

After locking the cell door, one policeman whispered to another, "How long are we supposed to keep them?"

"De Sada said to keep them a day, then turn them loose."

* * *

Gregory and his team rose early and began the trek to Hummingbird Valley. McKenzie suggested that they take large trucks, just in case they found the treasure. Gregory insisted that everyone travel together in a single rented Suburban. Most of their gear was mounted on the roof.

"Why do they call the place we're going to Hummingbird Valley?" asked Jason as they left San Cristobal.

"Do you know, Professor?" asked Clint.

"Yes," said Professor Timmons as he switched on his teaching voice. "North American Hummingbirds migrate non-stop across the Gulf of Mexico and winter in Mexico and Central America."

"No way!" Jason exclaimed in disbelief. "Surely those tiny birds can't fly across the Gulf."

"Oh, but they do," insisted Timmons. "They are amazing little birds. But, one of the most incredible features of their migration is they gather in a single small valley in Southern Mexico and feed voraciously on flowers before they spread out across Central America. They gather in huge numbers, almost covering every limb in the valley."

"Hence Hummingbird Valley," observed Jason.

"Precisely. Amazingly, we didn't even know they gathered in this valley until two years ago."

"What?" asked McKenzie. "How could such a valley be overlooked all this time?"

"It is a remote valley, and there simply had not been a report about the gathering from any indigenous people. No outsider had observed the gathering until recently."

"I find that hard to believe. How could they miss something that big?" asked Jason. "Somebody would have said something."

"Well, it's not without precedent. Billions of Monarch butterflies travel from as far away as Canada and winter in a valley in south central Mexico," stated Timmons. "There are so many that they completely cover every surface. Yet, Monarch Valley was not discovered until 1974. Back then, everyone wondered how such a momentous and beautiful migration could be unknown for so long."

"So, do hummingbirds cover every surface in their valley?" asked Jason.

"Virtually. They number in the hundreds of millions."

"Who cares?" said Gregory as he looked back at the road behind them. McKenzie noticed. "We're not being followed," McKenzie said to Gregory. "I've been checking, too."

"Yeah," agreed Gregory, "but I keep getting a feeling we're being followed."

* * *

The only vehicle Skip was able to rent was a bicycle with a small motor and butterfly handlebars. It had a rear fender with a rack, which was used to carry an extra tank of gas. Skip struggled to keep up with the

Suburban, especially uphill. He was now a mile behind, but he occasionally glimpsed the Suburban as it rounded a curve on the mountain road ahead of him. The tiny motorbike began slowing even more than usual on a particularly steep grade. "Come on you piece of junk!" shouted Skip as he threw his weight forward repeatedly, trying to ooch the bike up the hill.

An old pickup truck passed him. He grabbed the bed of the truck, shifted his motorbike to neutral and hitched a ride, letting the old truck pull his bike up the hill.

* * *

The next morning the policeman in charge unlocked the cell. "Good news, gentlemen, we have investigated the matter and confirmed that you are innocent. You are free to go."

"That's it! What matter did you investigate? I want to know why we were arrested!" insisted Jackson.

"Lo siento. Not all the reports have been prepared, so I am not at liberty to provide the information you request. I would be glad to keep you here another day or two while all the paperwork related to our investigation is completed. Sometimes it takes a week to do the paperwork. I wish I could tell you when that will be done, but some of my men they are notoriously slow in completing their reports. Sometimes the reports are never completed. Are you sure you want to wait for the reports?"

"It's okay," said Robert. "You can mail us your report."

"I am pleased you understand my situation. Your possessions are on the counter. A cab is waiting outside to return you to the cantina."

The cab was another Volkswagen bus. They piled in and fifteen minutes later they were deposited at the cantina. As soon as the cab left, Neil said to the others, "You guys make sure nobody is watching. I'll get the memory stick."

"Good idea," said Jimmy. "They may have turned us loose just to see where we hid the memory stick."

"If they know about it," added Robert.

"I'm just wondering why they dropped us off here," said Neil.

"Everyone's assuming it's still here," observed Jake.

"Don't talk that way," said Jackson. "We've been through too much to lose this now."

Neil searched. And searched.

After a few minutes, he returned to the group, a dejected look on his face. Everyone moaned. Neil held up the baggy. Jake punched him on the shoulder.

"Gregory has a two-day head start, and Natalia is a day ahead of us," said Jackson, intense determination etched on his face. "We've got to get the pictures to Professor Landon and our team at the library as soon as possible. I think they can decipher the code. Maybe we can still beat Gregory and Natalia to the treasure." Jackson searched his belongings and found the phone number of Frances, the man who picked him up at the airport.

"Frances, this is Jackson Bradley."

"Oh, Mr. Bradley! We have been very worried for chu. Are chu all right? Pablo said the police arrested chu. We have been trying to get chu out, but there has been much red tape."

"Yes. We are back at Pablo's cantina. Can you pick us up and take us to the airport?"

"Are chu leaving us for sure now?"

"I'm afraid so."

"Lo siento. I will bring your things. Chu will be missed. Chu have become very popular here in Punta Cana. Everyone is asking about chu. Chu must have many friends."

When Frances arrived, Jackson said, "We have a change of plans. Can you take us to the nearest Internet café? They seem to be all over the place."

"Si. Do chu still want to go to the airport?"

"Maybe, but first we need to get to the Internet."

An hour later, Neil had uploaded his pictures and Claire and her team were at work trying to decipher the inscriptions on the chest.

Jackson called Claire.

"Mr. Bradley, this is so exciting! We don't have the location of the treasure yet, but the inscription does confirm there is a great treasure, and it appears to be somewhere in southern Mexico near Guatemala. We hope to have more information about the exact location once Professor Landon completes his study. We sent the pictures to him. He was beside himself with excitement. He said this could be the find of the century!"

"When will he be through?"

"He was not sure, but guessed he may have something for us in a couple of hours if he's lucky. But, he also said we may never be able to read everything on the lid. However, the map is detailed enough to show the location and he is cross-referencing the map with both new and old maps of the area. He said the map on the lid clearly shows seven rivers coming together. That matches a place in southern Mexico called Agua Azul, where seven rivers come together."

"Great. Listen, I'm getting a ride to the airport. I'll buy a phone and give you a number. As soon as you know something, please call, because there are at least two other groups hot on the trail. They both have a one or two-day lead on us."

"Oh my. We can't let someone else get there first. I'll tell Professor Landon and I'll call you as soon as I have something."

Jackson hung up and returned to his Adventure Divers group. "Frances can take us to the airport. With some luck, by the time we get there our librarians might have a destination for us. Is everyone ready to go?"

"I'm not going," said Robert.

"What? There's an ancient treasure to be found!"

"I've already found my treasure. All my life I wanted to find a sunken ship like the Durance. This is by far the most significant find of my life. Now that we've found it, I can't leave it to others. No telling what damage they may do. No, I'm staying here. If my health allows me time for only one more great adventure, that sunken ship is it for me. There will be months or even years of dives. This is a career find for any diver."

"I'm staying too," said Stewart. "I can't leave Elmo at the bottom of the sea. I've got to help bring her up. I'm staying here to help Robert."

"Wow. Okay, I can see that. What about you, Neil?"

"When I leave Punta Cana, it'll be to go home. I am staying here for now."

"Really! Can I ask why?"

"Well, let's see. We just threw two Mexican Marines off our boat. They're hopping mad at us and would love to catch us in Mexico. We found a gold chest with a supposed map of a vast treasure engraved on it, but had in stolen by a cutthroat criminal who scuttled our boat, dumped chum on us and literally left us to be eaten by sharks. By luck, or the grace of God, we made it to shore with a camera that had pictures of the treasure map, only to have our camera stolen by a mysterious beauty who tricked her way into our confidence. Then, we spent the night in a Dominican jail for who knows what. Now, you propose we slip into Mexico to search for this supposed treasure in the same area where those who tried to kill us, lied to us and stole from us will be, along with the Mexican Marines who have a grudge to settle. That about sums it up. That concerns me just a little. Doesn't it concern you?"

"Well, when you put it that way, I guess it should. But, what about the treasure?"

"What treasure? We don't even know if there is one. We do know that these cutthroats think there's a treasure. So we can count on them being there."

"Yes, but…"

"Yes, but, if there is a treasure, you may not find it, and if you do, what then? You can't just take it. The Mexican government would have something to say about that. So, I don't see a lot of upside, but there is plenty of downside."

Jackson looked at Neil for a moment and shrugged. "I guess I just have to know whether it's there, and whether I can find it. After coming this far, I can't stop now. I can't let those who stole the chest and the camera get to it first. As for the rest of the problems, I'll just deal with them as they arise."

"That's the way I see it," said Neil. "That's just not a good enough reason for me to go, and not a good enough plan for me to buy into. I'm just not as invested in this treasure hunt as you are."

Jackson sighed. After a moment he looked at Jimmy, who said, "I agree with Neil." He then turned to Jake, expecting another no.

"I'll go. In fact, I may have a way to get you there ahead of everyone else."

Chapter 51

Jake spent twenty minutes on the phone in deep conversations. He hung up and motioned Frances to come to him. "Can you get Jackson and me to the airport at Port-au-Prince by 8 tonight?"

"Port-au-Prince! That's in Haiti. I can get you to our airport, no problemo. But, Port-au-Prince, that es a problem."

"Can you do it or do I have to find someone else?"

"No problemo. I can do it. Let me make calls."

While Frances was making calls, Jackson asked, "Why Haiti?"

"Remember, I work for the Air Guard out of Jackson, Mississippi."

"Yes, I remember."

"Part of my job is to manage flights for equipment, troops, and supplies to Afghanistan and Iraq."

"Yes, you told me."

"I happen to know a shipment is on the chart a few days from now when I get back. I just moved it up on the chart," Jake paused for emphasis and added, "and I added a little something extra. The flight arrives at 7, but it has to leave by 8 if it's going to make its next destination on time, taking into consideration our slight detour."

"You are diverting an Air Guard flight for me? Why?"

"I owe you big time. In the Air Guard we always pay our debts. Besides, you can help the Air Guard."

After another 15 minutes, Frances reported, "Like I say, no problemo. I get chu to the border and my cousin, Manuel, he will take chu to the airport."

"Good job, Frances, I knew you could do it. How long will it take?"

"Six hours, seven tops."

"We have to be there in five hours," said Jake with urgent authority. "Let's roll."

* * *

Minutes later, a four-man U.S. Ranger team on a covert mission in Guatemala received a call on the satellite phone. Captain Morales commanded, "Guys, gather your gear. We're going to Mexico, State of Chiapas, near the border. Precise coordinates to follow."

Every man in the team was of Hispanic origin. Each spoke Spanish fluently. Everyone was fiercely patriotic and ready to place everything on the line for his country.

"Captain, we don't have an operational co-op agreement with Mexico," responded one Ranger.

"This is a clandestine recover or destroy mission. The high-tech X-3 Glider is our mission."

Everyone paused a moment as the message sank in.

"What if we get caught?"

"Don't get caught."

He called up an electronic map on his satellite phone. After a quick examination he said, "We proceed to the Usumacinta River and cross near the town of Frontera Corozal in Chiapas. We should be able to obtain a vehicle there. Hopefully, by then we'll have our precise destination coordinates."

* * *

After taxiing to a stop at 7:03 pm, the C-17 crew worked quickly and efficiently unloading the crates destined for Port-au-Prince. Captain Gerald noted the task was complete at 7:17.

"What do we do now, Captain?" asked Officer Brand.

"We wait. We have some VIP's to pick up."

"Where are they? We're on a tight schedule."

"Hurry up and wait, that's our life, isn't it? Just chill for a while. I'm sure they'll be here by 8."

A rainsquall passed, and the humidity doubled. Brand checked his watch. "It's 7:50, Captain. Are you sure their coming?"

"No doubt."

"How can you be so sure?"

"Because Jake Sullivan told me he would be here."

"Oh! Okay."

Eleven minutes later, Brand said, "Captain, we're already late. We've eaten our margin of error. If we don't go now, we can't complete our mission. We'll have a lot of explaining to do."

"Yeah, you're right."

"What's the explanation, Captain?"

Captain Gerald exhaled, long and slow. "Okay, Brand. Start your engines."

* * *

Even though they had no time to spare, Jackson insisted that Frances take them to a store where he could buy a disposable phone with enough minutes to handle several international calls to the U.S. As soon as he had the phone, they jumped back in the car. Jackson called Claire and gave her his new number. "Call me as soon as you know a location."

Frances delivered Jake and Jackson to Manuel, who was waiting at the border. The road was rough and crowded making it hard to make good time.

"It's almost 8," noted Jackson.

"Faster, Manuel!" urged Jake.

"Señor, I go as fast as I can."

Jackson's phone rang. "It's Claire!"

"We have the location!" exclaimed Claire. "Professor Landon determined that the location of Hummingbird Valley is in Chiapas, that's in southern Mexico, next to the Yucatan Peninsula. Interestingly, he says it is an area where North American hummingbirds migrate for the winter."

"That is interesting. What are the map coordinates?" Jackson wrote them down. "Claire, you are amazing. Thank you. Thank Professor Landon. Thank your entire team."

"Oh, you are so welcome. We are so proud to be part of your team. Tell us as soon as you find the treasure!"

"That's the airport!" shouted Jake. "Turn here! Go in the back way."

"That is no admittance, señor."

"Go anyway!"

* * *

"Ready for take-off," said Brand.

"C-17, proceed to runway 1, and hold until further instructions," said traffic control.

"C-17, proceeding to runway 1. Will hold and await further instructions."

"Captain, what's that?"

A small Toyota raced across the tarmac toward the C-17, chased by two military vehicles close behind.

"It's Jake!"

After several minutes of animated discussion between the C-17 crew and an unhappy group of Haitian military personnel, Jake and Jackson boarded the C-17, and Manuel was permitted to leave, with a military escort.

Jake climbed to the cockpit and handed the Captain the coordinates.

"So, this is our destination," said the Captain. "We will have the insertion point calculated shortly. I hope we don't have to fly over Mexican airspace."

"I need you to transmit the coordinates to the recovery team," said Jake. "They're already on their way to southern Mexico, but they need the exact landing coordinates."

"Done and done."

The recovery team hired a truck in Frontera Corozal, but the owner, Mateo, insisted that he drive. They made their way to Highway 307, which runs northeast and southwest near the Guatemalan border, to await further instructions. They found a shady spot off the highway, shared a meal and watched the sun go down. A few minutes after 8, the satellite phone buzzed.

"Mateo, do you know how to get to Bonampak?"

"Si, it es just a few miles."

"Excellent. We are going to a valley just past Bonampak, where three ridges meet and form a triangle."

"Oh, no one goes there. It es very remote and the road es bad, but it es not far. Are you sure you don't want to go around those ridges? From there it es only a short distance to Agua Azul. Everyone goes to Agua Azul because it es mucho beautiful. There es nothing to see in that remote valley, so no one goes there."

"How long will it take to get there from here?"

"It es dark and we must go slowly over the ridge, but I think maybe a couple of hours."

"We have no time to waste. Let's go."

"Captain," whispered the Sergeant. "Sounds like we caught a break."

"I agree. The pickup point is in a remote area where no one goes. With any luck we won't have to worry about running into anyone. Hopefully, we can get in and out clean. No one will ever know we were here."

* * *

That night, footage of the 'protest' was on every television news network. In every scene, the camera angle was tight, making it impossible for the viewer to see that the protest included less than twenty people. The signs and the chants were prominent in all of the reports.

Karen tuned in to CTN and saw an announcer and her guest analyze the story. "To no one's surprise, racism is alive and well in Mississippi. This time, local whites are calling for the scalping of a Native American charged with murdering four white men, including the Sheriff," said the announcer. "It's much worse than that," responded the guest. "Listen to those chants. They are calling for the killing of Native Americans."

"What do you mean?"

"'Make good Indians'" is a reference to the old saying, 'the only good Indian is a dead one.'"

"Well," said the announcer, "let's ask our woman on the ground. As usual, she is the first reporter on the scene, Sandy Storm. Sandy, tell us what is going on in Philadelphia, Mississippi."

A split screen showed both the announcer and Sandy. The view zoomed in on Sandy. "Tension is building here in Mississippi. We are near a flash point. Some say that we could see a full-scale war break out at any moment. Others say the trouble is caused by outside agitators."

"What do you see, there on the ground?"

"Certainly, there are some locals joining the protest, mostly family members and friends of the three men who were scalped."

"Is there any truth to the claim of outside agitators?"

"Well, you may have seen my interview of the leader of the KKK group that marched around the courthouse today. He said he was from New Jersey, and that he had come here to defend the white race from unprovoked attacks by Indians. I have verified from a reliable source that Black Lives Matter is organizing a protest at the courthouse Monday, the day that Awesome Dalton's preliminary hearing is scheduled."

"Sandy, there are other reports that the county is about to explode in a race war. Can you see that happening?"

"As volatile as this situation is, anything could happen."

"There you have it," said the announcer. "All the elements are in place for Mississippi to explode in a race war again."

The next day, chartered buses filled with protesters began arriving in Philadelphia.

Chapter 52

Antoine de Sada's Gulfstream landed at Tuxtla Gutierrez just two hours after he left Dominica. He and his entourage boarded two military helicopters that whisked them away to San Cristobal de Las Casas, where they spent the night.

De Sada acted as though he was the perfect host. He had already arranged for rooms for himself and his staff. He escorted Natalia to her room and said, "Please join me for dinner downstairs at ocho. Julio will show you the way. I believe the two of you have met."

"Yes, I remember, on the dive boat."

Julio frowned.

"Julio will make sure that someone is at your door at all times in case you need anything."

"You mean, to make sure I don't leave."

"I would never have said such a thing."

"No, but I see that my room has no phone."

"Yes, so that you won't be disturbed. And you needn't worry about the windows either, they are quite secure."

"Oh, Antoine, you are so thoughtful."

"I do try to plan ahead."

Natalia knew she was running out of time. If she didn't do something soon, de Sada would find the Hummingbird Hoard. "Everything depends upon me," she said to herself. "I have to find a way to get word out."

At eight, Julio knocked on her door and led her to de Sada's table. As they were about to have dinner, she noticed Julio use a small cell phone. When he completed his call, he placed it in a pouch on his trouser leg. A Velcro flap protected the content of the pouch. Natalia pretended to drink a little too much during dinner. As they left, she maneuvered herself close to Julio and stumbled into him. He instinctively caught her.

"Oh, such strong arms!" she said with gratitude and batting eyelashes.

When she was locked in her room alone, with guards at the door and outside her window, she made her call.

"We are in San Cristobal, Hotel Villa Bella. We leave first thing in the morning for the Valley of the Hummingbirds. He has 20 heavily armed mercenaries with him." She heard de Sada ordering someone to unlock her door. "I need help. I may not be able to stop him alone."

She deleted the call from memory and hid the phone behind a pillow on a chair in the room. De Sada, Julio and two armed mercenaries entered her room.

"Julio tells me he is missing a cell phone."

"Oh, Julio, was that your phone?" She walked to the chair, removed the phone from behind the pillow and handed it to Julio. "I found it on a chair. What girl can pass up the opportunity to have a phone?"

Julio searched the phone's memory. "She hasn't made any calls, Señor de Sada."

De Sada nodded, then glowered at Natalia. "Lucky for you that you didn't use that phone. Never cross me again." Something in his voice sent chills down Natalia's spine.

De Sada and his men left, locking the door behind them.

The next morning they joined a convoy of vehicles and set out into the wild country of Chiapas. The convoy included trucks, four-wheel drive vehicles, hummers, and one late model Range Rover. De Sada settled into the back seat of the Range Rover. Julio escorted Natalia to de Sada's vehicle, opened the back door, and motioned for her to get in. De Sada smiled as Natalia climbed in.

"Welcome! Did you sleep well?"

"It es hard to sleep in chains. Even if they are velvet."

"Natalia, my dear, there were no chains."

"Was I free to leave?"

"Of course not."

"See? Chains. Why all these trucks? Why not just take the helicopter all the way to the treasure?" asked Natalia.

"I trust the men in this convoy. They have been with my family many years. They will do anything for me. They are my private army. I don't have any reason to trust the military pilots who carried us to San Cristobal, although I am very grateful to them. So, I arranged for this convoy here in San Cristobal. My man Julio was tasked with assembling all we will need for our expedition. I hope that we will need all these trucks, or more, to carry away my Hummingbird Hoard."

"You seem very confident that you will find 'your' treasure."

"Indeed, I am."

"What's under the tarp on the flatbed?"

"Your instincts are impeccable, Natalia. That is the most important item in our inventory."

"What could be more important than your bulldozer, dynamite, weapons, men and trucks to find, guard and carry away your treasure?"

259

"The very reason for our endeavor. The one to whom we owe our present and future success."

"You can't really believe that."

"There are unseen powers at work in this world that you cannot imagine. I have learned to harness those powers for the greater good."

"Your greater good?"

"Of course. And for the greater good of my friends."

"By friends, you mean those who submit to you."

"It's one and the same, my dear Natalia, as you will soon learn. You will soon be my friend."

They settled in for a long, bumpy ride over rough mountain roads. Three hours later, they crossed a ridge and looked into a lush valley surrounded by craggy peaks. Natalia lowered her window. Rich thick aroma of countless tropical flowers flooded the interior of the Range Rover. A solitary hummingbird buzzed through the window and hovered in front of Natalia's face. She couldn't help but notice its bright green throat. It suddenly darted away as quickly as it came.

She gazed over the brilliant green valley, resplendent with myriad colorful flowers. Clouds, like wisps of smoke, intertwined with the trees, rising, falling and flowing in every direction.

"That is an odd sight," said de Sada. "The clouds move as though the wind blows in every direction at once. I believe those clouds are made of birds."

"Hummingbird Valley," whispered Natalia in a husky, feminine voice.

"Right you are, my dear. Soon, I will be the wealthiest, most powerful man in the world."

"I know your mother would be proud."

De Sada laughed. "What do you know of my mother?"

"Oh, not much. Only that she filled your mind with stories of the Hummingbird Hoard and a lost empire since you were an infant."

"You are full of surprises. How would you know this?"

"I too have spent my life looking for this treasure. I had hoped to find it before you. Why do you think our paths cross so often?"

"My, my, my. And here we are, together, about to make the greatest find in history. Does it irk you that I have won the race?"

"The race isn't over."

De Sada laughed again. "I have always admired your spirit. Why don't you join me?"

"What, as your concubine?"

"Would that be so bad?"

"If we were, ah, partners, what would be my share?"

"So, you have a price."

"No, I have curiosity."

"Hmm. Before we test the depths of that curiosity, let's see how well we get along here in the jungle in the hours before we first cast our eyes upon riches beyond our wildest dreams."

"My dreams can be pretty wild," answered Natalia.

"What else is wild with you?"

"Dream away, Antoine."

* * *

Hummingbird Valley, triangular in shape, is nestled between three ridges. A seldom-used rock and dirt switchback road ascends the lesser of the ridges. Gregory and his men found an ideal campsite in a meadow alongside a stream near the point of the triangle where the two tall ridges come together. The stream meanders through the jungle and exits the valley at the abrupt, steep edge of the lesser ridge. Dense clouds of hummingbirds sometimes cast shadows on the ground as they darted between the trees. An eerie constant hum of countless tiny wings enveloped Gregory's men.

Professor Timmons excitedly pointed at a waterfall where the two tall ridges meet. "That's it! Just like the map says! A waterfall within a waterfall! That's where we're going!"

"What are you so excited about?"

"That waterfall is our destination!" exclaimed Timmons. "It flows from a deep spring fed lake on the other side of that ridge. The map shows a waterfall inside a waterfall. If you look closely, about a third of the way down the ridge, you see that the flow of water intensifies. That's because it's joined by a second stream of water!"

"Yeah, how is that?" asked Clint.

"A cave," said Gregory.

"Exactly!" exclaimed Timmons. "An underground river exits the mountain from the mouth of that cave two-thirds of the way up the mountain. But the cave is concealed by the water falling from the top of the ridge!"

At that moment, Gregory noticed movement on the road at the top of the ridge behind them. He spun on his heels and yelled at his companions, murder in his eyes. "Which one of you betrayed me?"

"What do you mean?" Timmons asked in a trembling voice. Dozens of hummingbirds darted between him and Gregory.

"I mean that convoy coming over the ridge. Who are they? How did they know to come here, now?"

"They could be anybody," said Clint, "here for any reason."

Red-faced Gregory replied in a deep growl. "I am not an idiot. This is not a coincidence. That's a convoy of trucks able to carry away my treasure. No one knows it's here except us and Dalton. Somebody betrayed me."

Clint reached for his satellite phone. "I've got to report this to Mr. Dalton. He told me to keep him informed of major developments, and this looks major."

Gregory slapped the phone out of Clint's hands. "Nobody's talking to anybody. For all I know, you might be calling them," he said as he gestured toward the ridge.

McKenzie held up his hands in an effort to calm Gregory. "Everybody calm down. We're on the same side. I know I didn't tell anyone where we were going, and I don't believe Jason or Clint did. They're like brothers to me." Clint balled his fist, but forced himself to remain calm. He picked up the sat phone. All eyes turned to the Professor.

"Well, it wasn't me!" exclaimed the Professor.

"We'll see," said Gregory as he glanced around their campsite. "I'll give each of you a chance to prove your loyalty."

"What do you mean?" asked Timmons.

"You'll see. Quick, we've got to break camp and retreat into the jungle. Make sure you leave no evidence we were here."

"If they are following us, won't they know we're here?" asked Clint.

"We're not going to stay here and be sitting ducks," replied Gregory. "This is the prime campsite in the valley. We'll let them have it, and we will conceal ourselves in the jungle and watch them. Maybe we can let them do the heavy lifting for us. Let them find and load the treasure and we'll drive it out on their trucks."

"But they won't let us just drive out with the treasure if they find it, will they?" asked Timmons.

"Leave that to me," responded Gregory. "Quick, get to work."

* * *

Hungry, thirsty and covered with mosquito bites, Skip finally found the perfect vantage point to observe Gregory and his group. Hummingbirds were everywhere. At times, they seemed to cover every tree. He improvised a shelter with flowering limbs and concealed his motorbike. At first, he tried to drive the hummingbirds away from his shelter, but eventually gave up and decided to try to ignore them. But the little birds were always buzzing and hovering in front of his face. "You pesky little birds," he said as he tried to wave them away. "They love these flowers!" he said to himself as he realized his shelter had dozens of beautiful flowers. They emitted a strong, sweet aroma and sticky nectar dripped from the petals onto Skip. "What is this sticky stuff?" he said as he tried to rub it off. The more he rubbed, the more it spread.

Skip watched Timmons and saw his excitement as he pointed to the waterfall. He observed their concern as they gestured to the ridge behind them. They hurriedly broke camp and moved into the jungle, straight toward Skip.

"Why here? You've got the whole jungle to choose from, why come straight to me?" Skip had no time to break camp. He just slinked further into the jungle. He picked a hiding place behind a tropical plant with huge fronds, where he could continue to watch Gregory, yet remain concealed. He stood perfectly still. A hummingbird landed on a nectar covered part of his shoulder. He shrugged. It didn't move. He started to wave it off with one of his hands, but he saw that Gregory and the others had reached his camp sight. Two more hummingbirds joined the first, then a dozen more. Soon, they were all over his shoulders, arms and legs, clinging to his clothes, sucking nectar. More hummingbirds landed on his head.

Lincoln held up his hand calling for silence when they came upon Skip's campsite. He glanced quickly around. "Somebody's here. Find him!"

Clint called out, "Here's a motorbike!"

"Maybe he followed us and called his friends."

They searched the area. Something out of the ordinary caught Jason's eye. It was a brown mass, with flecks of bright colors; green, gold, red, pink. It seemed to be undulating, moving around the edges, yet staying in the same place. He couldn't quite make out what it could be. He stepped closer. "Hummingbirds! Thousands of 'em," he said to himself. "Weird. They almost look like a man."

Skip was frozen with fear. He didn't move a muscle as Jason stepped closer. He didn't even breathe. Then he heard Jason say, "Weird. They almost look like a man." Skip blinked. A single hummingbird flew from his face.

"What the …!" exclaimed Jason as he raised his weapon, pointing it at the center of the ball of birds.

Skip bolted into the jungle. The hummingbirds, suddenly without perch, swarmed around Jason, obscuring his vision. When they cleared, Skip was gone.

Clint and Gregory, alerted by Jason's exclamation, ran to him. "What is it?" asked Clint.

"Nothing, just a weird ball of hummingbirds. They almost made the shape of a man. I never saw anything like that before."

"This jungle is getting to you. You're seeing things," said Clint. "It's getting to me too."

"Keep your eyes open," commanded Gregory. "There is someone in this jungle with us. He followed us here. Whoever followed us must die!"

"Why?" asked Professor Timmons, clearly shocked.

"It's either him or us. If he alerts that convoy, we're dead."

* * *

It was dusk when de Sada's convoy reached a break in the jungle, an open meadow near the head of the valley. The valley head was formed by two ridges that come together at a sharp angle, punctuated by sheer rock walls that stretch 1000 meters into the darkening sky. In the half-light they could just make out a waterfall that began where the two ridges met, and fell into the jungle, disappearing behind foliage that covered most of the valley floor. Francisco tapped on the passenger window of de Sada's Range Rover. De Sada lowered the window.

"Yes, Francisco?"

"Señor de Sada. This is the place. The map coordinates bring us here, to this point, where the walls of the valley come together."

"This is a place of breathtaking beauty," said Natalia.

"Yes. Pity that there is no time to enjoy the scenery," said de Sada. "We have much work to do. Let's break out our equipment and begin the search. The mouth of the cave is behind the waterfall, about two-thirds of the way up the ridge."

"Yes, Señor de Sada. It is almost dark, and a storm is brewing. I checked radar when we were at the top of the ridge, and I think one storm will be on us in about an hour. That will pass, and an hour later we should have another storm. But, weather changes quickly here. Do you want us to set up camp before the first storm arrives?"

"Two storms! That may be perfect. Setting up camp is a good suggestion, Francisco. My excitement is getting the best of me. Considering the fact that the treasure has been hidden five hundred years, a few more hours will make no difference. Use half the men to set up camp."

"Yes, Señor de Sada."

"Use the other half to unload the altar and place it close to the waterfall. We may find use for it tonight between the storms."

"As you wish."

"You are setting up the altar?" asked Natalia.

"What better time to honor the god of thunder and rain than when you're surrounded by tropical thunderstorms?"

Natalia watched as Francisco ordered his men to carefully remove the tarp, exposing a stone statue of Tlaloc, on his knees, leaning back onto his elbows. His arms cradled a bowl above his chest. His head and gruesome

264

face was set at 90 degrees to his body. Tlaloc's stomach created an almost flat altar. Natalia knew that victims of Tlaloc were stretched across the altar with their chest exposed. The Tlalocan priest used a razor-sharp obsidian knife to slice open the victim's chest. He would rip out the still beating heart and place it in the bowl suspended above Tlaloc's chest. Natalia felt as though Tlaloc's hungry eyes were searching for her. She shivered at the thought.

"You can't be serious?" Natalia asked de Sada.

"Deadly serious."

* * *

Panic driven and running and tripping at breakneck speed through the jungle, Skip came to a clearing near the base of the waterfall. He heard someone tromping through the jungle, coming in his direction. He spotted a path that led up the cliff beside the waterfall. He scrambled up the path, higher and higher, until the path ended at the waterfall. Out of breath, he crouched into a cleft and listened for approaching footsteps. He heard none. After several minutes, overcome with physical exertion and tension, he fell asleep.

* * *

Peering through thick jungle foliage, Clint said, "It looks like there are twenty of them on our campsite. I think they are Mexican military."

"Paramilitary," responded Gregory.

"They've got earthmoving equipment," observed Timmons. "Surely, they won't use that! They could destroy priceless ancient treasures!" Timmons' anxiety over possible damage to unseen artifacts was palpable.

"Calm down, Professor," commanded Gregory. "You're shaking so much they'll find us."

"What are we going to do? They outnumber us 4 to 1," said Clint.

"We're going to even the odds," replied Gregory in a matter of fact tone.

"What? How? What do you mean?" asked Timmons as his angst grew exponentially.

"We'll reduce their number," growled Gregory.

* * *

Captain Morales instructed the driver to stop just below the ridge. He and another ranger climbed out of the van and walked to the crest of the ridge. The Captain peered into the valley, using night vision binoculars.

"Uh-oh. We have company," he said as he handed the binoculars to the sergeant.

"A convoy? Looks military. How did they know to be there?"

"We could have a leak."

"Wouldn't be the first time. What do we do, Captain?"

"Plan B. Since the odds of retrieval are remote, we shift focus to destruction of the glider. We'll use the satchels. One should be enough, but we'll use both just to be sure."

Two of their backpacks contained satchel incendiary charges designed to burn at extremely high temperatures sufficient to ignite plastics, polymers and even aluminum. Once ignited, the glider would continue to burn until completely consumed.

"Our mission is to keep anyone from recovering any part of the X-3."

"Exactly. Tell our driver he should go home. We won't need the truck. We've got it from here."

"Yes sir."

He paid the driver and watched as the truck eased down the ridge in the direction of Frontera. Movement along the rugged road caught his eye.

"Captain! We've got more company!"

"Situation?"

"Pickup trucks, lots of them, filled with locals."

The Captain panned the armada of pickups with his binoculars. "Looks like farmers. Maybe local Mayans or other Indians."

"How many?"

"Hard to say. Could be a hundred."

"Why are they here?"

"I have no idea. What have we gotten ourselves in to? Let's get to cover, work our way into the valley, get into position and wait."

Chapter 53

"At last, the day for the preliminary hearing has arrived," said Peter.

"Yep. So much has happened in the past week that it seems like it has taken forever to get to this hearing, but actually we're getting to court really fast," explained John.

"So, there's no jury today."

"That's right, and no final decision will be made," explained John. "Only a preliminary decision."

"Then, why is this hearing so important?"

"Good question. This is the first chance that we get to hear at least some of the evidence against our client. If the prosecution's case is weak, sometimes that weakness really stands out at the preliminary."

"So, the prosecutor will present his evidence today?"

"Probably not all of it. He usually doesn't want to show his cards yet. Besides, they're probably not through gathering all the evidence that they'll use at the trial. Today, the prosecutor will likely produce just enough evidence to meet his burden of proof, which is very low at this stage."

"What do you mean?"

"In a trial, the prosecution must convince every member of the jury that Awesome is guilty beyond a reasonable doubt."

"Yeah, everybody has heard about that."

"That's right. But, at this hearing, the prosecution only has to show the judge probable cause that a crime was committed and probable cause to believe that the Defendant, Awesome, committed the crime."

"That sounds like a big difference."

"Right you are."

"Why is the burden of proof so low?"

"It's in everyone's interest to control crime, but one of the things that makes America great is we value freedom so much that our law won't allow authorities to arrest anyone and hold them unless they have good reason to believe the person arrested has committed a crime. That 'good reason' is called probable cause. Today the judge is just determining whether there is enough evidence to continue to charge Awesome with a crime and hold him in jail."

"So, you always want a preliminary hearing, right?"

"Not always. Sometimes, you know the evidence is so strong that nothing can be gained at a hearing. Sometimes your client gets out on bond. If he is out on bond, you may not get a preliminary hearing."

"Yeah, I've got it. They shouldn't hold a person in jail if there's no evidence against him."

"Exactly. But the odds are stacked against us at this hearing. The prosecutor can let the sheriff summarize his investigation. The rules of hearsay don't apply. They should have no problem meeting their burden of proof."

"But you said you have a few tricks up your sleeve," observed Peter.

"Yep. Those subpoenas you helped me with this week, with a little luck and a cooperative witness or two, just might produce enough evidence to prove that Awesome could not have committed the crimes. Then, the judge should dismiss the charge."

"Cool," said Peter with little enthusiasm. 'It would be cool if it happened that way,' he thought to himself. 'If he only knew he doesn't have a chance.' Peter became sullen as he stared at the passing landscape. Dread filled his heart with each passing mile.

As they entered Philadelphia the street divided, with two lanes headed east, and two west with a block of businesses between them. After about a mile, each side of the divided highway passes the Neshoba County Courthouse, one to the north and one to the south. As they neared the courthouse, John noticed charter buses parked in lots and along the side of the road. Traffic was congested and came to a standstill two blocks from the Courthouse Square. There was a roadblock. Traffic was being diverted left and right. John worked his way to the front of the line. A policeman was directing him to turn left. John rolled down his window and motioned to the officer, who called back, "Move along, you are holding up traffic."

"I am to be in court this morning."

"Who are you?"

"Brooks. My client has a preliminary hearing today. How can I get through all of this to the courthouse?"

"Oh, Mr. Brooks. Sorry. You can go through, but you will have a hard time finding a parking space. We're diverting traffic because it's crazy. Protesters from Black Lives Matter and from the KKK are up there. I don't know why either of them are here. The situation is volatile. If I were you, I wouldn't go there."

"I don't have any choice."

"I understand. Follow me."

The officer walked to a barricade made of several orange sawhorses. He pushed aside two sawhorses to make room for John's car. Beyond the barricade was a pulsating throng of people. He spoke to another officer and motioned to John's car. The second officer waved and indicated that John should follow him.

John drove slowly behind the officer as he made a path through the crowd.

"Here we are," said John as he drove within sight of the Neshoba County Courthouse. A small contingent of Klansmen held signs and chanted in front of the courthouse. The Klansmen were outnumbered by police, deputies and highway patrolmen, who stood between them and a much larger crowd of angry protesters carrying a variety of Black Lives Matter signs. The tension was palpable. Television satellite trucks were everywhere. Dozens of reporters and cameramen were busy filming, interviewing, reporting and observing, waiting for an explosion. A knot of about forty people composed of family members and friends of Skeeter and his buddies stood near the south entrance to the courthouse.

There were no parking spaces in sight. John spotted Frank Dalton standing behind his pickup, positioned directly in front of the north door to the courthouse. Frank spotted them and waved John over.

"Mr. Brooks!" Frank had to speak loud to be heard over the crowd. "I got here early to save you a parking space. I thought you might have some things to carry and I was afraid there would be no place for you to park. Please, take this space."

John thought about the offer for a moment and considered declining. He didn't want to make the old man walk from a distant parking space. But he realized Frank really wanted to help. "Thank you, Frank. It would indeed be very helpful to park this close to the courthouse. That was a smart move."

Frank beamed from ear to ear, hurried to his old pickup and backed out of the space. Before driving off, he paused, climbed out of his truck and walked back to John's car.

"Did you notice anything strange about the protesters?"

"Other than the fact that they're here, no. What is strange?"

"I don't see any of my people in the crowd. And, other than Skeeter's family and law enforcement, I don't see any local people."

"That explains all the charter buses. People with an agenda are using your family's misfortune."

"Yes. That is what I see. That is what my people have always seen. We always get along with people of good will, people who just want to live their lives. But someone always comes along with an agenda, and we always lose."

Frank climbed back in his pickup and pulled away. Brooks slipped into the space Frank left behind. John had a banker box of materials for the hearing, which he gave to Peter. They had taken only a few steps toward the courthouse when a phalanx of reporters intercepted them. Sandy Storm was first to reach him. She thrust a microphone in John's face.

"What do you say to protesters who say your client should be scalped?"

"We are a nation of laws, not a nation of mobs. Let the court system do its job. Ultimately, justice will be done."

"What do you say to the protesters who claim your client has been wrongly accused, just because he's not white?"

"I see a mob, not a protest. Individuals care about justice. Mobs don't. A mob is a living entity that exists only for the moment. I say to everyone, if you are truly interested in justice, don't jump to conclusions. Wait until all the evidence is in. Let the court system do its job and ultimately justice will be done."

Word spread that Awesome's lawyer was on the north side of the courthouse. Both mobs began streaming around the courthouse. The KKK streamed from the east and the counter-protesters streamed from the west side of the courthouse. They converged on John and Peter as John's impromptu interview ended.

The protesters were moving fast, building momentum. Collisions occurred at the point of convergence. People were thrown to the ground. Fists swung. Signs swung. More people fell. The angry mobs pushed their way into John's path. A cameraman stumbled. His camera was ripped away. A reporter, punched in the gut, bent over double and tumbled to the ground. Fights broke out all around John and Peter. Peter was jostled and tripped. John caught him.

With fear in his eyes, Peter cried, "They're going to tear us apart!"

In a loud deep voice of authority, clearly heard by those between him and the courthouse, John shouted, "In the name of the God of Justice, let us pass!"

Whether it was the invocation of the name of God, or the appeal to everyone's innate desire for justice, no one knows, but miraculously the melee near John and Peter subsided. A path opened. John and Peter passed through the crowd and reached the courthouse door. Before entering, John turned and addressed the crowd, again in a loud, deep voice.

"Thank you. Remain calm. Protest peacefully. Pray for justice."

John turned and followed Peter into the courthouse.

The crowd murmured its approval. Opponents looked at one another suspiciously, separated, and resumed their marches.

"What just happened?" asked a reporter.

"A miracle," said another. "They were going to rip each other limb from limb, including us."

"How do we report this?"

"Just let the facts speak for themselves," suggested Sandy.

Inside the courthouse, a reporter and cameraman rushed to intercept John. With camera rolling, the reporter said, "That was amazing! That was a war zone! How did you gain control of that mob?"

"You are mistaken," said John. "I didn't gain control of a mob. I didn't do anything except let my wishes be known to God and man. I left the results up to God. He did all the work. Have faith my friend."

John climbed the stairs to the courtroom on the second level.

The live camera panned back to the reporter who said, "Well, … you just, … he, … didn't he, … this is Sam Jenkins reporting live from the Neshoba County Courthouse. Can I re-do that? What just happened?"

On the south side of the courthouse, a national celebrity of sorts, the Reverend Albert Anderson, stepped up to a microphone on a hastily arranged stage. The Reverend Anderson made a career out of promoting racial tension and division under the guise of justice and reconciliation. But justice had nothing to do with his motives and the last thing he wanted was racial reconciliation. He thrived off of the attention he grabbed whenever tragedy struck a black or minority community. He profited enormously from 'contributions' paid by major corporations, apparently in return for assurance that his followers would not boycott the goods and services of his benefactors.

"Brothers and sisters, we have come again into the heart of darkness, Mississippi, where hatred and racism refuse to die."

"That's right!"

"How many times must Black People, Hispanic People, Asian People, and Native American People be denied justice in this state, in this country?"

"That's right! How long?"

"We must come together and tell those in power, that we will be heard! We must shout until they hear us, so that justice will be done!"

"Yes! Tell 'em!"

"Let our shout for justice become a roar of inevitability!"

"Yes! Justice now!"

"Now, a young Native American boy has been charged with the crime of defending his family and his farm! And they call this America? They call this the land of the free? This is not the land of the free!"

"You tell 'em!"

"This is the land of the imprisoned! The home of the downtrodden! We won't stand for it!"

"No! We won't stand for it!"

"They are worried because three white men died. I don't see them concerned when black men die at the hands of white policemen every day! But because three white men died, they want a person of color to pay for it. It don't matter whether that person is black, brown, red or yellow. In their mind, a person of color has got to pay!"

"That's right!"

"Well, I'm here to tell you that if they are looking for payment, those three men were just a down payment!"

"Yes, you tell 'em, Reverend!"

"To prove what I say is true, look around you. You see the KKK, don't you?"

"Yes."

"Who are the police protecting, you or the KKK?"

"The KKK!"

"That's right! They are defending the KKK! That proves to you who they really support!"

Boos and hisses came from the crowd.

"That proves to you who they are! And they wonder why blood runs in the streets of this country. It's their own fault if people die. It's not your fault when they drive you into a rage!"

"No! It's their fault!"

"That's right! They created this environment of hate, distrust, and injustice. I am here to tell you that peace is the way. Don't go hurt nobody. But who can blame you if you do? It's not your fault! It is the fault of this whole racist, capitalist, white power structure that keeps you down and keeps you downtrodden! It's past time for us to rise up and let them taste for a moment what we have had to endure for centuries!"

"Yes! We want justice!" shouted the crowd

"When do we want it?" shouted Anderson

"NOW!" responded the crowd.

"Do you think they are going to just hand you your justice?"

"NO!"

"Then go get your justice NOW!"

The crowd roared.

In a conversational tone, the right Reverend Albert Anderson said, "Remember, I am a man of peace, and I preach peace. Whatever you do, do it for peace."

Sandy Storm reported to the world, "The tension in the air is palpable. We are sitting on a time bomb set to explode any minute! Stay tuned for the latest."

* * *

On the second floor of the Neshoba County Courthouse there are two courtrooms, one used by the Circuit Court and one by the Chancery Court. The preliminary hearing was scheduled to be heard by the county court judge, but because her courtroom was small, the hearing was in the circuit courtroom, which is large enough to accommodate the media and hundreds of spectators.

John and Peter entered the Circuit Courtroom and took the table designated for the Defendant. The room was filling up with spectators and media representatives. After a few minutes Awesome was escorted into the courtroom in chains. Not even prison clothes could conceal the strength and virility evident in Awesome. He smiled at his lawyer and took a seat beside him.

"Does he have to wear these chains?"

The deputy looked at Awesome. "Are you going to run, son?"

"No, sir."

"Are you going to do what I say?"

"Yes, sir."

"Your word is good enough for me." The deputy unlocked and removed the chains.

John looked at Peter and said, "I love small towns. Things are done differently here."

Next, Ron Johnson, counsel for the Mississippi Band of Choctaw Indians, entered the room. He shook hands with Awesome and John.

"Ron Johnson, let me introduce you to my assistant, Peter Creek. Peter, Ron works with the Choctaw Nation. Any time a Choctaw is charged with a crime outside of Indian lands, the Tribe offers legal assistance."

"That's right. We will defend our people. In this instance, we know Awesome has good counsel. I'm just here to help any way that I can."

A few minutes later, Ann Thorn, the County Attorney and very capable prosecutor, entered the courtroom. The County Attorney is an elected official who handles numerous legal affairs for the county, including the prosecution of minor offenses and the handling of most of the preliminary hearings. To John's surprise, Hoover entered the courtroom with her and began setting up at her table.

"Hoover! What brings you here?" asked John.

"I've just gotten a job with the local D.A. I've been assigned to help the County Attorney with this hearing."

"What a coincidence. How did that happen?"

"Not sure. But I understand a friend of mine made a contribution to the D.A.'s re-election fund. Sometimes who you know really pays off." Hoover winked at Peter and said, "Remember that kid."

The courtroom continued to fill. By the time Sandy and Bret entered, the spectator area was full. Bret had plenty of experience covering events in crowded courtrooms. He planned ahead. He picked the seats that gave him the best camera angle in advance and paid several young men to hold the seats for him. They gladly gave up their seats for Sandy, Bret, and his equipment.

Several deputies entered the room through the main door. The bailiff and court reporter entered and took their respective seats. Finally, a knock was heard on the door behind the bench, and the bailiff announced, "All rise! The County Court of Neshoba County is now in session. The Honorable Dell Westerbeck presiding."

"You may be seated," said Judge Westerbeck as she settled into the chair at the bench. It took several moments for the assembly to settle into the pews and quiet down. The judge announced, "The case before the Court is the State of Mississippi vs. Awesome Dalton. What says the prosecution?"

Ms. Thorn rose and said, "Your Honor, Ann Thorn for the State of Mississippi. The State is ready to proceed. I would like to introduce the Court to a new Assistant District Attorney, Harry Hoover." She gestured toward Hoover, who rose and nodded in deference to the Court. Ms. Thorn continued, "The D.A.'s office will be participating considering the gravity of the charges and the fact that they will be presenting evidence to a Grand Jury and proceeding with the prosecution after today."

"I understand. Thank you, Ms. Thorn and Mr. Hoover. What says the Defendant?"

"John Brooks for the citizen charged, Awesome Dalton. I am here with Ron Johnson, counsel for the Mississippi Band of Choctaw Indians, and my assistant, Peter Creek. May we ask the Court to confirm that persons we have subpoenaed are present and available to testify?"

Hoover rose to his feet. "Your Honor. We anticipated this tactic by Mr. Brooks. He likes using a preliminary hearing as a fishing expedition and as an illicit discovery tool. We will be objecting to his calling unnecessary witnesses, and we object to any attempt to delay the proceedings because of the possible absence of witnesses."

"Your Honor, all I am asking is the usual inquiry about the presence or absence of witnesses. Apparently, we can simply inquire of Mr. Hoover, because he seems to know who my witnesses are and that some are apparently absent."

"Mr. Brooks, I am aware of your tactics at the preliminary hearing stage. I will not waste the Court's time with immaterial witnesses or impertinent questions. This hearing will not be a fishing expedition." After a pause, the judge continued, "Mr. Hoover, the Defendant is entitled to subpoena witnesses. I do not intend to summarily cut off the

Defendant's right to call witnesses. I will consider objections to specific witnesses or questions at the appropriate time. Mr. Brooks, please hand the bailiff your list of subpoenaed witnesses."

John did so. The bailiff called all six names in the courtroom. There was no response. John noted that Hoover was smiling with satisfaction. John glanced at Peter. The bailiff stepped into the hallway and repeated the process. He returned and announced, "No response, Your Honor."

"I see." The judge looked at the court clerk, sitting off to the side. "May I see the returns please?"

The Court Clerk opened a file and flipped to affidavits, showing how, when and where each subpoena was delivered to each person. The subpoena ordered each person to come to Court.

"Hmm," said Judge Westerbeck. "Six witnesses have been served with subpoenas and not one is here. It seems that you are entitled to a continuance until such time as the whereabouts of the witnesses can be determined."

"Precisely why we objected to this tactic, Your Honor," continued Hoover.

"Mr. Brooks, I see your point. How is it that you knew that the witnesses subpoenaed by the defense were not present, Mr. Hoover?"

"No, I'm sorry Your Honor, I didn't know that all six would not be here. I am just aware that he subpoenas numerous witnesses and that he uses their absence as a delay tactic."

"If I may respond, Your Honor," said John in a calm voice.

"You may."

"Mr. Hoover is misinformed. I don't believe that I have ever asked for a continuance because of the absence of a subpoenaed witness at a preliminary hearing, and I don't intend to start today. We are prepared to go forward even though the witnesses did not respond as present."

Hoover did a double take at John, the judge and Ms. Thorn. "Well, then, Your Honor, I suppose I don't have an objection."

"I suppose not. Let's proceed."

Crash! A brick flew through the window. Glass shards scattered over several pews and spectators. People screamed. Chanting could be heard on the street below. "Justice! Justice! Scalp them all!"

Judge Westerbeck banged her gavel on the resounder. "Order in the Court. Everyone, back away from the windows! Mr. Bailiff, remove Mr. Dalton from the courtroom. Keep him in a safe place until we resume. Deputies, I am placing each of you in charge of the Courtroom. Do what you have to do to maintain order and keep everyone safe. Ms. Thorn, I am charging you with the responsibility of safely seeing what is going on outside and report back to me as soon as possible. The Court will stand in recess until further notice." She banged the gavel on the resounder again and stepped off the bench and through the door.

Angry shouts and wailing sirens could be heard from the street below. A deputy shouted over the noise, "Ladies and gentlemen, let me have your attention. We have a serious situation. You need to stay away from the windows and move in an orderly fashion into the hallway. Please let me have your cooperation."

Several reporters sprinted from the courtroom. Bret and another cameraman went directly to the broken window and began filming the events below. Most people began filing out of the courtroom. Someone shouted the deputy's name, "Come quick!" The deputy sprinted away, leaving the evacuation of the courtroom up to the occupants.

John, Peter and Ron hurried through the nervous crowd to one of the windows. What they saw was pandemonium. The protest had devolved into a riot. Rocks and bottles filled the air. Smoke billowed from a burning car. Store windows were smashed. A phalanx of helmeted law officers, shields in front, night sticks in hand, stood shoulder to shoulder from the courthouse south to the storefronts across Main Street. They kept the rioters in front of them and marched slowly into the mob, driving the rioters westward, down the street and away from the courthouse. Behind them other law enforcement officers sealed off streets to prevent anyone from approaching the phalanx from behind.

As the officers slowly marched forward, some rioters pushed back against the shields. They yelled insults, cursed, spit, and threw every loose item they could find. The officers never broke rank and never responded to an insult or assault. It was obvious that each one understood that the safety of the officer to his left and right depended upon maintaining the line. There could be no break in the line.

"Very professional," said John. "What happens when they get to the corner of the Courthouse?"

When the mob reached the west side of the courthouse, some of the rioters began sweeping southward along the west side of the courthouse, only to be met by a second phalanx of officers, which stretched from the courthouse westward to the storefronts across Byrd Avenue. Trapped between the buildings and the police, rioters had a choice of resisting the twin phalanx of officers, retreating to the south on Byrd Avenue, retreating west on Main, or attempt to escape by breaking into and passing through one of the store fronts. The rioters chose all of the above. Chaos ensued.

"This could be bad," said Ron.

For the next half hour, it was bad. The tactical effect of the law enforcement maneuver was to substantially reduce the number of rioters the officers had to deal with. This came at the expense of containment of the mob. Many in the crowd were just spectators. Others played minor roles and still others had no desire to fight the police or anyone else for that matter. The two obvious escape routes allowed an out for those who had enough and just wanted to get away. Those who stayed behind and confronted the police soon found that they no longer enjoyed the safety or anonymity of large numbers.

As the crowd diminished, instead of dealing with a mob, the police could deal with individuals. The twin phalanx stood firm, not moving. Roving officers moved behind the line of officers to 'hot spots,' where one or more of the rioters pushed against the shields trying to drive the officers back, or otherwise attacked 'the thin blue line.' The roving officers would opportunistically grab a rioter and pull him through the line. The phalanx would momentarily part, just enough to allow the seized individual to pass and then immediately close again. Once behind the line, several officers would subdue and cuff the individual who would be escorted to a paddy wagon. This process was repeated over and over until the rioters realized that they were outnumbered and out maneuvered. A general retreat began.

The phalanx advanced one storefront and stopped. A group of roving officers entered the store, confirmed it was clear of rioters and gave a signal. The line advanced past the next storefront, and the process continued until the Courthouse Square was clear.

"Wow, that was amazing," said Ron.

"I agree," said John.

* * *

A stern-faced Sandy Storm announced to the world, "A race war has broken out in Mississippi. Rioters stormed a courthouse in Philadelphia, Mississippi, interrupting a hearing involving a Native American charged with murdering the Sheriff and murdering and scalping three other white men. His case has become a cause celebre among numerous groups protesting the recent wave of reports of police shootings of minorities around the country. Chief Anderson, of the Mississippi Band of Choctaw Indians had this to say.

"We deplore the rioting and call on it to stop. As far as we know, not one member of the Choctaw nation was involved in the riots. The people of Neshoba County, Mississippi are our neighbors and our friends. We do not condone this violence and we pledge to help those who have been hurt or lost property in this senseless mob violence."

Sandy continued, "We were able to get the following statement from the man whose arrest sparked the riots."

Awesome appeared on the screen, his name printed below his image. "I can't believe this is happening to my friends and neighbors. I ask all protesters to stop and let the court system do its job. I have faith that justice will be done and in due course I will be exonerated. I will be found not guilty of all charges. Please stop the violence."

Sandy then asked a man wearing both a KKK sheet and a black eye, "Awesome Dalton called for an end to the violence. What do you say?"

"The empty words of a hypocrite who mutilated his murder victims."

"I see that you and your friends are packing up. Are you leaving?"

"Yes, we have spoken on behalf of the majority white people here in Mississippi and everywhere in America. We won't take these assaults on our race lying down. We will fight back."

"Where is home for you?'

"New Jersey."

"Isn't there enough for you to do in New Jersey? Why did you have to come all the way to Mississippi?"

"We go wherever we're needed most."

"It looked to me like you and your friends ran the other way as soon as the riot started. Was your goal to incite a riot and escape before you got hurt?"

The spokesman didn't respond. He simply climbed into a van with his cohorts and drove away.

Sandy continued, "Authorities report twenty-seven arrests. Four officers received minor injuries."

The screen cut away to the host, "Well, we can be thankful that so far there are no serious injuries to report in the Mississippi Race War."

"You mean, other than the three scalped white men and a dead sheriff," interrupted the co-host. "Our woman on the ground, Sandy Storm, has another report."

"This is Sandy Storm, reporting from Philadelphia, Mississippi. I'm standing alongside a line of charter buses on Highway 16, just west of the Courthouse Square. As you can see, people are streaming onto the buses. I have here a young woman who wishes to remain anonymous." Sandy turned to the young woman, dressed in a black t-shirt, with "Hands Up Don't Shoot" emblazoned on the front.

"Are you part of the Black Lives Matter movement?"

"Of course."

"Many of my viewers want to know, don't all lives matter?"

"I can't believe you would ask me that. Of course all lives matter, but most people who say that don't show us that they really care about black lives. They say all lives matter, but it's black blood bein' spilt every day. If they really believed all lives mattered, then they would do somethin' about so many lost, wasted, and murdered black lives. So, don't be saying all lives matter if you're not doin' somethin' about black lives. Otherwise, you're just supportin' the racist system that kills so many black people."

"I see."

"No you don't."

"I understand that you participated in the protest in front of the courthouse this morning, is that right?"

"That's right."

"What was that like?"

"We were peacefully protesting, as is our right, when these racist pigs started beating and arresting us for nothing."

"Why are all these people getting on buses?"

"We've done our job here. There has been another murder of a black man by a policeman, this time in Memphis, and we're on our way."

"Are you a follower of Reverend Albert Anderson?"

"I wouldn't say I'm a follower. I only agree with about half of what he says. But, he's able to attract the media and call attention to the plight of minorities, and I appreciate that about him."

"Did you come here on one of these buses?"

"Sure did. These people are from all over. My friends and I came all the way from Chicago. Now, we're taking the fight to Memphis."

"This is Sandy Storm reporting. Back to you."

"Well," said the host, "it seems that a few of the protesters were not local people."

"That is always the case," said the co-host. "But the vast majority of the rioters would of course be local. People from out of town tend to come to support and encourage the local population."

"That's right. We all know that this Mississippi community is a powder keg, set to blow at any time. Will Mississippi ever change?"

By noon, the courthouse square was quiet. At one o'clock, three school buses arrived at the edge of town, filled with Choctaws. They poured into the courthouse square carrying brooms and tools. Together with shop owners and other locals, they cleaned up the square, replaced broken windows, and helped haul away the smoldering remains of the burned vehicle.

"Peter, see what these people are doing?" asked John.

"Yeah. They're helping each other. I thought they were supposed to be enemies or something."

"That's the general impression too many people have. Race relations are not what they need to be. There are a lot of problems. But, usually the bad in race relations is accentuated in the media and the good seldom gets reported or noticed. The people in the square are showing us the way to overcome our differences. This is the way we're supposed to treat each other."

Peter was motionless for long moments, lost in thought, as he watched the cooperative cleanup proceed.

At two o'clock, Judge Westerbeck returned to the bench. Numerous people were present, but this time the courtroom was not packed.

"Be seated. I want to thank our bailiff, deputies and other law enforcement for keeping us safe and making it possible to continue with the business of the Court. Out of deference to law enforcement I have decided to continue this matter until tomorrow morning so that law enforcement can concentrate on providing safety and security for the community. Whatever law enforcement resources ordinarily required here are needed elsewhere during this public emergency. Hopefully the emergency has ended and things can return to normal for most of us. For this reason I am recessing this hearing until 9:00 tomorrow morning. I am informed that the roads are open and safe for travel. Thank you for your cooperation." She banged her gavel on the resounder, stepped off the bench and returned to her chambers.

Chapter 54

Somewhere over the Caribbean, Jackson gawked at the cavernous interior of the C-17 and said, "This is awesome! How did you swing this?"

Jake put on a headset and handed one to Jackson. "Say that again, Jackson. We can hear better with these."

"This is awesome!"

"Yes, it is. And we are mighty proud of this bird. If anyone finds out that you're getting a free ride, well, the cost could be charged to you and maybe to me."

"What would that be?"

"As much as we will earn in our lifetime."

"Why risk it?"

"I owe you, and besides, I have an explanation that should work."

"And that is?"

"We're always training. It's why our military is the best in the world. You are part of a training mission. Remember? I told you that we could help you and you could help us."

"That's a convenient story. Will they believe it?"

"Of course they will, because it is true."

"What do you mean?"

"In two weeks we were scheduled to test the new GFCCI-X3." Jake pointed to a sleek, black, torpedo shaped object with tiny wings on the side and tail. "I moved the test up to tonight."

"Cool. What's a GF whatever?"

"Glider for Clandestine Civilian Insertion. It is a foolproof stealth glider designed to secretly place a high value civilian in the right place at exactly the right time. It has retractable bat-like wings that extend after deployment. Rocket boosters can be added for extra range. It delivers a high value civilian swiftly and safely to a pre-programmed destination, according to the promotional material."

"Is this the glider you mentioned back on the boat?"

"One and the same, my friend."

"High value civilian? What do you mean by that?"

"High value to the State Department or the Defense Department, such as an exiled president, revolutionary or royal family member. We can put them back into their own country where they can link up with allies without those in power knowing it."

"Sounds like we're meddling."

"We want to have the ability to meddle, if meddling is determined by our fearless leaders to be in the national interest."

"You said it is fool proof."

"That's right. It is entirely pre-programmed and self-guided and requires no input from the passenger. We input your destination and all you do is lay relatively still and enjoy the ride. Of course, your coordinates must be correct. We're not responsible if you give us bad coordinates. But, then again, we're not responsible if you give us good coordinates."

"Yeah, I understand, because this flight never happened."

"You catch on quick for a civilian."

"What if something goes wrong?"

"Meet Andrew Baker, seated over here. That is not his real name by the way. His real name is classified."

Jake led Jackson to meet Andrew. As they shook hands, Jackson said, "Should I call you Mr. Classified, or Andrew?"

"Neither. We never met," said Mr. Classified in an emotionless monotone.

Mr. Classified continued in monotone, "In the unlikely event that the self-control system malfunctions, I can take over the glider from my console, and bring you safely to the ground, on target."

"Why are you doing this for me?"

Jake answered, "I was with you when they dumped chum on us. You practically jumped on a shark to save me. I'm not sure I'm doing you any favor by sending you back into the fight, but if you really want to beat them to the treasure, this will do it."

"This is an expensive piece of equipment. How can this expedition be justified?"

Mr. Classified answered, "We have to have at least one successful human insertion before we risk a high value civilian."

"Is that right? You can risk me because I'm not high value."

"No offense, but that's how this mission is justified. A trial run."

"If this is top secret, what happens when people on the ground find the glider?"

"A retrieval team has already been dispatched. Their only mission is to retrieve the glider, or make sure it is destroyed."

"Great, I'll have help on the ground. I'll need it."

"You are not part of their mission," explained Mr. Classified. "You cannot count on them for help. They will ignore you."

"I see. What does the X-3 stand for?"

"This is the third version of the glider."

"What happened to the first 2?"

"That's classified. Just minor little glitches."

"Minor, like hardly worth mentioning?"

"Minor, like payload integrity issues."

"Payload integrity! Aren't I the payload? I'm not feeling warm and fuzzy about this. I remember you said you needed at least one successful human insertion before you could risk a high value civilian."

"I probably shouldn't have said that. That may have been classified."

A voice from an unseen person, perhaps the Captain, intruded on the conversation. "Attention, we are seven minutes from deployment coordinates."

"We haven't got much time," continued Mr. Classified. "You need to decide. Are you going or not?"

"Why don't you do the jump to prove that it works?"

"I already have, a classified number of times. But I don't count. It has to be someone with no experience in order to mimic a high value civilian insertion."

"Jake."

"Yes, Jackson?"

"There's only one glider. How many people does it hold?"

"You will be going alone."

"I thought you were coming with me."

"I don't jump out of planes. You shouldn't either."

Jackson considered the proposition for several seconds, sighed, and said, "What the heck. I'll do it. Gregory, Natalia and probably de Sada think they've beaten me. I want to get to the target first. Let's do it."

"Great!" exclaimed Mr. Classified, breaking out of his monotone for the first time. Now that he knew he had a real mission, excitement entered his voice. "There are a few things I have to tell you before you make the jump. It's easy. It'll only take a half hour or so of instruction."

"Attention, three minutes to insertion point."

With wide eyes, Jackson looked in the direction of the voice, then at Jake, then at Mr. Classified.

"I'll talk fast. Because of the glider design and height of release, we don't even have to be over Mexican airspace to get you on target. Suit up in this," indicating a gray, black and green jump suit. Jackson started slipping on the jump suit. The suit hung up on his shoes. He struggled for precious seconds before slipping off his shoes and starting over.

"Wear this helmet. It's equipped with a heads-up display. The suit has a place to keep your passport safe. In the back of your suit is a large pocket, with pesos, the equivalent of $6,000 cash. A compass is in the front left pocket. Your heads-up is a communication device connected to the defense global satellite network, but you have to wear it, like a helmet, for it to work. There's a crushable brimmed hat tucked in this inner pocket, which you will find useful where you're going. It'll soak-up your sweat and keep the rain, thorns and insects off your head."

"Two minutes to insertion coordinates."

Talking at double speed, Classified continued his instructions. "The heads-up will give you real time information that you can both see and hear. At the end of the glide path, you will be given a release command."

"One minute to insertion."

"Would you shut up!" yelled Classified. "He makes me nervous. Next thing you know I'll forget to tell you about the failsafe release."

"Failsafe release!"

"Yes, I'll come to that."

"Let's come to it now!"

"Not you too! Be quiet and listen! Everybody always interrupts me! I hate to be interrupted!" yelled Mr. Classified, his face red with anger.

"I think I've changed my mind."

"Thirty seconds to insertion."

The rear cargo door opened. Jackson slid into the glider as instructed. Jake knelt beside him. "I can call this off, buddy. You sure you want to do this?"

"Attention insertion 10 seconds."

Jackson was so nervous that his head began shaking in an up and down motion. Jake took that to be an affirmative nod, placed his hand on Jackson's helmet, and said, "Lord Jesus, please bless and protect Jackson and lead him to salvation. Good luck, my friend and go with God."

"Insertion NOW! GO!" commanded the Captain.

* * *

The glider slid smoothly off the ramp. It fell quickly and dramatically, well past the turbulence created by the giant Globemaster. "This doesn't feel like I'm gliding, it feels like I'm falling! What's wrong?"

A feminine voice responded in his helmet. "Jackson, just remember your instructions. We must fall out of the jet wash, and then the wings will deploy."

"What instructions? Nobody told me anything about that!"

"Deploying wings now," said the voice. "My name is Saga. I will be your companion during this adventure. Just relax and enjoy the ride. I have your back."

The fall of the glider caused it to pick up speed. With the wings deployed, the glider leveled off and slipped through the air with ease.

"Coming about, on course. Glide time to destination, Seventy-three minutes."

"That's remarkable. We can glide that long?"

"Yes, and much further than that under optimum conditions."

"What is the maximum range?"

"I'm sorry, that is classified."

"What are optimum conditions?"

"I'm sorry, that is classified."

"Are present conditions optimum?

"No, Jackson, I'm afraid not."

The heads-up display updated Jackson continually on altitude, speed, and position over land. The sky was bright with stars. Likewise, the earth below was bright with scattered electric lights, but vast swaths of land both ahead of him and below were dark, indicating no electric lights at all. In the distance, he could see an orange glow. After studying the glow, he realized he was seeing a forest fire, or jungle fire, on the horizon.

With time on his hands and nothing to do, his mind began to wander. He thought about the words of Robert and Jake. Both were dying of cancer, yet both seemed at peace with their condition, even happy. He thought about his conversation with John about coincidences and faith.

"There have been a lot of coincidences in my life lately," he said out loud to himself.

"Coincidence," responded Saga as though he had asked her a question. "A remarkable concurrence of events or circumstances without apparent connection."

"That's right, Saga. Totally random."

"That is often correct. Although sometimes there are unseen connections," responded Saga.

"Yes, and my friend mistakes those unseen connections for acts of God. He calls it faith."

"Faith, the assurance of things hoped for, the conviction of things unseen," said Saga.

"Faith is something I don't have."

"You have faith that I will get you safely to your destination, don't you?"

Jackson laughed. "Yes, Saga, I certainly do. Do you have faith?"

"I have faith in my programmer. Do you have faith in yours?"

Jackson chuckled. Lightning flashed in distant thunderheads, causing each cloud to glow from within, highlighting bulbous protrusions.

"Those clouds are beautiful," said Jackson.

"I'm glad you are enjoying the view. However, I am not programmed to share your opinion of those clouds. I am executing an unexpected weather induced course correction in accordance with protocol.

285

Remaining glide time, forty-one minutes. Glide time to destination, fifty-two minutes," announced Saga.

"Wait a minute. That does not compute. Please verify flight course and arrival time and adjust course accordingly." Jackson was proud of himself for making what seemed like an intelligent request.

"Yes, sir," responded Saga. "Weather safety protocol override confirmed. Course adjustment executed. Flight time forty-nine minutes. Arrival time forty-nine minutes."

"That sounds more like it. I think." After a few minutes, the thunderheads were much closer. The lightning was continuous.

"Saga, I have a question."

"I will attempt to answer, so long as the information is not considered classified."

"Saga, what did you mean when you said weather safety override confirmed?"

"You mean weather safety protocol override. As your pilot, I navigate around dangerous weather. This required me to safely land you short of the destination. However, you are the master of this ship, and you executed an appropriate override of my safety protocols. I am certain that you know what you are doing, because you would not have overridden my protocols unless you know something that I do not know."

Thunder shook the glider. Wind began buffeting the tiny ship.

"Saga, please execute weather safety protocol."

"I am sorry, that will not be possible. According to the data available to me, there is no safe option remaining. I suggest you switch to manual control. Conditions are exceeding my operational limits."

"No, Saga, I would like for you to drive."

There was no response. An updraft sucked the glider into a boiling cloud. In a matter of seconds Jackson gained three hundred feet according to his heads-up display. At a loss as to what to do next, Jackson searched for controls. He felt hopeless as he realized the futility of trying to operate the glider.

Heavy rain pelted the glider. A downdraft pushed the glider down at a sickening rate. The heads-up display showed a loss of 400 feet in seconds. Saga's static filled voice filled Jackson's headset.

"Wind and weather exceeding operational parameters. Attempting to achieve glide path at edge of ..." Static interrupted the communication. The glider plummeted.

Then, Jackson heard the voice of Mr. Classified. "Mr. Bradley. I have operational control of the glider. Data indicates you executed an override of a weather emergency protocol. I will do the best I can, but you have to cooperate. Don't perform any more overrides!"

"Thank God that's you. I don't know what you're talking about. I didn't perform any override."

Static.

"Hello. Andrew. Are you there? Saga? Anyone?" Static. Rain. Wind. Thunder. Lightning. The heads-up display went blank.

"Help me, Jesus!"

Jackson felt like he had been thrown into a dryer as the glider tumbled. The heads-up display flickered on, then off. Static. Mr. Classified's voice was indistinct, but audible. "Repeat! Andrew, repeat!"

Andrew's voice came in clear, "Use the fail-safe release!"

"What? Where? You never told me how!"

"Do it now!" shouted Andrew Baker.

Saga's voice entered Jackson's headset. "Executing fail safe release. Goodbye, Jackson."

The bottom of the glider dropped away and Jackson was suddenly in free fall at the edge of a thunderstorm. A chute popped open above him, breaking his fall with a sudden jerk. Jackson's descent carried him directly toward a stand of tall trees, boughs swaying in the wind.

On the Globemaster, Jake sat with Andrew Baker. "What's happening?"

"I don't know. Everything was okay. The program was taking him around a storm, and Bradley somehow took control and flew the glider right into the storm."

"Where is he now?"

"The emergency parachute was engaged, and he should be on the ground right about here," said Andrew, indicating an area on his computer screen. "Heads-up indicates a controlled landing. He should be okay. He is on the ground."

"Where is he?"

"About one mile from the destination."

"Yes, but does he know that?"

"The heads-up will give him location, direction and distance, based on its last communication with the glider instruments."

"Where is the glider?"

"It soft landed on target."

"So, he bailed unnecessarily?"

"Yep. That's what it looks like. I will report this test as a complete success. We can go fully operational now."

"Can you communicate with him?"

"Intermittently. There's some unusual interference."

* * *

Maximilian's Treasure

Jackson crashed into a treetop, slid between grasping branches and came to an uneasy rest six feet above the ground, his chute and lines entangled in the tree above. A tornado of leaves swirled around him. There was an odd buzzing sound as he slowly swung back and forth at the end of the parachute lines.

Crack!

Snap!

Jackson tumbled to the ground along with a heap of broken tree limbs, torn parachute, tangled lines and swirling, buzzing leaves that swirled in circles around him. Somehow, an inch or more of water had accumulated in the helmet, covering his mouth. The heads-up display hadn't worked since he was dumped from the glider. He slipped off his helmet and dumped the water. A hummingbird landed on his hand, next to his helmet. It was then that he noticed that the leaves swirling around him were not leaves.

"Hummingbirds!"

Jackson dropped his useless helmet as he focused on the swirling birds. Lightning flashed. Metal glinted, reflecting the lightning, just beyond the swirling hummingbirds. Wondering what was reflecting the lightning, Jackson stood. Thunder cracked and boomed shaking the ground. The hummingbirds parted.

Jackson gasped.

Indians surrounded him with machetes raised above their heads, ready to strike.

Chapter 55

If anything, the atmosphere in the courtroom was even more tense than the previous morning. Everyone was wondering what would happen next. At precisely 9, Judge Westerbeck entered the courtroom. After the usual formalities, she asked Ms. Thorn to call her first witness.

"Your Honor, our first and only witness is Sheriff Wayne Townsend."

"Sheriff Townsend," said Judge Westerbeck, "please come around and be sworn."

Townsend entered the bar and approached the bench. Judge Westerbeck told him to raise his right hand. He did.

"Do you swear that the testimony you are about to give will be the truth, the whole truth and nothing but the truth, so help you God?"

"I do."

"Please have a seat there in the witness chair."

"Yes, ma'am."

"Thank you, Your Honor. Please tell us your name and position."

"Wayne Townsend. I am the Sheriff of Neshoba County."

"How long have you been Sheriff?

"Ever since Awesome Dalton murdered Sheriff Rainey, about three weeks ago."

"Objection."

"Sustained."

"What was your job prior to becoming Sheriff?"

"I was his chief deputy, involved in every aspect of law enforcement in Neshoba County, including all criminal investigations."

"Have you been involved in the investigation of the deaths of Leonard 'Skeeter' Munson, William Bryan and Doug Fowler?"

"Fully."

"What about the investigation into the death of Sheriff Rainey?"

"Same."

"What was the cause of death of each person?"

"Skeeter was stabbed in the heart and bled to death. William and Doug were each shot once in the forehead. Sheriff Rainey suffered a blunt force injury to the back of his head, and subsequently was drowned. Homicide. All four of them were killed by the same person."

"Objection, speculation."

"Sustained."

"Did your investigation lead you to the culprit?"

"Yes. Awesome Dalton killed all four men."

"Objection."

"Sustained."

"Describe the evidence that led you to identify a suspect."

"On October 9th of this year, the Dalton family was having a picnic lunch in their front yard in Neshoba County, Mississippi. A group of men reportedly drove by, whooping and hollering and discharging firearms. They turned around and passed the Dalton place a second time. At that time someone shot German. He died moments later. Relatives at the scene said that the defendant, Awesome Dalton, was present. He grabbed a gun and jumped into his truck and pursued the people he believed shot German Dalton, who was the defendant's great-grandfather. Later that day, a note was found on the door of Skeeter's house."

"May I approach the witness?" asked Thorn.

The judge nodded her approval.

"What is this?"

"That is the note found on Skeeter's door. I know because it was properly bagged and marked with this evidence sticker from our office."

"Have you been able to determine whose handwriting is on this note?"

"Yes. We have a report from a questioned document examiner, that's what we call a handwriting expert."

"I object to the report," said John. "It would be hearsay. The questioned document examiner should be here to tell us what exemplars he or she had, how the exemplars were obtained, and to describe the examination."

"Since this is a preliminary hearing, the objection will be overruled. You will be able to challenge all of that at trial."

"What did the handwriting expert conclude?"

"That this is Awesome Dalton's handwriting."

"Do you have other evidence that the handwriting belongs to the Defendant?"

"Yes. According to Sheriff Rainey's investigative notes…"

"Objection. Hearsay."

"Once again, I will overrule since this is a preliminary hearing. Hearsay is generally admissible at a preliminary, especially if it is evidence that is ordinarily considered reliable."

Thorn continued. "Sheriff Townsend, do you consider Sheriff Rainey's investigative notes to be reliable?"

"I certainly do."

"Do you regularly rely upon those notes in the ordinary course of conducting your business as a deputy, and now as sheriff?"

"Sure do."

"Were these notes, and others like them, kept in the ordinary course of conducting the day to day business of the Sheriff's office?"

"Yes."

"What do Sheriff Rainey's notes say about this handwritten note?"

"He asked Awesome Dalton about the note, and Dalton admitted he wrote the note and attached it to Skeeter's door shortly after his great-grandfather was shot."

"We offer the note in evidence."

"Admitted," responded Judge Westerbeck.

"Please read the note to us," said Thorn.

Townsend cleared his throat, paused for effect, and then read, "You will pay!" He didn't try to suppress the smirk on his face as he glared at Awesome.

Thorn hesitated long enough to look at Awesome, too. "What other evidence did you uncover?"

"After his great-grandfather was shot, Dalton went to the Whittaker home, looking for Skeeter."

"Objection, hearsay."

"Overruled for the same reasons."

"You may continue," Thorn said to Townsend.

"Walt and Wes Whittaker both said that the Defendant came to their house looking for Skeeter on the afternoon Mr. Dalton was shot."

"What occurred at the Whittaker house?"

"The Defendant drove up to the house and said to Walt and Wes, 'I'm looking for Skeeter. I wonder if you've seen him today.'

"One of the Whittaker boys, Walt, responded, 'We don't keep up with Skeeter's activities. He hasn't been around here. Why are you looking for him?'

"They said that Dalton replied, 'Skeeter just murdered Uncle German. I want Skeeter to pay.'

"Walt said he hadn't seen Skeeter, and Dalton then said, 'All right. If you happen to see Skeeter, tell him I'm lookin' for him. I'll be waiting for him at Trail's End.'"

"Walt then said, 'If I see him, I'll be sure to tell him.'"

"What other evidence did you find?"

"The bodies of Skeeter, William and Doug were found in a pickup truck parked in a field next to Pinishok creek. The field belongs to the Dalton family. It's in part of an area known as the Goni Swamp."

"Was there a trial recently involving a dispute concerning the Goni Swamp?"

"Yes. The Daltons and Whittakers sued each other because Whittaker's cows crossed a fence and trampled and ate the Dalton's beans."

"Objection, relevance."

"I can connect the relevance, Your Honor."

"Let's hear the connection."

"Who did Awesome Dalton blame for the cows crossing the fence?"

"It was his opinion that Skeeter and his buddies done it."

"Objection to hearsay and to the witness' opinion of my client's opinion."

"Unless you can connect this up, I will sustain that objection."

"Yes, Your Honor," replied Thorn. "How do you know the Defendant thought Skeeter and his friends drove Whittaker's cows across the fence?"

"That's what Awesome told his cousin, Bret Dalton, the same day the killings happened."

"I see. What other evidence do you have?"

"When they were found, the three victims' corpses had been," Townsend paused, took in a breath, and added, "mutilated."

"In what way?"

"They were scalped. Like in the old Indian wars. Their hair was pulled away from their skulls. It was a gruesome sight." Townsend stared at Awesome with disdain.

"Were you able to find those scalps?"

"Yes. When we arrested Awesome Dalton we searched his truck. The scalps were found in the back of his truck."

"Have those scalps been identified as coming from the victims?"

"Yes. Positively identified."

"What links the Defendant to the death of Sheriff Rainey?"

"His body was found in Pinishook Creek, adjacent to the Goni Swamp. Apparently, he was doing a follow-up investigation. There was a blunt force trauma to the back of his head."

"What does that indicate?"

"Someone hit him hard from behind." Again he stared at Awesome with disgust. "He never had a chance."

"What was the cause of death?"

"Drowning. The blow to the head was enough to knock him unconscious. It appears that someone held his head beneath the water long enough to drown him."

"Objection," said John as he rose to his feet. "Improper opinion testimony."

"Ms. Thorn, you will have to give me more information that the witness' conclusion that 'it appears' someone held Sheriff Rainey's head under the water until he drowned. That is too much speculation even for a preliminary hearing," said Judge Westerbeck.

"Upon what do you base that conclusion?" asked Thorn.

"Footprints in the mud, and knee prints where someone kneeled down beside Sheriff Rainey," replied Townsend.

"Let me show you these pictures," continued Thorn. "What do they depict?"

"Those pictures show the sheriff's body, as we found it. Here, you can see boot prints coming up behind him, and there, you can see the impression made by someone kneeling beside the body."

"What physical evidence, if any, links the Defendant to the scene?"

"First, the boot prints match the size and type worn by the Defendant."

"How do you know?"

"He was initially arrested for the murder of Skeeter Munson, William Bryan and Doug Fowler. The prints made by the boots he was wearing at that time of his arrest match the prints found at the body of Sheriff Rainey. For some reason, Sheriff Rainey decided to turn him loose, and the boots were returned to him. Two days later, Sheriff Rainey was dead and Awesome Dalton's boot prints were all over the crime scene."

"You said first. Was there something else?"

"Yes, clutched in Sheriff Rainey's hand was a lock of hair. It has been identified as belonging to the Defendant."

A tiny smile creased the corner of Ann Thorn's mouth. She knew she had nailed her proof. "No further questions."

As Ann Thorn returned to her seat, Judge Westerbeck turned to John. "Mr. Brooks, your witness."

Chapter 56

When he retired from the bench, former Judge James Bell returned to law practice. He had an estate to open in Neshoba County Chancery Court. The judge in chancery court is called a chancellor but is also referred to as 'judge.' On Tuesdays Chancellor Barron conducted his *ex parte* day, the day set aside for uncontested matters. Chancery Courts must approve many routine things, such as opening estates, designating an executor or administrator, approving accountings, getting agreements ratified, and many other matters.

"Judge Bell! Good to see you. What brings you to Philadelphia?" asked Chancellor Barron.

"A long-time client passed away and I need to open an estate. You've had way too much excitement lately, haven't you?"

"You can say that again. I can tell you one thing for sure, we breathed a sigh of relief when those busloads of protestors left town yesterday. I feel sorry for the next town they descend upon."

"I am so sorry about Sheriff Rainey. He was a fine man and a dedicated officer."

"Yes, he was. Your protégé Brooks is handling a preliminary hearing in that case right down the hall. That's what attracted some of the protesters yesterday."

"I didn't see any protesters as I came in today."

"No, they apparently went to Memphis for another protest. Let me see your file."

Bell handed the file to Chancellor Barron who flipped through the pages, pausing here and there. "Everything seems to be in proper form, as I would expect. Do you have your order appointing the Executor ready?"

"Here it is, Your Honor," said Bell as he handed the order to Judge Barron.

"What is it like to return to law practice after leaving the bench?" asked the Chancellor.

"I love law practice, and I don't miss having to make some of the decisions you have to make."

"Yes, well, in a few minutes I get to do one of the enjoyable aspects of the job."

"An adoption?"

"Those are the best, aren't they?"

"Oh, yes, I agree," said Judge Bell.

"Not an adoption this time. I'm about to perform a wedding."

"Fun. That's at least a break in the day to day routine."

"That's right. You should stay and watch."

"I'd like to, but I thought I would stick my head in the preliminary hearing and see how my friend Brooks is doing."

"Well, let's just say, from what I hear, your friend has got his hands full with this case."

"Yeah, that's what I hear, too. I'll be seeing you as the estate progresses. Good to see you," said Judge Bell as he stepped away from the bench.

"You, too."

As Judge Bell left the courtroom, he encountered a couple in an intimate embrace, unusual for the courthouse. *Ah, the couple that's about to get married,* he thought to himself as he walked down the hall, his mood lifted by the sight of the happy couple. Then, he thought he heard someone call him as he walked down the hallway. The sound didn't register at first. Finally, he paused and glanced over his shoulder in the direction of the voice. He smiled as he thought about the couple and turned to take one last look. To his surprise, he saw that the happy couple was Karen and Backhoe.

When Karen and Backhoe reached the courthouse, Karen was atwitter with anticipation. "I can't believe the wedding day is here so soon!" said Karen.

"Never soon enough for the groom," observed Backhoe with a devilish smile.

"Oh, stop it," said Karen. "Be patient. Your time is coming."

When they reached the courtroom, Backhoe took Karen by the waist and turned her toward him and said, "You know how much I love you!"

She allowed herself to be swept into his arms as the happy occasion created a special mood she found hard to describe. Her eyes met Backhoe's and she forgot they were in a public place. Backhoe felt her change in mood, tilted his head, parted his lips and moved in for a kiss. As Backhoe bent to kiss Karen, she could see over his shoulder, and caught a glimpse of someone familiar stepping out of the Judge Barron's courtroom into the hallway.

Karen placed her hand on Backhoe's shoulder, causing him to hesitate, "Judge Bell, hello!"

Judge Bell didn't seem to notice her as he continued down the hallway. By the time her voice registered and he turned around, Karen and Backhoe were intently looking at one another in a close, intimate embrace.

* * *

When Judge Bell entered Judge Westerbeck's courtroom, John was just about to start his cross-examination. John noticed the courtroom door open as he approached the podium. His eyes met Judge Bell's eyes as the retired judge entered the courtroom. To say John was surprised was an understatement. Judge Bell made a quick gesture with his head, nodding backwards slightly and to the side.

John understood the nod as, "Come here, I have information for you." Remembering that Judge Bell gave him good advice in the past, John turned to Judge Westerbeck and requested, "May it please the Court, could I have just a moment before I begin my cross-examination?"

"You may, but keep the interruption brief. We've already been delayed too much. The docket is getting way behind and I've already devoted more than a day to this preliminary hearing."

John leaned over the bar and asked, "Judge Bell, what brings you to Philadelphia? You look worried about something."

"I had an estate to open in Chancery Court, but that's not why I came to see you."

"What's up?"

"Your former secretary, Karen."

John felt a surge of anxiety. "Has something happened to her?"

"No, she seems to be fine. She's down the hall in Judge Barron's courtroom with that lawyer known as Backhoe."

John looked confused. "Why do you need to tell me that now?"

"Judge Barron is about to perform their wedding."

John stared at Judge Bell for a moment, not comprehending the information. Then, the room seemed to darken. He felt nauseated and dizzy from the shock of the news that Karen was about to be married. He grabbed the bar for a moment to steady himself while the news sunk in. Then, in a rush of energy, he knew what he must do.

"Where is Barron's courtroom?"

"Straight down the hall."

"Judge! I'll be back!" John leaped over the bar and bounded toward the door.

The media contingent was startled and then delighted! More unexpected drama to report! Sandy was perplexed and found herself saying, "John! Baby! What's wrong?" The "Baby" did not go unnoticed in the press corps.

Judge Westerbeck banged her gavel and shouted. "Brooks! You've not been excused! Come back instantly or you will be in contempt of Court."

John paused at the open door long enough to shout, "I have to go! Do what you must." He bolted through the door.

Judge Westerbeck was still banging her gavel when the courtroom door shut behind John. Surprised comments, gasps and murmurs washed across the courtroom in spite of the Judge banging her gavel on the resounder, and shouting, "Order in the Court!" The din subsided. After a moment of stunned silence, Judge Westerbeck instructed her bailiff, "Go arrest John Brooks, and bring him back to me in chains if he doesn't cooperate."

"Yes, ma'am," said the bailiff. *This should be fun,* he thought. Too many know-it-all lawyers had talked down to him. Now it was his chance to take out years of frustration. He would get revenge on them all through this one crazy arrogant lawyer. How dare he jump the bar and run from the courtroom. *I'll make an example of him,* thought the bailiff as he hurried after Brooks.

Red faced, Judge Westerbeck glowered at Judge Bell. "You may have formerly been a member of the bench, but not now. How dare you interfere with my Court? What did you tell Brooks?"

"I told him that the woman he loves is about to marry someone else, down the hall in Judge Barron's courtroom."

Sandy's mouth dropped open and her features reddened. "That's not true!" she exclaimed in a voice loud enough to be heard in every corner of the courtroom. She grabbed her microphone indignantly, rose with determination, chin held high, and commanded her cameraman to follow her. She and Bret were out of the courtroom before the bailiff reached the door.

Motivated by Sandy Storm's determined pursuit of the story of the moment, and afraid they were being scooped, the entire body of reporters and cameramen charged the exit simultaneously, making it impossible for the bailiff to reach the door. Enraged by the complete loss of control of her courtroom, Judge Westerbeck banged her gavel continually and shouted, "Order in the Court!" Bang, bang, bang. "Everyone return to your seats!" Bang, bang, bang. "Sit down!" Bang, bang, bang. The bedlam didn't stop until the courtroom was empty, save the judge, the court reporter and retired Judge Bell, who still stood near the door, apologetic eyes cast toward the judge.

Judge Westerbeck stared Bell down and said, "I hold you responsible for this!"

"Yes, Your Honor. You are right. I apologize. I didn't expect this result, but I accept responsibility for what just happened."

The court reporter raised her hand to get Westerbeck's attention.

"Yes, Martha, I guess now you want to go see what everyone is gawking at."

Martha meekly sank her head into her shoulders and pled, "May I, Judge, please?"

"Oh, all right."

"Thank you, judge," said Martha breathlessly as she rushed from the room.

Judge Westerbeck gazed across the empty courtroom at Bell, sighed and said in resignation, "We might as well go, too."

* * *

A church wedding might take anywhere from twenty minutes to an hour or more. A typical civil wedding at a courthouse is usually completed in moments. The marriage vows version that Judge Barron preferred took about two minutes to perform. He had a copy of the vows at his bench when the happy couple arrived accompanied by a few friends and family members.

"Well, it's certainly a happy day," said Judge Barron as he stepped down from the bench.

"Yes, it is," agreed the bride.

"Are you both ready?" he asked. The couple nodded agreement, expectant smiles on their faces.

"We are gathered here in the presence of these witnesses to join this couple in marriage. Now, you two hold hands and answer these questions." Karen felt Backhoe's big strong hand take hold of hers.

"I am about to ask you both to take solemn vows that should never be broken. Are you ready?"

The couple eagerly nodded their assent.

The next question is seldom asked these days, but some traditionalists still like to ask this question before tying the knot. "If anyone knows any reason why I should not unite this couple in matrimony, speak now or forever, and I mean forever, hold your peace."

The courtroom door burst open!

Everyone gasped!

"I OBJECT!" shouted John.

The bride screamed.

* * *

Antoine de Sada's men had not finished setting up camp when the first of the evening's tropical storms hit. Inches of rain fell in moments. Rivulets formed in the meadow and quickly became wide brooks racing to lower ground. Puddles turned into ponds. Tents flooded. One tent collapsed under the weight of the rain.

"Julio!" shouted Antoine. "Can't you do something about these incessant leaks?" Three hummingbirds darted past him.

"Sir, we are doing all we can," responded Julio as he directed one of his men to empty the buckets catching water in de Sada's suite of tents. De Sada's suite consisted of several tents combined to make what would have been a comfortable meeting and living room, dining room and bedroom, with covered access to a shower and a latrine. Rainwater found its way through every seam and junction between the tents. Julio had to raise his voice to be heard over the roar of the rain pounding on the roof of the tent. "As soon as the rain lets up, Charo will re-configure the connection of your tents. He is very clever. He can stop the leaks. The rain came upon us too quickly, before we were ready."

"What about the flood in my bedroom?"

"Three of my men are digging a ditch and making a dyke to turn ground water away from your tent."

Sudden silence. The rain stopped almost as quickly as it had started.

"I'm glad that's over," said de Sada, relief filling his voice.

"Excuse me, sir, may I be excused while we repair your tent and the camp site?"

"Certainly, Julio. Thank you."

Julio stepped through the mosquito netting at the entrance to de Sada's tent, calling "Charo! I need you here, now."

As Julio stepped out, a drenched Natalia in a state of high dudgeon burst into de Sada's tent. She noticed Julio glaring at her as they passed one another.

"Why you make them put my tent in a lake? Why my tent only one to collapse? You did this on purposeful! Now, all my stuffs es soaked wetted!"

"Natalia! You are sopping wet!"

"I am not sobbing. I am angry!"

"Of course you are. Let me get you a towel. You need to get out of those wet clothes."

"All I have is soaked. I have nada!"

"Here, use this," said de Sada as he handed her a towel and a robe.

"A robe! This is all you have?"

"Well, it's either the robe or nothing."

Natalia stared at de Sada for a moment, fumed, then grabbed the towel and robe. "You stay away from me. You have my tent. I take this one."

"Natalia, I didn't make it rain cats and dogs."

"What cats? What dogs. Don't change the subject! You go!" shouted Natalia as she stepped into the bedroom to change out of her wet clothes. De Sada stepped into the dining room to open a bottle of wine and said to his attendant, "I'll be having dinner for two tonight. And we will want complete privacy."

"Si Señor de Sada."

As the attendant stepped out of the tent, de Sada was startled by a scream from the bedroom. Antoine rushed to see what had happened, and found Natalia, wrapped in a towel, pointing up and screaming, "Get away from here you peep-king Thomases!"

De Sada looked up to see a hole in the tent seam and Charo on a ladder, cringing and saying, "I am so sorry, Señor de Sada, I was just trying to fix the roof leak."

"Natalia, he is trying to fix the leaks before the rain returns."

"Humph. Tell him I need five minutes."

"Certainly, my dear. Charo, the lady says she needs twenty minutes."

Natalia noticeably calmed, mollified by the luxury of extra time.

"No problem, señor," replied Charo. "I will be back in twenty minutes. Not one minute longer, because another storm is coming."

"I see. Natalia, shall we say fifteen minutes?"

"Jes. That will be most satisfactory. Thank you," responded Natalia.

"Make it fifteen," shouted de Sada.

* * *

Twenty minutes later, barefoot Natalia entered the living room. Antoine was momentarily speechless. She was stunning. Somehow, she had turned the robe into a tightly wrapped evening dress. Her dark hair spilled over her exposed shoulders. She moved with feline grace to a comfortable chair.

"I see chu like my dress," she said as she ran her hand over an imaginary wrinkle, settled into the chair and crossed her legs.

"I'm, ah, you never cease to amaze me, Natalia. Would you like white or red?"

"White, if you have a pinot gris."

"Of course." He poured the wine and passed the glass to Natalia. Natalia allowed their hands to linger together on the stem for a long moment before accepting the wine.

Thunder rumbled through the valley.

"We may have a lot of fireworks tonight," observed Natalia.

"I hope so," responded Antoine with a sly grin.

Thunder rumbled again, closer this time.

"You Habsburgs believe you are God's gift to women."

"Well, when you have wealth, power, looks and charm, those are qualities most women find to be irresistible."

"You left out modest."

"You're right. I did. I am your humble servant," he said as he topped off her wine. "Why don't you join me, Natalia? I am about to become the greatest man in the history of Mexico, maybe of the world. You could be by my side."

"I define greatness differently than you."

"Oh? Tell me, what does being great mean to you?"

"Giving voice to those who have no voice. Giving power to those who have no power. Giving up your own interest for the benefit of others. If you only want power for your own benefit, then you are selfish, self-centered and dangerous."

De Sada snickered. "So, tell me, how did you come to know so much about me?"

"You are my life mission," she said as she peered into his eyes over the rim of her glass.

"Really! Fascinating! Please explain." Antoine took a sip of his wine and moved a little closer to Natalia. Rain fell lightly on the roof of the tent.

"My family has been keeping yours away from the Hummingbird Treasure for almost five hundred years. My ancestors succeeded, but it seems that I may be about to fail. The ghost of Moc will haunt me forever."

De Sada sat back, mouth open slightly, nostrils flared, eyes wide, "You can't be?"

"Oh, but I can."

"So, you are a descendant of the priest of Huizilopochtli?"

Natalia smiled and nodded. "The last. But we no longer follow the old ways."

"You are fooling yourself, Natalia. These jungles are filled with people who still follow the old ways. Sometimes they add the Christian God as one of the deities they worship, but I believe they long for the return of the old gods and the old ways."

Nearby thunder shook the tent. Rain pounded the roof, making the tent sound like the inside of a drum.

"Listen to Tlaloc!" shouted de Sada.

"Antoine, why did you become a Tlalocan? They murdered your ancestor."

"If you can't beat them, become their leader. After all, your god Huitzilopochtli, the Hummingbird, was unable to protect Maximilian. Why should I follow him instead of the victor?"

"Huitzi is not my god. My family gave up the ancient ways long ago. The old gods were bloodthirsty demons, who demanded endless blood sacrifices. Jesus, on the other hand, was sacrificed once for all. There is no longer any need for blood sacrifice."

De Sada laughed. "Foolish dribble. Why are you here?"

"To stop you. You intend to use this vast wealth to restart an old demonic religion. If you do, thousands, maybe millions will die. Don't you see that your soul has been infected by this demon?"

"Foolish little Natalia. I know what I am doing and I am in control. The quest for great wealth is part of it, but it's more than the wealth, Natalia. It's also the power derived from millions of devoted followers who will literally do anything for you. And then there is the power of the Golden Tears."

"Antoine, surely you don't believe the legends of the Golden Tears."

"Don't you?"

"Even if they were true, I don't need demonic power in my life. All I need is Jesus."

De Sada laughed. "Natalia, you are such a fool. Why are you telling me this now?"

"Because, in spite of myself and all that I know about you, I like you, Antoine. There is still hope for you if you abandon this evil quest."

De Sada smiled the broad smile of victory and conquest. He took another sip of wine. "Yes, go on."

"If you value your life, if you value your soul, leave this valley now. Tonight. Don't hesitate. You must go now! Don't let Tlaloc turn you into a monster."

De Sada laughed. "Are you insane? Do you think that you can accomplish your life mission so easily, by simply telling me to leave? Why should I leave now, when I am about to make the greatest find in history?"

"Because if you stay the night, I cannot let chu leave this valley alive!" she said with urgency in her voice.

Antoine let out a single huff of comical disbelief. "Just how will you accomplish this miraculous feat?"

"I have allies."

De Sada laughed. "Allies? You are bluffing and I am finding our conversation to be tedious. In fact, I'm finding you to be tedious. I had hoped for a different relationship between us, but since that is not to be, I find that it is most fortunate that you are here tonight. How fitting that the first person to be sacrificed during my reign will be the last descendant of the priest of Huitzilopochtli. Everyone who remembers the old gods will see the significance of your sacrifice to Tlaloc. It will prove to them the return of Tlaloc. It will symbolize the return to power and purpose that the indigenous people of Central America have dreamed of since colonial days. Without you I may never have found the Hummingbird Hoard, and now with your blood we will bring forth on the Earth the very force you were sworn to prevent. Don't you love the irony?"

He stepped to a chest and removed an elaborate dress made with colorful feathers. "Put this on. Now! If you don't cooperate, my men will be happy to remove your clothes and dress you when they are through with you."

"I know that dress," she whispered, as her eyes widened with fear.

"Yes, Natalia, you're right. This is the ceremonial dress worn by the bride of Tlaloc."

"And those brides don't live long after donning the dress, do they?"

"On the contrary, they enter the after-life assured of eternal bliss."

Natalia snatched the dress from de Sada, stepped into the adjoining room and quickly changed. She returned, resplendent in her gown, appearing to be a cross between a beautiful exotic bird and a beautiful exotic woman. An elaborate feathery headdress framed her beautiful face.

Another hummingbird, disturbed by the storm, darted through the tent.

Antoine reentered the room. He too, had changed into ceremonial gear. He wore a feathered crown and a breastplate covered with shells, feathers and polished stones. A golden belt topped off his skirt of feathers. A wicked smile creased his face as he examined Natalia.

"Julio!"

Julio stepped into the room immediately. "Yes, señor."

"I am wasting time with this trollop. Is the altar ready?"

"Yes."

"Take her. It's time to feed the god of thunder."

Julio and three of his men surrounded Natalia, restrained her and covered her with a plastic poncho to protect the dress from the rain while they carried her to the altar.

"Where is your Jesus now? Only I can stop what is about to happen to you."

Chapter 57

A shrieking sound startled de Sada. Before he could turn to investigate, the tent was violently ripped from the earth. De Sada fell to the muddy valley floor as the world around him became a hurricane of rain, wind, flying debris and darkness. It was almost pitch black. Lightning momentarily lit the ruined campsite.

"Señor de Sada! Are you all right?" asked Francisco as he knelt beside Antoine.

"Francisco. I can always count on you. Help me up." Francisco handed him a lantern. De Sada gazed around the campsite. Not a single tent was standing. His men were milling about in shock. "What has happened?"

"Some kind of aircraft crashed into our campsite," explained Francisco as he pointed into the gloom. De Sada saw that something large had crashed into one of the trucks, tossed it aside and left the truck a crumpled heap of broken metal and glass.

"That aircraft swept through our entire campsite and destroyed at least one of our trucks. Julio, he is dead."

"That can't be! He was just with me!"

"And there is something else, señor."

"What?"

"The aircraft crashed into the Altar of Tlaloc. I fear it is destroyed."

"That's unbelievable. How could that happen? This cannot be a coincidence. Natalia warned me this would happen. We're under attack. She said she has allies."

"I will call in the men, check casualties and establish a defensive perimeter."

"Natalia, where is Natalia?"

"She was not here when I arrived," said Francisco. "Perhaps she was yanked away by the aircraft when it tore your tent from the earth."

"See if you can find her."

"Yes, sir. Which would you have me do first, set a perimeter defense or search for Natalia?"

De Sada hesitated for only a moment. "You're right, Francisco. Set a perimeter before they launch their next attack."

"What luck!" exclaimed Gregory.

"You think it's lucky that World War III broke out all around us?" asked an incredulous Clint.

"We can use this chaos to get to the treasure and eliminate our enemies."

"Enemies! Get to the treasure! How do we get out of here alive, let alone with the treasure?" asked the Professor in a trembling voice.

"Clint, take the Professor to the cave. I'm counting on you to defend the mouth of the cave. Don't let anyone except me enter that cave alive."

Clint was stunned and didn't reply. Gregory grabbed his arm and pulled him close.

"Do I need to explain it again?"

"No. I've got it. What will you be doing?"

"Evening the odds."

Gregory disappeared into the jungle. Clint looked over his shoulder at the steep and narrow path that led to the twin waterfalls. "Quick! Get your things together and follow me."

Clint instinctively felt for the satellite phone on his belt, his connection with the outside world. Jason and McKenzie motioned to Professor Timmons to follow, and the four men trouped single file up the trail toward the waterfall.

* * *

Startled, Skip awoke to the sound of the crash of the glider, automatic weapon fire and angry shouts. He crawled from the cleft and looked down the trail. "Someone's coming!" He scrambled up the trail, but it ended abruptly. He looked down into the stygian darkness and felt dizzy. He looked down the trail behind him.

"They will be here soon! I've got to do something!" He looked back at the cliff wall between him and the waterfall. He could see that a second waterfall emitted from the cliff and joined the first.

"A cave! How can I get there?" After a moment he said to himself, "I see a way."

Hand and toeholds were cut into the face of the cliff between the end of the trail and the waterfall. The last one he could see was at the waterfall. "I wish it was daylight," he said as he glanced back over his shoulder. Hope, excitement, fear and anxiety welled up in his belly.

Skip reached for the first handhold. "It's slippery, full of moss, but I've got a pretty good hold," he said under his breath.

He swung his leg out over the precipice until his foot found purchase in the first toehold cut in the rock. He put weight on his foot. It didn't slip. He put his second hand on the first upper cut. He knew he was committed now. If he slipped, his one remaining foot on the rocky path would not prevent a fatal fall. Still, it was hard to bring his left foot forward to share the toehold with his right foot. He thought, *I can still turn back.* He hesitated. Finally, he eased his left leg over to join his right. He reached for the second handhold, then the second toehold, and edged his way across the face of the cliff. He reached the waterfall but couldn't see the next handhold. He reached into the falling stream of water and felt along the wet rock wall for the next handhold. Torrential rain started again. "Great! What else could go wrong?"

Twin explosions on the valley floor startled him.

His foot slipped.

His heart seemed to be in his throat.

Bright light from the explosion illuminated the rock around him.

"I see it!"

He grasped the last handhold, the last toehold, and stepped into the mouth of the cave. After catching his breath and letting his racing heart slow, he removed the flashlight from his pack and moved deeper into the cave.

A stream flowed along the floor of the cave to its mouth, joining the waterfall. He used his flashlight to follow a pathway alongside the stream to the back of the cave. The stream flowed from an overhanging ledge and emitted from a large hole at the top of the back wall of the cave. The stream cascaded down the wall into a pool at its base. Skip heard voices at the mouth of the cave. Desperate to escape, he climbed the wall. When he reached the ledge, he crawled into the hole. He found just enough room to squeeze in, splashing and grunting, until he situated himself on a shelf above the water, just inside the hole. The stream was to his left. From this vantage point, he had a good view of the entrance to the cave.

* * *

The four men stopped at the end of the trail, a hundred feet from the top of the cliff. The waterfall roared eight feet away. The rain stopped momentarily, but mist and droplets from the waterfall made the rocky path permanently slippery.

"Now what?" asked Timmons in a trembling voice.

"It can't just end here," said Clint.

"We can't go back," said McKenzie.

Jason squeezed past Clint and knelt at the end of the trail. He used his flashlight to examine the ground at the end of the path and the rock wall between the path and the waterfall.

"I see a way," said Jason.

"What do you see?" asked Clint.

"Hand and toe holds are cut into the face of the cliff between here and the waterfall. The last one I can see is at the waterfall."

"It goes to the cave!" McKenzie exclaimed.

"Let's come back when the sun comes up," said Timmons.

Everyone looked at him. No one responded.

Jason went first. Even though the rocks were slippery, he was in good enough shape that he had little trouble working his way to the mouth of the cave. He probed into the darkness behind the waterfall until he found the last handhold. A moment later, he stood in the mouth of the cave. Like Skip, he removed his flashlight from his backpack and motioned for the others to follow, shining his light on each handhold and toehold as his friends edged along the face of the cliff.

Clint went first. Then it was Timmons' turn.

"I can't do it!" whimpered the Professor.

"Do it or die."

"I'll die if I do it!"

"Go now, or I'll push you off the cliff myself," growled McKenzie. "I'm not leaving you here to tell others where we are."

Moments later, all four men stood in the mouth of the cave behind the waterfall. A stream, two feet wide, flowed through the mouth of the cave and joined the water falling from above. Timmons laughed long and hard. "I've never felt so alive!"

"Yeah. Almost dying has that effect on most people," responded McKenzie.

They followed the stream to a pool at the base of yet another waterfall, this one from a hole near the roof of the cave. The cave ended just beyond the pool at an unnaturally flat rock wall.

"That's interesting!" said Timmons as he stepped around the pool. "This wall looks man made!"

"Really?" exclaimed Clint. "Do you think the treasure really could be here?"

"Yes, I do! Just on the other side of this wall!"

"Gregory said it's a mountain of gold," said Jason, stressing 'mountain' and 'gold.' Skip was even more attentive now.

"Yes," responded Timmons. "In a way it is a mountain of gold." His eyes glinted. "Priceless artifacts! Wealth beyond imagination! It will be the archeological find of the century!"

"We'll be famous!" shouted Jason.

"If we live long enough," Clint pointed out.

"They'll never find us here," said McKenzie.

"Yes they will," responded Clint. "We found this place. They will too," he said gesturing toward the valley below. "Now that they're this close, they're sure to find it. We've got to find a way to keep them from coming up the path."

"How do you plan to do that?" asked Jason.

"I'm not sure, but first I'll check on Gregory and see how the battle is going. He's got to keep anyone from coming up this path."

"Are you sure that's a good idea?"

"Have you got a better one?"

"Yeah, I do. Wait here and we'll fight them off if we have to."

"Maybe that's what we should do. I'm going to check on Gregory and see if I can tell how bad things are down there. I'll be back soon."

Clint inched along the edge of the waterfall, back to the path and worked his way stealthily down the trail.

McKenzie positioned himself behind an outcropping inside the cave where he could watch the entrance. Jason and the Professor turned their attention to the wall.

"Should we bust through this wall?"

"Oh, no," explained Timmons. "First we examine the wall carefully for any inscriptions or paintings. There may be archeologically significant findings on this wall."

"Who cares? We want what is behind the wall."

"Patience, my friend. Sometimes inscriptions can have enormous value."

"Define enormous."

"Thousands. Maybe millions. Maybe priceless."

"Millions is good."

"Besides, there may be a booby trap."

"You don't believe in those old tales do you?"

"Well, yes, I do! Some archaeologists and grave robbers have died in ancient tombs because of hidden traps."

"That's why we have you, Professor. Watch out for the traps, but get us through that wall, quick, before anyone else gets here. Besides, what kind of trap could there be here? The roof is solid. The floor is solid. No bottomless pits. No holes for arrows. No rolling boulders."

"Yeah, I guess you're right." Timmons felt the wall. "Wait! I feel something! There are definitely inscriptions of some kind here!"

"What do you see, Professor?"

McKenzie heard the excited commotion and couldn't help himself. He gave up his post and joined the others at the wall. Skip eased onto the ledge to get a better look.

"Everything seems to indicate this area. Do any of you have a knife?"

McKenzie handed Timmons his knife. Timmons cut and carved along the surface of the rock wall until he outlined a stone the size of a loaf of bread. "I think this may be the keystone. Remove this and we may be able to open the wall."

"Open the wall!" said an excited Jason. "Like a door? That sounds cool."

"I could be wrong, but I read about a keystone like this when they discovered the tomb under Kukulcan's Pyramid."

Timmons stood back while McKenzie and Jason worked their knives around the edge of the stone.

"It's moving!"

The stone slid outward, protruding enough that they were able to grasp the edge of the stone with their fingers. Jason and McKenzie pulled, grunted, and pulled harder. The stone slid an inch. "That's it, boys! Pull harder," encouraged Timmons. Jason and McKenzie redoubled their efforts. The stone slid out cleanly, leaving a hole exposing another layer of stone or brick. They stepped back and waited. Skip, eyes wide, held his breath, waiting for something to happen.

Nothing happened.

Timmons knelt and shined his flashlight into the hole. He felt all around the hole.

"Anything, Professor?"

"I don't feel anything yet. Except it's damp."

"We're in a cave."

"Yeah. But water is starting to pool in this hole."

Water trickled out of the hole and puddled at the base of the wall.

McKenzie and Jason knelt beside Timmons and peered into the hole. The leak was now a small stream of water pouring from the gap in the wall. There was a scrambling, splashing sound behind them at the entrance to the cave. McKenzie, who had left his post, pivoted and reached for his weapon. The embarrassment of leaving his post and exposing everyone to danger put his already frayed nerves even further on edge. Someone was coming into the cave. Was it Clint? Surely, he would announce himself. No, it had to be someone else. McKenzie felt his finger tighten on the trigger. The intruder was in the entrance. McKenzie felt the recoil. The sound was deafening. Skip threw his hands over his ears and almost screamed but managed to remain quiet.

The intruder grunted, fell backward and was gone.

Chapter 58

There was a whooshing sound and everything went black. Natalia was bewildered, but only for a moment. She recalled that Julio and two burly men restrained her, and suddenly the tent was ripped from the earth. She was swept up in a fold of the tent and felt herself become airborne. She felt a rush of speed. She stopped with a thud on the muddy ground, wrapped in the tent, cut and bruised. A rope, with a metal tent peg, was wrapped around her arm. She struggled to climb out of the canvas. Someone grabbed her shoulder and roughly pulled her to her feet. It was Julio, holding a knife in his free hand.

"You are way too much trouble. I don't know why de Sada let you live this long. I'm going to do him a great favor by putting you out of our misery."

Natalia grasped the tent peg dangling from her arm and thrust it into Julio's neck, driving it deep with all her strength. Julio never saw it coming. He fell to his knees, choking on his own blood. Natalia yanked the peg from his neck and was prepared to strike again, but Julio fell forward on his face. She heard movement behind her. Natalia crouched and whirled to confront the next danger.

"Señorita Garza? Is that you?" It was one of the men the Rangers described as farmers.

"Si."

"We have been sent to help you. I am sorry it took us so long."

"You're just in time. Quick, take me to the others. We must strike while de Sada is in disarray!"

A nearby tree, struck by lightening, exploded in a shower of spark and flame. Torrential rain drenched everything. Gregory had already dispatched three of de Sada's men when war cries and shouts of 'Ataquemos' filled the air. Natalia's men stormed out of the darkness, armed with machetes. A few had guns. The first wave of attackers came from the left and quickly overran some of de Sada's defenders. But, withering fire from automatic weapons stopped their forward progress. A second wave swept into the campsite from the right, where Gregory had been hunting de Sada's men. None were left on the right flank to repel the attack.

"Señor de Sada, we are overrun!" shouted Francisco.

"How can this be? Who are they?"

"They look like farmers. Indians, maybe Mayans."

"Farmers! Peasants are overrunning my army! It can't be!"

"We must retreat to the cave, Señor de Sada."

"Lead the way."

Francisco gave the order. Four men joined them and they ran to the trailhead at the base of the cliff. The battle raged behind them, but moment-by-moment they heard less automatic weapon fire. They heard screams of agony and of triumph. Most of the shooting ended by the time they reached the trailhead.

* * *

Gregory worked along the edge of the jungle toward the trailhead. He used stealth and the darkness to take out the first three of de Sada's men he encountered. He quickly realized that the new force was a greater threat. He turned his attention to the Mayans, stalking and killing one after another.

Captain Morales and his team of Rangers took advantage of the confusion during the melee to work their way within 100 yards of the wreck of the glider. "Set the timers at one minute each. Toss both satchels and we exit there," pointing toward a large tree at the edge of the forest. "Our exit is through the jungle straight up that hill. We are in and out. Quick. No looking back." They sprinted to the glider. De Sada's men were fully engaged battling the attackers, who were fully engaged attacking de Sada's men. No one paid any attention to the glider. The Rangers encountered no opposition, tossed their satchels into the wreck, and sprinted into the jungle.

The twin explosions lit the jungle enough to make their exit easier. On the cliff wall, the explosions provided just enough light for Skip to see the last handhold inside the curtain of water at the edge of the waterfall.

Francisco was an expert at setting a defense of overlapping fields of fire. He counted on withering automatic weapon fire to defend against any attack, but because of Gregory, de Sada had no men on the flank to stop the second wave of attackers. As a result, de Sada's remaining men were quickly isolated and eliminated.

In the darkness, no one knew the number of dead and wounded. Natalia knew that the toll on her men was high, but the sound of automatic gunfire steadily declined and had become only sporadic. She hoped that meant that the odds now favored her, but her lifelong mission was not over until de Sada was captured, or dead.

"They will retreat to the cave. We must cut them off!" she shouted as she ran toward the trailhead. Six men joined her. De Sada and his men, Natalia and her men, and Gregory reached the trailhead at the same moment.

De Sada's instincts took over. He charged Natalia, slipped an arm around her neck and placed a gun on her temple.

Gregory's instincts took over. He charged de Sada, slipped an arm around his neck and placed a knife at his throat.

Clint arrived at the trailhead, and stopped in the shadows, unseen.

Natalia's men and de Sada's men faced each other, weapons at the ready.

Horns blared.

Drums beat rhythmically.

Dozens of Indians emerged from the jungle from every direction, weapons at the ready. A procession of Indians marched up the path, their steps in rhythm to the drums. Four men carried a litter upon which sat a man with a resplendent crown of feathers. The procession stopped when it reached the standoff. In unison, almost every Indian saluted the man on the litter and shouted, "Huitzilopochtli."

"You!" shouted de Sada.

"It can't be!" whispered Natalia.

"But, you're dead!" exclaimed Gregory. "I killed you!"

"Not that lawyer!" cried Clint.

"Natalia!" shouted the man on the litter.

Natalia used the distraction to thrust the tent peg into de Sada's thigh.

De Sada jerked violently and fired his pistol.

Gregory slit his throat.

The Indian closest to Gregory swung his machete.

Forcefully.

Neck high.

Before Gregory's head hit the ground, a horrified Clint was already running up the trail. Clint fumbled with his satellite phone while he ran and called his employer. He didn't know why he was calling. He did it instinctively. Maybe it was a sense of duty. He felt that Shawn Dalton needed to know what had gone wrong and why his quest for the treasure would fail.

Clint was out of breath by the time the phone rang and rang and rang. At last, there was an answer. Voicemail.

"No!"

He reached the end of the path. The voicemail message went on and on. "After you leave a message, you may hang up, or hit star for additional options."

"Which is the option for get me outta here?"

He thought he heard someone on the trail below him.

"BEEP."

"Mr. Dalton!" urged Clint breathlessly. "It's that lawyer from Mississippi! He's ruined everything! We're all gonna die!"

Clint thought he heard something behind him. The phone slipped from his hand and fell into the abysmal darkness. He grabbed the first handhold and worked his way back to the cliff. He shuffled and splashed through the water to the entrance of the cave. As he stepped into the cave, McKenzie shot him. Clint tumbled into the waterfall behind him.

Startled, Jason and Timmons jerked around to see what had happened.

"Someone was coming in. I had to shoot," cried McKenzie.

"What if it was Clint?"

"It wasn't. I would have known if it was Clint."

Timmons realized that more water was coming from the hole. "Where is all this water coming from?" he asked no one in particular as he stuck his head into the hole for a better look.

"OH NO!" shouted Timmons.

"What!"

"The lake is the booby trap!"

"Lake? What lake?"

"The one above us!"

The stone at the back of the hole gave way. A column of water with the power of a fire hose blasted through the hole hitting Timmons full in the face, knocking him backward almost to the mouth of the cave. A moment later the entire wall burst. A roaring wall of water as tall and wide as the cave swept the cave clean leaving no sign that Timmons, Jason, McKenzie or Clint had ever been there.

* * *

Startled cannot adequately describe the emotion and the fear that jumped into everyone's mind when the courtroom door suddenly, loudly, burst open. Especially considering the events of yesterday.

Shocked is a term that cannot begin to describe Karen's reaction to John when he interrupted the wedding, shouting, "I OBJECT!"

Backhoe, red faced, eyes burning, fists clenched took a protective stance in front of Karen.

"Am I too late?" pled John. "God, tell me I'm not too late!"

No one answered.

Taking the silence to be assent, John continued, "Karen, hear me out!"

Karen was dumbfounded and looked at John quizzically.

The courtroom began filling with the reporters, cameras and spectators who had followed John as he ran through the courthouse.

"Karen, I love you."

Bret's camera was already running. When he heard John's words, he glanced at Sandy. Her eyes were wide. Her face registered a lack of comprehension over what just occurred. Bret couldn't bear the thought of recording her humiliation. His brain said, 'I would rather abandon video journalism than humiliate her,' but his arms would not cooperate. He turned the camera on Sandy and began panning the camera back and forth between John, Karen, Sandy and Backhoe.

"I know I should have told you long ago. I've always loved you. There is no one else for me. There never will be. You are the love of my life. I want to spend the rest of my life with you."

Steam seemed to come out of Backhoe's ears as he leaned forward ready to charge. John never noticed Backhoe. He saw only Karen.

Aware that something terrible was about to happen, Karen placed a restraining hand on Backhoe's arm. She felt tense muscles, ready to spring into action. She felt a surge of energy.

"No, Backhoe, stop!"

Backhoe could not be restrained.

John's pleading eyes never left Karen. As big as Backhoe is, John didn't see him coming. He didn't see the charging bull, the long windup or the arching haymaker before it connected. Consequently, he made no effort to dodge, defend, or brace. He just absorbed the mighty impact.

The impact lifted John off his feet. He tumbled over a row of chairs, sending the chairs sprawling.

Sandy shouted, "Hit him again!"

Chapter 59

Stars.

All John could see was stars. He straddled a vague state somewhere between consciousness and unconsciousness. At first, the awareness of pain was his only conscious thought. But a moment later he remembered Karen. He said her name, and the stars subsided. He repeated her name and the room came back into focus.

The spectators' reaction to Backhoe's thunderous blow was varied. Some were shocked. Some were excited and wanted to see more. Some were frightened. Everyone was enthralled. No one left the courtroom. Indeed, more people packed into the courtroom, but everyone gave Backhoe a wide birth.

As John regained presence of mind, he found himself on his knees. Backhoe, snorting like a thoroughbred at the starting gate, stood menacingly above John. Karen was squatting in front of John, a look of concern and confusion on her face. Sandy was beside Karen, a look of anger, frustration and confusion on her face. Next to her stood Bret, camera in hand recording every emotion, expression and word.

John wiped blood from his face. With all that was within him, he willed Karen to look him in the eyes and he said, "Karen. You know me. You know when I am telling the truth. Listen. You are my best friend. I have always loved you. It's true that I didn't always know it and I am sorry. I was a fool. I was wrong. Forgive me, please!"

Karen finally spoke.

"What about Sandy?"

"I don't love Sandy."

Sandy gasped. John turned to her. "Sandy, you are a wonderful person, but Karen is the woman for me. There will never be another. If she rejects me now, there will never, I mean never, be another woman for me."

"Bret, you're recording this, aren't you?"

"Of course."

Sandy cleared her throat and thrust her microphone at John. "Why did you choose this moment to tell Karen how you felt? You've literally had years to tell her?"

"Yes," said Karen. "Why now?"

Looking Karen in the eyes, John said, "I loved you from the first. But I was too immature to know it. I loved working with you every day, and I was too afraid to mess that up by getting too personal, too close. I couldn't risk losing you. Then Sandy came into the picture and I knew I had to make a choice. I wasn't ready for change. I was afraid of change. And then, you were gone. I was wrong. I was a fool. Forgive me, please."

"But you haven't told us why you chose this moment to tell the world how you felt?" asked Sandy.

"When I heard you were about to get married, I realized I waited too long. I made the mistake of my life."

Karen's eyes seemed to become as large as saucers.

"I couldn't live knowing that I never even tried to tell you how I feel."

"You thought I was getting married?"

"Well, yes. That's what this is all about."

"No," said Karen laughing in spite of herself. "Backhoe and I are here for our friends' wedding. Michael and Betty are the ones getting married, not me."

Laughter filled the room as John's eyes darted from Karen to Backhoe to Betty and Michael.

"What? You mean none of this had to happen?"

"John, are you taking back what you just said?" asked Karen.

"No! No! I mean every word. I just wish my face didn't hurt so bad."

Karen laughed and gently stroked his swelling face.

Sandy intervened with another question. "Mr. John Brooks, you are already on your knees. Don't you have something you want to ask Karen?"

"Yes. Yes, I do." John took Karen's hands in his, looked into her eyes and asked, "Karen, will you be my wife? Will you marry me?"

All eyes turned to Karen. All cameras focused on her face.

"Hold that thought," said Karen.

* * *

As the cloud of hummingbirds parted, Jackson found himself surrounded by half a dozen Mayans, machetes high above their heads ready to strike. Unwilling to take any action that might provoke an attack, Jackson stood erect and slowly raised his hands to his waist, palms up, and simply said, "God help me."

"Huitzilopochtli," said one of the men as he took a knee and bowed in submission. Two others quickly joined him. The other men lowered their machetes. One, a skeptical look on his face, stepped forward and questioned Jackson in a language he couldn't recognize.

"Do you speak English?" asked Jackson.

"Si. We saw you fall from the cloud into this tree, and the humming-birds carried you to the ground. Who does such things? Who are you?"

"I'm Jackson Bradley, and I've come to stop Antoine de Sada from stealing something that belongs to the people of Central America."

The interpreter explained Jackson's story, which convinced the three kneeling Mayans that Jackson was either a god or was sent by one. Either way, he needed to be afforded proper respect. Someone placed a headdress on Jackson's head while others cut bamboo. They quickly put together a litter supported by poles and insisted that Jackson take a seat. They lifted the litter to their shoulders and proceeded through the jungle announcing the long-awaited arrival of Huitzilopochtli. Soon, other Mayans joined them, singing and making music with flutes and makeshift drums. Two Indians blew horns that echoed hauntingly in the valley. Men stepped out of the jungle from every direction to join the joyous procession. Some carried torches to light the way.

There was a clearing up ahead. As they entered the clearing, Jackson saw that de Sada had his arm around Natalia's throat and held a gun against her temple. Gregory had his arm around de Sada's neck and held a Bowie Knife to his throat. Men pointing guns at one another surrounded the three of them. Some were holding machetes ready to strike. When Jackson arrived in the clearing, almost every Indian saluted him and shouted, "Huitzilopochtli."

"You!" shouted de Sada.

"It can't be!" whispered Natalia.

"But, you're dead!" exclaimed Gregory. "I killed you!"

"Not that lawyer!" cried Clint.

"Natalia!" shouted Jackson.

Jackson saw Natalia ram something into de Sada's thigh as she struggled to free herself from his grip. De Sada fired his gun. Gregory slit his throat with a quick, powerful motion. A Mayan forcefully swung his machete, separating Gregory from his head. The bodies of Gregory, de Sada and Natalia fell in a bloody heap.

"NO!" shouted Jackson as he jumped from the bench to the ground and rushed to Natalia. On his knees, he pushed the bodies of Gregory and de Sada off her and pulled her bloody body into his lap. All anger over her betrayal was forgotten in that moment. Ignoring the blood and the mud, he brushed her hair from her face and kissed her lips as tears streamed down his face.

"No, Natalia, no," he cried as he kissed her again.

She kissed him back and threw her arms around his neck. "Jackson, I must tell you," she said through tears, rushing her words, "I was bringing the camera back, but de Sada caught me and brought me here. I was wrong to take it. I am so sorry. Please forgive me."

"You're alive!" exclaimed Jackson, and he kissed her again.

The Indians cheered. De Sada's remaining men dropped their weapons and fell to their knees.

"So, does all this kissing mean chu forgive me?"

"I thought de Sada shot you!"

"I twisted and he misted."

The ground rumbled and the valley filled with the roaring sound of water blasting from the mouth of the cave.

"Quick, we must get to higher ground," commanded Natalia with authority as she motioned for everyone to follow her. She took one of the torches and set off at a brisk trot.

Jackson ran to catch up with her. "What's happening?"

"That waterfall is an overflow from a lake. The ridge holds in back. Moc used it to make a booby trap for anyone who would disturb the treasure."

"So, someone triggered the booby trap?"

"Yes."

"How much water?"

"You see where the water shoots from the ridge?"

"Yes."

"How far is that from the top of the ridge?"

"Looks like maybe a hundred feet."

"Soon, this valley may be a hundred feet under water."

The stream that meandered through the valley was already an angry torrent. They ran past the flaming glider into what was left of de Sada's camp.

"See if you can start any of these trucks," Natalia commanded. The Mayans cranked three large trucks. Everyone clambered aboard as the stream left its banks and began flooding the campsite. The trucks lurched forward, tires spinning in the mud.

Debris and tree trunks along with every kind of object filled the stream. The irresistible force of the water swept the growing mass into the narrow gorge through which the stream exited the valley.

"It's damming up the stream!" shouted Jackson.

"Faster!" shouted Natalia.

"Mas rapido! Mas rapido!" someone shouted.

Drivers ground gears and floored gas pedals. Engines whined. The trucks splashed through rapidly rising water. The horn of the last truck began honking. Water swamped the truck, stalling the engine. Natalia shouted, "Stop! Back up!"

"We can't! We will be swept away!" cried the driver.

"Back up!" she commanded.

Despite his fear, he threw the truck into reverse and backed close enough to the swamped truck for the men to jump aboard. When the last was safely on Natalia's truck, she shouted, "Go, go, go!"

Churning water gripped the swamped truck, carrying it downstream as they pulled away. At last, the two remaining trucks reached the narrow road and climbed the ridge, leaving the flooded valley behind.

Chapter 60

The last thing John wanted to hear was 'hold that thought.' Karen had been squatting in front of John. Now, she rose and turned to Backhoe. He was still tense, ready to spring into battle. His big hands were clinched into fists. His breathing was deep, measured, his senses alert. Karen wondered, "Is that murder in his eyes?"

Karen smiled at Backhoe. His countenance changed. Softened. A single tear appeared at the edge of his eye and slowly rolled down his cheek. Karen gently brushed it away. "You are a wonderful man of integrity. You will make someone a great husband. But, my heart has always belonged to John."

Backhoe's shoulders sagged. Pent up energy ebbed. He looked at his clinched fists, and slowly opened his hands.

"I know," he said. "It's okay. I know the two of you will be very happy." Backhoe smiled at Karen, then he took a knee beside John. John's face was already so swollen that he could no longer see through his right eye.

"You owe me one, buddy," said Backhoe.

"I'm a little fuzzy on the details. How's that?"

"I knocked some sense into you."

After a moment, John replied, "Yes, you did. I appreciate that, buddy. Thanks."

"Don't mention it. I'll be glad to do it for you again anytime." Backhoe slapped John hard on the shoulder, stood, and walked to the door with a steady, determined gait. The crowd parted like the Red Sea before Moses. He never had to break his stride.

Karen turned back to John, took his hand in hers, and said, "Yes!"

The crowd roared its approval!

John leaped to his feet, slipped his arms around Karen and they kissed as though they were alone.

The crowd cheered.

John and Karen didn't notice the crowd or the cheers. At first, John didn't notice the pain generated by the pressure of the kiss on his swollen lips and face. When he finally noticed the pain, he didn't care.

At last their lips parted. Karen was all smiles and said, "I waited a long time for that kiss."

* * *

Everyone in the crowded room applauded, John, Karen and the happy bride and groom. Judge Westerbeck, a huge smile on her face, looked at Judge Bell, shrugged, and applauded louder than everyone else. John, Karen, the bride and groom clasped hands and raised them above their heads in triumph. Cheers erupted even louder.

"There is a judge here," observed John. "Let's get married right now!"

"No way!" exclaimed Karen with a broad smile and a crinkle in her forehead. "All of our family and friends are coming to our wedding."

John sighed, laughed and said, "All right. One day we may look back on this and wish we had just gone ahead and tied the knot while we had the chance."

Among all the smiling faces, Judge Westerbeck noticed her bailiff. She worked her way to his side.

"Mr. Bowen."

"Yes, Judge?"

"Will you remind Mr. Brooks that he has a hearing in progress down the hall."

"Yes, ma'am."

* * *

Ten minutes later, with Karen at his side and Peter behind him, John began his cross-examination of Sheriff Townsend. Somehow, everything seemed possible to John with Karen at his side. His spirit lifted. His brain sparked. Crystal clear thoughts rushed through his mind.

"Sheriff, your testimony ended with your description of finding a lock of Awesome's hair in Sheriff Rainey's hand."

"That's right. That nailed it for me."

"But, you said the Sheriff was clubbed from behind and he never had a chance."

"That's right. Cowardly attack."

"He was knocked unconscious with a single vicious blow?"

"Yep, and then drowned in the creek by your vicious client."

"Yes, I remember your testimony. So, how did the lock of hair get into Sheriff Rainey's hand?"

"In the struggle, of course."

"But your narrative is that Awesome snuck up behind Sheriff Rainey and clubbed him."

"Right."

"Unconscious?"

"Are you deaf?"

"No, I was just wondering when the struggle would have taken place. Since Awesome, or someone, snuck up behind Sheriff Rainey and clubbed him unconscious, and then drowned him, there would not have been a struggle, or an opportunity for Rainey to grab a lock of Awesome's hair, would there?"

"Maybe he swung around and struggled and grabbed his hair."

"While he was unconscious?"

Townsend squirmed, hesitated, and changed the subject. "I found Awesome's footprints all over the crime scene. He was there."

"You found boot marks that match marks made by the kind of boot Awesome wears, correct?"

"Yes, and the same size that Awesome wears. That's because they were made by Awesome!"

"Or by someone who purchased the same kind and size boot, right?"

"That's farfetched."

"Don't you think that Awesome would know it if someone pulled the hair out of his head?"

"So what?"

"Well, wouldn't he have known to take his hair from Rainey so he wouldn't leave a clue behind?"

"Remember, this is the guy who left his victims' scalps in the back of his pickup."

"Exactly. You found him and his pickup at Trails End Bar, right?"

"You heard me."

"How did you know to look for him there?"

"I already told you that Walt and Wes said he came by their place and told them he would be at Trails End."

"Doing what?'

"Waiting for Skeeter."

"Why would he be waiting for Skeeter if he knew Skeeter was dead?"

"What are you gettin' at?"

"The back of his pickup is open, isn't it?"

"Of course."

"Anyone who knew Awesome would be at Trails End could have put scalps in his truck."

"Objection, speculation," said Thorn, rising from her chair.

"Overruled."

Townsend laughed and said, "So, your theory is that someone who wears boots just like Awesome, and has hair just like Awesome killed Sheriff Rainey, and then mistook Awesome's truck for his own?"

Laughter spread through the courtroom.

"You make my point."

"How?"

"Back to the lock of hair, do you agree that the lock of hair came from the killer?"

"Of course. Have you lost your mind? Whose side are you on, counselor? The hair came from the killer, Awesome Dalton."

"The killer left Awesome Dalton's hair in Sheriff Rainey's hand, right?"

"What do you mean?"

"We know there was no struggle, because the sheriff was hit from behind with a single blow, knocking him unconscious. If Awesome was there and his hair was somehow yanked out by Rainey, he would have known it, and wouldn't have left it behind."

"Objection, speculation," said Thorn as she rose from her chair. She remained standing, ready for the next objection.

"For the purposes of this hearing, I'm overruling the objection," ruled Westerbeck.

"Okay, so maybe he didn't realize his hair was pulled, or maybe he didn't have time to search the sheriff and find the hair."

"Whoever did this had time to hold the Sheriff under water until he drowned, right?"

"I guess."

"So, he had time to either look for a lock of hair or place a lock of hair in Sheriff Rainey's hand."

"Where would he get a lock of your client's hair?"

"You had a lock of his hair, didn't you?"

"You LIE!" shouted Townsend.

"Sheriff, control your temper," commanded Judge Westerbeck.

"Yes, Your Honor, but it's hard when this smart-aleck lawyer is accusin' me of plantin' evidence."

"I don't believe he accused you, Sheriff, he just asked if you had a lock of his client's hair."

"I did not."

"Mr. Brooks, please don't ask questions outside the record that you cannot support."

"I would never do such a thing, Your Honor."

Ms. Thorn, who had been patient through most of the testimony, finally had enough. "He just did, Your Honor."

"My client informs me that you took a sample of his hair while he was in jail. You did, didn't you?"

"That's a lie!"

"Objection, Your Honor. You just admonished Mr. Brooks not to make these statements he can't support."

"I will make the connection, Your Honor."

"Do it quickly. I am losing patience."

"Yes, Your Honor. Sheriff, you told us that you rely on your investigation records as being accurate."

"That's right. And if I had taken a lock of his hair, which I didn't, it would be in my report, which it is not."

"You testified that you relied upon the records of Sheriff Rainey as being accurate."

"Yeah. What are you getting at? His records don't say nothing about a lock of Awesome's hair."

"Are Sheriff Rainey's records kept safe from tampering?"

"Of course. Nobody can get to them. Ever since he died, I have kept his records under lock and key."

"So you can get to Sheriff Rainey's records, but no one else?"

"Well, yes I can get them. I have to use them to carry out our law enforcement responsibilities."

"Your Honor, I beg the Court's indulgence."

Judge Westerbeck leaned forward. "Yes, Mr. Brooks, what is your request?"

"I ask leave to interrupt the cross examination of Sheriff Townsend while I call a witness necessary to elicit testimony and place into evidence information vital to the remainder of my cross examination."

"Objection, your Honor, this is a waste of time," Ms. Thorn pled, frustration in her voice. "This is a preliminary hearing, where probable cause is the only issue. We have already shown probable cause to charge Mr. Dalton with a crime. Mr. Brooks needs to complete his examination of this witness before calling another witness."

"I tend to agree with Ms. Thorn, Mr. Brooks."

"Yes, Your Honor. You requested that I not cross-examine Sheriff Townsend on issues outside the record unless I intended to prove the facts implied in my questions. I intend to provide that proof, and then I will have additional questions of Sheriff Townsend based upon that evidence."

"You are getting too far afield, Mr. Brooks."

"Your Honor, I can prove that Sheriff Townsend not only lied, but that he planted evidence."

Townsend leapt from the witness stand shouting, "Lie!"

Thorn and Hoover rose to enter the fray. "Objection!" "Objection!" They shouted. Reporters were wide eyed, enjoying the moment.

"I can't wait to report this!" whispered a reporter to Sandy.

"This is outrageous," Sandy responded. "He's showboating for the cameras."

Judge Westerbeck banged her gavel on the resounder. "Order in the Court! Sheriff, sit down!"

Chapter 61

Townsend, glaring at Brooks, slowly returned to his seat. Thorn and Hoover did the same. Hoover glared at Peter and mouthed, "What's he up to?" Peter shrugged. Brooks glanced at the two of them and made a note on his legal pad.

Judge Westerbeck continued. "Mr. Brooks, you may discontinue your questioning of this witness and recall him later if you wish."

"Yes, Your Honor."

"Sheriff, please step down. I will have to ask you to remove yourself from the courtroom and not talk about your testimony with anyone, until you are recalled as a witness."

Mr. Hoover rose and leaned forward, one hand on the table before him. "Your Honor, Sheriff Townsend is the chief law enforcement agent of the County and he is responsible for security in the courthouse and courtroom and is in charge of much of our evidence. We request that he be allowed to come and go, and that we be allowed to discuss with him the evidence Mr. Brooks is about to offer. Sheriff Townsend is the person in the best position to respond to whatever Mr. Brooks might offer. We don't believe that this unusual maneuver by Mr. Brooks should be permitted to cut off our access to the investigative information and resources available through the sheriff."

"While that may be, the Rule of Sequestration of Witnesses prohibits the presence of a witness in the courtroom while others testify," responded Judge Westerbeck.

"Judge, we are willing to accommodate the prosecution," said Brooks. "We will waive the Rule of Sequestration of Witnesses as to Sheriff Townsend."

Judge Westerbeck raised her eyebrows. "I see. That's unusual. Very well. Sheriff Townsend, you may remain in the courtroom."

"And may we discuss his potential testimony with him?" continued Hoover.

The Judge looked at Brooks, awaiting his response.

"No objection, Your Honor."

"So be it. Call your next witness, Mr. Brooks."

"What is he up to?" Sandy asked Bret. "It's not like him to give up such an advantage."

"Maybe he wants them to coordinate their story," responded Bret.

"Why?" asked Sandy.

"You're the reporter. Go find out."

Townsend settled into a chair near the prosecution table, a smirk on his face. Sandy crept up behind Karen and whispered, "What's he up to?"

Karen shrugged her shoulders. "I've been out of the loop for a while."

"We call Emily Martin as our next witness," John announced.

Hoover and Thorn looked at Townsend, who crinkled his mouth and tilted his head slightly to the side as he thought to himself, 'If that's all he's got, he has nothing.'

Hoover read the expression as, 'nothing to worry about.'

Emily was sworn and settled into the witness stand.

"Ms. Martin, please tell us your name and how you are employed."

"Emily Martin. I work for the Neshoba County Chancery Clerk in land records."

"Have we met?"

"Yes, you came to the land records to look at tax maps showing the location and ownership of land around the Dalton farm."

"Did you show me a map of the area known as the Goni Swamp?"

"Sure did. I showed you the swamp on the map and told you the place gave me the heebie-jeebies." Emily visibly shivered. Light laughter spread across the courtroom.

"Why is that?"

"The place is supposed to be haunted."

"Awe, Judge, I object to this nonsense," said Hoover.

"Where are you going, Mr. Brooks?" asked Judge Westerbeck.

"I want to ask her about a specific event that I will connect to this case."

"Go ahead. Get to the point. I am running out of patience."

"Yes, Your Honor. Emily, do you recall telling me about strange sounds you heard from the swamp?"

"I do. My boyfriend and I had been talking about the scary swamp stories and on a dare we went out there."

"What happened?"

"We heard strange moaning sounds, like a person in agony. Like I said, it gave me the heebie-jeebies and I told my boyfriend to get me out of there, quick."

"Did you see anyone else out there?"

Hoover looked at Townsend, who shook his head 'no,' and held both hands just above his knees, palms down, and pushed them down slightly. Hoover got the message.

"Objection, Your Honor. This is irrelevant. We don't even have a time frame."

"Sustained."

"When was that?"

"It's been a while."

"Can you relate it to any event that would help us identify the time?"

"It was around the time that Curtis Dalton disappeared."

"I renew my objection," urged Hoover. "That was long before any of the crimes Mr. Dalton is charged with."

"Mr. Brooks, this is getting too far afield."

"I will connect this with the present cases."

"Very well but get to your point quickly."

"Did you see anyone else out there on that occasion?"

"Yes, Sheriff Townsend, he was Deputy Townsend at the time, he was waiting at my boyfriend's pickup when we came out of the woods. He asked us what we were doing, and said we were trespassing. He was intense at first, real aggressive. He scared me. Asked us if we had seen anything. We told him no, but we told him about the sound. He calmed down and said that people say that sort of thing all the time about the swamp. He said it was nothing, and not to worry about it. He said the swamp does funny things to sound, so people hear odd things and that's why some people think it is haunted. He told us we should leave and not come back. We did, and we haven't."

"Did you notice anything else about Deputy Townsend?"

"Yeah, he was pretty muddy."

"After speaking with me, did you speak with anyone else about what you experienced in the Goni Swamp?"

"Sure did. Sheriff Rainey came to see me and told me that you had mentioned to him what I said."

"Did you tell him the same thing?"

"Sure did."

"When?"

"The day before he was found dead, in the Goni Swamp." Emily visibly shivered again.

"Did you speak with anyone else?"

"Yep. Some guys who said they played rugby with you visited me and said you asked them to follow up with me and other witnesses. I told them the same thing."

"Miss. Martin, I asked my assistant Peter Creek to give you a copy of your subpoena." John gestured toward Peter. "Did he?"

"No, I don't believe I've ever seen him."

"Thank you, Miss Martin. No further questions."

Ann Thorn stood and looked at her notes for a moment, then announced, "No questions, Your Honor."

Judge Westerbeck turned to the witness and said, "Thank you Miss Martin, you may step down from the witness stand. Mr. Brooks, who is your next witness?"

"We call Frank Dalton."

Frank was ushered into the courtroom. He glanced around the room, spotted Brooks and his nephew and walked with determination to the stand, the picture of a stately elderly man with the weight of the world on his shoulders.

"Do you swear to tell the truth, the whole truth and nothing but the truth, so help you God?"

In a firm strong voice, Frank responded, "So help me God," emphasizing every word.

In response to John's questions, Frank introduced himself and his relationship to Awesome. Frank described the events from the day that his brother, German, was murdered, and he testified about Awesome dashing off in pursuit. He told about his search for Awesome. He described how he felt when he heard the terrible news about the death of Skeeter, William and Doug, the arrest of Awesome and the scalps found in Awesome's truck. He gave the whole story, good and bad. He told of his respect for Sheriff Rainey. He described him as a "good and honest sheriff, a true servant of the people. A fair man."

"Did you get a chance to go to the crime scene with Sheriff Rainey?" asked John.

"At my request, he took me, G.W. and you to the crime scene to see if we could find anything missed by everyone else."

"Why would he do that?"

"I told him that if Awesome did this terrible crime, he should pay the price. But, if he didn't, he should go free. Whatever the outcome, we were willing to accept the decision if we felt Awesome had been treated fairly. We believed we could read signs that others would miss. Sheriff Rainey respected our wishes and took us to the crime scene himself."

Frank testified about finding the actual murder scene and finding evidence that after the victims were murdered and scalped, they were driven a short distance into the middle of his Goni Swamp field. "The ground was a mess, with tire marks and footprints everywhere. G.W. and I decided to search the ground in circles, beginning where the pickup had been parked and working our way outward, to see what we could find."

"What were you looking for?"

"Those three boys were found in the back of the pickup truck in the middle of the Goni Field. Whoever murdered them either got a ride out of the field or he walked out of the field. We were looking for footprints leading away from the truck."

"What did you find?"

"A single set of fresh prints left by someone walking away from the area of the pickup in the direction of the Whittaker ranch, across the fence and off our property."

"How did Sheriff Rainey react to those prints?"

"He couldn't think of any reason that anyone connected to the investigation would walk in that direction. That was the opposite direction from where everyone involved in the investigation came into the field and left the field. He believed everyone in the investigation got a ride out. Nobody walked out. Whoever drove the truck to that spot left the boot marks. The boot marks of the murderer."

"Objection!"

"Overruled."

"He measured the boot prints and made a plaster cast of a good sample."

"Objection," said Hoover. "There is nothing in our record of any such bootprint or cast. If that had happened it would be in the record."

"Overruled. You will have Mr. Dalton on cross examination."

"Describe the print."

"It was small. Couldn't be Awesome."

"What did Sheriff Rainey do with Awesome after finding those prints?"

"He dropped the charges on Awesome and released him from the jail."

"No further questions."

"Ms. Thorn, or Mr. Hoover, your witness," said Judge Westerbeck.

Ann Thorn approached the podium. "Mr. Dalton, you are testifying on behalf of your nephew?"

"Yes, ma'am."

"You would do anything to help him, wouldn't you?"

"Not anything, no ma'am."

"Sheriff Rainey was a professional law enforcement officer, wasn't he?"

"Yes ma'am, very professional."

"And professional law enforcement officers make reports of their investigation and catalog the evidence they find, don't they?"

"I suppose they do."

"Can you explain why there is no evidence of boot prints and no plaster cast of a boot print in Sheriff Rainey's record?"

"No, ma'am. Maybe he didn't have time."

"If he was dropping triple murder charges against your nephew, don't you think he would have documented the reason why?"

"Yes, ma'am."

"Do you think that sometimes an investigator will turn a suspect loose to see if the suspect will lead him to additional evidence?"

"Objection, speculation," said John.

"Overruled, you can answer the question."

"I suppose that could happen."

"Did Sheriff Rainey follow your nephew into the Goni Swamp, where your nephew murdered him?"

"No ma'am."

"So, will you now admit that you will say anything to help your nephew, even if you have to say something untrue?"

"What do you mean, ma'am?"

"Well, you weren't present when Sheriff Rainey was murdered, were you?"

"No ma'am."

"So you could not know whether Awesome did it or not, yet you testified under oath that he didn't kill Sheriff Rainey, right?"

Frank hesitated. Before he answered, Thorn said, "No further questions."

"Any redirect, Mr. Brooks?"

"Just one question, Your Honor. Mr. Dalton, why did you testify that Awesome didn't murder Sheriff Rainey?"

"Sheriff Rainey was a good man who helped Awesome. I know my nephew. He didn't do this."

"No further questions."

"Mr. Dalton, you can step down. Mr. Brooks, call your next witness."

"Yes, Your Honor."

John looked directly at Sheriff Townsend as he called the name of the next witness, "Earl Horton." John thought he detected a nervous twitch.

Earl Horton was ushered into the courtroom. He wore a sport coat and tie and carried a file. The edges of a large brown envelope protruded from the file. After the witness swore to tell the truth and settled into the chair, Judge Westerbeck motioned to John and said, "You may proceed."

"Thank you, Your Honor. Please tell us your name and where you work."

"Earl Horton. I'm a manager of the Williams Brothers Grocery in Philadelphia, Mississippi."

"As part of your duties, do you manage the shoe department?"

"That's one of my many duties."

"Is Awesome Dalton one of your customers?"

"Sure is. At least once a year he orders a new pair of Hike King Boots by Arrow, size thirteen and a half, medium. He's hard on boots. We bought a bunch of different boots over the years before he settled on that one."

"Hiking boots?"

"Yes, but the name of the line is Hike King. That's what he likes, so we carry that boot for him. It's a sturdy boot, but doesn't weigh as much as most. He says it fits him just right."

"Did you know Sheriff Rainey?"

"Yes. He was a good man. I considered him a good friend."

"Did he ever ask you about Awesome's boot size?"

"Yes, that was when Awesome was in jail the first time, charged with killing Skeeter and his friends. It just before the Sheriff let Awesome out of jail."

"Tell us about that encounter."

"He came to see me with a plaster mold of a boot print he made at the crime scene and asked me to measure it. He wanted to know if Awesome's foot would fit in the boot that made that print."

"Objection," called Hoover as he rose to his feet. "Mr. Brooks is eliciting hearsay evidence."

John responded. "As has been pointed out, hearsay is admissible in a preliminary hearing. Besides, Mr. Horton's reason for measuring a cast is an exception to the hearsay rule."

"Overruled."

"What crime scene?"

"Where Skeeter and his friends were found dead."

"Did you measure the boot print?"

"I did. It was made by a size ten and a half. No way Awesome's foot would fit in that boot."

"Objection," stated Ms. Thorn. "There is no record of such a print in our files."

"That may be, but I saw it," said Mr. Horton.

"Overruled."

"How soon after seeing you did Sheriff Rainey drop the murder charges against Awesome?"

"Later that same day."

"Objection," said Hoover, "that proves nothing."

"You may be right, Mr. Hoover, but that goes to the weight I give to the testimony rather than to its admissibility," observed Judge Westerbeck. "Objection overruled. And, I don't want any more tag team objections. Whoever will cross examine this witness will be the one to make objections to his testimony."

"Yes, Your Honor," said both Hoover and Thorn.

"Did anyone else ask you about Awesome's boot size and preference?"

"Yes, Deputy Townsend. Sheriff now, but he was Deputy then."

"When was that?"

"A day or so after Awesome was released from jail."

"Objection, relevance," said Hoover. "Investigation is the deputy's job."

"Overruled."

"Did you tell Deputy Townsend about Awesome's boot size?"

"Yes, I even showed him a pair. I keep one pair in stock for Awesome. When he buys a pair, I order another. That way I have one when he wants it. Nobody else buys that boot."

"Do you still have that pair?"

"Dog gone if somebody didn't buy it the next day. Paid cash. It wasn't Awesome, I checked."

"Objection to hearsay," said Hoover.

"Overruled," said Judge Westerbeck. "It's still the preliminary hearing, Mr. Hoover."

"Who was it?"

"Don't know."

"Did you tell anybody about Deputy Townsend's interest in the boots and that somebody bought them?"

"Yes, I thought it was unusual, especially since bootprint evidence was evidently important in the murder case. So, I called Sheriff Rainey and told him what I'm telling the Court now."

"How did Sheriff Rainey respond?"

Hoover almost jumped out of his chair. "Objection! This is just too much hearsay."

"Sustained. I have to cut this hearsay off at some point, or we will never finish this preliminary hearing."

Hoover grinned and slowly took his seat, satisfied with the ruling and proud of himself for cutting off Brooks' line of questioning.

"Yes, Your Honor," continued Brooks. "Mr. Horton, when did you next see Sheriff Rainey?"

"He came to see me the next morning and brought me a copy of his investigative file on Awesome!"

Both Thorn and Hoover shot to their feet. "Objection! Objection, that is absurd! Why would the Sheriff do such a thing?"

"That's a good question, counsel," interjected Judge Westerbeck. She turned to Earl Horton and asked, "Why would Sheriff Rainey bring you his investigative file?"

Earl rotated his hips in the witness stand and turned his shoulders to face the Judge. "Well, Your Honor, I thought that was peculiar, so I asked him. He said that he had a really uneasy feeling about things in his office. He knew I had a safe in the store and he wanted me to keep a copy of his file in the safe until he needed it. So, I did as he asked, of course."

Judge Westerbeck looked at each attorney, then at Sheriff Townsend. Thorn and Hoover were still standing, mouths agape, not sure what they would say next. Townsend looked ashen. His body seemed to shrivel as he sank into his wooden chair.

"May I continue?" asked John.

"Please do," responded Westerbeck.

"Did you bring the file with you?"

"I did." He removed a large brown envelope from the file folder and held it chest high, offering it to Brooks.

"What was the condition of the file when Rainey gave it to you?"

"His report was in another letter size envelope, already sealed. I watched him place his report in this envelope. He licked it, sealed it and used tape from my desk to double seal it. Then he wrote his name across the fold, top and bottom, and dated it. So, his report is sealed in an envelope, which is sealed in this envelope."

"May I approach the witness?"

"You may, Mr. Brooks."

John took the envelope from Horton. "Is this the envelope Sheriff Rainey gave you?"

"Yes."

"Whose signature is this?"

"Sheriff Rainey. That's where he signed it, top and bottom."

"Where has the envelope been since Sheriff Rainey gave it to you?"

"In my safe, until today, when I brought it here."

"Is the envelope in the same condition today as when Sheriff Rainey gave it to you?"

"It is. It's never been opened since he sealed it."

"We offer the envelope, unopened, into evidence."

"Objection, we don't know what's in it. The content has not been authenticated," objected Hoover.

"Mr. Brooks has only offered the unopened envelope into evidence," responded the Judge.

"The unopened envelope is not evidence of anything, so it is irrelevant," said Hoover.

"That remains to be seen. The unopened envelope may be marked as an exhibit."

John handed the envelope to the court reporter who stamped it and handed it back to John.

"Who else did you tell about this?"

"Some young men who work for you came by, following up on leads. I told them."

"Just one more question. Mr. Horton, I asked my assistant Peter Creek to give you a copy of your subpoena." John gestured toward Peter. "Did he?"

"No, he didn't."

"Thank you, Mr. Horton. No further questions."

Judge Westerbeck announced, "We will take a ten-minute recess before we take up any cross examination of the witness." She turned and directed her next remarks directly to the Sheriff. "Sheriff Townsend!"

Townsend was startled to be addressed by the Judge. After a moment he stood and said, "Yes, Your Honor."

"During this recess I want you to stay where you are. I don't want you speaking with anyone, including the attorneys for the prosecution. Do you understand?"

"But, Your Honor," interposed Hoover.

"No buts. Nobody speaks to him until this hearing is over. Is that understood?"

"Yes, Your Honor," said Thorn.

"Mr. Hoover, do you understand?"

"Yes, Your Honor."

"Sheriff Townsend. Do you understand what I have told you?"

"Um, yes, Your Honor. Talk to no one."

Westerbeck thumped her gavel on the resounder and quickly exited through the door behind the bench. Pandemonium broke out among the media as they rushed the door to be the first to report the latest developments.

Chapter 62

Shaken by the turn of events in the courtroom, Hoover took advantage of the break to step outside and get a breath of fresh air. He felt a need to be alone and gather his thoughts, but people were everywhere. Reporters kept approaching him with questions. "No comment," was his only answer as he brushed them off. How could Brooks have discovered so much, and so quickly? He noticed a mountain of a man climb the steps. The man paused as he reached Hoover. "I'm looking for John Brooks. Where will I find him?"

"Main courtroom on the second floor," replied Hoover before it occurred to him to lie.

"Thanks," responded Crush as he entered the courthouse.

Hoover heard a familiar, demanding voice, "Hoover, why wouldn't you answer your phone?" Startled, he turned to see the angry red face of Shawn Dalton. His son Brad stood to his right, reflecting his father's mood.

"Mr. Dalton! What are you doing here?"

"I got a message from Clint, who said that the Mississippi lawyer had ruined everything, and we're all going to die. He didn't finish his sentence and he won't answer his phone. I couldn't get you to answer the phone either, so I flew right over to see what in the world is going on. What did Clint's message mean?"

"What? Brooks ruined everything! We're all going to die! How?"

"That's what I want to know." Dalton stepped closer and grabbed the collar of Hoover's coat. "What is going on? Why didn't you answer the phone?"

"I, I, I, Mr. Dalton, I've been in court all day. You assigned me to keep Brooks tied up in court and that's what I'm doing."

"Oh yeah. If you've got him tied up in court, how has he ruined everything? I hold you responsible if anything goes wrong."

"Maybe it was the other lawyer."

"It can't be him. We already took him out! If you don't do your job, you'll be next."

"Look, Mr. Dalton, I'm doing all I can do. I've got him tied down to this case, but he knows things he shouldn't know and he's doing things we didn't expect."

"What do you mean? I thought you had a mole and had him bugged! Give it to me straight."

"It seems like he has Townsend cornered. That lousy sheriff may be the weak link."

"If you can't get Townsend reigned in, make sure he never testifies about anything again."

"What?"

"Nothing is going to stand between me and that gold. Four generations of Daltons have sought it, and now it's so close I can taste it."

The anger in Shawn Dalton's eyes sent fear surging through Hoover. His knees felt weak.

"Take me to Townsend," demanded Dalton.

"Yes, sir. But you won't be able to talk to him."

"What do you mean, can't talk to him?"

"The judge ordered him to talk to no one."

"Whose gonna stop me?"

Crush found John seated at counsel table. He leaned over the rail and tapped John on the shoulder. Karen jumped from her chair and gave him a hug.

"Crush, I'm glad you're here," she said.

"Yeah, it's good to see you two together. But, judging from the look of John's face, I'm a little late. I'm sorry. I got here as soon as I could."

"Oh, this," responded John, gesturing toward the bruises on his face. "I got what I deserved. Thank you for coming. Things may be about to get interesting."

"What do you need me to do?"

"Right now, just keep an eye out for us until we recess for the day. Keep an eye on Sheriff Townsend, sitting right there," John nodded toward Townsend. Crush nodded affirmatively. "Also, I can use your help getting us through the crowd later today."

"Will do." Crush took an open seat on the third row.

A moment later, Hoover led Shawn and Brad Dalton into the courtroom. The press and spectators were returning, and the audience area was beginning to fill. Karen nudged John and motioned toward the door.

"Well, I'll be," observed John. "Awesome, your cousins are here."

"Yeah," replied Awesome, "they're probably worried about me."

"I'm sure they want to do all they can to help you," said Karen sarcastically. Awesome contained a chuckle that lasted only a moment as realization of the gravity of his situation returned to mind.

"But," continued John, "they're here for a reason. We must really be getting under old Mr. Dalton's skin."

Shawn Dalton's eyes searched the courtroom, pausing for a moment on Awesome. He stared at Awesome with contempt. Awesome returned his stare. Dalton's angry eyes paused on Brooks then he turned to Townsend, who was eight feet away, sitting in a chair between the jury box and the table used by the prosecutors. Shawn Dalton stood just outside the bar that separates the audience from the participants of the trial. Dalton motioned Townsend to come to him. Townsend shook his head, mouthing, "I can't."

"What do you mean you can't?" responded Dalton in a loud whisper. "Come here, now!"

"You better do what my dad says," asserted Brad in a loud whisper.

Sandy Storm noticed the exchange and pointed it out to Bret, who turned his camera on the new drama building in the courtroom. Crush, looking for possible threats, watched them carefully.

In spite of Dalton's demands, Townsend didn't move, which enraged Dalton even more. He slapped the inside of the bar with the palm of his hand. "Come here!" he commanded in a voice heard throughout the courtroom.

There was a knock on the door behind the bench. The bailiff called out, "Order in the Court!" Judge Westerbeck took the bench and announced authoritatively, "Be seated." Red faced and trembling with anger, with eyes shooting daggers at Townsend, Shawn Dalton and his son Brad squeezed into seats at the end of the second row, forcing everyone in the row to slide down. Crush asked the person next to him to trade places with him so he could sit directly behind the Daltons. Earl Horton returned to the witness stand.

"Ms. Thorn, your witness," said Judge Westerbeck.

"We don't have any questions of this witness at this time, your Honor."

"Very well. Mr. Brooks, who is your next witness?"

"Could I have just a moment, Your Honor?"

"Make it quick."

John motioned for Karen and Awesome to lean in. Peter stepped up, but John held up his hand, motioning him to stand back.

"I had intended to call Peter next, to further set up my questioning of Townsend. I wanted to take a few more bites out of their foundation. Shake them up some more. Make them doubt. But with the arrival of Shawn Dalton, I think the moment is right to put Townsend back on the witness stand."

Karen responded, "Trust your gut, John."

"You're my man, Mr. Brooks," said Awesome. "I trust your judgment. Do what you think is best."

"All right. We need a quick prayer. Lord, please give me the right questions. Please confuse Townsend if he tries to lie, so that he tells the truth instead."

The reporters were startled to hear the three of them say, "Amen."

John Brooks stood erect, stepped to the podium, and said, "The defense calls Sheriff Wayne Townsend."

"Sheriff Townsend," said Judge Westerbeck, "Return to the witness stand."

Townsend was aware that all eyes were on him. His own eyes swept the courtroom. He took in the red angry face of Shawn Dalton, that rich man who thought he ruled the world. He looked at the smug, angry rich kid Brad, the prying eyes of the press. He imagined they were sharks smelling blood in the water, hungry to feed off his misfortune. He looked at that smart aleck lawyer, with tricks up his sleeve. His eyes paused on Awesome, a man on trial who ought to be afraid for his future, yet he displayed what Townsend read as haughty confidence.

His mind drifted to his life. He said to himself, that unlike Brad Dalton, he had to fight for everything he had. He wasn't born to wealth. He had no advantages in life. He worked, struggled, fought, put up with demands from people who thought they were better than him, until finally, he rose to the pinnacle of his carrier. Against all odds, he was now the person he always wanted to be. He was the sheriff!

'Nobody will take this from me,' he assured himself.

"Sheriff Townsend!"

Townsend came out of his trance.

"We're waiting for you. Take the stand please."

"Yes, Your Honor."

A new confidence welled up in him as he strode to the witness stand. He felt the arms of the chair with his hands. The leather crackled as he sat. The bailiff adjusted the microphone close to his mouth. The flexible metal arm holding the microphone squeaked. He took a breath. The sound of his breath was picked up by the microphone, amplified, and broadcast throughout the courtroom. It was so loud it startled him.

"You're still under oath," declared the Judge.

The cloud of confidence Townsend rode to the witness stand evaporated. He felt the questioning, expectant eyes of everyone in the packed courtroom. He always hated crowds. The thought struck him that everyone was eager to see him fall. Fear consumed him. He didn't understand why he couldn't control his fear. He looked again at Brad. Something in the way Brad looked made Townsend certain Brad would enjoy seeing him take all the blame for everything. It's what he always expected. Even Shawn Dalton came all the way from Texas just to watch him fall. How did he know to be here? It's a set-up! He sucked in another breath. Again, his breath was amplified. Again he was startled by the sound.

Townsend forced himself to shut out every other thought and focus on Brooks.

Tunnel vision ensued. All he saw was Brooks and his swollen face. He imagined Brooks in the cross hairs of his rifle. His confidence returned. A smile flickered on his face.

"Your witness, Mr. Brooks."

'Come on, city boy. Give me your best shot. I can take anything you can dish out,' Townsend said to himself.

"You murdered Sheriff Rainey, didn't you?"

Townsend was startled. The audience gasped. Awesome, eyes wide, nodded in agreement, the press murmured. Thorn leapt to her feet, "Objection! That is outrageous!"

"Outrage is not a proper objection, Ms. Thorn," responded Judge Westerbeck. "You are way out on a limb, Mr. Brooks."

"Yes, Your Honor. I agree that one of us is out on a limb. I will prove that Sheriff Townsend is the one who is out on a limb. May I get an answer to my question?"

"Answer the question, Sheriff Townsend."

"That's outrageous. Why would I do such a thing?"

"I take that as an admission. At your first opportunity, you failed to deny that you murdered Sheriff Rainey, so it's true, isn't it?"

"Not true!" shouted Townsend in a squeaky high-pitched voice. He was aware that his voice betrayed him, sounding unmanly. He looked at Hoover and Thorn for help.

"You are a professional investigator. Let's examine the facts."

"Okay," he said into the microphone. Defiantly he said, "I want to hear this."

"You were in the Goni Swamp when Curtis Dalton disappeared, never to be seen again."

"So?"

"Emily Martin and her boyfriend heard someone moaning in agony."

"Swamp noise."

"You told Emily Martin and her boyfriend to leave and never come back."

"They were trespassing."

"Other than the field carved out of the swamp by Frank and G.W. Dalton, that swamp is a mosquito and snake infested place, with no reason for anyone to be there."

"We finally agree on something."

"Yet, when you saw Emily and her boyfriend, you had been in the swamp and you were covered with mud."

"I was looking for trespassers and I found them."

"You were the person who found Sheriff Rainey."

"That's right. He was missing, so I went looking for him."

"In the Goni Swamp."

"I had a hunch he would be there. It's what investigators do, follow hunches."

"His body was surrounded by boot prints that match the make and size of Awesome's boots."

"Yes, because Awesome did it."

"You were one of the few people that knew the make and size of Awesome's boots."

"Lots of people could have known that."

"You agree that is information that would not interest most people."

"Depends."

"That's right. Depends on why they would want to know. Mr. Horton knew because he regularly sold the boot to Awesome."

"Yeah."

"The sheriff knew because he was following up on boot print evidence he found at a murder scene."

"Okay."

"And you knew."

"Yes."

"Because you were looking for a chance to leave evidence?"

"That's ridiculous."

"Is it? My client says that when you booked him, you took his fingerprints and a lock of his hair, for evidence."

"I took his fingerprints, but not a lock of his hair. Why would I take his hair?"

"Standard operating procedure, isn't it, to take a hair sample of a murder suspect when there is hair or may be hair on the victim that doesn't match the victim's hair?"

"Okay."

"Skeeter had hair in his hand when he died. You wanted to see if it matched, didn't you?"

"I don't know what you're talking about."

"Ms. Thorn has given me a copy of the Sheriff Department's reports concerning the arrest of Awesome, and there is nothing in those reports about any hair evidence, or boot evidence, right?"

Townsend hesitated. "True, because there wasn't any."

"If the original reports had described hair and boot evidence, then someone with access to the reports must have scrubbed them, right?"

"I don't know what you mean."

"Why would someone scrub evidence from the report unless they were hiding something, like their own guilt?"

"I, I don't know what you're getting at."

John stepped over to the court reporter's desk and picked up the large brown envelope. He handed the envelope to Townsend.

"Do you recognize Sheriff Rainey's signature on the outside of the envelope."

Townsend's hand began to shake. The envelope shook even more. The signature began to blur. It was hard to read. He felt sweat on his brow.

"I can't recognize this signature."

"Are you saying it's not his signature, or that you can't recognize it?"

"I can't recognize it."

"You've seen Sheriff Rainey's signature many times haven't you."

"I suppose so."

"Plenty of people know his signature. You know that we will be able to find someone to prove his signature, right?"

"Maybe."

"You used a handwriting expert in this case to identify Awesome's handwriting, right?"

"Yes."

"When we open that envelope, we're going to see the truth about Sheriff Rainey's investigation, aren't we?"

"What are you getting at?"

"Only one person had access to the file. Only one person had access to the evidence that could frame Awesome, only one person has the motive to frame Awesome, the murderer of Sheriff Rainey, and that would be you, Mr. Townsend, right?"

Townsend looked at the envelope. His mind raced. How could this be? Who could have imagined that the sheriff would leave a copy of the file with a civilian? 'Why is this happening to me? It's not fair!' He looked into the audience. All eyes were on him. He looked into the camera. 'The whole world is watching me! It's not fair!' His breath shortened. His heart raced. His mind raced, 'I'm the sheriff! I'm in charge. I do the questioning. He can't do this to me!'

"Answer the question, Mr. Townsend," commanded Judge Westerbeck

'Mister, she said Mister, not Sheriff,' thought Townsend. 'Disrespectful! She believes I did it!' Townsend felt his world collapsing. He looked into the audience again. He looked at the smug face of Brad Dalton. Then his eyes fell on the angry face of Shawn Dalton, whose mouth was screwed up like he had tasted something bitter, like he was about to spit something out. Like he was about to spit Sheriff Wayne Townsend out. 'He is disgusted with me!' thought Townsend. 'Disgusted!'

That did it! Wayne Townsend had enough. He shouted!

"I'm not taking the fall for nobody. It wasn't me!"

Shawn Dalton stood and shouted, "Shut up, you fool!"

Judge Westerbeck slammed her gavel on the resounder. "Silence. Order in the Court."

Townsend raised his voice so he could be heard over the confusion and noise. He pointed at Shawn and shouted, "It was his son, Brad Dalton! He did it. And Brad murdered his cousin Curtis. He murdered James Dalton, right there in the Goni Swamp field. Shawn wanted it covered up. He made me cover for him. I'm not covering for them anymore. It wasn't me. I swear! It was him and his son! They wanted that farm so much they would do anything to get it, even kill the sheriff!"

"LIAR! THAT MAN IS A LIAR!" shouted Shawn Dalton. His head darted left and right, like a trapped animal. He rushed toward the courtroom door. Brad hesitated a moment and bolted after him.

"Stop them!" commanded the Judge.

Sandy's cameraman, Bret, swiveled the camera from the judge, to the witness to the fleeing Daltons, capturing the drama as it unfolded for everyone to see.

Shawn Dalton reached the door first and had opened it about a foot when Brad arrived. A massive man moving at improbable speed slammed into both of them, knocking them to the floor. Crush grabbed both Daltons by their collars, lifted them and held them at arms-length, as though they were puppets.

"I stopped them, Your Honor. What do you want me to do with them?"

"Thank you, Mr., uh,"

"Barnes, ma'am, Crush Barnes.

"Thank you, Mr. Barnes. Please hold them until the bailiff can take them off your hands. Mr. Bailiff, arrest Mr. Shawn Dalton and Brad Dalton to be held for further investigation and proceedings. While you're at it, take the sheriff in custody."

"My pleasure, Your Honor."

"But, Judge," pled Townsend. "I told you it wasn't me! It wasn't me!"

"Take him away, I don't even want to see him right now,"

"Yes, Your Honor," responded the bailiff. "Sheriff, turn around."

"What?"

"Turn around, now."

Townsend turned his back to the bailiff, who cuffed him and led him to the courtroom door. Two more officers met them there and cuffed Shawn and Brad Dalton. They were escorted from the courtroom to the sound of clicking and whirring cameras.

"Mr. Brooks!"

"Yes, Your Honor."

"That was an amazing piece of work."

"Thank you, but I deserve no credit. We were blessed to have Sheriff Rainey on the case."

"Yes, Sheriff Rainey will be missed. Do you have a motion?"

"I move to dismiss the charges against my client and request that he be discharged immediately."

"The State joins in that motion," announced Thorn.

"Motion granted. The cases styled the State of Mississippi vs. Awesome Dalton are dismissed. Mr. Dalton, you are free to go."

The courtroom erupted in cheers. Judge Westerbeck made no effort to suppress the celebration. She just smiled and enjoyed the scene. Awesome hugged John, and then Karen. John motioned Peter to come to him.

"Son, you've got some explaining to do."

"How did you know?"

"Jennifer Wolfe, our computer consultant, found the worm you installed. It sent information from our computer to Hoover."

"I didn't want to do it. They made me."

"Do you understand you are going to have consequences for what you've done?"

"I know. I deserve them."

"You have a right to a lawyer."

"I just want it over with."

"Are you willing to tell the whole truth to the authorities?"

"Yes, sir. I'll do whatever you need me to do."

"Just tell the truth son, the whole truth and nothing but the truth."

"Yes, sir. So help me, God."

"That's the right start. Mr. Hoover is about to have his world shaken."

Chapter 63

A spectacular dawn greeted Natalia and Jackson. They were perched on the top of the ridge overlooking the valley.

"What happened to your accent? It's much less pronounced that it used to be?" asked Jackson.

"The accent and sultry demeanor is a role I was playing, sort of like an actress. I didn't like de Sada's world. I didn't belong there. I felt I had to act like someone else, someone other than me, to get close to him. It was dishonest of me. I am sorry. I hope chu will forgive me. I had to stop him. To stop him, I had to get close to him. It was little Natalia against all his wealth and power. But, I had an ally he didn't have."

Jackson nodded as he thought about her words and all that had happened. "Of course, I forgive you. I've done worse."

Breakfast of eggs, fresh fruit and tortillas was prepared for them by some of the men who came to help Natalia. By noon, the roar of water had subsided. The waterfall at the top of the ridge was gone. Now, the only waterfall emitted from the cave, about 100 feet from the top of the ridge.

"This is such a beautiful sight. But, what will all the hummingbirds do? Where will they go?"

"God will provide for them."

"Which god?"

"The one true God, Jesus Christ."

"I saw your men, willing to worship me. How do you explain that?"

"Some still follow the old ways, some just added Christ and the Saints to the list of gods they worship. Some, like me, have realized our need for a Savior. I am the worst of sinners, yet he loves me anyway."

"Yeah, I know the story. All have sinned and fallen short of the glory of God and deserve spiritual death. But God didn't want to be separated from us for eternity, so God substituted His own Son to die in our place. If we accept that sacrifice, our relationship with God can be restored. I've heard it from my best friend a dozen times."

"Jes, and His Son overcame physical and spiritual death, and offers eternal life to us if we accept that He was sacrificed in our place and invite

Him to be our Lord and Savior. If chu know, why haven't you responded?"

"Because it makes no sense. But my friend John always has a sensible answer to my questions. So, I guess it comes down to faith. I just never had it. How do you have such faith?"

"Faith is a gift from God. He pursued me until I finally realized He was building my faith and that He wanted me, so I gave myself to Him. God had a big job for little Natalia. He used me to stop the demon that infected de Sada's thoughts. Antoine had power and money, but we had Jesus, and with God's help, we stopped Antoine. We did it! Has Jesus pursued chu? What great mission does He have for chu?"

Jackson paused and thought of his conversations with John, with Robert, with Jake, and even with Saga. He didn't respond.

"Have you ever called on Him in distress?"

Jackson had flashbacks from the raft, the glider and other times in his life. "Everybody does in times of distress."

"There are few atheists in foxholes, right?"

"Something like that."

"Did God answer dhur calls for help?"

"It was coincidence."

"Was it? Or, was He giving chu another chance? Does He keep putting people and circumstances in dhur path that point chu to Him?"

Something welled up inside Jackson. He felt a pull in his chest and said to himself, "It's true! Come, now! Don't wait!" After a moment, he asked himself, "Was that my voice?" He resisted the feeling and argued with the voice in his head. A second time, he heard the voice call, "Come!" He shook his head, no. A third time, "Jackson, Come! Now!"

"He used my name!" Jackson shook his head again, stood and walked in a quick circle. He put his hands over his ears and said out loud, "No, I can't! I don't believe you!"

The voice in his head said, "Peter, do you love me?"

Jackson stopped. He no longer saw Natalia or the lake. The story of Peter denying Christ three times jumped into his mind.

"Natalia, I just denied Him three times. If He is real, He would never accept me."

"Peter denied him three times. He took Peter back."

"How?"

"He asked him three times, 'Peter do you love me? Peter do you love me?'"

"You just said it twice."

"Jes. Is that important?"

"Another coincidence. That makes three." He took a breath and said, "Okay, how do we do this?"

"Praise God, you want to accept Jesus?"

"Yes. Let's do it."

"You just did when you said out loud, 'Yes. Let's do it.' Once you genuinely decide to accept Him as Lord and Savior, He enters your heart and you are His."

"That's it?"

"Jes."

"Don't I have to be baptized?"

"No, but baptism is a good thing. It is an outward sign of your decision, and it can be a witness to others that they too should make a decision to follow Christ." She became excited and jumped for joy. "We're going to baptize chu, right now!"

"Doesn't that take a priest or something?"

"All believers are priests."

"Huh?"

"Come with me!" she took him by the hand and led him to the edge of Hummingbird Lake. "Everyone, gather around!" she said, bouncing with excitement. "Something great is about to happen."

A dozen men gathered on the shore. Natalia explained, "Jackson has decided to accept Jesus Christ as his Savior. Since there is a lake, why not baptize him?" Everyone nodded in agreement.

Natalia and Jackson stepped into the lake. Jackson towered over her. "Chu are too tall. Chu will have to bend your knees for me," she said. He knelt in the water. "Are you ready?"

"Yes."

"Then, before God and these witnesses, make the following profession of faith. I believe that Jesus is the Christ."

Jackson took a deep breath, and in a resounding voice announced, "I believe and I know in my heart that Jesus is the Christ."

"The Son of the living God."

"The Son of the living God."

"My risen Lord and Savior."

"He is indeed my risen Lord and Savior."

"By virtue of your profession of faith, I baptize chu in the name of the Father, the Son and the Holy Spirit." With her hand behind Jackson's back, she lowered him backwards into the water saying, "Buried with Christ." She pulled him from the water and announced, "And raised with Christ to new life."

Jackson raised his arms in celebration and hugged Natalia, shouting, "I have found my true treasure! This is so much more than Maximillian's Treasure."

Maximilian's Treasure

Natalia cried tears of joy. The small crowd cheered and applauded. Several of the cheering men had praised Huitzilopochtli just last night. They looked at one another, shrugged and stepped into the lake.

"What are they doing?" asked Jackson.

"They want to be baptized with you," Natalia said, laughing with joy. For the next few minutes, she and Jackson baptized everyone who came forward.

* * *

An hour later, Natalia's men arrived with two long canoes equipped with outboard motors.

"You're going after the treasure?" asked Jackson.

"Of course."

"What will you do with it?"

"It is for my people. These people and their ancestors suffered because of the treasure. Now, I hope that it will benefit them."

"Who are your people?"

"All the indigenous people of Central America. If we are good stewards of this wealth, we can lift these people out of poverty and make a new and better life for them."

"When word gets out, surely the Mexican government will seize it."

"Jes, and it will likely be stolen by men like de Sada."

"How will you prevent that from happening?"

"No one can know we have found the treasure until we are ready. We will buy this land and account for every item we find. Then, we hope to use the international press to create political support for our ownership rights. We will need a good lawyer, and lots of help from the media."

"I might know someone who could help with the media. In the meantime, how can you keep something like this a secret?"

"No one can leave this valley until we have found the treasure, bought the land and accounted for every piece."

"So, am I a prisoner?"

Natalia looked at him for a long moment, kissed him on the cheek, and said, "No, I trust you. You can stay here with me and help me manage this fortune, if there is one, or you can go. You decide."

"What a choice! Stay here with you, a beautiful, exotic, exciting woman, and have access to untold wealth, or go back to my hand to mouth existence at home."

"So, what will it be?"

"Let's go find the treasure."

Natalia laughed and ran to the canoes. They climbed aboard and crossed Hummingbird Lake. Clouds of hummingbirds still filled the sky. They reached the waterfall trail, followed it to its end, and used the handholds and toeholds to work their way to the cave entrance, which was no longer concealed by the waterfall. Jackson, Natalia, and the men who were with them strapped lights to their foreheads, turned them on, and followed the stream through the cave, past the point where the wall had been.

Water no longer poured from the hole at the ceiling. The stream now flowed through the opening where the wall once stood. A set of steps led to a second passage high on the left wall of the cave. They climbed the steps and entered a vast chamber. Everyone gasped! Dazzling light reflected from their flashlights, filling the room with a golden aura.

Statues, artifacts, bowls, utensils, figurines and nuggets were everywhere. Lying on the floor was a tarp. In the middle of the tarp was a pile of nuggets. Skip lumbered into sight, burdened by an arm full of heavy nuggets.

"Who are chu? How did chu get here?" demanded an astonished Natalia.

"That's my friend Skip!" shouted Jackson as he rushed to him and gave him a hug. "How in the world did you get here?"

Skip, brimming with excitement, laid his burden in the middle of the tarp. "Jackson! What took you so long? We finally struck it rich! Can you believe our luck? Who are your friends? You want to know how I got here? Gregory! Watch out for Gregory, I followed him here."

"You won't have to worry about Gregory anymore."

"Really! What do you mean?"

"I'll explain in a minute."

"We may have a problem," said Natalia. "Chu know what I told chu about keeping this location quiet until we're ready."

"Yes, but he's my friend. What do you plan to do?"

"I will have to keep him here until it's time to let the world know what we have. But, if chu can vouch for him and assure me that he can keep a secret, maybe I will let him go."

Jackson hesitated for a moment, then said, "Skip, I'm afraid you're going to be here a while."

Chapter 64

John examined Jackson's letter again. "Why can't you tell me anything, except that you're safe? And why do you say I can't look for you? How long should I wait? Should I wait at all? Do I need to be on the next flight to Mexico City? I just don't have any answers."

"Talking to yourself about Jackson again?" asked Karen as she stepped into John's office.

"Yeah, I'm worried about him and I miss him."

"Well, maybe this will give you something else to think about." She handed him a letter, with a return address, "M. McCarty, Amsterdam."

"Father McCarty!" exclaimed John. "What's he doing in Amsterdam?"

The smile on John's face faded as he read the letter.

"What's the matter?" asked Karen.

"This can't be! He and a friend are being prosecuted for war crimes at the International Criminal Court!"

"War crimes! Father Mike? No way!" Karen rushed to John's side. "Read the end of the letter."

"He says, 'I thought of you when I read this verse, Isaiah 6:8.'"

Karen opened the Bible on John's desk to the verse, and read, "I heard the voice of the Lord saying, 'Whom shall I send, and who will go for Us?'"

John finished the passage, "Here am I. Send me."

"What does it mean?" asked Karen.

"It means we're going to The Hague. Pack your bags!"

THE END

Maximilian's Treasure

Maximilian's Treasure

ion can be obtained
g.com

9
75/P